LAWMAN

BOOK 1

TALE OF A GUNFIGHTER

COLD WEST PUBLISHING
AN IMPRINT OF CREATIVE TEXTS PUBLISHERS, LLC

LAWMAN
Book 1: Tale of a Gunfighter
by Kevin Hogge

Published by Cold West Publishing
An imprint of Creative Texts Publishers, LLC.
www.ColdWest.com

The following is a work of fiction. Any resemblance to actual names, persons, businesses and incidents is strictly coincidental. Locations are used only in the general sense and do not represent the real place in actuality.

Kindle Edition

TALE OF A GUNFIGHTER

This book is dedicated to my loving wife Marsha who is my
inspiration and my rock.

TALE OF A GUNFIGHTER

CHAPTER 1

I hate trains. They're loud and I'm always bored just sitting there with nothing to do. This is the third time I've traveled on this iron horse and my impression hasn't changed much. This time, I'm riding from Abilene, Kansas to Maple Ridge, New Mexico. The trip will take almost two days and it seems all I can do is count telegraph poles as the Central Union Pacific, rolls westward, rail by rail. I've tried to sleep but the noise from the trucks on the rails, combined with the chatter from the other passengers made that almost impossible. I managed to dose off a couple of times but some kid would start crying, or the train would hit a bump in the tracks and ruin that. With nothing else to do, I'll just relax and continue counting these poles to pass the time.

The train has stopped twice already. The first time I stayed onboard with no reason to walk around that little makeshift town. We stopped on a slight bend in the track which gave me a good view of the side of the locomotive. I watched the engineer and brakeman as they moved the boom from the water tank, which luckily was on my side, then fill the boiler. That was interesting. But, with the loss of air circulating about, the summer sun soon increased the inside temperature considerable. The second time, I got off and had a beer in a little tent saloon then to the outhouse. There was a lady selling apples on the boardwalk, next to train station. I bought two and tackled those once we were back onboard. You don't see many apples in these parts, not as fresh as these at least. Now we're rolling once again. I'll bet we stop at every water tank and mud-puddle town between here and New Mexico.

My name is Ernest Evans but most folks call me Ernie. Some people call me a gunman but that's a title I've tried to avoid. I spend my time working for the Kansas Cattle Buyers Association, tracking down ranchers who scammed them on a light herd, or stuck them with sick cows. My primary job is to collect the money these ranchers were overpaid and return it to the KCBA, minus my fee. Unfortunately, some of these men would rather turn to a leather holster than a leather wallet, in response to my request that they settle up.

I hate to admit it but I make my living with a gun, no matter how I try to justify it. I killed two men, in a fair fight, in a Dodge City saloon a couple of years back. Somehow, it caught the attention of Mr. William Murphy, head of the KCBA up in Abilene, nearly two hundred miles away. The men thought I'd cheated after I won three hands in a row and went straight for their iron. They were slow and luck was on my side. I dropped them both before either man was fully cocked. The KCBA thought they could use a man with my particular skill so they offered me this job.

I usually ride Bruiser, my Palomino Morgan but Maple Ridge is a stretch from Abilene. That's a long way to ride a horse, so once again I'm taking this train. As expected, I'm heading out to see a rancher who was overpaid and I aim to come back with eight hundred dollars of my client's money. I'll show him the papers that list each head with the amount due. I'll try to reason with him but if he chooses his pistol instead, I'll make him number six and take whatever I can. I don't like to kill. Dead men don't pay and I always come back light. That never seems to bother my clients. They see me as much as a deterrent as a collector and the KCBA wants the word out that they won't be cheated.

There's always the law to contend with. I'm careful to meet with these ranchers in the presence of others, usually introducing myself to the town marshal first. Even when I know where I'm headed, I'll stop in the marshal's office just to be seen and to know who I'm dealing with. They look at me as some kind of bounty hunter but I hate that description worse than gunman. It seems that things really haven't changed much over the years. This job makes it extremely hard to shake the past.

Life itself was a challenge for Ernie Evans. He was a product of the Civil War, with only distant memories of a happier time. His childhood was derailed when he was ten years old and completely torn away at age twelve.

It was September 1861 when U.S. Senator James Lane led his Redlegs in a raid on the town of Osceola, Missouri. The town was decimated, with everything of value either stolen or destroyed. This was not the first battle the Evans family had seen and surely would not be their last. As retribution for the pro-slavery guerilla tactics of the Missouri Bushwhackers, nine men were captured and executed in a mock court martial.

When Lane and his men left Missouri, they took with them 350 horses, 400 head of cattle and 200 slaves. This was only one of many raids perpetrated by the North as several Missouri towns were plundered and burned. Their actions served only to intensify the resolve of the bushwhackers, who crossed the Kansas border in unwavering retaliation. Joseph Evans, Ernie's father, was a part of those raids.

Missouri was their home and Joseph Evans saw it as his responsibility to protect his family from the Jayhawks and northern sympathizers. As they tried to impose their Yankee ways on the new territories, bushwhackers met them with a brutal pushback. From the early skirmishes near their home Ernie had come to know William Quantrill. He'd also met Jessie James on several occasions. He didn't realize it at the time but his father was a part of their vendetta and was as rough as they come. He never saw that side of him, or the other Gray Ghost with whom he kept company. This caused reality to come as quite a shock for a young boy.

Ernie was twelve years old when a neighboring farmer and the Methodist Parson from Osceola, showed up at the front door of their farmhouse. The year was 1863, May 3rd to be exact. His father had joined the war effort for the South late in '61 and now wore two stripes, on his way to becoming a sergeant. He had officially become a soldier and donned the Confederate gray in October '61. It was after the Yankee raid on Osceola but he'd been enthralled in the battle for much longer. The border war between Missouri and Kansas had been raging since the mid-1850's. For them, the war came early, long before Ft. Sumter and continued long after Appomattox.

On April 22, 1863, Corp. Joseph Evans had been deep in the fight to keep Admiral David Porter's ships away from Vicksburg and the waiting forces of Gen. Grant. Their supply ships were slowed but not stopped. Col. Evans was manning artillery fire from the banks that day, when he was struck by shrapnel from enemy fire and killed at the height of the exchange. Corp. Evans never received his third stripe.

After the death of his father, Ernie set his mind on taking his place as the man of the family. But at the age of twelve, that came with many obstacles. On a number of occasions, the ominous sounds of cannon fire and skirmishes came dangerously close to their farm. Ernie learned to stand guard and returned fire when he could. He engaged in the art of gun play early and became cold to the carnage. The increasing sense of insecurity was shared by all but he was determined to stand tall and protect the family. He was a boy trying to be a man, scared to death and could only cry where he knew no one would see.

With the need for contact away from his mother and younger brothers, Ernie spent time in town when he could. There he became better acquainted with the rebel forces and bushwhackers who supported the South but lived outside their ranks. Using the war as their excuse, many of these men murdered innocent people and raided their homes for personal gain. With no understanding of the political or philosophical differences between each faction, young Ernie was easily persuaded to follow along and soon joined in on the Kansas raids.

He was intent on avenging his father's death and saw his participation as necessary to replace his father's voice and his gun. Young Ernie was eager to fight the enemy but in his rides with the bushwhackers he never saw anyone in uniform. He rode near the back on his first raid and couldn't understand why they were invading a farmer with little more than a few cows and plow horses. The scene was far from what he'd expected when they lit out earlier that first day and one he planned never to see again. He wanted to fight Yankee soldiers, not Kansas farmers who simply supported their cause.

Ernie was equally as naïve about his role with these men. They had no need for the gun hand of a boy. He was there only to carry the presence of Joe Evans' memory. Going back to May 1858, most of these men, including Ernie's father, had thrown in with Charles Hamilton. They'd joined his march to execute abolitionists near Marais des Cygnes, on the Kansas - Missouri border. Now they were using their talents to pillage and terrorize farmers and townsfolk.

Several years his senior, Ernie had come to know a number of older teen-age boys in town. Also fascinated with the aura of the bushwhackers, these young men were beginning to join in as look-outs and to provide cover fire for the men who orchestrated these raids. Ernie's better nature soon played on his conscience and he began to spend less time with the bushwhackers, though his friendships with the older boys remained.

As he grew older and the war finally ended, Ernie began spending time again with Tom Bainbridge and Clayton Emerson. They had stayed in the fight until Quantrill was killed in May 1865. By now, he had caught up with them in stature and felt pretty much their equal. Soon after, they were rumored to have spent time riding with the James Gang, though they were never arrested, or named among their numbers. Ernie turned down their offers to join in. But he too, was eventually questioned, after a mid-day bank robbery left two men dead and three thousand dollars gone. He spent more time on the farm after that but even that would eventually play out.

Mrs. Annie Evans grew weary of their small farm and sold it in '71 to move in with her sister in Liberty. There, she found work in Fisher's Dry Goods Store. It was a small establishment but one the westward wagon trains had patronized for years. Ernie drifted a bit until he ended up, strangely enough in Kansas, where he took on work in the stock yards, east of Ft. Dodge. It was here that fate would have him meet Mr. William Murphy.

-

It was a dry August afternoon when Ernie reached Maple Ridge. He exited the train with the gear he'd brought along, then asked the clerk at the train station for directions to the nearest livery stable. The first order of business was to rent a horse and saddle, then find a real saloon for a beer. The constant motion of the train had made him a bit sick. He couldn't wait to have a saddle under him once again, with his feet squarely planted in the stirrups.

The town appeared busy as he walked out of the station and looked south. The tracks seemed to draw a line as to where the open range ended and the town began. Looking north of the tracks from the platform, there were a few corrals and barns close by. Just south of the mountain range a number of roof tops were visible, above the tall grass. But the growth of the town was entirely to the south of the train station. There was a "Town Limits" sign on Grayson Street just beyond the tracks but it didn't seem necessary. The town limits were as obvious as a line in the sand.

With his saddlebags and scabbard over his right shoulder, Ernie made his way to Fredrick Street and headed south toward the Double Deuce Corral, two blocks down. He checked his pocket watch as he began his walk. It was now 2:30 pm. His train had arrived on schedule, he had ample time to cover his plans for the day and saw no reason to rush. It was Ernie's first trip to New Mexico and this little town was pretty much what he'd expected. It was originally built from the remains of an abandoned outpost. Folks moving west found it as a good place to stake a claim and rebuilt the temporary structures the army had left behind. To Ernie, it was just another little town along the tracks. But to the people he encountered in the street it was their home and the result of much hard work and sacrifice.

Fredrick Street was stirring with busy folks going about their day, as Ernie slowly walked along. The blacksmith shop seemed to be the loudest place around with the distinctive clang of the anvil ringing against the buildings. There he noticed a man shaping a new tongue for a wagon, which had been pulled up close to the door. The man looked up and nodded as Ernie watched. He was impressed by his skill and stood for a while watching as he turned a piece of hot steel into a work of art. I wish I could do that, Ernie thought, as he tipped his hat in approval and walked away.

There were two livery stables on Fredrick, with the Double Deuce Corral being the largest. It had been built by Jim Williams a few years back, as his personal stable. When he decided to sell, Ralph Thomas quickly stepped up to acquire the property. Christening his new enterprise, the Double Deuce, he wasted no time in proudly raising a large sign on the front of the barn. It showed a two of spades and two of hearts, prominently fanned above the name. It was a little crooked and less than professionally done but no one had the heart to make fun of it.

The Circle K was the other, on the corner of Fredrick and Fourth Street. It was run by a young fellow from Santa Fe. His prices were cheaper and he claimed to know a lot about horses. But he didn't know much about people. Most folks chose to pay the difference and trusted their horses with Ralph, crooked sign and all.

Ernie had no problem in finding the place. But once he'd acquired a fast horse and saddle, he found it hard to break himself free of Ralph. He was closing in on his sixtieth birthday and Ralph was rather looking forward to crossing that threshold. He'd fought with the 4th Infantry Regiment in Georgia during the war and never thought he'd see his fortieth. Since then, each one seemed to come with a sense of victory. Ralph stood about five foot six inches and weighted one hundred forty pounds on a good day. He always had a joke to tell and Ralph loved to laugh. He'd stroke his gray beard and tell an old joke that folks had heard a hundred times but he still made them laugh. It wasn't the jokes; it was Ralph and his way of having so much fun laughing at his own yarns.

If you were new in town, he'd want to know everything about you and where you were from. Ernie wasn't saying much but Ralph kept pushing. He didn't take offense. He knew they were friendly questions from an old timer, curious about the world. Ernie finally pulled away, leaving Ralph with very few answers and scratching his head.

Saddled up, he walked the horse over to Grayson Street, where most of the business took place. It was the obvious center of this little three street town. It too, was busy with folks going about their day, from store to store. As Ernie scanned the street, he saw a number of cafés, a hardware store and the land office, among others. Finally, there it stood, The Alhambra Saloon, "just what I was looking for," Ernie said with a grin.A beer was the next order of business, after which he had to get to work. He would first contact the marshal just to get acquainted then ask directions to the Cahoon Ranch and its owner, Mr. Larry Cahoon. But for now, a saloon and a beer took priority over it all.

The town of Maple Ridge, New Mexico was the result of a vision, sacrifice and hard work, of a number of people. Not the least of which was Henry Grayson. It was September 1860 when Henry decided to settle in New Mexico. The Grayson's had left their Missouri home four months earlier, to avoid the coming war. Henry and Mary decided to keep their children from the devastation and headed west to California and a more peaceful environment.

Departing from the wagon train in Santa Fe, Henry and his family continued southwest toward Albuquerque. They rode with a Kansas family; they'd come to know on the trail. They too were destined for California and for very similar reasons. The Grayson's destination had been San Jose but they were finding it difficult to leave New Mexico. The tranquil and inviting atmosphere of the mountains and skyline was very different from what they had left behind. They couldn't see California as being any better.

Approximately twenty-five miles southeast of Albuquerque, they made their way through the Manzano Mountains. It was a small mountain range with a clear canyon pass that would take them to the 6,000-foot elevation of their current destination. The Manzano, which is Spanish for "apple tree", is on the southern tip of the Sandia-Manzano Mountains and the only place in New Mexico where maple trees grow in the wild.

Henry was oblivious to the rarity of what he'd found but he was captivated by the beauty of it all. Conflicted as they were, this seemed to be the deciding factor which kept the Grayson's in New Mexico. As they rode, Henry was insistent upon bringing several along. He picked out a few saplings, at separate places along the way and harvested each to replant at their new home, still unaware, of where that might be.

Albuquerque was enticing but too settled for Henry's new ambition. He was insistent upon making it on his own and was now looking for the invigorating feel of a small town and the open range. Their travels brought them to a man who told of an abandoned outpost, two hundred miles to the northeast and just south of Cimarron. Henry was intrigued, then realized he'd come all this way, simply to turn around and go back to where he'd started. So, with a heartfelt good-bye to their friends, the Grayson's turned east the next morning and trailed back toward Santa Fe.

The trail to the old outpost was wide and passable, with the buildings just as described. Henry could not believe it all sat there, unused and unscathed by settlers or Indians. Many were rundown and in need of much repair, while several of the building were unusable. These would be demolished with the old timbers and boards reused where they could. The remainder would be used as fire wood, with nothing going to waste.

Henry Grayson and his family were the first to settle on this grassy patch of flat land. With its access to water and a busy westward trail, he immediately saw its potential. It seemed their final decision to abandon California had been made. Along with Henry and Mary, was their son, Bobby and their youngest, Maggie. They were none too happy when they saw the desolate buildings. When Henry announced it to be their new home, the children thought he'd lost his mind. But Henry was set on building their legacy upon this place.

Others soon caught on and quickly saw the makings of a small town taking shape. Tracks were eventually laid near the edge of their new town, heading for Cimarron. Thinking ahead, Henry petitioned the Union Pacific and with the help of others, built a small train station. It was initially very confusing for the engineers and brakemen. There set a train station but it wasn't a stop? Henry was never sure if it was his persuasion, or the confusion, that finally got them on the schedule. But once they did, the place exploded. A year later, Henry was elected as their first mayor, with the dusty street at the center of town, named in his honor. Maple Ridge was now officially on the map.

Grayson Street was the center of town and the hub of commerce. Henry had considered it to be their main street from the beginning, long before it had a name. They grew slowly at first, as the old temporary buildings were demolished and new comers started to set up and stake their claim. New permanent structures were soon erected to replace the old buildings, with this dusty street as their anchor. Henry planted his maples strategically along the street and nurtured them like children. He envisioned that someday it would be lined with their offspring and he would plant each one himself.

Maple Ridge had come a long way since those early days. Henry was now semi-retired and showing his years. But he was still active on the town council and spent enough time at the mercantile to be a nuisance. Not much his son, Bobby could do about it though. Henry did own the place and Bobby wouldn't think of telling his father he was in the way.

Ernie remembered Mr. Cahoon from the cattle drive in June. He'd come into Abilene from the southwest trail, which was more commonly used by the remaining Texas drovers. It seemed odd, that he would drive in from that direction, given the purpose of that trail. The Texas longhorns were always separated from the other herds. They would drive in from the south, miles away from other cattle heading to market. Ranchers and farmers from Missouri and Kansas would shoot any trail boss, driving these big odd-looking cows on their land. With their five-foot-wide horns and long legs, they looked and acted differently than any cow these mid-western farmers had ever seen. They were mean, hard to control and left a trail of dead cows, everywhere they trod.

Longhorns were known to carry ticks, which caused "Texas Fever". It had no effect on them but could thin a passing herd within days, after picking up their unwelcome bug.

The Cahoon party hadn't intended to drive their beef on that trail. However, the green-horn drovers, boys really, relented after the herd came to a near stampede and finally settled down three miles from where they should have been. Inexperienced and unable to move them back on the range, they let the cows decide and stayed on their current course. Now walking the ruts left by the last string of longhorns, they were picking up their little parasites along the way.

Mr. Cahoon was probably lucky, all things considered. After the KCBA spotted ticks in the herd, they isolated the affected cows to contain the spread. Their quick move, made the losses much lighter than average. Mr. Cahoon, if he's smart, will pay for his mistake and allow me to go on my way.

The Alhambra Saloon was a welcomed sight and Ernie was glad to be back in his element. The first thing to catch his eye was a card game, which had garnered the attention of a number of onlookers. He resisted the temptation of joining in and chose instead, to settle in at the bar. Ernie looked back and gave it a second thought, then ordered a beer and wisely kept his focus on the task at hand.

"Howdy, stranger what can I get for you?" The bartender asked. He was a man of small stature, with a deeper voice than Ernie would have expected from someone his size. Noticing his attire and mannerisms, he surmised the man to be a Monte or Faro dealer, filling in behind the bar.

"I'll have a beer," Ernie replied.

"Coming at you," the bartender said, as he turned to fill Ernie's request.

Watching the movements of those around him, he was gaining a prospective of the men in town. He hoped it would help him determine what he might expect during his short stay. As a stranger, Ernie didn't seem to be drawing anyone's attention, which was a good sign. Being close to the train station, he suspected they were accustomed to strange faces. He expected some of the saloon's patrons would know Mr. Cahoon and perhaps a couple worked on the Cahoon Ranch. Remaining anonymous was important and not allowing Mr. Cahoon to know of his presence in town, was imperative. So far, he was satisfied and felt no cause for alarm.

"Thanks," Ernie said, as the bartender drew his beer and set it next to him on the bar.

"You new in town?"

"Yeah, just here for a couple of days," Ernie replied, with a slight smile as he removed his hat and laid it next to him on the knotty pine bar.

He didn't mind being friendly but wanted to keep the conversation to a minimal. The bartender seemed to catch on and immediately backed off.

"Looks like a nice town," Ernie continued, as he reconsidered and didn't want to appear rude.

"Yeah, nice folks, peaceable enough," the bartender replied.

"I'm just here for a couple of days, some business to attend to in town." Ernie decided to satisfy the bartender's curiosity to avoid suspicion and establish a friend in town for his short stay.

"I just arrived on the train," Ernie added, after taking his third healthy sip from the heavy glass mug. "Seems like a quite enough place."

"Yeah, I like it here," the bartender replied, as he turned his attention to a cowboy who'd stepped up with an empty mug, expecting a refill.

Ernie took a relaxing breath and thought of how to put the rest of his afternoon to good use. As he leaned in, he gazed through the large beveled mirror behind the bar, watching the reflection of the room behind him. The saloon was larger than most of those he'd frequented in Abilene. The large windows provided an ample supply of light, which illuminated the thick cloud of cigar and hand rolled cigarette smoke. Ernie took another sip of beer and watched as it swirled its way to the ceiling and over the tops of the batwing doors and into the street. The abundance of empty tables was typical this early in the day but Ernie surmised they would all be full come sundown.

Mentally running through the next few hours, he decided to start as usual with the marshal's office. He was reluctant to ask the bartender for directions, expecting the question would raise an unnecessary curiosity. Ernie slowly finished his beer and collected his hat, as he electing instead to stroll about and find it for himself. With a tip of his brim, he walked toward the afternoon sun.

The air was dry with a light breeze, which stirred up a covering of dust, as he stepped onto the boardwalk. The sun was now leaning heavily to the west, reminding folks to finish their business, as afternoon would soon become evening. For Ernie, there was no rush. He took the extra time to stroke the nose of his newest companion for a bit, to get better acquainted with his rented sorrel bay.

As he assembled a mental picture of the town, Ernie slowly looked around, to get a feel for his environment and take in the lay of the land. As a stranger standing on the street corner, he could only see what was before him. The history behind each structure, or the personalities and struggles of those in the street, could not be seen. He had no way of knowing but Ernie Evans had walked into something much bigger than himself, or his purpose for being in Maple Ridge. The people here were in more trouble than they knew and only a few had the foresight to realize it even existed. It seemed too many folks had the attitude that as long as it didn't affect them, they had no reason to get involved.

As he stood on the boardwalk in front of the saloon, Ernie studied the street, building by building. He momentarily studied the placement and size of each structure until he focused on the last building on the corner of the block. There he saw the sign which read; "Marshal's Office". He couldn't help noticing the cleanliness of the street. The boardwalks were swept, with the buildings all well maintained and accented by the swaying of the maple leaves in the afternoon breeze. He noticed right off that it was different than Fredrick Street but he wasn't surprised. On Fredrick, he saw the livery stables, a blacksmith shop and a large wood shop. This was where men who got their hands dirty made a living. Grayson was the center of town and obviously where the town's business took place.

"It's time to go to work," Ernie said aloud, as he untied his new friend and saddled up. Sitting square in the saddle, he felt more like himself, with a fine horse under him, as he pressed his boots firmly in the stirrups. As he slowly walked the horse down the street, he passed the Cattleman's Diner on the left and planned for that to be his next stop, following his visit with the marshal. Yeah, this is a nice town. Ernie thought, recounting his earlier conversation with the bartender.

As he stepped through the doorway, it took a moment for Ernie's eyes to adjust from the bright sun, to the dim lighting in the small office. The scene was quite normal as he looked around the room. There were two desks placed approximately four feet apart, with a small potbelly stove centered between them, about one foot from the outer wall. Marshal Delbert Smith was sitting at his desk writing a complaint against a young drover, who he'd arrested earlier in the day. It was a boring task but one he had to complete, prior to bringing his prisoner before Judge Kellum. The young man seemed to be the marshal's only customer, as he quietly sat on a cot in the cell to the left, repeatedly shuffling an old deck of cards.

"Afternoon, Marshal," Ernie said, as he tipped his hat back a bit and walked toward the desk, extending his hand.

"Afternoon, what can I do for you?" Marshal Smith asked, in a deep orotund voice. He rose to his feet and accepted Ernie's greeting with a firm hand shake. Marshal Delbert Smith was fifty-two years old and stood five foot ten, which made him a tad shorter than Ernie. He was just shy of two hundred pounds, with gray hair and a bushy gray mustache, which covered his top lip and part of his mouth as it trailed down to his chin. His trail worn hat was wide, with a tall crown, which Ernie assumed had been white some time ago. He seemed pleasant but to the point and Ernie wasn't interested in wasting his time, or the marshal's.

"My name is Ernie Evans. I'm here on business for the KCBA, thought I'd better stop in to introduce myself."

"I don't think I know who that is, friend. You need to be a mite clearer about your purpose." The Marshal replied.

"I'm sorry," Ernie continued, as he adjusted his stance. "I work for the Kansas Cattle Buyers Association. I'm here to see a rancher who was overpaid for his herd. I have the papers here to verify the amount." Ernie slowly reached for his inside coat pocket as he spoke. He unfolded the duplicate bill of sale for the cows, along with the list of those who hadn't survived the tick infestation. Reaching for the papers, Marshal Smith asked; "Who are you looking for?"

"A fellow named Larry Cahoon," Ernie replied.

The friendly tone, which began with their introduction, came to an abrupt halt. Marshal Smith withdrew his hand and immediately seemed to no longer have any desire to review the documents before him. Ernie felt their cordial beginning instantly turn cold. He'd seen this reaction before and the look on the marshal's face said more than any string of words could have conveyed at that moment. Ernie immediately knew this was personal for the marshal. He was either inquiring about a friend, or adversary and it was the very reason for the marshal's office to be his first contact.

"I'm sorry, did I say something wrong?" Ernie asked, with a slight but confident smile. He knew what he'd said and he knew what was coming next. This was by no means his first foray into this conversation.

"I don't think you know what you're getting into here, friend." Marshal Smith had retaken his seat and now showed a face with a stern and somber demeanor.

"I'm not planning to get myself into anything, Marshal. Just to collect the eight hundred dollars owed to my clients and I'll be on my way."

As the exchange bantered, Ernie seemed to be the voice of authority. Although he knew the marshal wore the badge, he felt he had gained the moral authority by pressing forward to calmly exercise his responsibility.

"You can look at it anyway you want, Mister. But you're fixing to get yourself into a deep pile of horse shit. My advice to you is to ride on out of here and forget about collecting someone else's money from Mr. Cahoon."

"I can't do that, Marshal. My job is to collect what's due and I aim to do just that." Ernie kept his voice low and respectful but he could see the frustration in Marshal Smith's face when he wouldn't relent.

"You a gun hand, Mister?" The marshal asked, as he looked toward Ernie's sidearm.

"No sir, I never draw first but I came here to do a job."

"You think you're going to waltz in there and show Mr. Cahoon some papers… And he's going to fork over eight hundred dollars and let you walk out, pretty as you please?"

"That would be his best response, Marshal. But if he chooses otherwise, then I'll have to deal with it."

Frustrated that Ernie wouldn't take his advice, Marshal Smith chose a stronger tact, explaining Mr. Cahoon's stature in town and the type of men he had working for him. The drovers he'd hired in the spring were green. They didn't represent the hardcore ranch hands and wranglers, who worked full time on the Cahoon Ranch. These weren't men to be trifled with and Marshal Smith knew Ernie was setting himself up for real trouble if he persisted. Undeterred in his task, Ernie knew the marshal would offer no support. He finally asked the location of the ranch, which was reluctantly provided, then cordially tipped his hat with a smile and made his way to the street.

The Cahoon Ranch was a fifty thousand acre spread, southwest of town and south of the C.S. Ranch. Small in comparison to the Maxwell Land Grant, Cahoon worked a large herd of cattle, with a renowned string of thoroughbreds that were second to none. A man of Scottish heritage, he'd made his way to America prior to the start of the Civil War. He'd saved enough money farming in his native Scotland to buy two fares on a merchant ship, for him and his wife to make it across the Atlantic. Making land in Charleston, S.C., he initially found work in a cotton gin and saved enough to make the trip to New Mexico. There, he took on work at the C.S. Ranch, where he learned cattle and the art of breeding champion horses from Charles Springer, owner of the C.S.

From the beginning, he had his eye on the open range to the south and vowed to own it all and make his mark in America. He'd read about the Cattle Barons in Cheyenne, Wyoming and fancied himself to be of their caliber. Guarding his empire with force, when deemed necessary, Larry Cahoon wasn't a man who tolerated intruders with forbearance. Still, Ernie had a job to do and would meet the challenge with grit and a steady hand.

The Abilene office of the Kansas Cattle Buyers Association employed four men. Their jobs were primarily to act as brokers for their clients and negotiate pricing with the ranchers to maximize their member's profits. They also maintained the day to day operations of the association and kept in contact with their members. Mr. William Murphy was head of the association and kept a firm grip on their bottom line. He was a rotund man, who enjoyed his success and usually dressed in the finest frocks from Kansas City. He was never seen without a cigar clutched in his teeth, with a swirl of blue smoke trailing close behind.

He and the board met weekly to review each transfer of stock and the profits earned by their members and in turn, for themselves. Mr. Murphy was always eager to remind their members of the increased cash flow they received by allowing the KCBA to do their bidding. He was very convincing when proclaiming the value of their small membership fees and nominal percentage of sale profits. They had come to accept his self-importance. But their main benefit was realized when a herd was found to be of less value than expected. That's when Ernie Evans would get involved.

William Murphy would boast of their role when counting profits but became irate when a herd was later discovered to be short. His buyers became inevitably on edge at the discovery of an overpayment to a rancher. They were the first to get the blame and many were fired to make a point and set an example for the others. The men who ran the slaughter houses in Chicago and New York knew when to apply pressure to their Mr. Murphy. They also knew when to stand back and allow him to revel in his own grandeur. The northern buyers were of sufficient ego to match wits with any of Mr. Murphy's buyers on the day of auction. They were, however, happy to defer to his techniques when their money found its way to the pockets of some undeserving rancher. By their calculations, it all balanced out.

The current situation with Larry Cahoon was the main topic of discussion for Mr. Murphy and the board in this week's meeting. The herd had been purchased on behalf of the owners of a Chicago slaughter house, who'd promptly paid their draft in full upon purchase. Now, they were looking to the KCBA to make good on the eight hundred dollars in overpayment. They had been lucky this time. The potential loss was light and Ernie was currently in New Mexico to rectify the problem. The board approved an eight-hundred-dollar bank draft, issued to their aggrieved member. Now, they owned the loss, lock, stock and barrel.

Mr. Murphy expected this to be wrapped up quickly. Although he would use this as an example of their exemplary service, a debit of this amount didn't look good on the books and he wanted it back as quickly as possible.

Upon leaving the marshal's office, Ernie untied his horse and decided to walk him down past the Mercantile and the Land Office, to the Cattleman's Diner. He knew he would earn his pay on this trip and immediately began thinking of ways to pull this off, without getting himself killed. Slow and patient, Ernie thought.

As he entered the diner, he could smell the combination of burning mesquite and an array of chilies and spices, used in their menu of Mexican specialties. With his mind set on a large rare steak, Ernie removed his hat and took a seat close to the door. The restaurant was larger than it appeared from the street and again, he wondered how many of the patrons had a connection with the Cahoon Ranch.

Waiting for his steak, Ernie sat with a large mug of Arbuckle coffee and pondered his plan for the next day. A couple of folks spoke, as they walked by. He responded in kind but immediately turned to his coffee, discouraging any small talk, or inquiry as to the stranger's purpose in town. As with the saloon, Ernie needed to remain as anonymous as possible.

As his plan began to formulate, he felt less on edge, with a sense of optimism easing his mind. He knew his normal tactics wouldn't work. The nonaggressive and non-intimidating demeanor of a businessman was in order. Ride right up to the front door with the mild-mannered attitude of a banker, no sidearm and no rifle scabbard. He would back off if challenged and evaluate the opponent. Upon arrival, Ernie would ride in and dismount in a slow unassuming manner and carefully walk up to the front door. He would offer no hint of his intention to fulfill his purpose at all cost.

Ernie played out the various possibilities in his mind, as he devoured a plate of beef, with gravy and boiled potatoes. As he devised a plan to deal with each perceived possibility, he wasn't sure at this point, if his first visit would be his last. After cleaning his plate, Ernie decided the next step would be finding a hotel. He sat for a bit, finishing his coffee and still pondering his options. With his appetite satisfied, he paid for his meal and headed back to the street.

The afternoon sun was approaching the mountain tops to the west as he mounted up and slowly walked his bay down the street. He headed back in the direction of the Double Deuce, as he looked for a hotel along the way, hoping he would find one close by.

"Back so soon, young fellow?" Ralph Thomas was pulling straw into one of the stables as Ernie dismounted and walked his horse to the back of the livery.

"Yeah, I'll be staying in town for the night, thought you might want to keep him here 'til morning." Ernie replied, as he held the reins and stroked the nose of his new friend.

"That will be fine. I'm still going to charge you, though." Ralph said with a laugh.

"I know," Ernie replied with a grin. "Where's the nearest hotel?"

"The Byron Hotel, down to the next block then over to Jacob Street, you can't miss it." Ralph replied, as he leaned against his pitch-folk and pointed in that general direction.

Ernie took his saddlebags and rifle scabbard then tipped his hat and made his way down the street. Still wondering what tomorrow would bring, he decided not to dwell on it for the evening.His focus now, was a clean hotel room and a good night's sleep.

The Byron Hotel was easy to spot. It was two buildings from the corner of Fourth, across from the telegraph office and was the tallest building in town. It was fancier than Ernie had expected. He could tell by the large well-furnished parlor, that it would cost more than he wanted to pay. He didn't feel like looking for another, so he paid the three-dollar nightly rate and took the key to room 214. As he entered the room, he smiled at his surroundings. It was a large room with a high ceiling and a big spiraled post bed. An oak wash stand was centered below a framed painting of fox hunters. Next to the bed, he saw a round pedestal table with a large lamp. It appeared to have been trimmed and topped off with coal oil. I'll sleep good tonight, he thought.

CHAPTER 2

Through the open window of his hotel room, Ernie could feel the cool breeze of the morning air as he awoke. The dim offerings of light, now projecting across the room, announced the start of a new day. He couldn't remember when he'd enjoyed a better night's rest. As he roused and began to contemplate the tasks of the day, he thought of what was before him. He knew it wouldn't continue on as calm or serene.

Ernie was learning his way around town a bit and easily made it over to the Double Deuce Corral to pick up his horse. Again, he found himself to be the target of Ralph's questions. Only this time he turned the tail on ole Ralph and began asking the same of him. To Ernie's surprise he was happy to oblige and immediately began with a proud story of how he had donned the Confederate gray. Ernie was intrigued and quickly gained a new level of respect for his new friend. He now knew there were at least two Johnny Rebs in Maple Ridge.

The Early Bird Café, on the corner of Third Street and Grayson, was the busiest place in town this time of day. JT Belcher prided himself on being the first establishment to open each morning. But he was also the first to close each afternoon. JT started early and could always count on a large crowd. After the morning rush, he would feed whatever prisoner Marshal Smith had locked up over at the jail. Then back to the Café to prepare for lunch and his same mid-day rituals. He was normally closed by two o'clock but by then he'd put in an honest day's work. Ernie had planned for the Café to be his first stop after leaving the Double Deuce.

He tied the bay to a hitch rail near the corner of Third Street and removed his rifle from the scabbard. As he turned toward the café, Ernie saw two cow hands walk in before him with a less than friendly look on their faces. They stood out from the others he'd seen, all with a smile or calm demeanor ready to start a new day. He walked in behind them as the men loudly took a seat and demanded instant service. Without hesitation a waitress brought coffee and asked for their order, obviously bypassing a number of folks, who'd been waiting much longer. No one said a word and most were reluctant to look their way. When the waitress finally came to his table, Ernie's curiosity was getting the best of him.

"Who are they?" He asked, motioning to the men.

"They work for Mr. Cahoon." The waitress quietly replied.

"So that means they push folks around and obviously scare the hell out of you?" Ernie asked.

"Yes sir… I'm afraid that's about right. They get what they want and we only hope they'll pay before they leave. Usually they don't." She confessed, shrugging her shoulders.

"And you put up with it?" Ernie asked, planning to stop his inquest there.

"You obviously ain't from around here." She quietly replied, before walking away.

Ernie watched the men from the corner of his eye, as he slowly ate and finished with a second cup of coffee. The men left before him but he was getting the impression of something he didn't like. He began to wonder about Marshal Smith's ability as a lawman.

The relaxing night he'd spent in a fine hotel had been a welcome change from trying to sleep on the train. Now he needed to be alert and mindful of every step and every word. If all went to plan, he'd complete his task before noon and skin out of town today. Based on what he'd seen in the Café, he would need to be at his best. This display was obviously a glimpse into what made the marshal so nervous. It was becoming clear that he was walking into exactly what the marshal had warned against.

Ernie stood for a spell, there on the corner of Third and Grayson just looking around. He pondered the oddity of what he was seeing. The town looked peaceful and the people seemed content, as they went about their business. Yet here were two men, frightening everyone in the Café without a complaint or challenge. It seemed all too normal. Cahoon had a tight grip on the town and it was becoming more obvious by the minute. Ernie wasn't sure if the townsfolk were under a constant threat, or if they'd simply become accustom to their way of life without the fortitude to fight back. He wondered about the marshal's role in this as well. Ernie's curiosity was stirring. Was the Marshal complicit, or was he too complacent?

It was early yet. Ernie wanted to arrive at the ranch around 10:00 am. Everyone should be busy by then, with their focus on the chores of the day. The men would be dispersed around the ranch, or out riding the lines. There would be no concentration of men around the bunkhouse, or near the main house. He felt that would be an appropriate time to do business. Arriving too early would cause alarm and appear unusual.

Ernie stood there awhile, leaning against a post a few feet from the corner. As he pondered, he heard a man approach and turned to see the marshal walking toward him.

"Good morning… Ernie is it?" The marshal asked with a smile.

"Good morning, Marshal. That's right, Ernie Evans." He replied.

"Yeah, that's right, I remember. How are you this morning?

"Fine, sir," Ernie replied.

"Did you get a good night's sleep here?"

"I did, thank you. That Byron Hotel is quite a place." Ernie replied.

"You picked the best. That's the fanciest place in town."

Well, I didn't pick it. It's a little rich for my blood. Ralph at the livery sent me there."

The marshal just chuckled. "Ole Ralph, he's a character. There are a couple of other hotels, where you could have slept just as well, for less money. The Grand Hotel is just a block down, on your right." The marshal added.

"I figured as much," Ernie replied. "By the time I got there, I was too tired to hunt for another."

"Are you still planning to go out to Cahoon's place today?" The marshal asked.

"I am, Marshal. But I thought I'd wait a bit. I don't want to get there too early, while all the ranch hands are around."

"You'd best take my advice and call it off. You're looking to get yourself killed out there and there's not a thing I can do to help you." Marshal Smith was making one last plea to keep Ernie away from Cahoon.

"I can't do that, Marshal. Like I told you, I have a job to do." Ernie replied. "Marshal, there's something odd going on here. Can you tell me about it?"

"I've already told you, if you were listening. My advice to you is to go on about your business and forget this foolishness." Marshal Smith then tipped his hat and walked away. He wasn't of the mind to get more involved in this conversation.

Ernie stood for a moment, recapping their talk as well as the marshal's demeanor. He then slowly strolled up the street toward the saloon, which was still closed. Everyone looked normal and going about their business but Ernie could feel an undertow that he could not explain.

His ride to the ranch took the better part of an hour. The air on the southwest trail was cool, which was good for the horse. It would conserve his energy, should they need to make a sudden break for it. Just over the ridge within sight of the main house, Ernie approached a stand of pinyon pines. A perfect spot to stash his rifle and revolver, he thought.

He tied the horse, then carefully placed his cartridge belt and revolver next to his scabbard and fully loaded Winchester. He'd keep them close to the road, for easy access, should the situation turn hot. The stand of trees gave a good place to protect the horse and provide cover if pinned down. His only remaining protection was a small, short barreled, "poker gun", which he kept in his inner left coat pocket. With his plan in place, Ernie took a deep breath and made his way to the main house.

As he reined up to the hitching post in front of the house, Ernie saw three ranch hands approach, all wearing sidearms. The men weren't smiling and he knew the party was about to start.

"Can I help you, Mister?" The first man stepped up, as the two stayed back a couple of paces. They were obviously there to provide cover, if needed and to let Ernie know they were ready, if he meant to bring trouble.

"Morning, Gentlemen." Ernie dismounted and smiled with his best businessman impression.

"I'm here to see Mr. Cahoon. Is he around?"

"Who's asking, Mister?" Raymond, the ranch foreman, walked up close and didn't offer a friendly gesture, or any information.

"My name is Ernest Evans. I'm here to see Mr. Cahoon about the herd he drove up to Abilene a couple of months back."

"What about it?"

"Well, I think that would be Mr. Cahoon's business. Is he about?" Ernie was calm but persistent.

With no further questions the foreman turned and walked to the house. All the while, his men held their position without speaking, or any show of expression, as Ernie stood quietly taking in the lay of the land. The house was large and meticulously designed. It was obviously the centerpiece of Mr. Cahoon's success. Unfortunately, it was in the open with little cover. Ernie felt certain that was by design. The front lawn was finely landscaped with a few well-placed trees but nothing that would provide cover for a man who didn't want to be seen.

There were several men working around the stable, about fifty yards to the north, all wearing sidearms. Just down from the stable, to the left, stood a large barn also with armed men in clear view. A bit unusual, Ernie thought. You wear your sidearm when you're out from the ranch, for varmints or undesirables. But not while you're working close to the ranch, it just gets in your way. This place is heavily defended, he thought but wondered why? The front door, the windows and the full front porch, showed limited access in or out. It was unusual for a ranch to be so closely guarded. The purpose of these men was obvious and Ernie knew he was being closely watched.

As he waited, Ernie thought back to last fall when he'd made a trip to the Oklahoma Territory, to pay a visit to Harvey Brewer. Mr. Brewer's losses were three times that of Larry Cahoon's. He worked day to day and his net worth was meager in comparison. Settling his debt with the KCBA wasn't possible, even if he'd wanted to. Problem was, he wasn't open minded enough to even try.

Ernie didn't have the time to learn much about Mr. Brewer, some things you learn the hard way. He was a man with a mean temper and a reputation of turning to his revolver early in a disagreement. Ernie hadn't the time to even review the bill of sale before Mr. Brewer became angry and demanded that he leave. Upon hearing the amount, Brewer's face became blood red and he immediately reached for his Colt. Ernie responded in kind and placed a bullet in Harvey Brewer's forehead, before his revolver was level.

Hearing the shot, Mrs. Brewer ran in and fell at her husband's side. Ernie quickly snatched her to her feet and demanded she bring him all the money in the house. She now feared that he would kill her as well, though he had no intention of hurting this lady. She nervously opened the safe and gave him twelve hundred dollars, which was bundled in a small box. Mr. Brewer would have been given the same option, had his temper not gotten him killed first. Ernie stuffed the cash in his coat pocket and slowly walked to the door, as the sobbing Mrs. Brewer lay across her husband's lifeless body.

As he cautiously walked through the doorway, he saw two ranch hands running to the house. Ernie quickly saddled up and made his escape with the sound of gun fire at his back. He wouldn't make the same mistake today.

Larry Cahoon was a man of stocky build and looked to be in his late fifties, as he slowly stepped out onto the porch. He was freshly shaven, with a small well-groomed mustache and dressed in the finest attire. He looked like money. His gold watch chain, glistened in the morning sun, as it swung against his black and gray vest, which tightly held in his well-fed stomach. As Ernie approached, Cahoon stood cautiously with two fingers resting in each lower vest pocket. Ernie looked once again to the men standing on his right and then moved forward to meet him at the bottom of the steps. The three ranch hands stayed in close proximity.

"Good morning, Mr. Cahoon. My name is Ernest Evans."

"You'll have to forgive me foreman, Mr. Evans. He's a wee bit touchy and a mite protective of the place when strangers are about." Mr. Cahoon spoke firmly and with a heavy accent. His demeanor was calm but showed the traits of a guarded and suspicious man.

"That's quite alright, Mr. Cahoon. I appreciate you taking the time to see me. May we step inside, where we can speak more privately?" Ernie was proud of how the words were rolling off his tongue. Not one to speak so properly, he had to quickly think of each word to make himself appear much more educated than he actually was.

Entering the house, Ernie was conscience of his surroundings. He carefully studied the windows, which displayed the magnificent lawn and each door, as they related to the parlor. He was also watching Mr. Cahoon's eyes. Ernie was careful not to be seen as overly curious, or to have an ulterior motive. He would obviously become suspicious, if he noticed Ernie paying too close attention to his surroundings. But knowing his environment was imperative. Drawing a mental picture of the ranch, from the pines to the furnishings in the parlor was necessary. Ernie needed to develop some type of advantage, should a second visit become necessary.

"Please, have a seat, Mr. Evans." Mr. Cahoon pointed to a deep red French Provincial sofa to their left, which was positioned across from two high back maroon leather arm chairs. As he took a seat, a second gentleman, dressed in a black English cut suit, with a clean silver banded Stetson, entered the room. Turning to take a seat next to Mr. Cahoon, a nickel-plated Colt, with pearl grips, came into clear view. His purpose became immediately obvious.

"Mr. Evans, this is Gregory McElliott. He's... let's say, my business manager." Mr. Cahoon just smiled, as he knew Ernie would understand his meaning. Without a reply, Ernie simply nodded, which prompted no exchange from Mr. McElliott.

"Mr. Cahoon, I'm with the Kansas Cattle Buyers Association. It seems there was a small problem with the herd you delivered to Abilene back in June, nothing to be alarmed for. Turns out, a few of the cattle you drove in picked up Texas Fever and had to be put down." Ernie slowly removed the bill of sale and a list of the affected cows, from his pocket as he spoke.

"The office copy of your bill of sale and this listing of the sick cattle, is all here for your review. You can wire the main office in Abilene to verify if you'd like but it's all here. The purpose of my visit is to collect the eight hundred dollars of overpayment and be on my way." Ernie calmly arranged the papers on the mahogany table between them and quietly waited for a response.

Larry Cahoon sat motionless for a moment, as he stared at the papers before him, then looked toward McElliott and broke into a very contemptuous laugh.

"Mr. Evans, did you come all the way from Kansas for this?"

"Yes sir, I did. I would appreciate it if we could settle this matter now, so I may be on my way." Ernie was calm and showed no sense of concern, though he knew he was being mocked.

"Well, you should be on your way but I'm afraid you'll be leaving empty handed, Mr. Evans. We sold you a good herd and I'm not of the mind to give you eight hundred dollars." Larry Cahoon spoke with a low firm voice and would not relent. McElliott shifted his weight in his chair, away from his sidearm, apparently anxious to get involved and earn his pay.

The situation, at this point, was of no surprise to Ernie, as he carefully measured his current position.

"Mr. Cahoon, I can't just leave. This is a proper bill and my boss would be quite upset if I were to return, without settling the matter. We hope to see you again next year but that wouldn't be possible, with this outstanding bill unsettled." Ernie wasn't sure how far he could push the issue but he knew they would become suspicious, if he relented and left too soon.

"That's not my concern, Mr. Evans. I'll just sell to someone else next year."

"It's not that easy, Mr. Cahoon. You see, word travels. One buyer gets stuck with sick cows and all the buyers find out. I promise you, the others won't take the chance, if they feel they might also come up short."

"Actually, it is that easy, Mr. Evans. Mac, see our friend to the door." Mr. Cahoon rose to his feet as his earlier smile, was now more of a scowl. As he slowly walked from the room, Gregory McElliott rose to his feet and carefully draped the right side of his long coat over the back of his black leather tooled holster. The look on his face was as if he only hoped Ernie would make one wrong move.

Carefully and without a hint of provocation, Ernie slowly walked to the door, with Mac only one step behind. As he reached for the door knob with his left hand, Ernie's right went for the poker gun, in his left inner coat pocket. He quickly drew the pistol and pressed the barrel to Mac's throat, just to the left of his adam's apple, then moved in almost nose to nose.

"Now Mac, we can do this a couple of ways, one you live and one you don't." Ernie quickly removed Mac's Colt, with his left hand, as he spoke. Cocking the hammer, he pressed the revolver tightly to Mac's stomach.

"Now, you're going to call Mr. Cahoon back to the parlor and we're going to try this again, you understand?"

Mac stood for a moment with a look of anger, which obviously had no effect on his opponent. With no hint of fear in his eyes, Ernie tilted his head a bit and pressed the gun barrel a little harder.

"What's it going to be, Mac?"

Without breaking his stare Mac complied and nodded with the quiet utterance, "Okay."

Ernie motioned for him to turn. As he did, the poker gun was replaced in Ernie's coat pocket, with Mac's revolver now firmly gripped in his right hand. Being summoned, Mr. Cahoon returned to the parlor with a surprised look, that Ernie took great pleasure in perpetuating.

"Mr. Cahoon, it seems that you misunderstood my polite manner and apparently thought I was asking that you make good on your bill. We're going to do this again. Only now, it's one thousand dollars, for the extra trouble you've caused me. Now, you go to your safe and bring me the money. I will write you a proper receipt, then Mac here and I will be leaving. You make sure your men stand down and Mac will be back for dinner. Otherwise, Mac will make a fine dinner for the coyotes. It makes no difference to me."

Larry Cahoon was furious but didn't say a word. The arrogant attitude, he and Gregory McElloitt had displayed only a moment earlier, was now gone. He seemed a bit more compliant, with Mac's revolver staring him in the face. Without delay, Mr. Cahoon walked to his desk and unlocked the top right-side drawer. Before he reached in, Ernie turned and placed Mac between Larry Cahoon and himself.

"Just in case you have any ideas, Mr. Cahoon, I'll drop Mac in a second, if you come up with anything other than a cash box. Just so we're clear."

The look on the rancher's face was as though his plan had been just as Ernie suspected. He slowly closed the drawer and turned to a portrait of Mrs. Cahoon, centered between two large windows. Ernie could see the contempt as he slowly lifted the painting from its hook and carefully set the bottom of the frame on the hardwood floor. A black recessed wall safe was now clearly visible.

Blocking Ernie's view, Mr. Cahoon turned the dial until the combination dropped each tumbler into the open position. He slowly turned the handle on the door and once again, Ernie reminded him that money was the only acceptable item he should withdraw from the safe's contents. Mr. Cahoon counted ten one hundred-dollar bills and smacked them on the desk.

"You just messed up bad, Mister. You won't make it out of here alive." Cahoon said, in a low, confident voice.

Ernie picked up the money and as promised removed the bill of sale from his pocket. After laying it on the desk, he pulled the pen from the ink well and signed under the words: 'Paid in Full'.

"You must be crazy." Larry Cahoon said, in disbelief.

"No sir, I ain't crazy, just doing my job."

Ernie backed away, with Mac's Colt still firmly planted in his side. As they walked backward to the door, he instructed Mr. Cahoon to call his three guard dogs to the porch. It was time to have a little talk about what would soon be taking place. Once gathered on the front porch, Ernie set in on the bunch of them.

"What's the matter with you people? I came here to collect an honest debt and you act like I'm stealing money out of your pocket. Now we're square and ole Mac and me, we're going to be on our way. You follow me and I'll kill him and any of you dumbasses who take a shot at me."

Ernie untied his bay and lifted a coil of rope from the horse tied to the next post, throwing it over the saddle horn of his own. He slowly walked him up the road, with Mac and himself on the right side of the horse, out of full view of Cahoon's men. He had determined that his only way out, was to walk Mac and the horse, back to the pines. He'd leave him tied there, for whoever found him first. The coyotes or Cahoon's men, Ernie couldn't care less who won the contest.

Upon their arrival, Ernie tied Mac to a pine and collected his rifle and gun belt. He knew Cahoon's men would be on his heels and there was no time to waste. Without a word, he saddled up and threw Mac's Colt between the trees, some ten feet away. With a roll of his spurs, Ernie and his mount headed northeast and out of sight.

Marshal Smith had been away from town for most of the morning. He'd left early, riding out to the smaller spreads to see the farmers who'd settled on the outskirts of town. It was a routine that he followed each week without fail. For him, it seemed to be the right thing to do. He'd ride out, from time to time, just to check on folks. He'd make sure they were okay and wanted to be seen around in case anyone needed help. He'd given thought to the stranger a couple of times during his ride. He hoped he'd taken his advice and left without confronting Larry Cahoon, or his men.

Prior to becoming marshal of Maple Ridge, Delbert Smith had made his living as a bounty hunter. He knew what it was like to live by the gun. He thought he'd seen all kinds but he'd never run up against men as ruthless as those who worked the Cahoon Ranch. He didn't see this stranger as any different and suspected if Ernie had persisted in his plan, someone would find his body somewhere along the trail, between town and the ranch.

He had no desire to challenge Cahoon over the death of some stranger. He'd been put in that position before and been threatened to back off, as Cahoon put pressure on his cronies on the town council. Henry Grayson was sick of his manipulation of the law and stood against Cahoon. But as usual, he was out numbered. The mayor immediately forced the marshal to turn the other way, if he wanted to keep his job. Not so eager to get himself killed, he did as he was told and dropped the whole thing. It had always stuck in his craw and he hoped someone would eventually get even with that crotchety old bastard.

It had been two years since Ben Willis challenged Cahoon's men. Ben and his wife had a small spread, to the south of the Cahoon Ranch where they managed a growing herd. Ben realized one morning that he was missing a few head and rode out to find them. He soon discovered them in a small cut, on the south end of the Cahoon spread, which was routinely crossed by travelers. Ben approached, to drive his cattle back in the open, when he was challenged by two of Cahoon's men.

"Where do you think you're going? You're on private land, Mister." One of Cahoon's men barked, as he reined his horse in front of Ben's.

"Those are my strays. I came to get 'um back." Ben said.

"Well, they are on the Cahoon Ranch now, looks like you should have kept a better eye on 'um." The men started laughing and tempting Ben.

"I don't care whose land they wandering onto, I'm taking them back."

"Go ahead, see how far you get." The men were no longer laughing and now hoping Ben would stand his ground.

Ben persisted and reined his horse around the men, to get a better look at the brand. Confirming it to be his, he cut out the missing head and started to drive them back. Cahoon's men watched for a bit and let him do the hard work of turning them in the direction of his spread.

"Where are you going?" Cahoon's man asked.

"These cows are mine and I'm driving them back to my spread." Ben said, as he rose up defiantly in the saddle.

"You're got one chance to ride off, Mister. And I ain't telling you again." Each man now, had his hand on his revolver.

When Ben passed the men, they each drew their sidearm and shot him out of the saddle. To make their point clear, they tied his lifeless body across his saddle and whacked his horse, sending him in a dead run back to the Willis Ranch.

Emma Willis was in a panic when she arrived in town that afternoon. She was afraid to remove Ben from his horse and hitched him to the back of their wagon, then rode five miles into town. She hoped her husband might still be alive. He was a good man, who worked hard to provide for his family. But the cold and callous way of Cahoon and his men left his family devastated.

Later that evening, Cahoon's two ranch hands were in Jack's Saloon, drinking and causing their usual disturbance. When one was approached, he defiantly told Jack that he'd get some of what they'd given Ben Willis, if he didn't back down. Word soon got to the marshal. He and Deputy Wilcox immediately went to the saloon and arrested the drunken cow hands.

Early the next morning, Cahoon came in with six riders demanding they be released. When Marshal Smith refused, Cahoon just laughed and made his way to the mayor's office. In less than an hour, both men were freed and on their way home. Marshal Smith never forgot that. He'd spoken to Judge Kellum about it several times but without an indictment that he could back up, there was nothing the judge could do. The whole thing had only made the marshal's hatred for Cahoon grow deeper.

There were other incidents. This was the only killing but these men had been responsible for a number of beatings of innocent men in town, all with no accountability. All designed to keep Cahoon's heavy hand on the townsfolk. Marshal Smith had been powerless against them and they reveled in it. He'd only hoped that someday he could make it right.

CHAPTER 3

Ernie made it back to town just ahead of the Cahoon posse and tied up in front of the ticket office, at the train station. Deputy Marshal Brady Wilcox was making his rounds in the area, when four of Cahoon's men came blazing up the dusty street. Not knowing what was taking place, he saw it as no coincidence that they came in on the heels of this stranger who'd just ridden in. Partially obstructed, by a taller sorrel standing next to him, they didn't initially see the bay as they passed by, still in a gallop. This gave Ernie an extra few seconds to be ready when they turned back.

Deputy Wilcox immediately crossed the street and was about to confront Ernie when the men turned back and spotted his horse. Ernie gave the deputy a quick rundown as he watched the men approach and asked him to stay close by. He suspected these men were ready to burn powder and needed to keep Deputy Wilcox as a witness to whatever was about to take place.

The men dismounted in the street, leaving their horses untied, as they walked toward the boardwalk, in front of the ticket office.

"You'd best come out, stranger," Mac shouted. He was still furious that he'd been had.

Deputy Wilcox slowly walked out of the office to calm the situation, where he was quickly challenged by Raymond Adams, Cahoon's foreman.

"You'd better back off Wilcox, if you know what's good for you." He shouted.

"I don't want any trouble, Raymond. Let's work this out." Deputy Wilcox was over his head and didn't want to be involved in gun play with these men. After an additional cold stare, he backed up two paces, away from the door. He knew he was no match for these men. Standing there, not knowing what to do, he remained silent, waiting for Ernie's move. He suddenly wished the marshal was in town.

Ernie stood in the doorway for a moment, watching the stance of the four men. I'll take Mac first, then the foreman. The other two will likely run, he thought. He backed away from the door, out of sight and drew his Colt. He then opened the gate and spun the cylinder. "Six live rounds, that should do it," he whispered.

With his revolver fully cocked, Ernie held it low. He slowly walked out the door, standing side to his opponents and looking over his right shoulder directly at Mac.

"The bill is paid, Mac. You'd best go on about your business."

"You are my business, you son of a bitch. Now return the money, or I'll drop you where you stand."

"That's not a good idea, Mac. I don't think you're that fast. I'm drawn and cocked; seems I have the advantage." Ernie stood with his Colt pointed down but ready to fire. He was as calm as a preacher on Sunday.

Deputy Wilcox backed away a few more steps. His heart was pounding, as a crowd began to gather. A slight breeze was kicking up dust and blew open Mac's coat, revealing his sidearm. He immediately draped his coat over the back of his black leather holster, bringing his pearl handled Colt into full view.

"I see you found your revolver, Mac." Ernie said. He wanted to rattle him a bit, to take him off his edge.

"You should have kept it, asshole. Now I'm going to kill you with it."

Mac was getting angrier by the second, all he wanted was revenge. Ernie kept his cool, watching the movements of each man. He watched their eyes, their stance and their gun hand. He could tell who would move first by the way they stood and the way they moved their head and eyes. Only Mac and the foreman were reading his position. The other two kept looking to them, not knowing what else to do. They never looked at him and appeared scared, just as he suspected. Ernie waited them out for a few moments. He goaded Mac a bit more, hoping he would draw first.

Suddenly, his right shoulder moved and Mac went for his Colt. Ernie leveled his revolver and caught him square in the chest. As his body hurled backwards, the Colt left his right hand and landed several feet away. The foreman drew a split second later and met the same fate, as he fell back onto the man behind him, knocking him down as well. Ernie immediately turned to the drover to his left, who was backing away with his hands in the air, too afraid to speak.

Deputy Wilcox stood there, without movement. He didn't know what to do. Arresting Ernie never entered his mind and it seemed that little else had as well. Ernie slowly walked out, as the man who'd fallen, was now on his feet and backing away.

"I don't want any trouble, Mister." The young man pleaded.

"Go home, boy. I ain't going to hurt you." Ernie replied. He placed his revolver back in the holster, then checked Mac and the foreman, to make sure they were both dead. Deputy Wilcox was still standing on the boardwalk, as the crowd was now threefold what it had been earlier.

Ernie walked back to the boardwalk and up to the deputy, who still didn't know what to do next.

"As I was saying, Deputy, Mr. Cahoon owed a bill for some cattle and didn't want to pay up." Ernie knew the deputy was rattled and just wanted to mess with him a bit.

"You just killed two men." Deputy Wilcox shakily replied.

"I know. It was a fair fight and I have you as a witness, right?" Ernie asked. He wanted to make sure the deputy and half the town, would see things his way. Once regaining his composure, Deputy Wilcox walked out to the street and began to disperse the crowd. He now wondered if he should arrest Ernie but quickly dispensed with that thought. Settling on the need to get the two dead bodies off the street, he made himself busy and sent for the undertaker.

Marshal Smith had just made it back to town and heard the news, before he reached his office. In the rare occasion where he galloped a horse in town, he spurred his mount and didn't let up until he was in front of the ticket office. Ernie was on the boardwalk, watching as the marshal and the undertaker reached the scene at about the same time. As the undertaker and Deputy Wilcox tended to the bodies, Marshal Smith made a bee-line for Ernie.

"What happened here?" Marshal Smith asked. He was sure Ernie was involved, without having to ask.

"Ask your deputy, Marshal, he saw the whole thing."

"I'm asking you, I'm sure this is your handy work." The marshal had expected trouble since the moment Ernie left his office but this wasn't how he thought it would turn out.

"I went out to the Cahoon Ranch and collected what he owed. He wasn't too happy about it and put these fellows on my trail to get his money back."

"So, he paid you and then changed his mind?" Marshal Smith asked. He knew there was more to the story than Ernie was telling.

"Not exactly, I had to persuade him to pay up." Ernie replied. He was scratching his three-day old whiskers, as he spoke and being intentionally vague.

"Yeah, I thought so. Damn it man, I told you something like this would happen. You're not going anywhere, until I get to the bottom of this," Marshal Smith replied. He wasn't cowering to Larry Cahoon but he knew he'd be in big trouble with the mayor, if he let Ernie off too soon.

Marshal Smith walked out and grabbed Deputy Wilcox by the sleeve. He pulled him aside and pushed him for a full account of what he had witnessed. Wilcox explained what had taken place, as he gave the marshal a full explanation of what he'd seen. In short, Ernie had tried to talk them down and then killed both men in self-defense. Satisfied that he had his deputy as a witness, Marshal Smith felt he would finally have an edge. When Larry Cahoon shows up, he knew the mayor would press him to make an arrest but he'd stick by his guns, this time and do what's right.

Mayor E. J. Sterns was forty-six, five foot seven inches and one hundred fifty pounds soaking wet. He was educated in the law and had lived in Santa Fe before moving to Maple Ridge five years ago. He'd come to set up his own practice and was doing quite well at the time of Henry Grayson's retirement. He'd never held public office but many in town supported him as the new mayor, so he decided to run. It wasn't something he'd thought about previously and if he'd lost, he wouldn't be overly disappointed. He won by a wide majority and had been mayor ever since. He was in his office, when he heard about the shooting and immediately left to find Marshal Smith. He knew there would be hell to pay and he wanted no parts of the mean side of Larry Cahoon. He needed to press the marshal and make sure the shooter was behind bars before Cahoon and his men hit town. He only hoped that would calm his temper, to some degree.

When he arrived at the scene, both dead men were stretched out in the undertaker's wagon, covered by an old blanket. At this point, the mayor didn't know their names, only that they were two of Larry Cahoon's men. When he learned they were Mac and Raymond, he knew Cahoon would expect someone to hang.

"Delbert, what the hell happened here?" Mayor Sterns asked, as he removed his handkerchief and nervously wiped the sweat from his forehead.

"According to Wilcox, Cahoon's men came up on this fellow and threatened to kill him. He tried to talk 'um down but they drew on him anyway. Looks like a fair fight, Mayor." Marshal Smith replied, as he spoke with authority and stood his ground.

"That may be but you'd better lock him up for now."

"I can't do that, Mayor. This fellow was in his rights to protect himself." Marshal Smith wasn't about to back down now.

"Maybe so but Cahoon will have my ass, if he ain't in jail when he gets here."

"What, better him than you?" Marshal Smith asked.

"Don't get smart with me, Delbert. You know exactly what I mean."

Ernie just watched as the two men talked. He could see the fear in Mayor Sterns' eyes.

Cahoon was on the front porch with a glass of afternoon tea, waiting when the two ranch hands rode up to the house alone. He'd expected to see Mac ride in first with his money and a report that their unwelcome guest was in the hereafter. Instead, he would hear that Mac and Raymond had taken that trip. Outraged by the news, he slammed the glass he was holding, against the porch column, with shared glass and its contents flying in every direction.

"Get me six men. We're going back into town now." Larry Cahoon shouted. His face was blood red, as he walked back into the house to get his revolver and holster.

Mayor Sterns didn't know what to do. He couldn't think straight and was very concerned for the town's safety and what was certain to come. Larry Cahoon had gained greater control over the town in the past few years. It had been subtle but persistent and many of the townsfolk were reluctant to stand up to his ways. The mayor thought it possible that Cahoon would kill two townsfolk in retaliation, if they didn't hand Ernie over to them. Or at least, put him in jail. He finally convinced the marshal to bring Ernie to his office, so they could discuss the matter. He was certain that Cahoon and his men would be there soon enough and hoped he could make sense of the situation before they rode in.

By the time Cahoon and his men arrived, Ernie had given the mayor his account of the story, with the exception of the events at the Cahoon Ranch. He knew that would come soon enough but wanted to be sure he was clear on the shooting, before bringing up that "difference of opinion".

"You have no idea of what you've just done here, do you?" Mayor Sterns asked.

"I did my job, Mayor." Ernie calmly replied.

"Your job? You come into our town and risk the lives of everyone who lives here, is that your job?" Mayor Sterns was outwardly shaking in his fine city bought boots and getting worse by the minute. Ernie knew nothing of their politics but he didn't need anyone to tell him that the mayor was owned by Larry Cahoon.

"The only life I've risked today was my own. If you're that afraid of this man, then why don't you folks stand up to him?" It sounded a bit disrespectful but Ernie was sincere in asking. It would never occur to him to back down, if he felt he was threatened. Mayor Sterns just stared back without reply. Although he was unwilling to admit it, any answer to that question, would be an indictment of his own fears.

"I told you yesterday to go on your way. I told you what kind of man you would be dealing with. But you did it anyway." Marshal Smith replied.

"You're the law in this town. Why don't you do something about it?" Ernie asked.

Marshal Smith stood for a moment, pondering his answer before he looked up. "Because he and the town council won't let me, that's why!" Marshal Smith replied, looking directly at Mayor Sterns. He knew he was right but still waited for the Mayor's excuse and expecting to be fired on the spot. EJ Sterns just turned away without a word.

The thunder of horses on the street and the accompanying noise from Cahoon and his men, set the mayor further on edge. He knew this would be a fiery few minutes and hoped Marshal Smith could keep Ernie from being killed, before it was over. He'd believed his story and quietly agreed they'd deserved it but he'd damn sure keep that to himself.

The campaign money and support the mayor had received from Cahoon had long since been satisfied. But he acted as if he owned the mayor's office. Since there had been no pushback thus far, he had every reason to believe that he did. He could never push Henry Grayson but EJ was naïve. Cahoon had enjoyed a free hand over the mayor's office since the day he was elected. EJ was a small-town lawyer, not a politician. When Cahoon offered him money to support his campaign, EJ thought he was interested in his ideas for growing the town and keeping the peace. But it wasn't his politics he was after; it was his power. The mayor controlled the marshal and that made Cahoon's contributions worth every penny.

Larry Cahoon walked past the secretary and didn't bother to knock, as he bolted through the mayor's office door. Six men trailed in behind him, itching for a shot at Ernie.

"There he is. I ought to kill you where you stand." Cahoon shouted. His face was as red as before, with no semblance of reason entering his mind.

"Hold on Mr. Cahoon, we've got this under control. Let's just talk about it, before we go any further." Mayor Sterns was shaking as he spoke.

"Under control? He's standing here wearing a gun, instead of in a jail cell, while two of my men are on a slab. You call that under control?" Cahoon's hand was on the butt of his revolver as he spoke, with each of his men following suit.

Marshal Smith stepped in, to place himself between Ernie and Cahoon, as the mayor stepped back a couple of paces. He got the distinct impression that the mayor wasn't going to interfere this time. He reveled in the possibility of finally being allowed to do his job. Looking the irate rancher in the eye, he pointed to the men behind him and instructed

Cahoon to tell them to stand down. With no immediate response, Marshal Smith pressed on and threatened to clear the room if they didn't comply.

"You don't talk to me that way, I own this town." Cahoon bolstered.

"You might own him." The marshal replied, as he pointed toward the mayor, without breaking eye contact with Cahoon.

"But you don't own me," he concluded. Cahoon was stunned by the marshal's reply and looked toward the mayor, expecting his support. Mayor Sterns stood without saying a word.

"You're talking mighty big, Delbert. You looking for this gun hand to back you up?" Cahoon was surprised and insulted that Marshal Smith would face him in such a manner.

"I need to get this resolved and I don't care if it's you or anybody else, I'm going to do my job." Marshal Smith felt a real sense of relief, with no intention of backing down.

Cahoon pondered for a moment, as he looked first at Ernie, then back to the marshal. He soon relented and without words motioned for his men to wait outside.

"Now," Marshal Smith began, "this fellow shot those two men in self-defense. There are probably twenty witnesses who will back that up. What I want to know is; what happened at your ranch?"

"This son of a bitch came to my home and robbed me of one thousand dollars." Cahoon said, as he shouted and pointed to Ernie.

"I didn't rob him, Marshal. You knew I was going there and why." Ernie was calm in his reply and was quietly enjoying Larry Cahoon's dilemma.

"You told me it was eight hundred, he said one thousand. So, which is it?" The Marshal asked.

"It was eight hundred, until Mac pulled a gun on me. Then I persuaded him to make it a thousand, for my trouble. I even left him a receipt."

Marshal Smith finally pushed Ernie for the full story, without being vague, as he'd been before. Ernie complied, accurately describing each detail, as Cahoon repeatedly interrupted, calling him a liar. The marshal called him down each time, which Cahoon didn't take too kindly. Once Ernie finished, the marshal turned to Larry Cahoon.

"Now it's your turn. How do you see it?"

Larry Cahoon had never been expected to explain himself. In his world, what he says goes and that had included matters in town as well, until today. His story was very different from Ernie's and Marshal Smith wasn't buying it. Mayor Sterns stood back without comment, which didn't go unnoticed by Cahoon.

"What do you have to say, EJ? You're being too quiet about the whole thing." Cahoon asked.

"I think you need to drop it and go home, Mr. Cahoon. It looks like this fellow is in his rights here." Mayor Sterns was standing up to Cahoon for the first time and not as shaky as he'd been only minutes ago. But this time, he knew he really had no choice.

As the conversation came to a conclusion, it was obvious that Larry Cahoon wasn't going to get his way this time. Ernie Evans had been very careful as always, to cover his way, both in and out of the situation. By doing so, he reduced the possibility of getting caught in such a trap. He didn't realize it but he'd just opened a can of worms that no one in town would come near. And it would become his reluctant responsibility to fix.

Without another word, Cahoon left the mayor's office in disbelief. No one had ever spoken to him with such disrespect and this stranger was the cause of it all. He found himself as perplexed, as he was angry. He thought of rushing Ernie in the office but knew someone would get shot. He didn't want to take the chance of it being himself and eventually saw the whole idea as too risky. The ranch hands were on the boardwalk, when he stepped out. They were eager to make a move, if the boss would give his permission. Cahoon chose instead to think this thing out but had no thought of leaving town, without Ernie's hide.

Cahoon stood for a bit, pondering, there on the boardwalk, just south of the Early Bird Café. Folks on the street were still watching and wondering what he might do next. At this point, so was he. It was now just past 3:00 pm, with an unbelievable turn of fate having unfolded in the past four hours. He'd been relieved of one thousand dollars by a stranger in his own home. His two best men had been shot and killed in the street and now he was being treated as though he had no stature in town. This was not going to stand.

He began walking, slowly down the street, as his men following close behind, without conversation. Folks on both sides of the street quickly backed away as they approached but still kept a curious eye on the men as they walked by. His men stayed quiet. They knew any comment would only spark a new outburst and waited for him to break the silence. When they crossed to the next block, Cahoon instructed his six men to follow him, as he pushed open the batwing doors of the Alhambra Saloon.

Marshal Smith and Mayor Sterns knew he wouldn't drop the matter so quickly. Their meeting at the mayor's office was only the first round and this wouldn't be over until Ernie was out of town… or dead.

Everyone knew about the shooting. About half the town, had either witnessed it, or arrived at the scene shortly thereafter. Ernie was building a quiet undertow of support, though he didn't know it and hadn't asked for it. The Cahoon Ranch employed a lot of men and was the source of much of the town's economy. Even so, Larry Cahoon's heavy handed way and belligerent attitude was getting to be more than most folks were willing to tolerate.

Ernie was the first man with the grit, to face down Cahoon, much less kill his gun hand and smartass foreman. This alone was beginning to make Ernie Evans the most popular man in Maple Ridge. Others around town began to think; this stranger comes to town and takes on Cahoon and here we are letting him push us around all these years. Store owners were finally seeing an opportunity to stand up for themselves. They were tired of putting the Cahoon Ranch first and their most loyal patrons at the bottom of the list. It just wasn't right. In the matter of hours, these men were talking to one another and quietly drawing unity amongst themselves.

As Cahoon and his men sat in the saloon, seething and plotting their vigilante move against Ernie, several townsfolk made their way to the mayor's office. When they arrived, the Mayor, Marshal Smith and Ernie were still there discussing the situation. They'd concluded that getting Ernie out of town as soon as possible was the smartest thing to do now. They had no way of knowing what else was stirring and were looking for the best move to quiet this thing, as soon as possible.

They found themselves in a quandary. As the townsmen stepped up, to put a stop to Cahoon, getting Ernie out of town became less of an option. Marshal Smith had sent Deputy Wilcox back to the train station, to buy Ernie a ticket for the next eastbound departure. The train he'd planned to take had left, which meant he would be in town until the next train the following day. The marshal suggested he stay in a jail cell for the night, to keep him safe but Ernie wouldn't hear of it. There was no doubt that Cahoon would return and they only hoped it wouldn't be until the next day.

When the men entered the office, Marshal Smith initially assumed he would now have them to contend with. He seemed to finally have the mayor on his side. Now he suspected these men would show their fear and cause the mayor to reconsider. Much to his surprise, they immediately began shaking Ernie's hand and thanking him for standing up to Cahoon. Ernie didn't take so kindly to their gratitude. He stood there, somewhat disgusted by them, wondering why they wouldn't stand up for themselves. They didn't know why Ernie had come to town and obviously didn't care. All they knew at this point; was someone had finally stood up to Larry

Cahoon and Gregory McElliott was dead. That in itself made Ernie a hero in their eyes.

Most of the Alhambra's patrons quietly left, when Cahoon and his men arrived. They knew there was a fight coming and no one wanted to be caught in the middle of whatever that might bring. Cahoon chose the large round table next to the stairway, for his men to gather. It was away from the bar and used primarily by folks who wanted some degree of privacy, usually for a private game of cards. He wanted folks to know they were there and why. What he didn't want, was someone skinning out the back door to warn the marshal, with something they'd overheard.

"I'm not waiting until tomorrow," Cahoon said, in a low but deliberate voice. "We're going back and drag that murdering bastard out of there. Once we've got him, we're going to take him down to that cottonwood by the tracks and string him up."

"How we going to get him out, Boss? He ain't going to walk out and give up." Lemual White asked. In the absence of Mac or Raymond, he was taking the lead but finding it difficult to stay on track with Cahoon's train of thought.

"I'll make that marshal bring him out. There's only him and that murderer in the office. EJ ain't going to do nothing. We're going to EJ's office and demand they turn him over. We'll surprise them and take him out at gun point. There's only Delbert and the stranger to contend with, you men can pull that off." He said.

The men knew they would be pushing their luck. But there were only two men to face in the mayor's office and there were seven of them. They'd be facing down the law but they had Cahoon to back them up. What worried them, was the man who'd just killed Mac and Raymond. None of them were that fast and they all knew it. They didn't have much of a choice and relented to follow their boss's lead.

Cahoon was now burning with rage. His best two men were dead and now he was being challenged. He needed a show of force and decided to go back to the mayor's office and get Ernie now. They wouldn't take a chance on him leaving town. And Cahoon wasn't about to let Mayor Sterns, or Marshal Smith stand up to him like that and get away with it.

With their decision in place, they all stood, adjusting their cartridge belts and checking their sidearms, one last time. They walked out single file, then turned to make their way south, on the boardwalk. The heavy sound of boots on the wooden planks and spurs clanging in the background, gave voice to the coming fight. Those in the street knew trouble was afoot. Some crossed the street to watch, while others, especially those with children, headed away from danger.

Cahoon and his men walked down Grayson Street, crossing Third Street, then past the Early Bird Café, to the mayor's office. He stopped on the boardwalk in front of the mayor's door, as his men gathered behind, determined to make them come to him.

"EJ, come out here and bring that killer with you." Larry Cahoon shouted. He and his men stood on the boardwalk with their hands on their sidearms, intending to draw as much attention as possible. Allowing his "bought-and-paid-for" mayor to stand up to him would not do. He'd put a stop to this and hang that thieving murderer for the whole town to see.

Marshal Smith stepped out and stood in front of Cahoon and his six men. He tilted back his hat and for the first time, he had the upper hand.

"Go home, Mr. Cahoon, this matter is settled. You got no more business here."

"Oh, I've got business here. And you're out numbered, Delbert. You send that murderer out here, now. I'll deal with him myself. You tell EJ I'll deal with him later." Cahoon spoke loudly, wanting everyone on the boardwalk to hear. He controlled this town and that wasn't about to change now. Cahoon's men stepped up closer, to challenge the marshal. They were ready to go in and drag Ernie out, as they'd earlier planned.

"Hold up there." The marshal said, to the men. "I wouldn't move so fast, if I were you... Ernie, come on out!" The marshal turned and shouted.

Larry Cahoon was perplexed by the statement and initially thought the marshal had given up quite easily. He was soon met with a surprise, as seven armed men walk through the doorway and onto the boardwalk.

"Eight against seven, Mr. Cahoon. I'd say it's time to call off your men and go home. You got nothing to gain here. This man obviously collected an honest debt and this ain't worth getting more people killed over." Marshal Smith had a growing audience, as the back and forth intensified and the number of men standing behind him doubled. He wouldn't think of backing down. He was making things right, considering past incidents. He wanted his town to see that he had a backbone and wasn't afraid to do his job. Cahoon wasn't about to fold his hand but given the situation, he knew it was time to draw another card.

"Okay, Delbert... I can see we're getting nowhere here. No need to get innocent folks shot up." Larry Cahoon couldn't give in but saw no way of making this happen to his satisfaction, from where they stood. Instructing his men to back off, he made one last promise to Marshal Smith before turning to leave.

"I'll be back, Delbert." Cahoon replied, as he looked to the men behind the marshal, "You men better think about what you're doing. And EJ, I'll deal with you later." He shouted.

Cahoon and his men slowly turned to gather their horses, as the marshal and his backup stood their ground until they were saddled up and out of sight.

Ernie had no way of knowing what he'd just done. His purpose in town was to collect a debt and be on his way. Now he stood as the man who'd given the town an opportunity to stand on their own. The merchants had become tired of Cahoon and his ways and the marshal was tired of not being allowed to do his job. The mayor saw it differently and was immediately concerned about the consequences.

Larry Cahoon had played a major role in town since the time Henry Grayson was elected mayor. He'd helped in turning this abandoned outpost into an actual town. He was involved in financing the building of the train station and wrote letters on Grayson's behalf to add their town on the schedule to Cimarron. With his assistance, Maple Ridge was given a name and a purpose. Cahoon felt the town owed him and gave no regard to the others who'd worked equally as hard to see their plans through. He'd considered his help to be more valuable than the others and it had become a debt they could never re-pay.

He'd used intimidation, through the force of his men to get what he wanted. He always took full advantage of his position to control the town council. When it began, it had been subtle and more of an irritant in exchange for his business. Over the past few years, especially after Henry's retirement, it had become much more obvious. The people of Maple Ridge were now threatened by his demands. He bragged about how much money he spent in town when in fact, he'd left the merchants holding the bag, as often as not. Still, they were forced through fear of life and liberty, to provide him with their best, at the expense of others.

They were all weary of the status quo and now a few were thinking there might be a way out. They'd never seen Cahoon back down but the more prudent among them were warning that he had not. The expectation from them was for a different tactic by Cahoon, with more men. The fight had just begun.

CHAPTER 4

Cahoon and his men left town in a cloud of dust, making as much noise on the way out, as they did coming in. He didn't find it as easy as he'd expected. But he was certain the town's sudden burst of disrespect would disappear, once he'd dealt with that stranger. There were too many folks around to take him as he'd planned. Things would be different, come morning. They wouldn't be so eager to face the number of guns he could bring back. Justice would be his.

It was late afternoon when Cahoon and his men reined up next to the big barn. Most of his plans for the next morning were already taking shape and he was anxious to get them in motion. For what he had in mind, there was little time to bring it all together by dawn. He and Lemual would assemble thirty men, with a plan to set out on the town at first light. They would hit the streets from different directions, with enough force to overwhelm the men who'd stood behind Marshal Smith. He'd put a stop to them and take Ernie Evans in the confusion.

There were forty-three men working his spread. Some were there for the pay and were good at ranching. Others were hired for their reputation with horses. They were never involved in the business end of things. But there were others, men who were hired simply because they were good with a gun.

These were the men who protected his power and made sure he got what he wanted. They watched the ranch and everything that moved. When Cahoon had a problem, they were called upon to deal with it. This time, he called on his ten best gun hands and twenty additional men. He'd set out on Maple Ridge with the likes they had never seen. They would get Ernie Evans and teach Marshal Smith a lesson, even if he had to burn him out.

Marshal Smith was sure he would return with force and knew the worst was yet to come. Cahoon was predictable and always turned to intimidation and the strength of his men, whenever things didn't immediately go his way. That applied to shop owners, as well as ranchers, who got in his way. He'd stood up to Cahoon before, usually to be poked fun at and forced to back down. Cahoon would intimidate the mayor and get what he wanted without regard for the law. There were times, when he was sure Cahoon's men had confronted him, just to remind him their boss was in charge.

Ben Willis had been the most unfortunate example. He'd stood up for himself and actually tried to do something about it. Everyone in town had wondered what he was thinking. He obviously under estimated Cahoon's men and believed they weren't as tough as folks had said. This time, it could be even worse. Mac, his personal gun hand, a friend of twenty years and Raymond, his foreman of seven years, had been gunned down. Now, the town was doing nothing about it. Cahoon had come a long way since he left Scotland. What he couldn't buy or build, he would take and it had always been that way. He wasn't of the mind to allow that to stop now.

There were only a few men in town with the background to understand Cahoon and Marshal Smith was one of them. He knew what he was like the first time he saw him. He'd spent enough time on the trail and in other small towns to see his kind many times over. The thing is, his brand may live in different towns and have different names but they were all the same.

Ernie Evans had no problem with sizing up Cahoon's type. When you've been on the wrong end of a Colt, as often as he could boast, you learn to read people early. Ernie could read the marshal as well. He was obviously a man of character but Marshal Delbert Smith had been held back and put on a chain a long time ago.

When they met the day before, he didn't seem to have much fight. It wasn't in his eyes but Ernie couldn't see his heart. After finally facing down Cahoon, it was a very different story. Marshal Smith showed a fire in his eyes, which could only come from deep within a man's soul.

The ranch hands gathered at the bunkhouse at dusk to stow their gear and grab some grub. Cahoon waited until they were fed and rested a bit, then called out the men he'd planned to include on this ride. His meeting with the men didn't take long. They all knew about the shooting and were ready to make things right, for the boss. No one really cared much for Mac, although most were quiet about it. But they did like Raymond, their foreman of seven years.

This was nothing new for them. Most of these men were handy with a sidearm and had put it to use more than once. Some worked there to avoid the law, while others were hired for their past reputations. Cahoon had relied on men like these to make his ranch successful. He'd called on them before and expected they would be ready to ride for him again.

Ernie and Marshal Smith left the mayor's office, still discussing the situation. EJ had been of little help. With each thought they had for averting trouble, EJ seemed only to be counting dead bodies. Having enough of that, they excused themselves for the more optimistic atmosphere of the Cattleman's Diner. Ernie was ready to leave town and make his way back to Kansas. That wouldn't be until 3:00 pm the next day. He'd done his job and didn't initially consider this one to be his fight. But he now felt obliged to help out, since it was sure to happen before he left town. Given the marshal's situation, he needed every steady hand with a gun that he could muster. He seemed to have very little back up. All Ernie had seen so far, was a hand full of store merchants and one green deputy.

The marshal's concerns were mounting and Ernie could see it on his face. They had a fight coming and it would take more guns than he'd seen. Ernie knew he would be involved in at least one more encounter, with these men. There was no way of avoiding that. He was willing to oblige but didn't plan on hanging around for their next dust up with this bunch. He'd made enemies of these people and would stay close to Marshal Smith for now. He didn't know anyone from the ranch, with the exception of Cahoon himself. He'd killed the only other men he'd spoken with there. Ernie knew he'd be a sitting duck for a late-night ambush and that wasn't out of the realm of possibilities.

Over supper, the marshal reluctantly explained his past encounters with Larry Cahoon. Most of what he told Ernie made him angry to recount and somewhat embarrassed to admit. He had a total lack of control in upholding the law, with no support to protect their town. For Ernie, it explained his earlier reluctance to provide any information. The marshal's biggest worry now was protecting the people of the town and keeping the mayor out of his business.

He knew they would show up early the next morning with a large posse of men. The problem was, he didn't have the manpower to cover them. If they rode in, as he expected, he was sure they would separate and roam the streets, shooting out lights and windows. His greatest fear was a fire. Intentional or not, it would be devastating. It required more men than he could deputize, if he had any chance of holding them off. But Ernie had a different idea.

As the marshal continued to speak, Ernie began thinking of ways to meet them head on, away from Maple Ridge. He had an idea. It was military in nature and he didn't think it would be that difficult. He'd heard many times of how General Lee had defeated the Yankees in battle with a much smaller force. He'd relied on the determination and will of his soldiers against men who didn't want to be there in the first place.

He figured that a number of Cahoon's men were ranchers at heart and would fall in that category. He didn't know who or how many but they had no choice but to play the odds. Ernie was willing to help but they had to do it his way. He'd lay out the strategy but the marshal would need to fill in the blanks. He'd need to determine where this would take place and how many guns he could depend on.

The marshal became convinced that Ernie's idea could work. He knew where he could make this happen, if he had enough men. He also knew the townsfolk and the surrounding ranchers. He began to think that he might find enough of them willing to make a fight. Ernie wasn't much help there but he knew one, Ralph Thomas. He was an old Johnnie Reb and certainly knew the tactics. Marshal Smith laughed and conceded that Ralph hadn't yet crossed his mind. But he was surely a good place to start. He continued to think of other names and quickly came up with what they needed.

The marshal's job now, was to round up enough of these men with grit and a gun, to make Ernie's plan work. As their strategy started to take shape, Marshal Smith's thoughts went back to his days on the trail. He'd brought in a number of men who had robbed or killed yet continued to evade the law. It was amazing how their attitude would quickly change, when the gun was suddenly in their face. He'd often suspected Cahoon would do the same, if confronted alone but he was never alone. Always relying on someone else's gun to do his work, Cahoon got his way and was never held to account. Marshal Smith now saw his chance and with Ernie's help, he was ready for a fight.

Ernie was confident that with the right men, they would make this work. They would ride out within a couple of miles of the Cahoon Ranch and set up behind the cottonwoods without being seen. The same cottonwoods Ernie had passed earlier that morning, on his first ride to the Cahoon Ranch. A couple of scouts could trail out to the ranch early. They'd watch the men as they saddled up, then high-tail it back, with a head count. This would give Ernie the information he'd need to string out his men. They could take on the intruders from front to back. Guerrilla warfare; just like old Johnny Reb.

Marshal Smith knew that Cahoon would ride the lead until they hit town. Once there, he would back off and let his men do the dirty work. He wanted that position. All he could think of at the moment was being at the lead of his posse, facing down Cahoon, as the others took his men by surprise.

After sending for Deputy Wilcox, Marshal Smith began to make a list of the men he felt would be willing and able to pull off such a risky ploy. He came up with twenty. As he explained their abilities to Ernie, he became more confident, that these men could actually make this work.

Deputy Wilcox was unaware of their conversation and was stunned when Ernie explained their plan. Wilcox was young and had never been involved in a shooting. What he'd seen Ernie do earlier in the day was as close as he'd ever been and that scared the hell out of him. His biggest concern at the moment was that he might be involved. Marshal Smith had no intention of that. He'd stay back and watch the street. The hard work would fall on a few shop keepers, who would be willing to burn power, should gun play find its way into town.

Cahoon picked out the thirty riders to accomplish his vendetta. He'd considered each man, one by one and how they might stand up under fire. His selection was careful. After the crew had eaten and stowed their gear, he wanted only those men around the big barn. He needed to keep some good men at the ranch, while others weren't cut out for what he had in mind. His choice was clear and his men would be ready at dawn. He'd see to it they never challenged him in this way ever again, he'd make them pay. He would get Ernie Evans and teach the town a lesson.

Their conversation seemed to make Deputy Wilcox rather nervous. Marshal Smith carefully explained his part once again, to be certain he had it right. It was imperative that he understood and would only tell the people he was sent to fetch. He didn't need Wilcox getting spooked and he couldn't take the chance of him running his mouth. He was firm in his directive and made sure that Wilcox would do as he was told and no more. His job was to contact the fourteen men on the marshal's list and have them meet up at the marshal's office at 9:00 pm. Meanwhile, he and Ernie would contact the six men in town who'd shown up at the mayor's office earlier in the day.

This was no easy task. Gathering fourteen men on such short notice and so little information, took all the persuading Deputy Wilcox could muster. It was, however, easier in town. Ernie Evans had made a name for himself in a few short hours and those who'd been around for the multiple showdowns, were aching to get involved.

Deputy Wilcox was back in town before dark, with the assurance from each man that he would show up. But no one could be sure until they walked through the door. It started about 8:30 pm, as Wilber Scott walked in with his sidearm and two Winchester 73s under his arm. Ernie wasn't sure why he'd brought them in the office, unless it was simply a show of vigilance. But he was ready to fight and that was all Ernie and the marshal were concerned with at the moment. Once Wilber arrived, they began filing in one by one. By 9:10 pm, every man on the list had gathered in Marshal Smith's office, ready to take a stand. He was stunned.

Marshal Smith didn't yet believe this would put a stop to Cahoon's ways. His current objective was keeping a bloody fight out of town. Ernie and the men, on the other hand, were intent on stopping him for good. After hearing Ernie's plan, most of the men were sure they could see this thing through. They intended to neuter that old bastard, if not kill him. At the very least, he would be easier to control and the law could keep him in check. To them it was worth the risk.

It was after 10:00 pm when the meeting ended. There was little time for most of the men to head home and be back in time to ride. They chose instead to stay in town and bunk at the corral or the floor of the marshal's office. Mr. JT Belcher, who owned the Early Bird Café, was among them and promised to have coffee and breakfast ready for the men at 3:00 am. This would give them time to mount up and be in place before Cahoon and his men left the ranch.

The two men selected as scouts would be the first served. They'd be the first to saddle up and strike out ahead of the marshal and his posse. With a few hours' sleep, then a hot meal, they would be alert and ready to make a fight. Ernie saved the three dollars for a room and stayed with the men. Marshal Smith, who lived in town, elected instead to go home for a few hours of shut eye.

3:00 am came quickly but every man was awake and ready to ride. They hurriedly gathered their horses and gear, then checked their weapons. Marshal Smith made sure they were each well stocked with ammo. JT left for the Café, before most were awake. He fired up the stove and put two percolators to work first. As the men gathered, he served up eggs and bacon. There wasn't enough time for biscuits but no one complained since it was on the house.

It was still dark, when the scouts broke out in a gallop. The others soon finished up and quickly saddled their mounts. Ernie repeated his plan for the men as they tightened their cinches and stowed their ammo. He assigned each man to their position in the line and made sure they would be ready when reaching the stand of trees. There was no room for error. He would check their position upon arrival and make ready for Cahoon and his men.

The last thing Ernie needed was three sticks of dynamite, which concerned Marshal Smith just a little. Still, he obliged and rustled up three sticks of Nobel from the store room. "What he'll do with them, God only knows," Marshal Smith mumbled to himself, as he mounted up. The posse quietly walked their horses to the edge of town. Once they were beyond the tracks, they spurred their mounts and broke out for their pre-dawn ride. The sleeping townsfolk had no clue of what was happening just beyond their windows.

-

Henry Grayson was known by all as the father of Maple Ridge. He'd paved the way for those who followed and they were mindful of the role he'd played. When he came upon this tract of land, Henry saw its potential and set his sights upon building a new town. He started out with only his wife Mary and their two children. Their first task was to clean out the sturdiest building and call it home. A worthy goal by any stretch but he had a vision of prosperity for others as well. Henry was an educated man but no stranger to the land or hard work. He was the first in his family to even finish school, much less earn a law degree. His father had been a dirt farmer all his life and had little use for lawyers. Still, he supported Henry and wanted more for his sons than he ever had. Of the three boys, Henry was the only one with the motivation to finish his schooling and make it beyond the handles of a plow.

Once they'd secured their new home, Henry began scouting the area and soon found a number of large ranches to the west and southwest. Cimarron was to the northwest. But that was a day's ride by wagon to gather supplies and to have contact with others. He was convinced that a small town in this place would be more convenient for the ranchers to the south. He realized there was immediate opportunity for commerce.

Others soon began to gather. Like Henry, they were headed west following the trail and joined in when they too, realized the potential. This soon drew the attention of Larry Cahoon. He saw this new town as an asset to his growing ranch and seemed very supportive at first. He was eager to help with men and money. Soon, his motivations became increasingly clear. It became obvious to most folks that he was building a town for himself.

The town quickly took shape. The old buildings were rebuilt with the main street straightened. Looking ahead, they also marked off two additional streets to the east and west for additional growth. Each building was constructed in proper order. They kept to their plan, with the canvas tents removed one by one, as everyone worked together. Cahoon routinely sent a few of his men to aid in building the stores on the dusty street. He also providing a portion of the lumber and timbers needed for sound structures.

Cahoon was present for each of the town meetings. He soon dominated the decisions, claiming his money would be spent his way. Henry kept him from claiming too much power and he backed off for a while. He settled on letting the townsfolk do it themselves and save his money and manpower. He would get the benefit of a closer town anyway, he concluded. But once the town saw enough growth to name a mayor, he decided it was time to make his presence known again.

Henry hadn't practiced law since arriving in Maple Ridge. They had little need for a lawyer but his abilities and connections were of great benefit to them all. He had written the town charter, opened the mercantile, established a land office and provided the territorial legislature with a meticulously scaled map of Maple Ridge. Cahoon became jealous when Henry was elected mayor and irate when the main street was named for him. Cahoon thought that honor should have been his. Still, he stayed quiet and only exerted pressure where it was monetarily beneficial to him.

Jim Williams and his wife Sarah settled in Maple Ridge just after the Grayson's and were at the forefront of the town's growth. Sarah and Mary talked many times of opening a dress shop but early on there was no one to sell them to. The ladies who'd settled there were too busy making a home. And besides, there was still nowhere in town to wear a fancy dress, if they had one. They planned to wait a while but Mary Williams' time became un-expectantly consumed with the care of their son, James Jr. He'd been the victim of an unfortunate accident, which had him bed ridden for almost a year. It required his mother's full attention but eventually he was back on his feet. Mary had lost interest by then and never pursued her ambitions.

Jim and Henry on the other hand, opened the first mercantile in town and began making money from the first day. They bought supplies from Cimarron, full price at first, then sold them for a fair profit. It was still a good deal for folks close by. Soon they were buying wholesale and having their shipments delivered to them. Jim had since passed away and after Henry's retirement, Bobby had become the proprietor of the mercantile and doing well. Bobby Grayson was at the forefront of this fight and eager to put a stop to Cahoon.

-

Ernie's two scouts set on the ridge, to the east of the Cahoon Ranch, before first light. They sat for nearly an hour, before there was a stir around the bunkhouse. As the sun was rising, the men gathered and saddled their horses. Cahoon just walked the area barking orders and working himself into a lather. Once they were sure of the head count and weapons, the scouts spurred their mounts and headed back to the waiting posse.

Marshal Smith knew the area better than Ernie and made the final decision on their exact location. Once the horses were secured and out of sight, he placed the men around the trees, past the turn in the trail. It provided a landmark, which would be visible to all. Stringing out about a hundred feet to the east of the road, all the men kept to one side to avoid any crossfire. Marshal Smith insisted on taking the lead position furthest away, while Ernie took up the rear. Before splitting up, the marshal turned to Ernie; "I have to ask. What are your plans for the dynamite?"

"To stop them dust chokers from turning back. When this thing starts, the last in line will try to retreat and go back for more men. I'll land a little surprise, close to the back few horses. They will throw their riders and spook half of what's in front of them. The rest will become disoriented and lose their focus. Believe me; I'll scare the hell out of them."

"What about the other two sticks?"

"We'll see." Ernie replied, with a smile.

They would make their surprise when the last man was out of the turn. As night turned to day, their wait was less than twenty minutes, when Ernie heard the sound of hooves coming their way.

As Cahoon's men cleared the turn, Marshal Smith and his posse had an unobstructed view of each mounted rider and their leader. The marshal was the only man still in the saddle. He held his horse back a ways from the trees, out of sight and waited for Cahoon to reach his position. He was the first to break cover and bolted out in front of Larry Cahoon, with the butt of his Winchester firmly planted on his right thigh.

"Hold it right there." Marshal Smith shouted.

Larry Cahoon reined up his horse, as his men began bunching up behind him. Ernie and the marshal's posse were still holding up behind the trees and brush, leaving the initial impression that Marshal Smith was alone.

"Delbert, I thought yesterday that you'd gone crazy, now I'm sure of it. If you don't move out of my way, I'll blow you out of that saddle." Larry Cahoon shouted. He had set out to show the town he was boss. Leaving the marshal on the trail would show them all that he meant business.

Cahoon's threat was Ernie's cue to make his move. With a loud whistle he stepped out, behind the last rider. Each of the twenty men came into clear view, with their rifles trained on Cahoon's men. The posse stayed close to the trees for cover but quickly made their purpose known. Startled by the sudden presence of a score of rifle barrels, each of Cahoon's men instinctively drew his sidearm. Confused and looking unsuccessfully to Cahoon for direction, several anxious men opened fire. Their lead hit the trees where the rifle barrels or hat brims were most visible but little else.

Ernie saw the last few riders in the pack begin to break early, as he'd expected. He quickly reached for the dynamite in his right coat pocket. He grabbed a match from his vest, then lit the short fuse and lobbed the stick in their direction. The smoke-filled air and sounds of gun fire was distracting and could have affected Ernie's distance. Still, he landed the explosive close to the men, just as he'd planned. The impact took the closest three horses off their feet, immediately killing one rider and his horse. The concussion of the blast took two additional riders out of the saddle, sending their horses in a dead run away from the fray. The sheer noise of the blast echoing in the trees disoriented the rest, momentarily bringing all gun fire to a halt.

Cahoon and Marshal Smith, were away from the impact and did not lose their concentration on one another. The noise of the blast did, however, serve to move their words into action. Cahoon drew his Colt from anger but much slower than was required. Marshal Smith had laid the Winchester across his lap and responded by reaching for his sidearm. With a sense of duty, he fired, hitting Cahoon in the gut and dropping him to the ground. As his men watched him fall, their returning fire intensified, bringing the forces on both sides back into the fight.

Marshal Smith dismounted, almost jumping from the saddle. He rolled away, taking cover behind an uprooted tree trunk, as his horse made a break for the trees. He immediately looked back to Cahoon, who was still lying in the road. He wasn't moving and the marshal still wasn't sure if he was dead or alive. Ernie simultaneously stepped out to take aim on those who were beginning to re-engage in the fight. Stepping out too far from cover, Ernie was now in clear view of one of Cahoon's men. Several others were now caught in the middle, with no means of retreat.

At this point, there were a number of downed men, from both parties. In the smoke and excitement, Ernie could not tell who was who. He'd spent only a brief amount of time with the marshal's men, not enough to recognize them so quickly. What he'd remembered so far, were their hats and the color of their coats. There were two men before him, who he knew to be Cahoon's. Both, without a doubt were dead where they lay. One was pinned under the horse, which was shot out from under him. Obviously crushed by the weight of the massive animal, the man and his horse lay dead in the grass. One of the men he recognized from the night before was lifeless and no doubt dead, lying next to the tree he'd used for cover.

Ohhh…something's wrong, Ernie thought. There was a sudden ringing in his head, which became increasingly louder than the chaos around him. The grip he held on his Colt loosened, despite his best effort to hold the two-pound revolver level. His knees began to buckle. His heart was now racing and the numb feeling he initially noticed in his back was hot, as the pain intensified. The last thing he realized, seconds before his eyes closed; Oh my God, I'm shot…

CHAPTER 5

That was the morning of August 6th... Ernie didn't see the light of day again until the afternoon of August 8th. He was unconscious when they brought him in, which turned out to be best for everyone involved. Dr. Rowe didn't revel in the thought of digging a bullet out of the back of a conscious man. They always fought against him to avoid the additional pain, placing their life in further jeopardy. He was dirty and bloody, when the Marshal and Bobby Grayson brought him in. They had packed the wound the best they could and left the rest to the doc. It took Dr. Rowe and his nurse a while to clean him up and dig out the bullet. Once he was cleaned and bandaged, they laid him in bed and hoped for the best.

When he awoke, it took several minutes for his mind to catch up and make sense of where he was and how he got there. Slowly remembering the gun battle, he began to wonder about the events of that day. Questions were quickly formulating but answers were non-existent. He tried to sit up, then laid his head back on the pillow and asked for some water. The nurse who was with him at the time, saw him stir and immediately left to fetch the doc. Still disoriented, Ernie saw her as she came back into the room, with the doctor closely behind. His eyes were squarely focused on Ernie's.

"Can you hear me, son?" Doc Rowe asked, as he checked the bandage on Ernie's back and right shoulder. He needed to make sure he hadn't opened the wound or caused any bleeding.

"Yeah, I hear you, what happened? Where am I?"

Miss Abigail Bainbridge was leaning in to give Ernie a sip of water, as she answered; "You're in Maple Ridge, Mr. Evans. You've had a rough couple of days. Everyone in town is praying for your recovery." She was about the prettiest thing Ernie had ever seen. It didn't hurt that she was the first thing he'd seen in two days. Those green eyes and auburn hair caused him to forget everything else for a brief moment.

"Please, call me Ernie. Mr. Evans sounds so...old." Ernie smiled, as his attention now turned to flirting with Miss Abigail.

"Mr. Evans, this is Dr. Rowe. He's been taking care of you."

"Doc, where's Marshal Smith?"

"He's over at his office, told me to come fetch him as soon as you were awake. Reckon I best do that now. Things have changed a bit since you took that bullet, son." Doctor Rowe smiled and patted Ernie on his good arm, as he turned to gather his hat and make his way to the street.

"What the hell does that mean?" Ernie asked, as he continued to focus on Abigail. He was thinking of the possibilities that stood before him.

"I think the marshal would be the best person to answer that question." She just smiled.

"What's your name?" Ernie asked, as they were now alone.

"Abigail... Abigail Bainbridge." She said, with a smile. She offered no information and had promised herself to keep some distance between them.

"Are you married, Miss Abigail?"

"Now that ain't none of your business." Abigail answered. She tried to suppress a smile but the harder she tried, the more obvious it became.

"I never said it was...Are you married?"

"No."

"Well, that wasn't so hard, was it?"

"I reckon not." Abigail conceded. She was flattered and enjoyed the attention but she knew who he was. She knew him the moment they brought him in. Or at least, after they'd cleaned him up. For her, he would be hard to forget. To this point, she was sure he hadn't recognized her. Her family name apparently did not ring a bell and her father's facial features were obviously not as apparent to Ernie, as they were to most who'd known him.

"Miss Abigail, when I get out of here... and able to walk down the street...would you like to have dinner with me?"

"Well, it sounds like somebody's feeling better," she replied with a giggle but refused to answer. They'd only met that one time and she was much younger but she expected he would recognize her at any moment.

The mood was suddenly broken. The door opened and an elated Marshal Smith appeared with Bobby Grayson and Deputy Wilcox close behind.

"Man, we were worried about you. How are you feeling?" Marshal Smith asked, with a wide grin, which was closely matched by those standing behind him.

"Better, I guess. Looks like I caught a bullet. Sorry I let you down, Marshal." Ernie replied.

"You didn't let me down. Hell, you made this thing happen. If they'd made it to town, there's no telling how many innocent folks could have been hurt or killed. I was afraid they were going to burn us out. I'd say you did just fine...up 'til you got shot." Marshal Smith began to chuckle a bit, which garnered a painful laugh from Ernie, in response.

"What about Cahoon, I saw him go down. That took guts, Marshal."

"Cahoon? Well, he took a bullet. But we don't know much about how he's faired since. They didn't call for the doc, so I wired the marshal in Cimarron." Marshal Smith replied.

"According to him, Cahoon's there and not doing so good." Marshal Smith showed no sign of remorse.

"We lost two men, Ernie." Marshal Smith continued, in a more somber tone.

"Yeah, I saw one of them fall," Ernie replied. He and Marshal Smith knew the risks but still, they'd hoped to get all of their men out alive.

Getting Ernie further involved at this point, would be futile. The surprise attack at the cottonwoods had temporarily stopped Cahoon. But his men were still around, with some promising a raid on the town. So far, only a few of his men had been seen around town. They'd made a nuisance of themselves the day after the shooting but there appeared to be no one in charge. Marshal Smith had immediately backed them down and let them know their ways would no longer be tolerated. He didn't think they believed him but they left and didn't take the chance. Cahoon had been wounded, with three of his ranch hands killed that morning. His men didn't know at this point, if he would live or die. They weren't sure what to do now and were afraid they could be arrested, with no one to get them out. It seemed that law and order was taking its proper place and Marshal Smith was gaining control of his town. With everything in him, he would not let it go.

Marshal Smith had received a wire from Cimarron Marshal, Henri Lambert, informing him of Cahoon's condition. He also had news that Mrs. Rachel Cahoon had put out a bounty on Ernie's head. She was looking for a gunman, who would be up to the task. Word around town, she was willing to negotiate top dollar to satisfy her anger. Her animosity toward Ernie was understandable but the fact that Marshal Smith was the shooter that took down her husband, had seemed to escape her mindset.

Larry Cahoon was still alive but grimly wounded. He'd been gut shot at close range but managed to survive. Once they got him back to the ranch, Mrs. Cahoon stopped the bleeding, then took him to Cimarron. There, he would be away from further danger. She felt very uneasy as they entered the town. Cimarron was a haven for some bad hombres and very different from the people she knew in Maple Ridge. It was then she realized she'd never been there. It was odd that she felt Larry's safety, rested in one of the most dangerous places in New Mexico.

Mrs. Cahoon had two of their men scout around a bit and wasting no time in spreading the word. It was a hard town, one of the deadliest in the west. A number of residents in Maple Ridge had come from Cimarron, looking for the quiet and safety the town had to offer. These folks had pulled up stakes to make a better life for their families. Little did they know, the worst of what they'd left behind would soon be heading their way.

Men like Clay Allison and those who rode with William Quantrill and Bloody Bill Anderson, frequently spent time in Cimarron. It was expected that men of this element would revel at the chance to once again be on the hunt. With the amount of money Mrs. Cahoon could pay, the line would surely be long.

Marshal Smith stayed in contact with the marshal's office in Cimarron. Any movement of these men was being watched. Marshal Lambert always had a number of saloon regulars, eager to spill the beans on whatever they heard. It wasn't due to their civic minded virtue. They were just looking for a way to stay on the marshal's good side. The reward was usually a lesser stent in jail for a drunken brawl, or a look the other way for a lesser infraction.

Deputy Brady Wilcox was charged with keeping an eye on the Cahoon Ranch. He stayed perched near the trees on the ridge, where he could see any strange movements, or visits by unknown characters. If he did, he would immediately high-tail it back to town and report to the marshal. The men in town were vigilant as well. With the deaths of Tom Johnson and Herbert Brumfield, they were serious about protecting the town. Tom and Herbert had volunteered to make a stand that morning. Although they understood the risks, these men didn't expect to pay the ultimate price to protect their town. Folks from all around were helping their families, now those who rode with them, felt it their duty to see this thing through.

There seemed to be no way to keep the coming confrontation out of town. Again, the marshal thought about getting Ernie away from Maple Ridge as soon as possible but given his current condition, that could be days. Marshal Smith expected the current conflict would come to their streets before his train rolled out. His other concern was the lack of Ernie's gun. He'd been their strength and inspiration two days ago but there was no way he could help them this time. For now, they would keep their eyes peeled and their weapons ready.

Ernie still had the eight hundred dollars, which belonged to the KCBA. He knew William Murphy must be out of his mind by now. Unable to wire the money, or even a message, he sent for the marshal's help. He liked Abigail but he wasn't that smitten. Unsure if he could trust her, or even the doc, he turned to Marshal Smith, knowing he could be trusted. The marshal was eager to oblige and immediately deposited the funds in the Maple Ridge Bank. He provided the name and address, just as Ernie had scribed and made sure he had a proper receipt. It was common practice to take small amounts of money to the telegraph officer, for a wire transfer. But the marshal was better satisfied transferring this amount through the bank.

When he arrived at the telegraph office, there were three telegrams for Ernie from the KCBA. The marshal collected them on Ernie's behalf but didn't need to read the content to know what they were about. He sent the telegram, along with the bank information as requested. Then on his own behalf, he sent another telegram to Mr. Murphy. He explained the situation and left his name for a return message.

The KCBA was relieved to receive the funds transfer but William Murphy was very concerned about Ernie's current situation. He pondered over what he should do. Not sure if he should send men, he wired the marshal with a request to do so and inquired further into the shooting. William Murphy was a hard man but loyal to those who were loyal to him. Ernie had gained his trust and always been faithful in his duties. Murphy felt he owed his support in return, if he was in trouble due to his job.

Marshal Smith's reply answered Murphy's question, with the mention of Clay Allison. That was all he needed to send men to Ernie's aid. Allison had been a troublemaker in Kansas. Abilene and Wichita had been besieged by him only a year earlier and it was common knowledge that he was in Cimarron. In a healthy state, Ernie would have no problem facing down the likes of this man. But wounded and unable to shoot, he was a sitting duck.

A somber mood hung over the Cahoon Ranch. While Cahoon was still unconscious in Cimarron, Mrs. Cahoon's fears ran headlong into reality. She'd never been involved in the operations, or the finances of the ranch and now realized the urgency of learning the art of ranching. Her optimism for his recovery was fading with each hour. The refined Mrs. Cahoon was feeling the impact, as her life was rapidly changing. There were no children. No one to groom and no heirs for whom they could pass along a legacy. Even with her friends, employees and vast holdings, Mrs. Rachel Cahoon was alone.

With the absence of her husband's authority and the loss of their foreman, trouble quickly began to brew amongst the men. Most worked together to carry on the tasks of running the ranch but a few saw it as their opportunity to assume Raymond's position. They began fighting amongst themselves. Each one seemed to have a sound argument, as to why he should be in charge. Mrs. Cahoon was unable to control them, until Lemual White stepped up. Lem was one of their head wranglers and took the reins to avert near chaos, among the men. She watched his tactics closely and quietly learned from his words and actions. The shooting was only two days ago but things were changing rapidly.

She wasn't allowed to see their books. That was his job and she'd never had the need to get involved. It had never occurred to her, that someday she would be forced into this position. The movement of cattle and horses, purchases and sales, overhead and payroll were all kept from her. But she'd heard enough to know that cash flow was a very important part of her husband's business. She had also come to know Mr. Kinsey, from the bank in Maple Ridge. She'd noticed how he seemed to have an eye for her, each time he met with her husband. It wasn't overt, just a subtle smile here or there, enough to let her know he would be sympathetic. She would provide no more encouragement than he'd mustered on his own but she would use this to her advantage.

Mrs. Cahoon quickly developed a workable plan for running the Cahoon enterprise. She needed three advisors, she concluded. First there was Lemual to run the operation and manage the men. Mr. Kinsey would advise her on the finances and Charles Springer to keep her centered and to watch her back. He had been a friend to her for years and she'd always trusted him. He'd guided her husband in the early days and she knew he would do the same for her. When she decided to send one of the ranch hands to ask for his help, she knew he would oblige.

Springer arrived the next morning as expected. The fair Mrs. Cahoon was out at the corral in boots and a floppy hat, asking questions and talking with a group of ranch hands. He almost laughed at the scene. But given the seriousness of the situation, he knew she would never forgive him if he did. Under that fair façade, which showed strength and persistence, he saw a woman who was scared to death. She was elated to see Mr. Springer and immediately broke away from the men.

"Charles, I'm so glad to see you," she said, almost in tears.

"Now, now, my dear…It will all work out. Larry will be back soon and things will be back to normal." He smiled and took her arm, as they began their slow walk back to the house. Again, he almost laughed in amusement, at her hat and dirty hands but he couldn't let it show.

"They will come back you know. That stranger and Marshal Smith are out to get Larry. If he does live, they will find a way to get him."

"What are you talking about? I thought he was shot by a robber. That's what your man told me." Springer replied.

"It was a robber. The man came here and stole one thousand dollars from us, then went back to town, where he was protected by the marshal." She was frantic in her explanation, as the bits and pieces were making no sense to Charles Springer.

"Then how did he shoot Larry?" He asked.

"They shot Gregory first and then Raymond, you remember Raymond. Then the next day, they shot Larry." Her story was making no sense. But still, Charles Springer was getting the impression that his old friend's methods of management were at the heart of the problem.

"How do you know all of this? Did you see any of what happened?" He asked.

"No, I didn't see it but Lemual and the men told me what happened," she replied.

"From their point of view, I would suspect." Mr. Springer added. "I wouldn't be so quick to believe any of this, Rachel. I think there's a lot more here than you know." Charles Springer was reluctant to say more but he was sure the truth would find its way through all the obvious lies.

He was quite disappointed as he sorted out the facts and immediately implored Mrs. Cahoon to be careful in her decisions. She felt that she was being careful and intended to protect her husband and the ranch at all costs. Her thoughts were irrational at times and naïve at best. Still, she held to the belief that the marshal and Ernie were after her husband. She would do all she could to protect him.

Unwilling to get further involved in the situation, Mr. Springer recommended several men who could take on the tasks of ranch foreman and 'business manager'. Though he was uncertain of what description his friend had for that job. He left the ranch, concerned for her wellbeing. He promised that he would be back to check on her and asked that she be careful about how she listened to the advice of others. Charles Springer left that day with the feeling that his friend had dug himself into a hole from which he may never recover.

With no regard for the safety of others, Rachel Cahoon persisted. Her men put out the word in Cimarron that she needed a gun hand. He was to protect her husband and to get even with the men who'd tried to kill him. The word around town spread quickly, which soon brought four men to Mrs. Cahoon's door. They were eager to take on the task. Little did she know; these men were of a ruthless caliber that she had never encountered. Her poorly thought out plan, based in anguish for her husband, would put a number of innocent people in peril. The results would surely be on her hands and she was dangerously naïve of her actions. Tom Bainbridge and Clayton Emerson answered the call, with two of their crew riding along.

There wasn't much time for William Murphy to take action. He had three men ready to send right away but it would be two days before they arrived in Maple Ridge. He knew the town would soon find itself in danger and accepted some measure of responsibility, especially for Ernie. Without hesitation, he contacted three ex-lawmen. He paid their expenses, along with fifty dollars per man to make the trip to Maple Ridge. They were the best around to aid the marshal in the expected fight. Each man had experience facing down the worst of them and had worked under men like Bat Masterson and Dog Kelly. Their last order before leaving town was to see Ernie Evans safely home.

Deputy Wilcox watched Charles Springer, as he made his way to the Cahoon Ranch around mid-morning. A lone visitor, who seemed to be an elderly gentleman driving a black and red two-seater buggy, didn't appear to pose any threat. However, the four men he observed the following morning was a much different scene.

Trail worn and heavily armed, these were surely the men he was waiting for. He watched, as two ranch hands met the men in front of the house then stood around, obviously talking for a spell. Eventually, they entered the house where things remained quiet for close to an hour. Finally, the men stepped out the front door of the lavish house with Mrs. Cahoon walking closely behind. With a tip of their hats, each man mounted up and headed north. Their identities were unknown but Wilcox was sure they weren't there looking for a job on the ranch. As soon as they were out of sight, he spurred his mount and high-tailed it back to town.

Dr. Josiah Gregg had kept a close eye on Cahoon, since the moment he'd arrived. The sporadic attempts he'd made to speak, or open his eyes, were a good sign. But given the number of days he'd been under his care; the doctor had expected more. He'd lost a lot of blood but the wound was clean with no signs of infection or fever. He expected his patient would live, which was more than he anticipated the afternoon his bloody carcass was carried through his office door.

His nurse carefully fed him a diet of soup, full of the nourishment necessary to strengthen his body. It was often laced with a small dose of morphine, to ease the pain and help him rest. Doc Gregg knew he must rebuild the much-needed red blood cells, for the body to heal itself. All he could do was to watch and wait. Still, it would be some time before this man would walk out of his door.

Two of Cahoon's men stayed in town, under orders from their new boss. This quiet lady, who they rarely saw, was now showing the attributes of her husband. Moreover, the tenor of her commands appeared amplified, with such firm unequivocal orders emanating from her small frame. Cahoon was down but the fight was far from over.

As Ernie tried to sit up, an overwhelming sense of hopelessness came upon him. Lying there alone, he tried to stop his thoughts from reaching back into the past. But the quietness of the dark room offered no distractions. He began thinking, as he'd done many times before, of life when he was a child. Back before his father died, when he could be a real boy, without the cares of the world. But as usual, his thoughts wouldn't grant his heart the time to revel in the pleasant memories of a kinder time.

Instead, he was drawn to the anguish of his father's death and the hopeless look in his mother's eyes. That was the day he could no longer be a boy. He was forced by the harshness of reality to assume the role of a man. The tragedies of war and the uncertainty of life, had hardened the heart of a child. But the man he had become was still searching for finality.

He thought of Margaret Ann back in Osceola and how she'd tried for so long to win his heart. With his entire conscience mind, he wanted to let her in but his emotions were cold. It could have been very different, he thought... If only. But the past could not be changed, he concluded. For better or worse, it had made him who he was. It was one of those rare moments, when his heart seemed to melt and he felt an uncomfortable sense of humility.

Ernie was consumed in the moment, as the sights and sounds of his past embraced his entire being. He'd learned not to dwell on days gone by but the still darkness was devoid of distraction. In all his thirty-two years, he'd never been under a doctor's care. It was unsettling for a man who lived by the gun. Now he was finding himself in a place he'd never been, alone and dependent upon others.

Ernie was determined to dispel this torrent of unwelcome emotions. He carefully pulled himself out of bed and stood on his own for the first time in days. Weak and somewhat wobbly, he took a few steps. He tried moving his right arm but it was tightly wrapped to his chest. He looked around the room for a moment. Then his eyes focused on the window and the dim moon light emanating from the street. With a deep breath, he unhanded the spiral bedpost and made his way to the door under his own power.

His first few independent steps, offered a welcome relief. His legs steadied and he felt the warmth of his muscles as they tightened and successfully moved him forward. Exiting the door, Ernie entered a dimly lit hallway. To his right, he noticed two closed doors and what appeared to be a large room at the end. Straight ahead, was an open arched doorway, which was obviously a waiting area or parlor. To his left, he saw the reflection of the white porcelain knob, on the outer door, leading to the street. He slowly made his way outside and immediately felt stronger, as he inhaled the cool night air.

Ernie took a seat on the porch and knew he wasn't on Grayson Street, as he looked around. I must be at the edge of town, he thought. The flickering street lights began about one hundred feet away, where the boardwalk abruptly ended with two steps trailing down to the patchy grass. He turned to focus on the building where he stood and realized it to be a house. Above him he saw a swinging sign, which read: "Henry C. Rowe, Medical Doctor".

This was a much-needed distraction from his mind's visit into the past. Ernie was glad he'd taken the initiative to move about. After a few moments to adjust, he thought; I ain't as bad off as they said, I feel pretty good. As he finally shook off his uncomfortable soul-searching exercise, Ernie took another deep breath. His mind then turned to Abigail; I think Miss Abigail can help cure my ills, more than she knows. He thought.

The conversations around town were becoming more dramatic by the day. Some had pronounced him dead while others were sure the doc had removed his right arm. Still, Ernie was alive with all of his limbs. He was asleep on the porch when Dr. Rowe entered his room to check on him at first light. Panicked by the absence of his patient, he immediately became convinced that Ernie had been taken in the dead of night. As he bolted out the front door, Dr. Rowe almost tripped over Ernie's crossed feet. His legs were comfortably extended where he sat, still quietly asleep in the white pine rocker.

Marshal Smith's concerns were mounting. The information from Deputy Wilcox gave a picture of what was to come and it wasn't good. The four men, who were seen at the Cahoon Ranch, were now in parts unknown. The marshal didn't have the men to deputize a posse, or the time he knew it would take to track them down. Besides, he didn't know where to start and their trail north was cold by now. His only option as this point was to wire Marshal Lambert in Cimarron, to see what information he could offer.

Maple Ridge was normally a quiet town and traditionally well served by the marshal and one deputy. However, over the past few days this had changed dramatically. After their recent showdown with Cahoon, he knew what would eventually come as a result. There was no doubt, things were about to turn nasty. Marshal Lambert was sincere in his attempts to provide assistance. He was tired of these men ravaging his town. If he couldn't catch them in Cimarron, maybe he could track their movements to Maple Ridge and put a stop to them there.

He'd heard talk of the four men, who rode south to the Cahoon Ranch. And he knew they'd been seen talking with their ranch hands, currently in Cimarron. Marshal Lambert didn't know these men by name but he did know that a couple had been bushwhackers in Missouri. The war had been over for sixteen years now. But these men weren't the kind to forgive and forget. Nor would they put aside the skills they'd perfected, on their many Kansas raids.

-

It was May of '78 when Ernie and Bobby Jenkins were having a beer in a Dodge City saloon. Two young Texas drovers soon came in and struck up a conversation, as they too, ordered a beer and took a seat at their table. They seemed to be amiable young fellows, as their conversation started out light hearted and fun. Ernie was shuffling a deck of cards, as they spoke. He and Bobby had been waiting for a couple of cow hands to show up, so they could start up a game.

As they settled in, they began learning each other's style and tell-tale signs of a good hand. The pot began to go back and forth, with no immediate winner or sharp turn of the cards. They were relaxed, asking questions about each other's past and enjoying the game before them. The back and forth went on for about thirty minutes. Soon, the two began losing and couldn't seem to get back in the black.

"I'll take two." Ernie said, as Bobby was currently the dealer.

"One for me." One of the young men requested.

"I'll stand," replied the other.

"Dealer takes two." Bobby announced.

They sat for a bit, studying their cards after each man had anted up.

"Three sixes. What are you boys holding?" Ernie asked, with a smile, as he laid his cards face up on the oak table.

"I got nothing." Bobby said with a laugh, as he shook his head and slapped his cards face down, in the center of the table.

"Me either." One of the young men replied, without a smile, as he and his friend showed their cards without further comment.

As they watched their money find its way to Ernie's stash, Bobby took note, as their attitudes turned sour and the look on their faces became cold. Ernie was enjoying the game thus far with his two-hand streak, not paying much attention to his new friends' demeanor.

With the next hand, the two were quiet. It became obvious, even to Ernie, that they were intent on winning back their money. As the cards rolled out, luck still was not on their side. Unfortunately for them, Ernie drew another good hand and chose to take only one card. The look on his face didn't give away his hand but requesting only one card, showed he was a player. Taking a chance, as they both were running low, each man took a risk and went all in. They hoped to bluff him out of whatever he was holding. Again, Ernie came up with the winning hand, three in a row.

"You're a cheating bastard!" One of the drovers shouted, as both men pushed back their chairs and came to their feet. Ernie knew what was coming and eased his hand down, to unlash his sidearm. Each man went for their gun but both were too slow. Ernie went for his Colt, as he simultaneously stood and cleared leather. He fired first on the man to his left, whose gun had barely cleared its holster. He immediately turned to the man to his right. His pistol was now leveled, as Ernie aimed his Colt. He fanned the hammer, hitting the second man dead in the chest. Bobby had now backed off. His ears were ringing, as he tried to focus on the scene through the smoke from Ernie's reply to their threat.

The two men lie dead on the floor, with blood soaking in the pine boards. Deputy Marshal Wyatt Earp heard the shots and pushed open the batwing doors in a rush. He went straight for Ernie. As Deputy Earp began asking questions, several patrons of the saloon intervened. They each gave their version of the fight, with all proclaiming it as self-defense. Satisfied that Ernie was within his rights, Deputy Earp turned his attention to the two dead bodies on the floor and the task of getting them to the undertaker.

News of Ernie's speed and accuracy immediately began to spread. The reality of the event was quickly surpassed by the creativity of its inevitable exaggerations. He wanted no parts of it, as he was asked about the details. He'd simply considered it to be something he was pushed into, with no choice but to respond. For William Murphy, it seemed his attitude about the whole thing, was as intriguing as his ability. Having this man's steady hand standing for the KCBA was a must and he just would not take no for an answer.

Ernie was surprised by the offer and more skeptical than reluctant at first. He had difficulty believing that someone would pay him as a hired gun and he didn't think he liked the idea all that much. Mr. Murphy became more persuasive, as he sweetened the pot. Ernie eventually could not say no. Three years later, he still wasn't sure if he'd made the right choice. But here he sat, on the front porch of Dr. Rowe's house helpless as a child.

Doctor Rowe could espouse a number of reasons why he didn't want Ernie sitting on the porch. The most obvious was the possibility of who might see him there. He tried to coax him back into the house but Ernie wouldn't hear of it. The passing of first light had now become sunrise. Ernie sat, watching the bright illumination appear above the horizon. At this time of year, the sun would rise above the plains, between the mountains to the east. The beams of light, bouncing off the rocks for that few minutes each morning was breathe taking, even for Ernie. He couldn't remember the last time he'd watched the sun rise. It was then he decided to do it again tomorrow, hopefully with Miss Abigail enjoying it with him.

Standing in his long-johns, Ernie carefully made his way to the dusty street. He stood for a moment, staring at the busy folks starting out their day, just a couple of blocks up. His legs were steadier than they were during the night, when he first ventured out. He was tied of this.

"Doc, get my britches." Ernie said, with an air of enthusiasm.

"What?"

"My britches, I want them. And cut this damn bed sheet off my chest, so I can move my arm."

"That's a bad idea, son." Doc Rowe replied.

"I don't care, just cut this thing off and sling it up or something, so I can move around." Ernie pondered for a moment and realized he'd just had a very close call.

CHAPTER 6

A heavy storm hovered over Cimarron, on the afternoon that Larry Cahoon finally became responsive. The lightning cracking to the east was ominous and amplified the rumbling sounds at six thousand feet. Cahoon was startled by a loud burst of thunder. He gasped and struggled to focus as his eyes opened and he tried to sit up. His mind was at a loss, with his inability to rise to his feet. Something was very different. He tried once again to focus on the room and gain some perspective of his surroundings. Doctor Josiah Gregg assisted his efforts. Still, it took a moment for his mind to settle in and begin asking questions or even remembering that he'd been shot. Dr. Gregg was careful that Mr. Cahoon didn't exert himself. But it didn't appear this incident, had taught him much of a lesson.

"Where am I?" He demanded.

"You're in Cimarron, Mr. Cahoon. You suffered a pretty nasty gun shot. Now, I need you to stay calm and not move around too quickly." Dr. Gregg replied. He didn't know Cahoon but he did know of his reputation. His first impression was as he'd suspected, with no expectation that it would improve.

"Where's my wife?" He asked.

"She's not here, sir. She went back to the ranch but two of your men are waiting outside."

"Get them… I want them here now." Cahoon barked. His memory seemed to return very quickly, without the help of others. It was a good sign but his temperament was of great concern to Dr. Gregg.

He'd never met Larry Cahoon before they brought him in that day. The gun shot was severe and those who brought him in were very helpful and concerned that he would die. It seemed to be a normal reaction, he thought. But as the days went by, the attitude of those who stood guard became intimidating. There was an air of uneasiness in the office, which Dr. Gregg could easily have done without. Even the Misses showed signs of an unreasonable expectation. It was disconcerting for the doc and he felt uncomfortable in his own office. Tending to other patients had become a challenge as well. Folks were uncomfortable with Cahoon's men standing guard over the entire office. Doc Gregg was finding this very difficult to explain. Now that Cahoon was awake, he wasn't sure what to expect.

Marshal Lambert had paid close attention to Cahoon's condition. He also took great interest in who frequently visited and routinely had a deputy stop by in the afternoons. Deputy Lewis made his usual call by Doc Gregg's around 4:00 pm. Cahoon was sitting up in bed, illustrating the demeanor he'd heard so much about. Two of the cow hands were there, providing him with an update on the ranch and the situation back in Maple Ridge. He was satisfied to hear that Ernie had been shot. It almost made his own agony worth it. But now, it was Marshal Delbert Smith he wanted.

When Deputy Lewis walked in, they all went quiet, wondering why he was there again. Cahoon saw the badge and asked in a gruff voice; "What can I do for you?"

"I just stopped in to check on you, Mr. Cahoon." The deputy replied.

"Why, what do you want?" He asked again.

"Marshal Lambert just wants to keep an eye on things. We know what happened down in Maple Ridge. The marshal doesn't want that to spill over into Cimarron." Deputy Lewis replied.

"Well, there's no reason to think you'll have problems here, deputy. My business is in Maple Ridge. But, as you can see, it looks like I'll be a while getting back there." Cahoon replied, in less than a cordial manner.

"We just want to keep an eye on things." Deputy Lewis repeated in a calm respectful voice. "Can I get you anything?" He asked.

"No but thank you." Cahoon replied, surprised by the gesture.

"Well, I hope you're better soon." The deputy replied.

He tipped his hat as he left but neither Cahoon nor his men returned the respect. They only looked at him with distrust.

As he thought of how to get even with the lot of them, another notion struck him, which changed the whole dynamic. The guy in Abilene who sent Evans here in the first place, he's the one who caused this whole thing. Cahoon thought. He couldn't remember his name right off. Ernie hadn't called him by name that day at his house, only referring to him as "the boss". That was the guy he'd sold the cattle to and the man who was responsible for this.

He had the papers in his file, his name would be there. He was the man he wanted. As soon as the deputy was out the door, he turned to his men with a new plan.

"I need a couple of men to go to Abilene." Cahoon announced.

"What, Texas?" One of the young men asked.

"No, Kansas and that old bastard who bought that herd back in June. He's the one who started this and got me shot in the first place. I want him."

"What do you want us to do, Boss?" The ranch hand asked.

"I want you to get my money back and make him regret the day he decided to come after me." Cahoon replied.

He caught himself at that point and realized that he wasn't talking to Mac, or even Raymond. The men he'd trusted and had his full confidence for all these years were dead. He was talking to ranch hands. They were there, only to sit with him and to make sure he was safe until Mrs. Cahoon returned.

Thinking more clearly, he curtailed his comments and sat quietly for a while. Cahoon found himself in a real quandary. Mac had been responsible for the less dignified aspects of their enterprise and always kept Cahoon's hands clean. Now he would need a new front man who could handle the job and keep it from crossing his trail.

William Murphy had dispatched three men on the morning train, heading for Maple Ridge and ready to lend assistance to Marshal Smith. A wire confirming their schedule was sent to the marshal, with express instructions to utilize their talents to the fullest extent. They were the best. Each man had worn a badge and worked the cow towns during the tough times. They would feel right at home. Rolling into town to back up the marshal was the right thing to do. This was nothing out of the ordinary for any of them. Like Ernie, they knew no fear and would show the same grit, when facing down Cahoon's men.

Cahoon, on the other hand, was making plans to send two men on an eastbound train to deal with Mr. Murphy. Those details would be a few days coming but he knew what he wanted. When sending for Mrs. Cahoon, he instructed that she bring the papers from the safe regarding the sale of cattle from the spring drive. In that file, would be the information he needed to be sure he had the right man, when exercising his vendetta.

Just a week earlier, he thought, he would have sent Gregory McElliott to handle a task of such importance. Then there would have been Raymond but he too was dead. It wasn't just his personal condition fueling this fight. He had to settle for the deaths of his friends and the three ranch hands who were killed during the ambush on the trail. These had to be accounted for. Larry Cahoon ultimately blamed William Murphy for it all. He had lost much in the past few days but it wasn't in his character to reason why. He could only blame others when the fact remained, if he had done the honorable thing and settled an honest debt, none of this would have taken place.

It had been several years since Ernie had seen Tom Bainbridge. After the war, they had spent time together in town and ran with some of their same acquaintances, including elements of the James Gang. But their friendship wasn't as close as it had been before. Tom had soured on Ernie and questioned his reluctance to ride with the bushwhackers and uphold his father's good name. Although he'd ridden in several attacks and fought in a number of skirmishes, Tom didn't consider that to be enough. He began to hold a grudge against Ernie. Tom had since married and tried to settle down. But his old ways were ever present and always boiling near the top. Regardless of his efforts to restrain himself, it seemed that Tom Bainbridge just couldn't shake the past.

Ernie was in Liberty, visiting his mother when they crossed paths on Mill Street. It was the first time they'd been face to face in years. He was surprised to see his old friend and didn't realize he'd harbored such feelings of resentment. When they met, Tom had with him his wife and ten-year-old daughter. The fortuitous meeting began cordially as Ernie could recall but soon turned as Tom began to question him about the past.

He continued to push him for the reasons why he'd stopped riding with the Gray Ghost and wouldn't let up. Ernie was a bit shocked and tried to play it off as having been a long time ago. Tom wouldn't hear of it. With his wife and daughter standing only a few feet away, he became increasingly angry, to the point of challenging Ernie and tapping his sidearm with his thumb. To Ernie's surprise, the conversation quickly devolved into a confrontation with Tom initiating gun play.

Ernie was always faster and prevailed with the lead from his revolver, now buried deep inside Tom's right shoulder. As he fell, Ernie immediately kicked his revolver away. He stood over him and watched as a crowd began to gather and create their own version of events. By the time a deputy and the doctor arrived on the scene, Tom was sitting against a post, coiled in pain. His wife and child were now sitting on a bench, crying and holding each other tightly.

Reluctant to interact with the sobbing Mrs. Bainbridge, Ernie stood away from the buildings, as he spoke with the deputy. It was a busy street and there were many who'd heard the commotion and saw the way Tom had challenged him. With the collection of witnesses and Ernie's demeanor, the deputy made a decision on his own to drop the matter. He saw no need in bothering the marshal. It was so obvious he didn't even take down the names of all the folks who wanted to tell the story from their perspective.

Ernie felt bad about losing an old friend and didn't understand his purpose for pushing him like he did. But the thing that bothered him most was the need to shoot the man, in front of his family. He didn't say anything to Mrs. Bainbridge but as he turned to leave, he looked toward the sad little girl, then removed his hat and very calmly said; "I'm sorry."

With Tom's recovery came the eventual loss of his family. They stayed together at their farmhouse, for a while but Tom was intent on moving on. He knew it wouldn't be possible, with a wife and child tagging along. So early one July morning, he packed his saddlebags and headed west for New Mexico. They hadn't seen nor heard from him since.

Tom knew his old friend, Clayton Emerson, had made his way to New Mexico some time back. He'd joining up as a trail hand, pushing cows west with Clay Allison as his trail boss. Allison had been hired by two cattlemen, Irwin Lacy and Lewis Coleman. They'd herded their cows together and pushed them to Colfax, New Mexico, near the Maxwell Land Grant, just west of Cimarron. His pay for driving the herd was three hundred head, ten percent of the total stock, upon arrival to their destination. Allison settled down for a while with Clayton as his ranch foreman. But as the removal of squatters from the Maxwell Land Grant intensified into the Colfax County War, Allison went back to his old ways.

He initially supported the Santa Fe Ring and helped to separate a number of settlers from their homesteads. But as the conflict intensified, Allison changed sides, when those who'd settled under the old Mexican Land Grant, were pushed off their land. Clayton Emerson rode along and was present at the murder of Rev. FJ Tolby. He felt he was back in his element and rode with Allison until the end of that conflict. Emerson stayed in Colfax County and worked as a ranch hand along the way. He'd primarily made a name for himself as a gunman and gambler. Upon the arrival of Tom Bainbridge in Cimarron, they joined up and ran outside the law, making money any way they could.

When the two men heard of Mrs. Rachel Cahoon's vendetta, they saw a way to get back in the fight and make some cash along the way. They weren't concerned with her reasons or the validity of her revenge, legal or otherwise. When they first met with her at the ranch, Mr. Cahoon was still unconscious and not expected to pull through. Now that he was recovering, she summonsed them to meet her at his bedside for clear instruction from him.

His meeting with the men was full of questions. He'd held his plans, thus far, close to the vest and offered them no useful information. But he had a multiple of questions concerning his interest in their skills. He asked where they were from and what they'd been doing since they arrived in New Mexico. They weren't very talkative but their actions told him what he needed to know.

When he learned they were from Missouri, they became his initial pick for the job in Abilene. Cahoon ended the meeting by telling the men to stay close by but that was all. They were frustrated that he hadn't given them anything specific, or offered any money but that was his intention. They had to be ready but for what was only for him to know.

It was just before 8:00 am, when Miss Abigail stepped onto Dr. Rowe's porch, ready to start a new day. She noticed one of the high back pine rocking chairs, pulled out to the edge of the boards as she approached but thought little of it. As she opened the door to step into the front hallway, she heard voices coming from the kitchen at the back of the house. A bit odd, she thought, for Doc Rowe to have a visitor this early in the day and he surely wouldn't be attending to a patient in the kitchen. She was met with quite a surprise, as she entered the room, to find Ernie fully dressed and having coffee with her boss.

"What are you doing here?" She asked, in an admonishing voice.

"I got tired of lying in that lumpy old bed." Ernie said, with a grin. Doc Rowe just looked at her with a smile, waiting for a reply.

"Well, you should be in that lumpy old bed, you're not well enough to be up and around."

Ernie had been up and about since before dawn, which was enough to convince the doc, that he was progressing quite nicely. Besides, moving around was good for his muscles and blood flow, helping the healing process.

"I think he's fine, Abigail," Doc Rowe replied. "Besides, we might need that lumpy old bed for someone else." He concluded, with a proud chuckle. When Ernie first arrived, he wasn't sure he'd ever make it out of that bed on his own. Now he sat at his kitchen table having coffee, Dr. Rowe was quite pleased.

Ernie had dressed with a little help from the doc. His right arm was now in a sling, with a bandage wrapped around his shoulder and upper torso under his shirt. He was also wearing his cartridge belt, with his sidearm turned backwards in the holster, just in case. As they talked, Abigail felt more confident that he was actually better. She was surprised at the strength of this man, to handle himself so well after the physical trauma he'd experienced. He hadn't yet pulled on his boots and Miss Abigail was happy to oblige.

As they talked, her thoughts went back to that day when she was a little girl. Prior to this, she'd remembered that her father was shot by a bad man. Shortly thereafter, he'd left her mother and her alone. She'd blamed him for that as well. She was oblivious to the reasons that her father had argued with the man that day. Only that he was shot and her life was forever changed. But she never forgot the gesture when this man looked at her with a sad face and said; "I'm sorry." That's all he said, as he turned and walked away. Now she was getting to know this man and realized he wasn't a bad man at all.

Ernie began to think that he would be well enough to travel in a few days. Now, he had to decide if he would stay, or actually go back to Abilene. At this point, he wasn't sure. With time to reflect, he thought again of how his confrontation with Cahoon had put the entire town in peril. He was torn between leaving and staying to help them bring this to an end. Then there was Abigail. There was something about her that warmed his heart. It had been a long time since a woman had turned his head. He was afraid he'd make another regretful decision, if he left too quickly. But what if he stayed? He didn't have any real roots in Abilene and he was making friends here. Besides, they needed him. It had been a long time since he was actually needed for something.

The coffee he'd had with Doc Rowe, had fueled his energy a bit but Ernie was hungry. He felt well enough to move about and was confident that his left hand was sufficient to do the job, should he be confronted in the street. As he stood and placed his hat firmly on his head, Ernie turned to Doc Rowe; "Doc, do you mind if I ask Miss Abigail to have breakfast with me?" The question was directed at Doc Rowe but Ernie smiled and turned to Miss Abigail for an answer.

"I have work to do," she quickly replied, looking to her boss for a comment.

"Oh, go ahead. It's quiet here and your patient may not be as strong as he thinks. You should go along, just in case he's moving too fast." Doc Rowe said with a smile.

"Well, if you think it's okay." She happily replied.

"You pick the place, Miss Abigail but make it somewhere close by in case I give out." Ernie looked at Doc Rowe and winked.

"Okay but only if you drop the Miss and just call me Abigail."

"That's fair enough," Ernie said, as he stood with an approving smile.

As they slowly walked up Jacob Street, Abigail was still surprised that he hadn't recognized her. She was beginning to think that if he hadn't realized who she was by now, that he probably would not. It was a long time ago and she was only a young girl. She realized a lot had changed since then.

She wasn't sure what to do, if anything. They'd just met and he'd likely be heading back to Kansas in a few days. But if he stayed, it could create a problem that she would eventually be forced to address. How would she tell him and if she did, when? How could she bring it up and how would he react? What if he remembered and discovered that she'd known all along and kept it quiet? She was beginning to think this wasn't such a good idea after all but she liked Ernie. There was something about him that made her feel safe. She knew it would come but not today, she decided.

Jacob Street was normally the quietest of the three major avenues in town. Most of the larger buildings were on Grayson where the majority of the town's business took place. The backs of those buildings were easily seen from Jacob, as they rose above the single-story structures. This was true of the noise as well. Some of the bustle from Grayson Street would amplify, as it echoed between the buildings and alleys. Fredrick Street was to the east of Grayson, where the stables and blacksmith shops created most of its activity. It was far enough removed from Jacob, to have any effect on its quieter mood.

There were a few two-story boarding houses on Jacob but the tallest building was the Byron Hotel, a few blocks down. It was the largest and fanciest building in town. Abigail lived at Blake's Boarding House on Jacob, just past Second Street. They passed it on their walk to the Café but she thought it a bit early to provide that information to her new friend.

There was still room for growth here, with a number of vacant lots. Those usually had a couple of hitching post, on one side or the other. Folks frequently used those to keep their livestock off the street. Just past Third Street, was the municipal outhouse, strategically nestled behind a couple of cottonwood trees. Maple Ridge was a nice place and Cahoon and his men aside it was a good place to raise a family. Abigail had quietly eyed a parcel on Second Street, where she envisioned a small white house with a picket fence. The part she hadn't yet figured out was who would be sitting in that other rocking chair on her porch.

Winston's Café was busy as they entered but there were still tables from which Abigail could choose. Ernie was polite and asked her to decide. That was nice, she thought. He was minding his manners. This was rather new for him and he consciously kept a check on his language and mannerisms. It had been a long time for him. He didn't want her to know that and he didn't want to mess up.

As they sat, making small talk, Abigail kept an eye on Ernie's movements. She still wasn't sure he was up to the walk back to Doc Rowe's office. She cautioned him not to eat too much. Ernie could see the concern in her eyes and wondered if it was a sign of her deeper feelings. He rather hoped it was but still held his emotions close. He was afraid of allowing his heart to get involved too quickly, though he remained open to the possibilities. He never expected this, when he left Abilene. But much had happened since he arrived in Maple Ridge, just a week ago. Something was different and he now saw the potential for a new way of life, away from the gun.

Marshal Smith was mindful of every movement in town. Each person, he didn't personally know, was carefully watched. Anyone known to have ties with the Cahoon Ranch was followed from the time they arrived, until they saddled up to ride out. In addition, the marshal had now taken on the task of meeting daily with Mayor Sterns, to keep his nerves in check. He was enjoying his new authority in town. It made him feel like a real lawman again. The past few days had been quiet, with only a few of Cahoon's men having been seen in town. Three had been there the day before. They'd picked up supplies from Grayson's Mercantile and Dawson's Dry Goods but they were respectful for a change. They'd paid for their order without question and left without causing their usual commotion. They were even respectful to Shorty Williams.

Not so long ago, two of these same men had been in town giving him a hard time. By the time Marshal Smith rounded the corner, a crowd had already gathered next to the store. He didn't know who'd caused the disturbance but he'd heard the ruckus as he was heading to the café for lunch. Pushing his way through the crowd, the marshal saw two bloody faced men, landing their last punches, before falling out from exhaustion. He instinctively knew that cow hands from the Cahoon Ranch must be involved. It was early in the day for them to be so rowdy. But they had a history of ignoring the law and usually got away with whatever they stirred up. Three of them had come into town earlier, to pick up supplies at Dawson's Dry Goods. One driving a twelve-foot buckboard, the 'big-rig' as Cahoon's men called it and two men on horseback.

When they arrived, their order was still being pulled, which they saw as an opportunity to give Shorty a hard time. With no regard for the other patrons, the three began blocking his way and pushing him around. They saw it as entertaining to bleatingly interfere with his best effort to get their wagon loaded and off the street.

Shorty was a friend to everyone. Folks in town didn't take kindly, to those who would make fun, or pick at him while he worked so hard to be like everyone else. He was slow but that was never a problem for those who knew him. At thirty-one years of age, Shorty was barely five feet tall and had a difficult time keeping up. When he was ten, a horse rolled over him, breaking his leg and injuring his back. It was almost a year before James Williams Jr, could walk again. His back was never the same. Now he walked a little bent over with an obvious limp but the constant pain in his back wasn't so obvious. He never complained and no one knew how bad it hurt at times. Still he worked hard and did a good job at the store. Shorty took great pride in being accepted as an equal, among those who knew him best.

After a few moments, a couple of men had enough of it and called out Cahoon's ranch hands. Taking advantage of Shorty was like picking on one of their kids. Although he was older than the men who stepped in on his behalf, they still saw him as someone they were obliged to protect. Shorty's father had passed away a few years back and he lived with his momma on Jacob Street. He took care of her as much as she took care of him. Still, he needed help with the little things that most folks took for granted and everyone in town was quick to oblige.

The town fathers had tolerated these men but Marshal Smith had become weary of the whole thing. He'd haul them in and lock them up for a while. He knew the mayor would make him turn them loose as soon as he heard of the arrest. The best he could hope for was to piss them off and ruin their day.

No one expected they would stay away entirely. They had a business to run and the town needed their commerce. It was a matter of who showed up, not if. In the past, either Cahoon or Raymond would routinely send in men with instructions to cause a row. Their tirades were designed as reminders for Marshal Smith. The marshal was convinced that Cahoon wanted him to arrest his men. This would give him the pleasure of riding into town to exercise his authority over the mayor and remind Delbert of who was in charge. It also made him look like a big man in front of his men. To Marshal Smith, those days were over. He now had the authority; any lawman would expect and he would not relent.

The marshal had informed Mayor Sterns of the extra help, he had coming from Abilene. He thought that would ease his mind a bit but all he could see was gun play in the middle of town. He only hoped this thing would be over before EJ had a stroke.

Bobby Grayson was beginning to make a name for himself as well. His father wasn't too pleased that he'd gotten tied up in this thing but the store's patrons knew he was on that morning ride. Bobby had earned a new level of respect. He'd never worn a sidearm in town but now he wasn't seen without one. The same went for several of the townsfolk. Marshal Smith could see a new level of confidence in his town. He knew this was the calm before the storm but at least they were showing grit. If they got used to it, hopefully they would stand up when it really counted.

The distant sound of its whistle, announced the arrival of the 3:00 o'clock train, as she made the final turn. The marshal heard the call and made his way to the small yellow building, to meet his expected visitors. As three men, dressed in long dusters and carrying Winchesters stepped onto the platform, Marshal Smith immediately approached, confident they were the lawman from Abilene.

"Afternoon, gentlemen. I'm Marshal Delbert Smith. We appreciate you coming all this way to lend us a hand."

"We're glad to help, Marshal. Where's Ernie Evans?" One of the men asked.

"He's over at Doc Rowe's office, recovering. He's coming along nicely, though. I'll take you over there in a bit." The marshal replied.

The men introduced themselves as Dick Bryant, Toby Harris and Ernie's old friend from Dodge City, Bobby Jenkins. Marshal Smith could tell that these men had worn a badge by the way they carried themselves. Each man walked with a confident stride. They seemed to know what was moving on their left and right flanks, simply with a roll of their eyes, or a slow but purposeful turn of the head. It was obvious these men had a history. If the resolute and calculated demeanor which Ernie had demonstrated was any indication, the town of Maple Ridge was now in good hands.

Marshal Smith's first task was to get his backup deputized and make them legal. He'd expected their first stop to be his office but relented when they approached the Alhambra Saloon. Their plan, since the last stop was to have a beer and relax a bit before moving on to more pressing matters. Their impression of a train ride wasn't much different than Ernie's and they too were pining for a good horse and saddle. Without comment, Marshal Smith gladly obliged and chose instead to provide some general information over a beer, where he knew they would be more comfortable.

The presence of the Kansas lawmen was immediately noticed in town. The usual stranger arriving on the afternoon train was a normal occurrence and garnered little attention. But these men were different. They had a way about them that made their presence known, without saying a word. When they entered the saloon, all conversation came to an abrupt halt. Marshal Smith just grinned, he suspected word would make its way to the Cahoon ranch soon enough.

Cahoon had improved considerable over the last few days. Enough so, that Doctor Gregg felt it was finally time to send him home. He'd been up and around, with no sign of bleeding. The doc was sure he'd heal as quickly at the ranch, as he would there. He was still surprised that he hadn't died in his office and was glad he hadn't. Given the attitudes of those around him, Doc Gregg was sure they would have held him responsible, if he had. He hated to think of how that could have turned out.

Mrs. Cahoon had come in the day before. She'd arrived in their carriage, hoping he might be well enough for a ride. If the Cahoon's had lived in town, Doc Gregg would have sent him home a couple of days earlier. By contrast, if Mrs. Cahoon had ridden up in a buckboard, he would still be reluctant to allow him to leave.

Larry Cahoon was anxious to get home and tend to the matters of ranching. But his retaliations against Marshal Smith and William Murphy were never far from his mind. Mrs. Cahoon settled up with the doc for his services, as two of their men helped him onto the leather padded seat of the carriage. As Dr. Gregg saw them ride off, he breathed a sigh of relief, he was glad to see him go.

Cahoon had a lot on his mind and a lot that needed to be done. He'd lost five men, who had to be replaced. Raymond's shoes would be the hardest to fill but he had to find a new foreman, soon. Then there were the finances. He dreaded the process of determining how much money he'd lost, while he'd been away. Near the top of the list was Murphy, the man in Abilene. He wanted to pay him a visit real soon. There was a lot at stake and Cahoon was eager to get started.

The young man, who'd driven Mrs. Cahoon up to Cimarron, carefully pulled the carriage up close to the house. He and the Misses slowly helped him out of the seat and to his feet, where he stood for a few moments, to gain his balance. He tried walking the steps up to the porch but stopped on his second stride, then motioned for her to take his arm. Making it inside and up the stairs, was more of a task than either of them had expected. When they reached their room, she saw him directly to bed, where he stayed for the rest of the day. His wound was holding but the three-hour ride from Cimarron had worn on him. He was still weak and he needed the rest.

He arose early the next morning and with her help made his way down the stairs. He was glad to have breakfast at his own table once more. It was a sight Mrs. Cahoon feared she'd never see again. Not one to count his blessings, Cahoon immediately turned to the business of the ranch. Mrs. Cahoon had been in charge since he'd left and asked if she could help. She tried to tell him what she'd learned in the past few days but he pushed her away.

He wasn't happy that she'd been in his books while he was recuperating. She was a bit surprised and disappointed by the look in his eyes but she soon conceded. Mrs. Cahoon was more concerned at this point that he'd gone headlong back to work, way too soon. He wasn't one to take advice and brushed off her request that he slow down. His concern now was to get things back in order and whipping his lazy ranch hands back into shape.

She tried once more to help by producing the names of three men, provided to her by Charles Springer. She was eager to assist in hiring a new foreman and again, hoped he would be grateful. Taking the initiative in his absence, she'd expected to see some gratitude in his face but there was none. Cahoon chose instead to turn to Lemual White. He'd been there for a few years. Cahoon wasn't sure how many but he was a man he trusted and had taken the lead after Raymond was killed. He'd ridden with them a number of times, concerning "other ranch business" and kept a cool head about it. Cahoon could depend on Lemual to keep their business to himself. He knew she was trying to help but Cahoon wasn't about to hire an outsider for this job. It came with too much inside information. She was put out by his lack of appreciation but kept it to herself. She hadn't stopped to consider that he was keeping her outside his operation as well.

He'd seemed a bit more engaged when she brought Clayton Emerson and Tom Bainbridge to his room in Cimarron. Their background was just what he was looking for, now that Mac and Raymond were gone. But any involvement they might have in ranch business would be for a specific purpose. Once completed to Cahoon's satisfaction, they would be paid and sent on their way.

He knew she was trying to help but Cahoon was quite disturbed when he discovered that she'd allowed these men into their home. You never bring men of their stripe to you and you never go to them. Given Cahoon's position, you send someone else and meet them on neutral ground. She had laid all their cards out and given these outlaws an inside view of their home. Cahoon was sure they had taken the opportunity to memorize the best ways in and out, should they choose to return for other reasons. He would start over with these men and make sure there were no misunderstandings as to where everyone stood. Cahoon employed men as rough as these and he expected a stern meeting between them and a couple of his gun hands would keep it all in perspective.

Cahoon was still weak but persistent in pushing his vendetta. He had in his employ, two men who had pulled a stretch in Yuma Prison. He'd hired them when no one else would touch them. It was time to call in his marker. He'd kept them close to the ranch, thus far. He had Mac and Raymond before and they lead the charge with their men. This always kept Cahoon out of the fray. He now had use for these men.

He would never admit it but the walk back to Doc Rowe's office was a bit much for Ernie. Abigail was none the wiser but if he'd been alone, Ernie would surely have stopped a time or two along the way. When they reached the office, Abigail suggested they sit on the porch for a spell and take in the mid-morning air. This suited Ernie more than she knew. As they sat in the white pine rocking chairs, he once again remembered the bartender's comment; "Yeah, I like it here." It sort of stuck in Ernie's mind and he was thinking he would like it here as well.

"I've never been one to pry, Abigail but you haven't told me much about yourself or where you're from." Ernie inquired.

"Well, I don't talk much about that. Besides, it's a bit early to be telling you too much." Abigail playfully pushed it off. She knew it was coming but wasn't expecting it so soon. She thought she'd have more time to ponder. To come up with a proper way of telling the story, without Ernie feeling that she'd been hiding it from the start. Abigail was surprised in the way he brought it up. A bit blunt, she thought. But maybe it wasn't blunt at all, just that she didn't know how to deal with the reality of his inquiry. She wasn't expecting the question and was doing her best to act normal. It was a simple question, one most folks answer right off. She knew he would eventually become suspicious if she revealed nothing about her past but it would have to come at another time.

"I recon you'll get around to it, when you feel like it. For me, I usually keep things quiet too. Shoot, I've told you more than I can remember ever telling anybody. Something about you…makes me open up and think with my heart a little…It's been a long time since I've done that, Abigail." Ernie stopped there, thinking he'd already said too much. Abigail smiled. She didn't expect that. Although she was glad to know how he felt, she wasn't sure if it made matters better or worse.

CHAPTER 7

At the end of his second day home, Larry Cahoon was in bed early. He was in pain and hurting more than he had in days. With a few shots of his finest Scotch, before retiring for the evening, he felt the pain subside and was sure it would help him rest. Mrs. Cahoon admonished him with a few "I told you so-s" but that only made him angry. He was getting tired of her now telling him what to do. He didn't like her interfering and became increasingly angry that she had allowed those outlaws in his house. How much thought does that take? He asked himself. He'd been a hard and callous man before but she was watching him spiral further into someone she didn't recognize.

He was a man who enjoyed Brandy and the finest Scotch. For him, it was a pleasant sacrament but the fact that he could afford the best, gave him a fuller sense of self-worth. He always drank in moderation. With the constant need for control, he would never drink in excess, or allowed it to dull his senses. But Cahoon was now finding the bottle to be his only remedy for controlling the pain. For the past two days, there was never a bottle far from his reach.

Cahoon was an early riser and positioned their bedroom on the east side of the house for a reason. He would arise with the dawn and enjoyed the view of the sun as it would crest above the horizon, reminding him to start a new day. But the dawn of the past two days, had not offered the promise he once enjoyed. His empire was in turmoil and finding a fast and permanent fix was out of his reach. His hold on the town was slipping and he knew the longer he stayed away, the harder it would be to regain control.

Lemual White was his best hope for now. He was a rancher at heart and Cahoon didn't expect him to replace Mac. But he would make a good foreman, although it would be a while before he could fill Raymond's shoes. He was now the most trusted man on the ranch. Lemual knew where he stood and the level of responsibility which had now been placed upon him. It was his time to make a move and make it fast. Lem would show Cahoon his ability by re-taking the town and Cahoon would make him the new ranch foreman, no doubt about it.

There was a lot at stake and the ranch's cash flow was the first to feel the hit. The downturn in supplies from town was already being felt and the expectation that his men pay up front, was unheard of. They didn't carry that kind of cash and with the exception of small orders, were now coming back empty handed. Cahoon realized that he was being challenged by more than the marshal and a stranger. The town was now showing a general disrespect for his men and in turn, for him. Much had changed in such a short time.

He still held to the illusion that he'd built the town. As time went by, his perception became more obscured from reality with regard to his true participation. As for the townsfolk, most were reluctant to give him credit for half of what he had contributed. For them, it hadn't been worth the cost. This made for a wide chasm, between the town and Cahoon. Unfortunately for him, there were more of them, than of him.

Lemual had routinely been among those sent to keep the townsfolk in check. He'd ride in with a few men and challenge a shopkeeper. If they refused to quickly fill an order, he and his men would break merchandise and run off the waiting customers. They'd do anything to cost the store owners money. They'd become so destructive that it wasn't worth the risk, forcing the store owners to relent and fall in line. Cahoon's men only hoped the marshal would make a move to arrest them. On the rare occasion that he did, Cahoon would have them out of jail and heading home in a matter of hours. It was all a well-orchestrated plan to remind everyone of who was in charge. Prior to Ernie's arrival in town, it had worked. Now Cahoon was intent on regaining that control and he knew it would require a dramatic move to bring them back in line.

It was late afternoon when Marshal Smith and his new deputies arrived at Doc Rowe's office. He was surprised to see Ernie dressed and sitting in the front parlor, with Abigail by his side. Ernie was equally as surprised, when he saw the ex-lawmen from Abilene following along. The sight of his old friend, Bobby Jenkins, from Dodge City, boosted his spirits.

"What in the world are you renegades doing here?" Ernie asked, as he rose to his feet.

"We came to save your sorry ass," Bobby said, with a wide grin.

"It looks like you're too late." Ernie replied, as he lifted his right arm, still in the sling.

"We can't trust you to go anywhere," Dick said, as he looked to Marshal Smith with a smile, waiting for his take on the situation.

"Well, I tried to warn him but he wouldn't listen," the marshal added, as they all ribbed Ernie, for getting himself into such a mess.

The light-hearted conversation lasted a while, as Ernie introduced Abigail and praised her for the great care he'd received. They teased her a bit for putting up with him, as she joined in the humor and seemed to fit right in. Ernie was pleased that she appeared so comfortable around his friends. As the conversation became serious, Abigail saw the need to excuse herself, before they settled in, for the task at hand.

"What's the deal here, Ernie," Dick Bryant asked, in a serious tone.

"I came here to collect a debt from a rancher, Dick. Now, it seems I've stirred up a real hornet's nest. No disrespect to the marshal but this guy has been running the town for years and taking whatever, he wants. He didn't take so kindly to me coming in and challenging his authority."

"Not to mention, you killed two of his men," Dick added.

"Yeah well, that too I reckon." Ernie replied.

"What's the latest on Cahoon, Marshal?" Ernie asked.

"He's back at home. Dr. Gregg, in Cimarron, sent him home two days ago, according to Marshal Lambert. I've had Wilcox watching the place but he hasn't seen anything unusual since he got back. My guess is, he'll send some men here in the next couple days and start up again."

"They won't have it so easy this time," Dick began. "We'll be waiting for them and I only hope one of them decides to draw down."

"I hope not," Marshal Smith replied.

"With all due respect, Marshal, I think that's what it's going to take. I understand you don't have the force to back up such a move but we do. I believe we'll have to cut him down a notch, to let him know we're serious. Remember, you'll have to deal with him after we leave. That is, unless we kill him first." Dick wasn't up to playing games with Cahoon. They'd come a long way to settle the score and they wanted it done quickly and decisively.

"What's your plan, Dick?" Ernie asked.

"We don't know this town, or who we're dealing with. I thought we should hang around the places where they would stir up trouble. I think we should stay low and not be so visible. We'll wait until they show up and rein down on 'um.'"

"I suspect they've heard you're here by now," Marshal Smith began. "When they come in, they'll be looking for you but they won't know who you are... or where you are. If they don't see strangers patrolling the street, they will get comfortable and start in. They make the most trouble at the hardware store and mercantile. When they do, they won't be expecting any opposition." The Marshal concluded.

Toby Harris had been quiet thus far. He was the quickest gun hand amongst them and probably the only one who could match Ernie but no one knew for sure. He was a deliberate man. It made him a good lawman but it was also the trait that scared most small-town politicians. Most didn't have the stomach for his kind of law. But anytime a posse was formed to catch an undesirable, he was the first one they turned to. Toby had no tolerance for people like Cahoon, or his men. Dick Bryant suspected if anyone was shot, Toby would likely to be the one behind the trigger.

He'd thought since they met, that Marshal Smith was weak. Like Ernie, he couldn't understand why he was allowing this to happen but he hadn't been privileged to the whole story. As he listened, Toby became a little angry. He'd never seen a marshal allow such things and had to speak up.

"Marshal, what are you doing about this? I mean, this is your town, ain't it?"

"Toby, hold up a minute." Ernie stopped him there, before he went any further.

"What?" Toby asked. "He's the marshal, ain't he?"

"Yeah but this is a complicated mess and Marshal Smith has been alone here. Believe me, he's a good man and we need to help him fight this thing." Ernie put a stop to Toby before he went off on the marshal. He'd seen him do it before but there was no call for it this time.

"No offense, Marshal. I was just asking." Toby replied.

"This has been a long time coming," Ernie continued. "This Cahoon owns the town council and the mayor. Every move Marshal Smith has made so far has been pushed back. I didn't understand it either at first but after being here a while, I have a good idea of what this man has had to put up with. I'm telling you; he has grit and I want him on my side. Hell, I saw him shoot Cahoon. He's the one who put him down." Ernie concluded.

Marshal Smith had been silent thus far, making no attempt to refute Toby's impression. After Ernie was done, he just looked at Toby with a stern eye and replied; "You need to be a mite more careful what you say, when you don't know what you're talking about." The look in the marshal's eyes told Toby everything he needed to know.

"Sorry, Marshal. No offense to you, I need to get a handle on what's going on here. I'm just asking." Toby had been rebuked and that didn't happen very often. It told the others a little about Marshal Delbert Smith as well.

Dick Bryant soon broke the silence to clear the tension from the room. "Well, now that we have that out of the way," he replied. Everyone took a deep breath and chuckled a bit.

"Marshal, we need to know what you plan to do this evening. Do they show up around here at night?" he asked.

"Yeah, most nights until lately. A few will come in for a card game, or just to get drunk." The marshal replied.

"Where do they go?"

"Either the Alhambra or Jack's Saloon."

"Ernie, are you up for a walk to the saloon for a beer?" Dick asked. It was then that Abigail walked down the hall and heard the question.

"If he doesn't stay too late," Abigail interjected with a smile, as she stepped in the doorway.

"You heard that. I can go but you'd better have me back here at a reasonable hour." Ernie laughed, as they all looked to him, realizing that their old friend had been smitten.

In his parlor, where he normally conducted business and reveled in his success, Cahoon sat with an open bottle of Scotch, pondering his current situation. He thought back to the early days, just after he'd taken ownership of this vast section of open range and all the plans he had at the time. As he looked around his opulent surroundings, he marveled in the transition and how successful he had become. Still, he was unwilling to consider the hard work of those who'd helped him build this beautiful place. Only that it was his and he had built it all from his own perseverance.

Cahoon had never trusted anyone, with the exception of Mrs. Rachel Cahoon and now he was pushing her away. By contrast, Mrs. Cahoon was a quiet, petite lady, with good up-bringing, who had always appreciated everything they owned. But circumstances had changed her since the shooting and through fear, she was becoming more like him.

She had depended on him since their marriage in Scotland and trusted his instincts when he decided to come to America. He had always provided and she'd never worried about the future. A few days ago, she was struck with the fear of being alone and the future suddenly appeared very uncertain.

Mrs. Cahoon felt her world collapsing around her and following in his footsteps was the only thing she knew to do. As uncomfortable and afraid as she was, she felt it was necessary and entered a world she knew nothing about. She was scared to death when she'd invited those outlaws into their home. She didn't know any better than to reach out to these men, with hopes of stopping those who'd tried to kill her husband. She was certain they would return if he didn't die and she couldn't allow that to happen. She had never considered the possibility that her husband was on the wrong side of the law and was shot as a result.

Cahoon didn't understand her fears or concerns and he didn't seem to care. Revenge for his pain and the loss of control over the town were consuming his every thought. He must be in charge, that's how it had always been. No one would take that from him. He would make them pay. They would rue the day they challenged him and he only wished that Mac had killed that murdering Ernie Evans when he had the chance. But Mac was dead and that opportunity had passed. Now it was up to him and he would prevail.

Cahoon and Lemual White had two plans to work out and both had to be kept very quiet. First, there would be a raid on the town and it had to be soon. Cahoon had initially considered a late-night fire ball through a store window. Fire in a small town was a devastating threat. With a little wind, it could consume an entire block in minutes. Cahoon decided not to take it that far. It wasn't a humanitarian decision by any measure but one of greed and the interest of the ranch.

He decided instead, to have a large number of men ride into town with the 'big-rig'. They'd make some noise to draw everyone's attention and then make sure Bobby Grayson gave him the priority he deserved and fill his order first. He would make it a long list of supplies, everything they'd needed but had been denied over the past few days. He wanted it all and any demand for payment would be met with force. Enough to prevent them from trying that stunt again. It would be a show of strength, to let them know that nothing had changed.

Grayson's Mercantile would definitely be the first target. Old man Henry Grayson had been a thorn in his side for years and Bobby had been acting tough, since that morning on the trail. They would get him first, to set an example for the others. Four men would hit Grayson's Mercantile, with Lem taking the lead. Two others would do the same at Dawson's Dry Goods. This wasn't new for Lem he'd done this many time, only this time he'd take more men.

Several men who knew Ernie Evans' appearance would trail along and scout the town looking for him. They knew he was wounded and expected him to be an easy target, if they were lucky enough to meet him face to face. Others would keep an eye on the marshal and join in the disturbance at either store, should their situation call for it.

Marshal Smith was sure to get involved and try to stop them. Cahoon had planned on it and hoped he would. If he walked in the mercantile, they planned to buffalo him and throw him in his own jail. They didn't want him dead. They wanted to make a mockery of him before the town and remove his newly found authority. Mayor Sterns would not be approached or threatened in any way. Larry Cahoon wanted to do that himself but that would be a few days after the raid. He would ride in and face down his little mayor. He'd bring this all to a stop and the town would be his again.

Then there was William Murphy in Abilene. That would take a few extra days to put in motion, with a couple additional days for his men to make the Kansas trip. Once there, they had to find Mr. Murphy and watch his movements and the activities around the KCBA office. They would stay close to town and learn all the streets and alleys without being too obvious. Trying to stay out of sight would be a waste of time, so they planned to spend time in the saloons. They would blend in with the other cow hands and drovers but not really join in. Be nice but not too nice. Stay close by but do nothing strange or unusual. They'd always keep an eye on the KCBA office and its chief officer, Mr. William Murphy.

There were only three people in the house at the time of their conversation in the parlor. Cahoon had always made sure he had complete privacy, with any such meeting. He was certain that Mrs. Cahoon was upstairs, where she usually found something to keep her busy. This time she was not. With a growing suspicion of her husband's actions, Rachel Cahoon remained in the kitchen for a spell, then ventured out onto the back porch prior to the men beginning their discussion in the parlor.

Slowly and silently, she made her way back through the kitchen and into the open hallway near the staircase. There, voices from the parlor could easily be heard, even whispers. They'd often laughed about the conversations they overheard during dinner parties. Things said by guests, thinking no one could hear. Now she was hearing things, which surely did not contain any humor.

Although she didn't heed his advice at the time, Charles Springer had opened her eyes and made her think for herself. She'd always known her husband to be a tough businessman and somewhat callous at times. But she really didn't know to what extent. She knew a good man would not do the things she was now hearing. Talking about such things as, planning a "raid on the town" or "making them pay".

Her suspicions over the past twenty-four hours had grown tremendously. His drinking and plotting seemed so out of character. But now she was coming to the painful realization that plotting and scheming, was the way he'd always gotten things done. Maybe he wasn't shot by men trying to kill him after all, she thought. Perhaps he was shot by men protecting themselves.

Her revelation made her sick and she wanted to throw up. Slowly, she made her way back into the kitchen and out the door. She wanted to get away and walked out to the pasture where her horse, Lillie was grazing. She stayed there for enough time to be sure the meeting was over and hoped he would come looking for her. If Cahoon found her outside with the horses, he would have no reason to suspect that she had overheard any of his conversation. Given his state of mind, Rachel Cahoon did not want him to know that she'd heard anything about his plans.

Cahoon sent one of his men back to Cimarron to find Clayton Emerson and Tom Bainbridge. He settled on a meeting with them near the canyon, just south of Coyote Creek, at 3:00 pm the next day. He didn't want to be seen with these men and he intended to keep their conversation away from town and any unwelcome ears. He'd gathered his files and the information he would need to nail down Murphy in Abilene. He'd make sure there were no mistakes.

The two men were Missouri Bushwhackers with no conscience for attacking a Kansas businessman. They knew this part of Kansas, which made Cahoon's task of finding Murphy somewhat easier. Along with them, he would send two of his own men as back up. Two of those who'd spent time in Yuma Prison. They owed him big time and he knew they would make sure his money made it back into his pocket.

By his third day home, Cahoon was carrying a bottle of Scotch in his hand and drinking straight from the bottle. Mrs. Cahoon was afraid and knew it had affected his judgment. She was greatly concerned about this sudden change. When she confronted him, he became irate and threatened her to mind her own business. In all their years together, this had never happened. He was a tyrant and she'd finally come to that understanding but his tact with her had always been respectful and protective. In the turmoil, even that was changing.

Lem hitched up Cahoon's carriage early that morning, for their trip to Coyote Creek. They would take four riders along to make sure they were covered and to be sure these bushwhackers understood who they were working for. Cahoon didn't expect the Kansas trip to take more than a week. He wanted it done quickly and clean. Get Murphy and make sure he knows it's Mr. Larry Cahoon's money he's returning, plain and simple. Shoot him, or leave him unharmed, he didn't care, just make it right.

He wouldn't drag out either of his vendettas. He wanted his money back and to regain control of Maple Ridge as soon as possible. Very soon, this would all be a bad memory and life would resume as it should be, with him in charge. With a bottle in his right hand, he and Lem rode off heading north.

The names Tom Bainbridge and Clayton Emerson weren't heard much around town. They weren't likely to be remembered in Cimarron. Nothing they ever did stood out as courageous, or special in any way. There were no notable stand offs, robberies or memorable gun play that could be attributed to either of them. But behind the scenes, they had made a living gambling, stealing and occasionally hiring out their gun, without ever being caught.

They hadn't pulled off anything of this magnitude since their days with Quantrill but felt their skills as gunmen were still the best. This job in Abilene would set them apart from the others and put them on a path to working more, for men like Cahoon. The cost of their gun would soon become very expensive.

It was justice as Cahoon saw it. William Murphy had sent his gun hand to New Mexico to seek him out and forcefully take money from him. Now he would send men to Abilene, to get it back. To him, it all made sense. The law wouldn't do anything about it. Marshal Smith had his chance, so it was now up to him. This was separate, from his problems in Maple Ridge. That was a different issue and Lem would rectify that very soon. This was ranch business and he would see that his money was returned, by turning Murphy's game around on him.

There were a number of wooden benches and rocking chairs lining the boardwalk on Grayson Street. Most were near the corners of each block, next to the fire barrel. Others were a few feet from the cafés and restaurant doors, usually beneath the windows. Michael King was probably the person who used them the most as he sat around, talking to folks and passing the time. Much of his day was spent hanging around Grayson Street. He'd walk from the Early Bird Café, then down to Grayson's Mercantile and back with little else to do.

Marshal Smith paid him to clean the office and jail cells once a week which only took him a couple of hours. Ralph Thomas paid him to clean stables, when he was too busy for the task. Others, like Bobby Grayson would pay him to do odd jobs here or there. JT felt a little sorry for him and usually asked him to stop by the Café to finish off some of the after-lunch leftover's, in exchange for a chore or two. He wasn't one to drink too much. But on those occasions when someone offered to buy him a beer, Michael would follow along and gladly join in. For the most part, he quietly sat around town and just passed the time.

He'd come to know everyone. His small talk had taught him more about the people in town than anyone realized. Some folks thought Michael wasn't all there but that wasn't the case at all, he was just plain lazy. Marshal Smith had used his knack for sitting and watching on several occasions. He'd found the information Michael could offer to be very useful. They'd always kept it quiet and no one was the wiser. The marshal had plans to introduce Michael to his new deputies and knew he would be of use to them.

There were rumblings around town about Cahoon's men coming in. Marshal Smith wasn't sure if someone at the ranch was talking, or if the townsfolk were just getting edgy. Michael was the perfect person to find the source of this information, without drawing suspicion from anyone. Either way, the marshal had a plan and he now had the fire power to face down Cahoon's men, even if it was in the street.

Those who'd seen Ernie's friends in town were beginning to refer to them as the "Lawmen from Abilene". They'd each taken a room at the Grand Hotel on Grayson, which was located down the block from the mayor's office and across from the Stage Office. This kept them closer to the center of town than the Byron Hotel and it was cheaper. They each arose at dawn on their second day in Maple Ridge. They slowly made their way to the Double Deuce Corral, then to the Café, where they planned to meet Ernie and the marshal.

Ernie was the first to arrive. He'd left Doc Rowe's early and paced himself along the way. He stopped a couple of times, to avoid being winded when he arrived. The walk was good therapy and much better than sitting around the doc's porch. Marshal Smith thought it would be best to get Mayor Sterns involved and invited him to join them. He was the second to arrive. As he and Ernie sat making small talk, Mayor Sterns was getting a different impression of this stranger. EJ had been angered by Ernie's actions and the way he had endangered the town. But he was now, seeing a man who'd been shot in the back in an effort to help and still he was willing to stay.

Ernie was seeing the mayor in a different light as well. On the day of the shooting in town, EJ had been a basket case with little sense of direction. The man Ernie now saw before him was an intelligent lawyer type, with a smart head on his shoulders. Their lone and unplanned meeting, would be of more value than even they knew. Until this moment, the mayor had only considered Ernie to be a hot headed, self-serving gunman. Ernie in turn, had only seen a squirrely little man, who was scared out of his boots. They each left that day, with a much different opinion.

By the time Ernie's friends and the marshal arrived, they'd finished their first cup of coffee and were ready to order if they hadn't shown up soon.

"Where's your sweetie, Ernie?" Bobby asked, with a laugh as they strolled in.

"She ain't my sweetie, you idiot," Ernie replied, with a grin.

"I don't know. You looked a might smitten to me."

"Go ahead, you're about to get tore up," Ernie replied.

"What, with your one good arm?" Bobby shot back, as everyone joined in, with a hardy laugh.

The light moment did each of them a world of good. It was a good way for the marshal and the mayor to get better acquainted with the "Lawmen from Abilene". And it helped set the stage for the more serious conversation, which was yet to come. As they settled in with their breakfast menus, Marshal Smith spoke up first, to begin with his thoughts for the coming days. He'd given this a lot of deliberation and had a few ideas to help them be better prepared for the coming showdown.

The marshal started by asking the men to come back to his office after breakfast. Each of the willing store owners, were to join them as well. He wanted them to be acquainted with Ernie's friends. Their take on this, was very important. Each of them would tell these men their concerns and about the tactics of Cahoon's men, as they wreaked havoc on their stores. It was also important for each man to become familiar with the physical appearance of the others. Should there be a confrontation in one of the stores things could get hectic real quick, especially if there was gun play. It would be smoky and loud and Marshal Smith wanted to be sure they would recognize one another right off.

They needed to settle on a few signals as well. They'd use a slight but subtle nod to let the men know if some of the patrons in the store were Cahoon's men. Then there were the logistics of who would be where and how to know where trouble was brewing. They also needed to avoid any suspicion, from the other Cahoon men, who could be waiting, to back them up. That was where Michael King would come in.

As they all sat, with their coffee and listening to the marshal, each man began to nod in approval. It was a good plan and even Toby Harris realized that he had judged the marshal's ability too quickly. Mayor Sterns sat quietly; a bit ashamed at his prior lack of confidence in Marshal Smith. He began to think, if he'd let the marshal do his job, they might not be in this mess. Ernie was watching the mayor's expressions. He could see the obvious embarrassment in his face, as he rubbed his forehead and wiped the sweat from his brow. He was a good man who was over his head. Ernie was getting a clearer picture of how this whole thing had taken place.

JT Belcher, Bobby Grayson and Ralph Thomas, were the men who Marshal Smith was relying upon to alert the others, when their adversaries arrived. They each knew everyone on the Cahoon Ranch and would be prepared regardless of who Cahoon decided to send in. The townsfolk knew what was coming and most had their eyes open and ready to take a stand. Marshal Smith had been watching this change take place for the past few days. He'd first hoped it would take hold with folks like Bobby Grayson, now it seemed to be contagious.

After their meeting at the marshal's office, Ernie and Bobby Jenkins walked down to Alhambra Saloon for an early beer. Ernie liked the place but hadn't been back since that first day. He now looked forward to relaxing there for a while, maybe join in a card game this time. There were only a few men in the saloon, as one would expect for that time of day and just what the two had hoped for. They chose a large round oak table with a deck of card carefully placed in the center. They took a seat and settled in, as Ernie reached for the cards with his left hand and began to shuffle. He found this simple task quite difficult, with his right arm in a sling.

"Time for this thing to go," Ernie abruptly announced. He then slipped his arm out of the sling and straightened his elbow for the first time since the shooting. Bobby just stared back.

"If you had a brain, you'd be dangerous."

"Why?"

"Cause the doc ought to be doing that." Bobby answered.

"Hell, if I listened to him, I'd still be laid up in a bed. No, it's time for this thing to go." Ernie replied, as he flexed his arm. Bobby just laughed, ole Ernie was still just as hard as nails, he thought.

"You remember how we used to do this, Bobby?" Ernie asked, with a mischievous grin, as he now shuffled the cards with both hands.

"Yeah and I remember the last time in Dodge, I thought I'd gone deaf. You fired that cannon twice in that saloon and my ears went numb." Bobby replied, as he shook his head and laughed.

"They were going to kill me, what did you expect me to do?"

"They got what I expected but I'll bet it came as a surprise to them." Bobby replied.

"You met Wyatt Earp, didn't you?" Ernie was now laughing out loud.

"Yeah but I don't think it was worth it."

Both Ernie and Bobby were having a good laugh, as the bartender walked up.

"Good afternoon, gentlemen. Man, it's good to see you again." The bartender said, in a jovial tone.

Ernie looked up to see the same bartender, who'd waited on him that first day.

"How are you, my friend?" Ernie asked. "You know, I never did get your name. I'm Ernie Evans."

"Yeah, I know who you are. I'm Garland, Garland Johnson."He was still dressed as dapper as the day Ernie first walked in.

"What will it be, Gents. It's on the house." Garland offered.

"We'll each have a beer," Ernie replied. "Are you sure that's okay?"

"Oh, I think it'll be okay… I own the place," Garland replied, with a proud smile as he walked away.

Ernie felt a sense of relief as he walked back to Doc Rowe's office. He'd decided to leave that afternoon and get a room at the Byron Hotel. With the extra two hundred dollars in his pocket, he could afford it and he would ask for room 214, he liked that bed. The sling that he'd worn for the past few days was now dangling out of his pants pocket. As he continued to flex the muscles his right arm loosened up and seemed to work just fine. Ernie had full use of his arm, with only a slight pain in his back, he felt fine. He was sure glad that was over.

When he walked into Doc Rowe's office, Abigail met him in the hallway and had a fit that he'd removed his sling. Ernie just laughed and waived his arm about to show her that it worked.

"I'm okay, Abigail," Ernie said. "Cahoon's men will be riding in town any day now and I need to be ready. I have to help."

"You've done your part, it's time for the others to step up and do theirs. I don't want you to get hurt again." She said, with concern in her eyes.

"Well, I'm glad you feel that way and I don't want to get hurt again either. But if I'm wearing this sling, I'll be a sitting duck."

"Not if you aren't there," she said.

"You know me better than that. I have to be there and I'll do my part to protect this town." Ernie replied.

He'd grown fond of Maple Ridge and liked the people. They'd been good to him and he was finding that he didn't miss Abilene all that much. He was also finding that he enjoyed Abigail's company more than he would admit, even to himself. He hoped she felt the same but his gut was telling him to take it slow and to be cautious.

"Abigail, I'm going back to the hotel this evening. I've been here long enough, it's time to go." Ernie said.

"Go, do you mean leave?" Abigail asked.

"No, I'm not leaving, just going back to the hotel. I don't need to be here." Ernie replied.

"Okay, as long as you don't leave." She said, with a smile.

"I'm not leaving." He quietly replied.

Ernie knew at that moment that she felt as he did and it gave him an unusual feeling in the pit of his stomach.

CHAPTER 8

It was 10:00 am when Lemual White and his men, slowly rode into Maple Ridge from the north trail. They crossed the railroad tracks two by two past the train station and headed straight down Grayson Street, looking from side to side. Michael King was sitting on a bench in front of the saddle shop, just past the Early Bird Café, three blocks away. He saw them as they reached the tracks. From that distance, he couldn't make out the likeness of either rider but still he had no doubt that they were Cahoon's men. He quietly stood and walked to the corner of Third, stopping next to the Café. Toby Harris was sitting on a bench, half a block away next to Grayson's Mercantile. When Toby looked his way, Michael gave him a short two fingered salute from the brim of his hat, to let him know the party was about to begin.

Their meeting at the Café had been two days ago and Toby had taken his assigned position at the mercantile each morning since. He was there as soon as the store opened and would move around from time to time to avoid suspicion but never out of sight of the mercantile's front door. Bobby Jenkins followed in kind as his assignment was Dawson's Dry Goods, across the street and two shops up from Toby's position. Ernie and Dick Bryant were sitting on opposite sides of the street, up from Second and saw the men ride in as well.

They instinctively knew the riders to be Cahoon's men and acknowledged it with a nod, as they started walking toward Toby Harris and Bobby Jenkins. Once Michael had gained Toby's attention, he walked inside the Café to alert JT. From there, he crossed the street and high-tailed it to Fredrick Street to let Ralph know they were in town. It seemed that everyone was now on alert. The town was busy as usual, with folks going about their business. The presence of a few of Cahoon's men in town was no surprise for most. And with townsfolk scurrying about, the presence of three strangers would go virtually unnoticed, by Cahoon's men.

The men reined up on Grayson, between Second Street and Third, with some tying up to the left as the others secured their lines to a hitch post on the right. As they dismounted, each man stood for a moment, obviously watching the street and running over their plan one last time. There were nine men in all. Four began a slow walk toward the mercantile, two headed toward the dry goods store, while three others moved toward Third Street. As the marshal's men watched their movements, they each saw the 'big-rig' as it rolled down Grayson Street and stopped in front of the mercantile. The two men sitting on the wagon's bench stayed in place, neither of them stepping down from their seat.

Toby made his way into the mercantile and gave Bobby Grayson a subtle salute off the brim of his hat, which prompted an acknowledging nod in return. Through the front windows, he watched their movements on the street. He saw the men separate, with four of them heading toward the mercantile door. Moments earlier, Bobby Jenkins had stepped into Dawson's, giving the same signal to him, which was observed by Shorty Williams as well. Marshal Smith and JT Belcher stood in front of the Café, waiting to see who would be headed where. It was all open at that point. No one knew where they would go, or even if they might be planning to make a stand in the street.

By the time Cahoon's men approached their destinations, each of the marshal's men were in place and ready for their move. Toby Harris and Bobby Jenkins were in their assigned locations. Ernie and Dick were at the corner of Third and Grayson, across from the Café, where JT and the marshal were watching. Ralph Thomas and Deputy Wilcox were on the corner of Second Street, watching from that angle. Cahoon's men hadn't seen any of their movements, or if they had, it didn't draw anyone's attention.

Dick and Ernie waited for them to enter the stores and watched the others, as they walked down the street, looking from side to side. It was obvious they were searching for someone and Ernie was sure it was him. He and Dick stepped aside and out of view until the men passed by, then made their move. Both men, made their way to the mercantile to back up Toby, while Marshal Smith and Ralph Thomas moved toward the dry goods store, from opposite directions. Michael King walked back to Third and stood as their lookout, watching the street from both directions in case another group came in from the south. JT stood near the front door of the Café, with the intention of turning the others away, if they tried to enter his place.

Each of the marshal's men stood back as Lemual White and his men walked about the stores, checking the situation before making their move. The lawmen watched as they looked toward one another, waiting for their cue to start a disturbance and challenge the respective store owner. Bobby Grayson looked to Toby and nodded as he moved his eyes toward Lemual White. Toby now knew their leader and the man to watch.

Lemual walked to the counter and pushed two patrons out of his way, then looked Bobby square in the eyes.

"I have an order to fill and I ain't going to wait. You'd best get to it now, shop-keep." Lemual spoke in a loud and demanding voice, intended for everyone to hear as he smacked his list on the counter.

"I have other customers who were here first, you'll have to wait your turn," Bobby replied in a calm but forceful manner.

"I don't reckon you heard me, shop-keep. You fill this order now, unless you want trouble." Lemual wasn't surprised that his first demand wasn't heeded. He expected as much and his men were prepared to make trouble in the store, until Bobby Grayson understood who was in charge.

"Maybe you didn't hear me, Lemual. You can wait your turn or go somewhere else. I'd rather you go somewhere else." Bobby's voice was equally as loud as Lemual's. He wanted his customers to hear him stand up to Cahoon's men but he wanted Lemual's men to hear him as well.

Toby slowly walked up behind Lemual, as he stood waiting for Bobby to buckle.

"I don't think you know what you've just done." Lemual said, with an arrogant grin.

The next sound they heard was the shattering of a large pickle jar, as it broke on the floor. Glass and pickle juice, flew in every direction. One of Lemual's men had walked up beside him, with the others to his right. He'd lifted the jar for everyone to see, then let it fall, crashing to the floor. Dick had moved behind the men, without being noticed and drew his sidearm. Holding it backward, he cracked the man in the back of his dirty black hat, as soon as the jar hit the floor. He immediately cocked the .44 caliber Colt revolver and aimed it toward the other two who were standing next to him. They were so surprised by his quick and deliberate action that they froze in place. By then, it was too late to make a move.

Lemual quickly turned in the excitement, only to have Toby standing in his face with his Colt cocked and aimed at his nose. As Toby backed up a bit, Lemual went for his gun, which prompted Toby to shoot him in the arm. His revolved was clear and cocked. He had all the time in the world.

"How stupid are you?" Toby asked, "I should have killed you but I think the marshal wants you to answer for this."

Dick was standing guard over the other two, who didn't make a sound, while the fourth man was still on the floor out cold. They knew it was useless to challenge Dick Bryant and neither one, was up to dying at that moment.

Ernie stepped to the door and looked down the street, expecting the others would come once they heard gun play. As expected, three of

Cahoon's men were running up the boardwalk, hugging the buildings as they worked their way to the mercantile. Ernie eased past the door jamb, with his revolver leveled as he shouted to the men; "You'd better stop there. I have a clear shot. I don't think you want to come any closer." JT saw them move up and slowly made his way past the corner of Third Street. He stopped next to the corner barber shop on Grayson Street, where he had a clear shot and good cover.

The two men in the dry goods store heard the shot before they'd made their move on Mr. Dawson and turned to aid the men in the mercantile. They hadn't noticed the marshal, or Ralph, as they stood in the back of the store and out of sight. When they turned their attention to the street, Marshal Smith walked up behind them with Ralph only a few feet away.

"Hold it right there boys," Marshal Smith shouted.

They each turned at the sound of his voice to see the marshal's Colt and Ralph's Winchester, pointed at each of them. Without a word their guns fell to the floor, with their hands out by their sides, in clear view. They had nowhere to go.

Marshal Smith marched them out into the street, with Ralph close behind as JT and Ernie moved in on the men on the boardwalk. They kicked their weapons away and turned them toward the street following Marshal Smith's lead and met him half way out. Deputy Wilcox holstered his revolver and ran up to meet them as both sides joined up. He was shaking like a leaf but no one had seen him, during the fracas.

"What do you want me to do Marshal?" Wilcox asked.

Before the marshal answered, he saw Dick Bryant enter the street from the mercantile, dragging one of Cahoon's men with two others in front of him and the barrel of his revolver. Behind him, Toby had Lemual White by his good arm, as he joined them in the street. The marshal hadn't seen a crowd this large since the day of Ernie's shootout at the train station.

Marshal Smith took a deep breath and said; "Lock 'um up!"

The two men in Cahoon's 'big-rig' had cut out. They eased down the street, as soon as they realized that gun play in the mercantile had resulted in bad news for Lemual. Reaching the corner of Fourth Street, they reined the horse around to Jacob Street and made their way across the tracks and back to the trail. Once they were out of town, Mark Ambrose, the wagon driver, popped the reins and put his horse in a dead run back toward the ranch.

Cahoon was in the parlor, hugging a bottle of Scotch when the men arrived. He'd pushed himself hard the past few days and was feeling the pain. The ride to Coyote Creek the day before had been harder on his gut, than he had expected. By the time he and Lemual arrived back at the ranch, he was finding it difficult to breath. After a few shots of bourbon, he turned in early, expecting he'd feel much better in the morning. When he awoke, he laid there for a bit and was relieved that the pain had subsided greatly. But after a walk to the corral and his talk with the men, it was back. That only served to make him more disgruntled.

He was alarmed when he heard the men at the door. It was too soon; their plan should have taken much longer to complete. There was no way that Bobby Grayson could have loaded his wagon that quickly. Not expecting good news, he slowly arose and walked to the foyer. He arrived just behind the maid, who'd opened the door and allowed the men into the entrance way.

"What the hell are you doing back here?" Cahoon asked.

"They got us, Boss." Mark said, in a humble tone.

"What do you mean, they got you?" Cahoon fired back.

"Talk man…I want the truth!" Cahoon clutched his side to combat the pain. His heighted state had only increased the discomfort.

"We waited in the wagon, like you told us to and expected Lem to come get us when he was ready. We heard them arguing in the store and I thought he'd got the best of Grayson. Then we heard a gunshot and saw Lem through the window when he fell."

"Is he dead?" Cahoon asked.

"No, he ain't dead, Boss. We ain't seen no reason why we should just sit there, so I rode off real slow, down the street a ways. When we seen the marshal and his deputies round them all up in the street, we high-tailed it back here." Mark Ambrose was almost out of breath from telling the story.

"Deputies, what do you mean deputies? He only has one." Cahoon asked.

"I know he used to have one but I seen three others wearing badges. I don't know who they was, Boss. I ain't never seen 'um before." Mark had become nervous, as he watched the look in Cahoon's eyes become increasingly cold. He half expected he'd take it out on him but he had no choice but to stand there and answer his questions. Cahoon stood in silence for a moment then began to shake his head, as he was obviously taking it all in.

"Go on," he replied in a quiet, somewhat calm voice.

"Unhitch the horse and go back to work. I got some thinking to do."

Cahoon stood for a moment, looking out across the front lawn of the ranch then slowly turned. As Mark rode off in the wagon, Cahoon pondered for a moment and clutched his aching side as he walked back into the parlor and a waiting bottle.

Mayor EJ Sterns was in his office when Cahoon's men rode into town. When he heard they were there, he collected his hat and walked outside, far enough into the street to see what was taking place. Gaining a little courage, he cautiously ventured up to Third Street, very close to the scene and stood just south of the Early Bird Café. He heard the gun shot from the mercantile and flinched, expecting the worst.

He stood there, watching, as JT walked up to the corner of Third to back up Ernie, who had just shown himself from the mercantile door. He'd never seen anything like this. It was like a bad dream to him. He thought of the marshal and his men and how they had put themselves in the middle of this without complaint. He saw Cahoon's men, as they carefully worked their way toward the mercantile and how Ernie had talked them down, without fear for his own life. He'd heard of such things but he had never seen anything like this.

When it was over and the marshal had arrested the men, EJ walked up to them and stood in the middle of the group as a show of support. No more running from Cahoon and no more fear of his men. He too was learning to stand tall and it was the greatest feeling he could imagine.

Marshal Smith wasn't done by any measure. Once they'd locked the nine men in his two jail cells, the marshal turned to Lemual White and called him to the bars of the cell.

"Now," the marshal began, "I can probably hold these other men for thirty days and I plan to keep them here to the last minute. But you and Harold Quinn will finally be held to account for killing Ben Willis." The marshal was both angry and satisfied that he could finally make that statement.

"You can't hold me for that, Marshal. I didn't do it and you can't prove no different." Lemual was shaken by the charge but still felt that Cahoon would intervene and get him out of it.

"You know you did it Lemual and you know I can prove it. I promise you; I'll have an indictment to Judge Kellum in the morning and then you and that other low life, will finally stand trial for murdering that good man. I think that should just about close the door on your boss. Larry Cahoon is finished, along with the fear that you bunch of worthless bastards have reined on this town." Marshal Smith stood tall, as he spoke, with all the authority that he was granted from behind his tin star.

Ernie and the others were on the boardwalk, up the street a bit from the marshal's office, when the crowd began to gather. Every curious onlooker in town had come out to shake their hands, or to go into the mercantile to see where it all took place. Ernie stood quietly, as he saw Abigail running toward him. He thought she would stop but she ran until she jumped in his arms. She held him so tightly around the neck that he could hardly breathe.

"I was so worried," she cried. "Don't you ever do that to me again." Ernie eased her back to her feet, as she now stood a few inched away, with tears in her eyes. He was both surprised and touched.

"I'm fine, Abigail," he said with a smile. "I told you I had to do this; it was my responsibility. I didn't know you cared that much." Ernie said with a grin.

"I do care that much and you should have known it." Abigail was becoming a little embarrassed, as she now realized, that half the town had just witnessed her display of affection.

Ernie stood for a moment, looking into her eyes, then finally spoke; "Well, okay then…that's good." He knew it sounded stupid but he couldn't think of anything else to say.

Abigail was amazed at his agility. With his wound only half healed, he moved faster than most. His strong, trail hardened body, didn't remember pain for long.

The mood in town was one of relief but Marshal Smith knew he had a long way to go, before this thing was settled. The men who rode in were all Cahoon's men. He was expecting a couple of strangers to be along, as Marshal Lambert in Cimarron had warned. After a quick walk to the telegraph office, a message was on its way to Cimarron for some clarification on these gun hands he'd talked about.

Toby Harris was getting itchy. When Marshal Smith returned, Toby was jawing with Ernie and Dick Bryant, asking when they planned to make a ride to the Cahoon Ranch to bring him in. The marshal heard the conversation as he entered his office and immediately chimed in.

"We're not going to arrest Cahoon, not yet anyway. I want Harold Quinn first." The marshal stated, as he joined in the conversation.

"He and that one yonder," he said, as he pointed to Lemual White, "killed a good man two years ago. It's taken me this long to finally get some justice."

"I intend to go after him this afternoon. How many of you want to ride along?" Marshal Smith asked.

"I think we'd all better ride along, Marshal. You can't be sure of what you'll find, once you get there." Toby added.

"You're probably right," Marshal Smith replied. "How about we saddle up and head on out there, get this thing done before dark?"

They were all ready to ride but for Toby and Dick, they still hadn't faced the man they came for. They'd have a quick lunch then head for the ranch, just hoping this rancher would give them an excuse. They'd come to do a job and to them, it was only half done.

Cahoon returned to the parlor and settled his morose, aching body into a large leather chair and reached for a bottle. Mrs. Cahoon watched from the door without words. Her heart broke, at the sight of this shell of her former husband. There he sat, consumed in his own antagonism for the world, drowning his pain and reality, in the first bottle that was within reach. She thought of all they had acquired and wondered why it never seemed to be enough. She'd always assumed it to be ambition, now she knew it was nothing more that rancid greed.

She'd heard the conversation with Mark Ambrose and realized this was the result of the plans he and Lemual had spoken of the day before. She pondered a moment and concluded that she wasn't displeased with the outcome. She wouldn't admit it, even to herself that she was glad. The implications of that would be far reaching. She was struggling with her current situation and began to think more of herself and less of her husband and the ranch. Life itself was changing before her eyes and the security she thought had been restored only days ago, was in peril once again.

Unwilling to concede, or even consider the fallout of his irrational decisions, Cahoon was still intent on getting his way. He wasn't of the mind to take the blame; it was their fault. The only thing he did wrong was to send in the wrong men.

Lemual – I never should have trusted him in the first place, he thought. He's to blame. If he'd been stronger and shown the level of force he was told to show, they would now have the town back under control. That was the problem and he knew exactly how to resolve it. Yes, that's what I'll do, he thought. When the bushwhackers return with my money, I'll set them on that ungrateful town and bring them to their knees. They've done it before, during the war and they can do it again. Yes…that's the answer. Now living in a world where his mind had been compromised by pain and alcohol, Cahoon felt a measure of satisfaction. He finally admitted to himself, that he'd lost this hand. But he had enough chips to stay in the game and this time he would succeed.

Nine men in two jail cells would be a challenge and Marshal Smith knew it. He knew he couldn't keep them all there and contacted the marshal in Cimarron for some help in the matter. He had no sympathy for any of them and for the time being he would enjoy every moment. From his desk, he could feel the temperature in the small office beginning to rise. He could only imagine how fast it must be rising in those crowded cells. Within minutes the men began removing their coats and some peeled off their shirts as well. A few had laid claim to a spot on the floor and Marshal Smith expected multiple fights to break out over this little piece of his smelly jail cell. He intended to let them fight it out. He wasn't going in there. If they wanted to kill each other, then more power to them.

He laughed when Molly, from the Café walked in. JT had always provided meals for his prisoners. That normally consisted of one at a time and usually days apart. It had never been a lucrative part of JT's business. When Molly saw both cells full, she just stood there.

"What do you expect me to do with all of them?" She asked.

"Feed 'um like you always do." Marshal Smith replied, as he began to laugh.

"How many is it?" Molly stood, with her jaw dropped.

"I don't know…Nine, I think."

"What do you mean, you think?"

"I'm just kidding, there are nine. Just bring whatever you've got left over. We'll let them sort it out."

It was coming up on 1:00 pm, by the time the marshal and his men had their prisoners housed and felt confident the street was secure. Dick and Toby had decided the Early Bird Café would be a good place to settle in for a good meal. Besides, they felt some kinship with their new friend JT and planned for everyone to meet there. Ernie declined their offer and decided to take Abigail to the Cattleman's for lunch instead. It was more expensive but he still had most of Cahoon's two hundred dollars burning a hole in his pocket. Bobby Jenkins snickered at him when he backed out but Ernie just grinned and didn't say a word.

Their lunch didn't remain private for long. Marshal Smith and EJ Sterns had decided to join in, where the mayor was proud to announce that their lunch would be paid by the Mayor's Office. It was the least they could do. Abigail was quite disappointed. She'd wanted Ernie all to herself. Ernie, on the other hand, was a little relieved. He'd had enough excitement for one day.

After lunch, they all gathered back at the marshal's office, ready to saddle up and make some noise at the old man's ranch. The morning had gone better than Marshal Smith would have expected. But he had to admit there would have been considerable more gun play, if Mac or Raymond were involved. Cahoon had the news by now, he had to. The wagon driver had skinned out of town, as soon as he heard the gunshot. He'd undoubtedly put the horse in a dead run, as soon as they were out of town.

They would be going in cold, which was all the better for the "Lawmen from Abilene". Marshal Smith hadn't been to the Cahoon Ranch in years and Ernie was the only one who knew the current lay of the land. They settled on six men, to ride out for the purpose of arresting Harold Quinn. He'd decided not to arrest Cahoon just yet. Since Ernie had the best bead on the place, he would ride lead.

The activity at the ranch was quiet, as they rode up to the hitching post on the right side of the front porch. The scene was very different than it had been on Ernie's first trip. No one approached as they rode up and there seemed to be only three men at work, outside the corral. No foreman, or gunmen, to interrogate them as to their purpose, or to stand between them and Cahoon. The men slowly dismounted and found it strange that no one had come from the barn, or out of the house. Slowly and with each man watching the house and the barns, Marshal Smith approached the door and hammered the large brass knocker several times. Shortly, a small elderly Mexican lady in a white apron opened the door and greeted the marshal.

"Good afternoon, sir. What can I do for you?" She asked.

"Good afternoon, ma'am," Marshal Smith replied, as he removed his hat. "I'm here to see Mr. Cahoon, is he available?" He asked, in a most cordial manner.

"No sir, he ain't well. I don't think he'll be up to having no company, I'll fetch the Misses." As she backed away, the door closed with two distinctive clicks. It was obvious to the marshal, that it was, both closed and locked.

The wait was only a minute or so, when Mrs. Rachel Cahoon reopened the door and stepped out onto the porch. She closed the door behind her, before she spoke a word, Marshal Smith got the distinct impression that she didn't want her voice to travel back into the house.

"You're Marshal Smith, aren't you?" She asked.

"Yes ma'am, I am," the marshal replied.

"Are you here to arrest my husband?" She asked, in a very quiet manner.

"No ma'am, we're here to arrest Harold Quinn. I'd appreciate it if you would call him to the house, without warning him. It would make it quicker and make my job a mite easier."

"What did Harold do, Marshal?" She asked, in an unsteady voice. Marshal Smith could see that she was visibly shaken.

"He and Lemual White were the men who killed Ben Willis two years ago. I've just now been given the authority to arrest them."

"I see. My husband has been standing in the way, hasn't he?" She asked, as tears began to run down her cheek.

"Yes ma'am, I afraid that's true. Are you okay, Mrs. Cahoon?" he asked. "Is there anything you need to tell me? We can help you, if there's trouble."

"No, not yet," she replied, "I have some thinking to do."

"Okay, I'm sure you know best. I'm always here if you need help." He offered.

"Thank you, Marshal," she replied, as she subtlety wiped the tears from her face. "I'll keep that in mind. I'll go out to the barn and get Harold for you."

Marshal Smith knew there was something amiss but didn't push the issue. The others knew it as well and figured that Cahoon was on a rant of some kind. Cahoon had no idea they were there. The maid knew better than to disturb him and Mrs. Cahoon was content for him to sit there in his own world. For her it was a bit of a relief and a break from his belligerent behavior.

Marshal Smith didn't take it for granted that Harold would be so agreeable to talk to the law. He and Ernie saddled up and slowly walked their horses in the direction of the barn where Mrs. Cahoon entered. Halfway down, they saw her walk out, with a man directly behind her. He immediately bolted to the north, at the sight of two riders coming toward him. The men spurred their mounts and soon overtook the unarmed man, corralling him between their horses. Marshal Smith quickly dismounted and drew his sidearm, as the man now had nowhere to go.

"Where are you running off to, Harold, you afraid of something?" Marshal Smith reveled in the moment and finally arresting the low life, who'd killed this good man.

"I ain't running from you, just don't want to be arrested, that's all." Harold replied, half out of breath.

"It looked like running to me," the marshal replied. "What are you afraid of, Harold?"

The others had waited at the house but at the sight of the man running from the barn they mounted up and joined in. Harold was now completely surrounded. Toby wished he'd try to get away. He had a mind to shoot him, gun or no gun. It had gone easier than the marshal had expected, still he wondered where Cahoon was and why they hadn't heard from him.

Mrs. Cahoon's demeanor gave Marshal Smith a glimpse into the turmoil which obviously surrounded the ranch. He didn't know what Cahoon was up to but he knew it was a great source of concern for Mrs.

Cahoon. This all seemed to be coming as a surprise to her and he wished she would allow him to help.

-

Four men boarded the east bound train in Cimarron at 9:30 on Monday morning. It would be 1:00 pm the next day, before they reached Abilene, Kansas. There were plans for a lot of poker along the way. Tom Bainbridge, Clayton Emerson and Cahoon's two men had their orders. They'd developed a specific plan, with Cahoon's approval. He expected them to return with his money and a stern lesson for Mr. William Murphy. Cahoon had additional plans for his Yuma parolees. With ten of his men now in jail, he would have further need for their talents, once this task had been completed to his satisfaction. They were eager to show their gratitude for being hired on, when no one else would. Cahoon knew they would do most anything he said. Although his empire was shrinking, Cahoon was still finding his men to be loyal.

The four were a good fit for such a job. Each had been involved in tougher scrapes than they expected on this trip. Whatever fight Mr. Murphy might put up, would be mild to what they were accustomed to. When the train made its stop in Maple Ridge, each man stayed onboard. They hadn't been on the train long enough to need a break and Cahoon didn't want to take a chance on his men being seen on an east bound train. His plan for retrieving his money was now in motion and he expected it would go better than Lemual White's screw up in town.

Marshal Lambert sent two deputies and his prison wagon from Cimarron to Maple Ridge. They showed up around 10:30 am, ready to haul a few men back and take some pressure off the jail. Marshal Smith was relieved, when he heard the snorting horse outside his office, although he was enjoying the discomfort of his crowded prisoners. He didn't have room for his now, ten inmates and laughingly realized that all good things must come to an end.

"Morning Marshal," the Cimarron deputy began, "we're here to pick up five prisoners. Marshal Lambert said he could hold on to 'um for a spell."

"Much obliged deputy, we can use the help...You hear that boys, some of you assholes are going on a little trip." Marshal Smith announced with a grin.

"We're glad to offer the help, Marshal. Which ones are going with us?"

"You can take those," Marshal Smith replied, as he pointed to the men in the cell to the left. "I'm going to cut out these two and put the other three in that cell yonder."

Lemual White and Harold Quinn were still holding out hope that Cahoon would get them out. For Lemual and his men, it had now been a full day since they spurred their mounts and rode away from the ranch. Harold's stay so far was shorter by a few hours but he too was wondering why they were still there.

Mrs. Cahoon's thoughts of meeting with Mr. Kinsey were weighting heavy on her mind. She was learning things about her husband that she'd suspected for a while. But now, her fears were proving to be true. If there's money I can take, where would I go? She thought. It's really his, so would I be stealing it? She wondered. It was all very complicated and she knew little about the world outside the ranch. She thought of Mr. Kinsey and the way he always looked at her. She had no intention of running to this man. That would only get him killed. She needed a friend and she knew she could trust him for advice. A month ago, she wouldn't have thought of such things but life was unpredictable and the world around her had changed. I'd better wait, she thought. But ideas were formulating and the possibility of life away from the ranch was becoming a reality.

She settled on making a trip to town, if he would let her. She'd never felt the need to ask before but given what she had learned about his obvious fight with the marshal, she thought it best. Approaching him had become difficult and she didn't know what to expect. Acting normal, as though she had no knowledge of the recent event, was the only thing to do.

She had one of the ranch hands to hitch up her carriage and then changed into a nice dress, as she usually did for such an occasion. Then came the test; "I'm going into town to pick up a few things and stop by the dress shop. Will you be okay while I'm gone?" She asked.

"You're not going anywhere," he replied.

"What? Are you now telling me what I can and cannot do?" She asked.

"I'm telling you to stay away from town. There are men there who want to kill me and you ain't going." Cahoon was forceful and adamant in his directive. She became afraid but wouldn't give in.

"How dare you talk to me that way. I'm going in town to have a dress repaired. What's the matter with you?" She asked.

"What's the matter with me? Well, I'm gunshot, I have five dead employees and ten men in jail. Not to mention, a ranch that's going to Hell. You've got enough damn dresses and you are staying away from that town." Cahoon was loud and forceful in his demand. He was becoming increasingly angry by the moment and she knew it would get even worse, if she pushed him any further.

Mrs. Rachel Cahoon had become a prisoner in her own home.

CHAPTER 9

Abilene had calmed considerably, compared to its earlier rough and tumble days. It began as a stage stop in 1857 but over the next ten years, it would see the greatest cattle boom on the plains. After the Union Pacific made its way through Abilene in 1867, Joseph McCoy saw the opportunity to build a real town in the midst of the sparsely populated prairie. McCoy began by building a hotel, stockyards and stables. The most important to him, was the Drover's Cottage, which he built as the headquarters for the Texans and eastern cattle buyers. Initially, it set in the middle of nowhere, with no trail access. The Texas ranchers, driving their herds north, couldn't find Abilene even if they knew it existed.

McCoy knew his work would be useless, if no one knew of his enterprise or the benefits to them. He printed thousands of flyers and had them distributed around the Texas ranches. They would announce, for one and all that Abilene, Kansas was open for business. Next, he paid to have the Chisholm Trail marked and cleared for the additional one hundred ten miles to reach their "Town Limits". His vision was finally a reality. The first year, Abilene saw only 35,000 head shipped through its stockyards but over the next four years, 440,000 head would be lead through their cattle gates.

As one would expect, the combination of drovers, money and whiskey, equaled trouble. Young men were routinely carrying more money at the time they settled up, than they'd likely seen in their short lifetimes. The merchants, saloon owners and soiled doves, saw it as their duty to separate them from their wages. A bath and new clothes was usually the first order of business, followed by the saloons and brothels. The opportunities, which abound, encouraged a swell of gamblers, gunmen and prostitutes to set up shop in Abilene.Competition for their money was fierce but keeping them alive and out of jail, was paramount. Dead or incarcerated cowboys can't spend money. Random gun fire aimed at street lights and windows, was commonplace and managing to keep these young men in line, was nearly impossible. Although one local newspaper declared that; "Hell is in session in Abilene", she still became known as the "Queen of the Cow Towns".

William J. Murphy came to Abilene, from Chicago in 1872, to set up the Kansas Cattle Buyers Association. He opened his office on Texas

Street and soon struck a deal with those who managed the Great Western Stockyards. Murphy's KCBA was seen as a direct competitor to Joe McCoy's Drover's Cottage. McCoy had established his enterprise on the south side of the Kansas Pacific right of way, opposite the stockyards. Murphy was two streets over and offered an alliance for the New York and Chicago buyers. Hiring the KCBA to manage their sales and shipments of stock was appealing and gave Mr. Murphy an edge. But the added benefit of retrieving unearned payments from those undeserving ranchers made the KCBA an enticing alterative.

Murphy's enterprise enjoyed continued success throughout the boom years but by the late 1870s, things were in a downturn. The expansion of the railroad west caused the number of cattle driven through Abilene to decline dramatically. Cahoon had a number of railheads at his disposal, with most closer to his spread than Abilene. Murphy initially found it hard to understand why Cahoon chose to drive his beef that far north and out of his way. It could be he'd alienated the closer buyers, forcing him to drive his herd the extra two hundred miles, to bring them to market in Abilene. His sick cows were now a memory, with the buyers paid and Cahoon's money back in the bank. The business transactions connected to this deal were settled but the job would not be closed, until Ernie Evans was safely back at home in Kansas.

The Cimarron train pulled into the Abilene station at 1:00 pm the following day. Cahoon's men were onboard. They'd traveled light and were off the train and out of the station before most folks had made it to the platform. Their conversations and planning for the coming days, had played out on the long train ride. Now they had a mind to sit back for a while, in a seat that wasn't rocking back and forth. They each needed a beer, without a lot of jawing about who had done what. Those stories had played out as well and it seemed the lies were getting deeper each time they were told. The Alamo Saloon, on Cedar Street wasn't far away and was the first stop on Tom Bainbridge's list.

The Alamo was the largest and most sophisticated drinking establishment in Abilene. The afternoon sun, glistened off the three glass doors on the west side of the building as the men approached, almost leading their way. Inside, there was a large bar, accented by brass railings on the south end of the building. There were gaming tables and an orchestra which played several times each day. From the back of the bar, hung a large beveled mirror, making the impressive room appear even larger than it was. The atmosphere was enough to break the tension between the men, which had been exasperated by their long eastern train ride.

Cahoon's ranch hands didn't cotton to these Missouri Bushwhackers. After making their deal at Coyote Creek, they had immediately taken the attitude of being in control, especially Bainbridge. He was pushy from the beginning and acted as though he had things completely under control. They had to admit that he was in the lead. But he wasn't pulling this off without each man doing his part. Cahoon's men had a role in Abilene as well but their main job was to make sure the money found its way back to New Mexico.

After ordering their first beer, the men decided that whatever they'd planned to do could wait until tomorrow. The music and girls had taken priority for the evening, as they each settled in on which Dove would lead who up the spiraled staircase. Tomorrow would be busy enough but for now, they needed to unwind.

Their plan was in place. They would each take a different street, to first locate the KCBA. Once it was found, they would all gather about, watching the movements around the office. Next, they would identify Mr. William Murphy. Neither man knew his favor but expected they could spot the "boss" by the way he dressed and especially if he was the man who had the door key. The combination of fine cloths and being the man who opened in the morning and closed shop in the afternoon would be enough to confirm their target.

At dawn, the men met in the lobby of the Merchants Hotel. There, they had breakfast then made their way in different directions as planned. They'd settled on staying in touch by meeting back in front of the Alamo Saloon each hour. As the men fanned out, they walked the streets, up one way, then back down the next street, searching for the office sign. Seth Leonard, one of Cahoon's ranch hands, was the first to find the KCBA office on Texas Street. He watched for a bit then made his way back to their meeting place. Along the way, he spotted Clayton Emerson and flagged him down. They had time before meeting with the others. Seth asked that he walk back to the office, so he could see it as well. Just to confirm that he had the right place. They stood across the street for a spell but there was no movement thus far.

When they arrived at their meeting place, Tom Bainbridge was there. Jim Holden, Cahoon's other man, was late arriving. He had walked the longer streets, from the train station, up to the stockyard and was a bit winded by the time he arrived. Once gathered, they walked back to Texas Street and spread out. It was approaching 9:00 am when a stout, well dressed, gentleman placed his key in the lock and opened the door. The clothing, the hat and the swirling smoke from a fat cigar, gave them all the assurance that he was their man.

EJ Sterns was the mayor of Maple Ridge but his first responsibility had always been the law. Initially, he'd expected that his position as an attorney and Officer of the Court would be beneficial to the town. It had played well in his "law and order" campaign. But he'd been ham-strung from the start, with threats and intimidation from Cahoon. He had made himself clear, from the day of Henry Grayson's retirement, even before EJ was sworn in on that rainy Monday morning.

Mr. Grayson's term as mayor expired on Friday, with everyone gathering for a small, farewell party at the mayor's office that afternoon. EJ felt it was private and hadn't initially planned to attend. But not surprisingly, he was invited and was honored to join in. The small farewell in the office lobby was later opened to the town. Those who walked by were encouraged to stop in and say a few words to Henry. Everyone was relaxed on that warm afternoon, reflecting on the growth of their little town. Henry's insight had been the root of it all.

As folks made their way in from the street, they would each have a sip of punch and a few words with Henry. It wasn't long, before Larry Cahoon and Gregory McElliott made their presence known. Not sure of what to expect, Henry took the lead, inviting Cahoon to the gathering and denying him the opportunity of some grand entrance. Henry was eager for this to be his last official conversation with Cahoon and took the opportunity to goad him just a little.

"Welcome to the party, Larry." Henry said, in a loud voice.

"Have some of this red punch, I'm not sure what all is in it but it's pretty good," he concluded. Everyone looked toward Cahoon, awaiting a reply.

"No, I never cared much for red punch, just stopped by to wish you a good retirement." Cahoon replied with a smirk.

"I'd say you really mean good riddance but either way... I thank you." Henry replied, as he raised his glass. Everyone chuckled, as he had garnered all the attention, making Cahoon the object of the conversation. It was his last official hurrah and using Cahoon to get a few laughs, was the best farewell he could have asked for.

In reality, Cahoon wasn't there to see Henry at all. He was glad to see him go. Cahoon had never been able to control Henry Grayson. Even with the influence he'd exerted over a number of the shopkeepers and the rest of the town council, Henry had never buckled to his pressure. With Henry standing in the way, he also had little control over Marshal Smith. That too was about to change. When EJ decided to run for mayor, Cahoon saw him as the opening he needed to run the mayor's office. Now, he was looking to get a head start, on his campaign investment by having a little chat with the incoming Mayor Sterns.

When Cahoon politely asked him for a meeting that afternoon, EJ truly had no idea of what was coming his way. Henry quickly noticed when they excused themselves, to one of the side meeting rooms. He knew what was coming. Once the three men were behind closed doors, Mac instructed EJ to take a seat. Cahoon began by recapping the amounts of his campaign contributions and how his men had assisted EJ on Election Day. Now it was time to let the new mayor know what he expected in return. Cahoon was ready to set the stage, for how things would be from that point forward. His tone was overt and EJ was stunned by the matter of fact attitude Cahoon was taking, regarding his new position in town. After he'd explained what all that campaign money was for, Mac took over to explain how things would work.

"First, we run the largest spread of anyone who either lives nearby or patronized the stores in town. Mr. Cahoon's money is what drives the Maple Ridge economy." Mac said, almost like a banker. "As a result, the ranch will get priority over others, when our men come to town for supplies." EJ was speechless. He had no reply for their demands and certainly no way of standing up to them.

"Secondly," Mac continued, "our men work hard. If they come into town to blow off steam, there will be no problems with Marshal Smith. You will put a bridle on him first thing Monday morning and keep a tight bit." Mac paused for a reply but there wasn't one. "Lastly, you will do what you are told and keep a lid on the town council, if you expect to see your little retirement party, with a bowl of that... red punch." Mac concluded his threats with a cold stare, which the new mayor realized was no bluff. Cahoon's favors had come with a high price and EJ was stunned to learn the extent of what that would be.

That was almost four years ago. Time had left its mark on Maple Ridge and on EJ Sterns. Finally, the time had come for him to make things right and the indictment against Cahoon's men was a good start. EJ wrote the indictment himself but passed it along to Ron Jarrod, the town's Prosecuting Attorney to file over his name. He'd wired Judge Kellum to make him aware of what was happening in Maple Ridge. The judge saw this as a breakthrough for the town and looked forward to executing his duty in court.

Judge Franklin Kellum was a man who respected the law. His commitment to the towns he served was a passion. The time he spent away from home was proof of his dedication. His wife persistently complained that he made his job harder than it needed to be. But, he was a man of principal, who saw law and order in these towns as his duty. He dreamed of a civilized west. Some of the towns he served gave him hope. But others, like Cimarron and now Maple Ridge, showed him the rougher side of the country's growing pains, as the westward expansion continued.

He was in town for his current court session and the timing couldn't have been better. He'd watched the town's autonomy shrink in the past few years and was saddened that the people of Maple Ridge hadn't stood up for themselves. His jurisdiction as a circuit judge, involved nine towns which gave him a better perspective than most. He saw the politics of each town, some more open than others but Maple Ridge had been a source of concern, that he knew would someday explode.

As the age of forty-three, he was younger than many of those who served on the bench. He was a serious man who had never given in to carousing or drinking and he wasn't lenient on those who came before him for such reasons. His concern was for the honest man, those who'd worked hard to build a dream and raise a family. He was good at reading people. A man who'd been wronged, or one who had exercised poor judgment, was subject to his common-sense interpretation of the law. Drifters, thieves and gunmen were judged by his stricter version.

He knew of Larry Cahoon, as did most people in the territory and he knew how he'd reached his status in life. The solemn judge wasn't impressed and he'd hoped that someday he could help the town make things right. When he arrived, he made the mayor's office his first stop. It was customary to meet with the mayor and the town's attorney, to get an overview of the docket. After which, he would routinely read the details in his hotel room, or in this case the lobby of the Byron Hotel.

The judge liked "The Byron", as he called it. The opulent surroundings, of its spacious lobby, gave everyone a sense of prominence. The judge quietly fancied himself in such a world but he knew the pay of a circuit judge would never afford him such luxury. He could have made more money, if he'd set up shop in Albuquerque or Santa Fe. But he felt a moral sense of accomplishment, by putting bad guys in jail, as opposed to helping them stay out.

There were only five cases on the docket for this trip. One cowboy charged with being drunk and causing a disturbance. One for petty theft in town and one against a drifter, who'd tried to steal a pig from a farmer just outside of town. But the two involving Cahoon's men, would consume most of his schedule. Sitting in the hotel lobby, the judge reviewed the three lesser cases first and quickly surmised the facts surrounding those. It was the Cahoon situation that garnered most of his attention. He wanted to be certain those cases were procedurally correct, with all content in order.

The complaints against the nine men would be tried as one. He'd probably throw this one out, had it been one intolerable farmer, raising a ruckus in a store. But this was a conspiracy of nine men, whose intent was to terrorize a town. That would get the full attention of the court. Mayor Sterns and Ron Jarrod had initially planned to file separate indictments against Lemual White and Harold Quinn but the judge decided to try them together.

Marshal Lambert had taken five of Cahoon's men up to Cimarron, which concerned the bunch of them. If they were separated, how could Cahoon get them out? After two days, they were beginning to believe he was going to leave them there and were sure he wouldn't have the pull to get the others out of Cimarron.

Lemual White and Harold Quinn were in the cell to the right and everyone knew why they had been separated. The incident at the mercantile was nothing, really. Even without Cahoon's help, they would be out of there and back to work in thirty days. Lemual and Harold were looking at a rope, if Cahoon didn't come up with something but no one had heard a word. Cahoon wasn't sure what was going on in Maple Ridge at this point.

He knew the marshal had been to his place and arrested Harold. Now, he had a total of ten men behind bars but that was all he knew. He didn't know how the marshal could have secured a warrant so quickly. He must have EJ and the Judge involved and apparently, they were giving him what he wanted. He never thought that Marshal Smith could come to his spread and arrest Harold then make it off his ranch alive. But he had and it was a strong message from the marshal of his intention for him.

He'd settled on letting the Maple Ridge thing stay as it was, for the time being. His focus now, when he was sober enough to think, was Abilene and the plan for retrieving his one thousand dollars. First things first, he thought. When they get back, I'll get my men out of jail and back on the ranch. From there, the issue of taking back control of Mayor Sterns and Marshal Smith would take priority. That would be the next job for the Missouri Bushwhackers and his Yuma parolees.

Cahoon had been on a two-day binge but he was sober now and the pain had relieved considerable. Mrs. Cahoon had stayed clear of him, since he'd confined her to the ranch. He had spiraled out of control and was as unpredictable one day as he was the next. This man, who had built this beautiful place and never taken his eye off the tasks at hand, had now lost all control. She was becoming more convinced that she needed to contact Mr. Kinsey at the bank. There had to be money available to her, if she decided to ride off. Or at the worst, she needed to know how she would manage if her husband was dead. Rachel Cahoon was beginning to accept that as a possibility, though she hated the thought. But given the trail he was on, she had to consider that as a possibility.

As evening approached, Ernie walked Abigail to the dining room of the Byron Hotel. It had been a busy day and he was glad it was coming to a close. He would never tell her but his back was hurting considerable. This was the first day he'd exerted himself in such a way but he didn't mind the pain all that much, given what he'd been through. He also considered that Abigail jumping in his arms didn't help matters any.

He'd stopped in the telegraph office on the way, just before meeting her at Dr. Rowe's office. It was important to him that Mr. Murphy knew how things turned out. He also needed to let him know that he appreciated his concern and to thank him for the help. Little did he know, William Murphy and the KCBA could use his friends back in Abilene about now.

The dining room was near capacity when they entered. It seemed that many of the townsfolk felt the need to celebrate and a hardy meal was customary for such an occasion. When Ernie and Abigail entered, several of the men stood and raised their glasses, as others applauded. Ernie was surprised and somewhat at odds with their gesture, though he smiled and thanked them. He'd come to understand the dilemma these folks were in, still he didn't understand why they had let it continue as it had.

Over dinner, which began with light conversation and their selections from the menu, Abigail carefully broached the subject;

"When are you going back to Abilene?"

"I'm not sure. What do you think I should do?" He asked.

"You know what I think, I want you to stay," she said in a low quiet tenor. "You can find work here and everyone likes you. You have been what this town needed, they just didn't know it," she added.

"Well, I do like it here…I don't know. You would be the reason I stayed." He couldn't believe he'd actually said it but...there it was.

"I was hoping you would say that," she replied.

Ernie had sworn to be careful and he didn't know if he'd just gone too far. He wanted to stay but this was all new for him. He was concerned that he might make a decision for his own reasons and somehow it would turn out badly for her. He couldn't have that. He quickly changed the subject, making a meaningless comment about the menu, as he changed his position in the high back oak chair. Abigail noticed, as he began to squirm a bit and realized that he was becoming quite uncomfortable. She was pleased that he'd actually opened up a little more but she was certain that would be all for now. Her mind was made up but she knew he still had to work it out in his mind…and in his heart.

After dinner, Ernie walked Abigail back to Blake's Boarding House, a few blocks up, on Jacob Street. The air was cool and the moon had just made its appearance over the mountain tops. She wished he would stay for a while but knew he had to go. It was there that she decided it was time for their first kiss. I'll be an old lady if I wait for him, she thought. So, she took the lead and said good night with a quick but deliberate show of affection. Ernie was taken by surprise and only smiled. As he walked away, the extra swagger in his step was obvious. Abigail grinned, with a sense of satisfaction, as she walked into the house. He hadn't said a word but she knew his ways by now and she saw it.

The "Lawmen from Abilene" would be leaving on the 10:00 o'clock train the next morning and Marshal Smith decided a farewell drink, with their new friends was in order. Mayor Sterns had really come out of his shell. He was disappointed in himself and was now doing his part to make things right. He felt increasingly responsible for allowing Cahoon to take control of him like he had. The respect these lawmen had afforded him during their stay had been gratifying and now they had invited him to join in for a drink. He was no longer an adversary of the marshal's office, he was now an ally, the way it should be.

It was close to 9:00 pm, when they all gathered at the Alhambra Saloon. Marshal Smith and Bobby Grayson arrived first and picked out two large tables, by the left front window. Bobby Jenkins, Dick Bryant and Toby Harris came strolling up the street, just as EJ pushed opened the batwing doors. Ernie was rounding the corner, when they walked in. He was the last to arrive. The marshal had tipped off the owner, Garland Johnson that they were coming and he was ready to celebrate with the crowd.

"First round is on the house," Garland announced.

This had been an important day for Marshal Smith and Mayor Sterns. They'd been at odds for years and were now finding common ground. Ernie was amazed at the change in attitude around town. Everyone he'd met when he first arrived had been cordial but he could tell from the beginning that something was wrong. He wouldn't have admitted it a week ago but he was glad he came to Maple Ridge and glad he could play a part in putting down a man like Cahoon.

His friends had been their salvation. Although the men in town were learning to stand up for themselves, there wasn't one of them who could have done what these men had done today. They were showing a sense of satisfaction; with the way they had handled the situation. Toby didn't kill anybody, although he wanted to and Dick Bryant was surprised by that.

This was a time for the marshal and the mayor, to stand back a bit and evaluate their respective roles in Maple Ridge. For EJ Sterns, it was time to stand up and do the things he promised during the campaign. Marshal Smith was seeing a clear path to do what he was hired for and wanted to do all along. Ernie Evans was in a different place. His dilemma now was deciding if he should stay or return to Abilene. He was becoming more attached to Abigail each day. Their relationship was growing and he couldn't get that kiss off his mind. He was surprised that she'd done that and recounted that moment many times during the evening. It was a timely celebration, for men who needed it. But in reality, they each knew that Cahoon would continue to make trouble.

-

Seth Leonard and Tom Bainbridge walked to opposite ends of the Texas Street and kept a close eye on the KCBA office. They took note of each man who entered and when they left. They needed to have a count of how many people they could expect to be in the office, at any given time. Clayton Emerson and Jim Holden walked to the next street and then made their way down the alley from different points. They counted the buildings from the north corner, to confirm they were in the right place, as they stood at the rear of the KCBA office. There was one back door and no window on that wall. It was locked and didn't appear to have been used much. There were no boot prints, or other signs of activity.

Tom was careful and planned to watch the place for a full day, to learn Murphy's pattern. He wasn't a man with patience and would have rushed the place to make a stand. But getting caught would be worse than not getting William Murphy and his money. He specifically wanted to know if there were any predictable times when he would be alone and for how long. If they could hit him with no one around, it would be faster and easier. There would be fewer people to contend with and fewer people to know what they looked like. Patience wasn't a virtue of either of these men but caution was paramount.

After leaving the alley, Jim Holden and Clayton Emerson fanned out and began randomly walking the streets, to get some idea of the deputies' patterns. They walked about, looking for a tin star and the demeanor of the man wearing it. They only saw two and neither seemed very aggressive. They just walked about and sat around, neither one appeared to give a thought to Texas Street.

There was little activity around the office. Those who had entered around 9:00 am were still there. It was now 11:30 and only one other person had entered. He stayed a while then left in the same direction in which he came. The predictability of this little office was quickly taking shape. Around 12:15, Tom and Seth saw the man they'd confirmed to be Murphy, step out of the office and onto the boardwalk. He stood for a moment, looking around, as he rolled an unlit cigar between his fingers. He turned to the south and began a tranquil stroll, as he removed a box of Diamond matches from his vest pocket and lit the Cuban Robusto. He was easy to spot. The swirl of blue smoke was as easy to follow as a Union Pacific locomotive. Staying back nearly half a block, the two men saw him enter Maxwell's Diner.

Tom suspected this to be his regular spot and hoped they would call him by name. As sure as he was of the man's identity, it was still an assumption. They hadn't exactly walked up to him and asked. Tom decided lunch at a nearby table would get him a name and an idea of what to expect from William Murphy when they came face to face. The diner was busy and loud. The clanging of silverware and multiple conversations, made Murphy's voice a bit hard to hear, from two tables away. But the waitress was easier to follow.

"Afternoon, Mr. Murphy. What can I get for you today?" She asked. That's all Tom Bainbridge needed to hear. They had their man and they were learning his routine. Easy as pie and they would get this thing done tomorrow, if the afternoon was as predictable, as the morning had appeared. It was 2:00 pm when Seth spotted the next and the last, visitor of the day as he entered the KCBA office. As before, he stayed a while, half an hour or so, then left, as the earlier gentleman had, obviously heading toward the stockyard. Seth was getting somewhat tired of hanging around but at 4:00 pm, Murphy's four employees all left together, meaning Murphy was in the office alone.

Clayton Emerson was within sight, just down the block. Seth slowly walked his way and discretely pointed toward the four men, who were now down the street, close to the corner. Clayton understood the gesture and watched the men as they turned but not knowing the significance of who they were.

"Murphy's men," Seth said, as he approached. "That means he's in the office alone."

"You think we should rush him now?"

"No, not yet, I'll find Tom. He just walked around the block. We need to let him decide, on how to handle this. Mr. Cahoon put him in charge, I ain't messing this up." Seth replied.

Seth found Tom Bainbridge a block over then walked back to Cedar Street, to find Jim Holden. Once all four men had gathered near the office, Tom watched for a while. Clayton hadn't lost sight of the office door and knew Murphy was still inside. What they didn't know, was if his men were gone for the day, or if they would return. Tom decided on waiting one more day. He suspected if they didn't return and especially if they left around the same time the next day, there would be a clear shot at William Murphy. They had all the time in the world. By Tom's measure, Wednesday had been a pretty good day.

-

The next morning, the "Lawmen from Abilene" had a big breakfast, at the Early Bird Café and no one was surprised when JT Belcher bid them a kind farewell, with breakfast on the house. They boarded the east bound train, just before 9:00 am, with a much different view of Maple Ridge, than when they arrived. A number of people had turned out to say good-bye. Ernie and the marshal were among them. Ernie was still wondering if he should be in that train.

"When you coming home?" Dick asked, as he shook Ernie's hand.

"I don't know, guess I'll be along in a few days," he replied.

"Don't lie to me. You ain't never coming back to Kansas, I can see it in your face. That gal's got you and she ain't letting go. You know it and I know it."

"I don't know." Ernie replied. "It is a tough decision, I got to admit that. Anyways, I'm still thinking on it. I'll likely be back in a few days."

"Who are you lying to, me or you?" Dick asked, as the whistle blew and he boarded the train.

"Adios!" Ernie shouted, as he waved good-bye to his friends. It was a common salutation in the Mexican culture of New Mexico but it wasn't one often heard, on the streets of Abilene. Dick Bryant and the others were sure their friend had just given them an answer.

That was Thursday morning. They would be making their arrival in Abilene around 1:00 pm on Friday.

-

The routine for Cahoon's men on Wednesday night was much the same as Tuesday. The Alamo Saloon was as intriguing as the night before but tonight they had a better feel for the place. The poker tables were at the top of the list for Tom Bainbridge and Seth Leonard. They'd been at odds; from the time they boarded the train in Cimarron. But they had worked well together during the day and decided to put that aside. Clayton Emerson and Jim Holden settled in at the bar and decided on a few drinks and a couple of Doves.

The Merchant's Hotel was a welcome sight by the time they stumbled in, each at different times. But as the sun rose, they each arose with it and dragged themselves to the lobby. Plans for day two, followed the pattern of day one. They had a good bead on Murphy's office. If his routine was the same today, as the day before, they would make their move around 4:15 and be out of town before sunset.

By 9:00 am, Bainbridge had Seth and Clayton watching the office to track their movements and comparing them to the day before. If their schedules and routines held, he and Cahoon's men would hit the unsuspecting Mr. Murphy at 4:15. Clayton would scout the street for four horses that were tied and saddled and looked like they would be up to a long ride. It would be a coordinated effort, where the timing of the robbery and stealing the horses, had to be simultaneous.

Mr. Murphy turned out to be as predictable as expected, down to the time he walked toward Maxwell's Diner. Tom stayed clear this time. He had no reason to get close enough for anyone to give thought to four strangers in town. Each man walked a different street most of the afternoon and took turns watching the office. They didn't chance being seen together and only met back on Texas Street, just after 4:00 pm to set in on the plan.

The men entered the KCBA at preciously 4:15 and stepped into the front office, quietly closing the door behind them. There were two doors at the back of the lobby area. Both were closed, with an open hallway to the left. No one came out, as they entered and the office seemed very quiet.

"Hello!" Tom said, then waited for a response.

"Who's there?" The voice which replied came from the office to the right.

"It's me," Tom answered. As the door opened, a man's voice could be heard, before he was seen. "Me? What me...who's here?" William Murphy asked, expecting to see an associate, or friend. As he entered the room, he saw three strangers, each holding a revolver and each one pointed directly at him.

"What are you men doing here?" He asked.

"We came to collect the money you stole from our boss." Seth replied.

"What money? I never stole any money in my life." Murphy began to perspire and was becoming very shaky.

"Yeah you did. You sent a gunman to take eight hundred dollars from my boss and then he upped the ante to one thousand. Now you are going to give it back, with the same courtesy, twelve hundred. You can get the money from your safe now, or I'll start shooting holes in you, until you do." Tom Bainbridge showed no fear in his demands. As the others watched, they suspected he was actually enjoying the moment.

William Murphy was petrified. He knew they would kill him, if he didn't comply. Slowly, he walked to the big safe, in the corner and carefully turned the dial. His mind was so rattled, that he could hardly remember the combination. Once opened, he covered any view of the safe with his rotund body and counted twelve one hundred-dollar bills. He quickly closed the door and turned the dial but it seemed they were only interested in that amount. They didn't press him for what was left. He took three steps and shakily handed the money to Bainbridge.

"You're talking about that rancher, in New Mexico. I didn't steal his money; it was an honest debt." He said slowly.

"So, you say, he sees it differently and sends you a little present." Bainbridge quickly spun his revolver around and forcefully hit Mr. Murphy, splitting his head, as he fell to the floor, with a loud thud.

The men holstered their weapons and hurried for the door, with Bainbridge in the lead. He carefully checked the street, before walking through the doorway, where he saw Clayton Emerson standing, with four saddled horses. The men quickly made their way out, mounted up and slowly walked the horses to the end of the street. It was there, a deputy marshal saw the four strangers and recognized one of the horses. He knew something was wrong and called out for them to stop. Seth looked him in the eye, without words and grinned, as they spurred the horses and high-tailed it out of town.

Neither Tom Bainbridge nor Clayton Emerson knew much about Abilene but they knew the prairie and they knew the trails. They had the money, now they had to get to Wichita, ninety miles to the south, before a posse could find their trail.

CHAPTER 10

The wagon that stopped in front of the mercantile was from the Cahoon Ranch and raised the attention of everyone who saw it. But the two men who jumped down and walked inside, were strangers to Bobby Grayson. He was surprised when they politely said they were from the Cahoon Ranch and offered up a supply list, asking that it be filled. Bobby returned the courtesy and gladly went to work, collecting the items and placing them on the wide pine countertop. He wondered why it couldn't always have been this way.

"I don't think I've seen you around before," Bobby said, with a smile.

"No sir, we ain't never been here. They asked us to come, since we was shorthanded. Reckon most of the fellows you know, are over yonder in the marshal's jail." The young man, who spoke up, sounded more like someone from town, than from the Cahoon Ranch. He was laughing and obviously not very closely attached to any of them.

"I think you're right, Bobby replied. "What's your name?" He asked.

"Henry sir, Henry Sutton." He replied, as he removed his hat. Henry didn't look to be a day over eighteen and from the looks of his face and his hands, he surely had no trail experience.

"How long have you worked for Cahoon, Henry?" Bobby asked.

"Only a couple of months," he replied.

"So, what's going on out there, Henry? I mean, since he was shot and his men ended up in jail, what's Mr. Cahoon doing out there?" Bobby asked.

"It's strange," Henry began, "he used to be out at the barn and corral every morning. Now, I heard he's drunk all the time, it's kind of different. Yesterday, Mrs. Cahoon tried to leave and come in town but he wouldn't let her."

"What do you mean she tried to leave?" Bobby asked.

Yesterday, she had me to hitch up her buggy, so she could come to town. I waited for a spell, then walked to the house. The maid, I ain't learned her name yet, she told me that Mr. Cahoon had been screaming at the Misses and refused to let her leave the ranch. She ain't been out the house since. I probably done said too much." Henry replied as he looked away.

"Wait a minute," Bobby replied. "Are you telling me, that Mr. Cahoon has his wife confined to the house and won't let her leave? Is that what you're saying?" Bobby asked.

"That's what she said. I usually see her in the mornings, out by the house but I ain't seen her today." Henry replied.

It wasn't unusual for Mrs. Cahoon to come into town, to visit the dress shop, or the grocery. Mr. Cahoon wasn't liked by most folks and he never came in alone. Mrs. Cahoon, on the other hand, was well respected in town and she was welcomed wherever she went. Given the circumstance, Bobby was now very concerned for her wellbeing. Marshal Smith needed to be aware of this and to consider the possibility that she was in danger as well.

"Henry," Bobby began, "I'd like for you to keep an eye on things. If you think that lady is in any trouble at all, please come here, as soon as you can and let me know. Would you do that for me?" Bobby asked.

"Sure," Henry answered, "I'll do that."

Bobby filled the order and sent Henry on his way but his concern for Mrs. Cahoon wouldn't leave his mind. He wasn't sure of what he should do at this point. Henry may have been a little over exuberant and he didn't want to cause more trouble, if it wasn't warranted. But on the other hand, leaving her there, with no help, could be a big mistake.

-

Deputy J. R. Simpkins saw the men on horseback and realized something was wrong. He recognized one of the horses and assumed they all must be stolen. The owner of the spotted Appaloosa was a cattleman, who regularly came into town. He knew the man who'd looked his way was a stranger to Abilene. He'd run headlong into the men at the corner of Texas Street and Third and immediately walked back up the block, looking for anything unusual. Seeing nothing out of place, he made his way back to the marshal's office. He knew they had four horse thieves on their hands.

Two deputies were in the office when he arrived. Marshal Johnson was at the stockyard where he saw them gallop by and instinctively knew there was a problem. He collected his mount and followed for a spell, to get a bead on their direction. The men hit the southern trail out of town in a dead run, he knew that following them alone would only get him killed.

He reined his horse around and headed back to his office, where he found Deputy Simpkins and the others readying their horses. They were preparing to ride after the men but Marshal Johnson wasn't as eager to tear out after these strangers, not just yet. No one knew why they were in town, or why they had stolen the horses and left so quickly. There was more to the situation than they were seeing from the street. He wanted to play this out, before anyone went riding after the wind. The marshal knew they were heading south and that meant Newton. It was the only town on the southern trail for the next sixty miles. And that Appaloosa would be easy to spot.

The first thing he wanted to know was why. The deputies went back to Texas Street, where the men had been spotted and began canvassing each building. Door by door, they either met with an occupant, who thus far, had seen nothing unusual, or simply rattled a locked door. When Deputy Simpkins reached the KCBA, he found an unlocked door and Mr. William Murphy lying on the floor, with blood on his cloths and in his graying hair.

He was lifeless, which left Deputy Simpkins immediately concerned that he might be dead. As he sat him up, Mr. Murphy began to rouse and reached for his hurting head. He wasn't initially sure of what had happened, or how long he'd been out. As he came around, he became more cognizant of his surroundings and to the extent of his trauma. Deputy Simpkins went to the door and called for one of the other deputies, to fetch the doctor and to alert the marshal.Mr. Murphy was shaken and weak, having problems forming his words at first. After a few deep breaths and a shot of whiskey, from a bottle the deputy found on a side board, he was sitting up with his memory beginning to serve him once again.

"Cahoon," he said slowly.

"I'm sorry, what did you say, Mr. Murphy?"

"The man said he was sent by Larry Cahoon, a rancher from New Mexico. He sold a herd up here in the spring." Murphy spoke, as he held his head with a wet cloth, which Simpkins had fetched earlier.

"The men who hit you, were there four of them?" The deputy asked.

"No, there were three." He replied.

"Close enough, the other one was probably on the street, stealing the horses."

When Doc Slater arrived, Mr. Murphy was sitting in a chair and sipping on another shot. He immediately examined his head and eyes and asked if he knew who he was. As he stood, he wobbled a bit. His vision was still quite hazy but he quickly regained his focus and his composure. The bleeding had stopped and was now replaced by a large lump on the side of his head. Mr. Murphy was considering himself very lucky. It was then he remembered the money, he'd forgotten about that.

"They stole twelve hundred dollars." He said slowly.

"They robbed you, Mr. Murphy?" The deputy asked, "Take your time and tell me how it happened."

"They came in and said they were here to get back the money that we recovered from their boss. Well, the money we stole, as they described it. He's a rancher, who was overpaid on a herd back in June. He told me how much he wanted and didn't bother with the rest. That's never happened before. That man, Larry Cahoon, gave our man in New Mexico a hard time down there. Then he sent them here after me. I guess I should have left that one alone." He concluded.

Murphy went on to tell the whole story and how he'd sent men to assist Ernie. The deputy stood surprised that these men would take such a chance. Marshal Johnson came in during his explanation and quickly caught up as Deputy Simpkins filled in the parts he'd missed.

"Where are they heading, Mr. Murphy?" The marshal asked.

"A little town in New Mexico called, Maple Ridge."

"Do you know anyone there?"

"Yeah, Ernie Evans, the man who works for me, he's still there." Mr. Murphy replied.

"I know him," Deputy Simpkins began, "he's a gun hand, Marshal. I'd heard he worked for the KCBA."

"He's not a gun hand, Deputy. He does good work for this company and he's honest. I need to wire Marshal Smith in Maple Ridge." Murphy replied.

"The men you sent, where are they now?" The marshal asked.

"They left New Mexico this morning, headed back here on the Union Pacific."

"Mr. Murphy, I need you to send that wire. I'm going to the train station to find out where she is now and have your men stop in Wichita. I'm sure that's where these men are heading. If your guys are on the train, they just might beat them there." Marshal Johnson replied. "Who are these men, Mr. Murphy?"

"Dick Bryant, Toby Harris and Bobby Jenkins." Murphy answered.

Marshal Johnson began to laugh to himself. "Well, I'd hate to be one of those guys and run into either of them. You hired the best."

Doc Slater sat with him for a while, just to be sure he would be safe alone. Mr. Murphy seemed to be over the worst of it. He'd have a knot and a head ache for a while but that was to be expected. He was now walking straight and thinking clearly. He hoped he could catch someone at the telegraph office, before they left. Marshal Johnson went straight to the train station to follow up on the train in route from Maple Ridge and the next stop for the west bound train to Wichita. It all made sense now, he thought. They couldn't wait in Abilene for the morning train. Stealing horses and riding south, was their only option. If all goes to plan, they will be riding straight into the men who'd just left their final destination.

-

Bobby Grayson ran into Marshal Smith a few hours later and told him about his conversation with Henry Sutton. Bobby had always liked Mrs. Cahoon. She was always kind and very different from her husband. He wondered if she knew and just ignored it, or if he'd hidden his ways from her for all these years.

He rather assumed that she didn't know but Bobby was sure that she would now find the truth hard to avoid. The marshal understood his misgivings but instead saw the opportunity of having an inside man, at the Cahoon Ranch.

Given the uncertainty of what was happening there, this was possibly the break he was looking for. Marshal Smith knew that Cahoon wasn't done. He was staying close to the ranch but only to regain his strength. It may take a few more days and the hiring of a few more men but he would surely come back with a vengeance. The marshal wanted to meet this young man and get him on his side. Bobby held to his concerns but was sure that Henry could be helpful on both counts.

Judge Franklin Kellum had read the indictments. He planned to proceed with the hearing for the murder case first, before turning his attention to the other matters on Thursday morning's docket. He would handle the rowdy cowboys as one case, for the sake of time and expected that would go quickly. With a light docket, he didn't anticipate the whole thing to run much past lunch. Attorney Ron Jarrod was prepared to argue the merits and strength of the indictment and expected the judge would hold the two men over for trial.

He contacted four witnesses from the saloon, including Jack the owner, who were willing to testify at trial. Mrs. Willis was contacted and agreed to be in court but was afraid to take the stand. For him, that was sufficient. He was sure that having her there, hopefully with some noticeable tears, would have the desired tug on the hearts of the men on the jury. This would, however, be a few weeks away. They had to make it past the hearing first but with the absence of Cahoon or a lawyer, he didn't see that as a problem.

They hadn't heard from Cahoon, or an attorney for the men. But after he sobered up, he had quietly retained a lawyer from Santa Fe. The accused were concerned as well. Thus far, they hadn't heard a word from Cahoon, or anyone else. Cahoon had in fact contacted attorney Teddy Black, in Santa Fe. He had hired him, not only for a possible trial but to make sure it never got that far. Cahoon was awaiting his arrival. Given how badly they'd screwed up, Cahoon didn't give a wit about Lemual White or Harold Quinn. He only cared about himself and he wanted them back on the ranch to ride with Tom Bainbridge, when he returned with his money. He also saw the possibility of getting them off, as the victory he needed to turn the tide. He was now depending heavily on his high-priced lawyer, to do just that.

Teddy showed up in town on the morning of the hearing. He knew there was little to work with and had no need to interview witnesses or confer with the accused. He had only one shot at getting them off and it was neither honest, nor ethical. He'd avoided the spectacle of arriving on the train and letting everyone know he was there. Instead, he'd taken the short train ride to Cimarron. There, one of Cahoon's men met him with the carriage, for a comfortable ride down to the Cahoon Ranch.

There was very little legal discussion to be had. There was no defense strategy, to be carefully planned, or laid in place. Instead, he and Cahoon simply assembled five men to serve as credible alibis. They would swear on the Holy Bible that both, Lemual White and Harold Quinn, were on the north range, pushing cows with all of them, on the day Ben Willis was killed. Their confession, in the saloon that night was nothing more than the ramblings of two drunken men. Teddy didn't have to prove a thing. That was the job of the prosecutor and the marshal. His job was to make sure there wouldn't be a trial. With a long line of spurious alibis, which no one could disprove, he planned to make sure the Judge wouldn't have enough evidence to hold them over for a trial.

Thursday morning was busy in Maple Ridge. Two deputies from Cimarron arrived in the marshal's hack, around 7:00 am, with five of Cahoon's men, shackled to the post in back. Trying to corral the eight rowdies in one place, with the two murder suspects in another, was a challenge. Added to the other three who were on the docket and now waiting in the courtroom, Marshal Smith had his hands full. Ernie had promised to help, if he were still in town, which he was.

Marshal Smith had been trying to pin a badge on his vest for the past week but Ernie wouldn't hear of it. Now, he would have to take the oath and display the deputy's star, if he was to fulfill his promise to help. Reluctant as he was, Ernie relented and raised his right hand, then pinned the badge to the left lapel of his dark blue striped vest. Although he planned only to help with the trial for a few hours, he was now a duly sworn deputy marshal of Maple Ridge, New Mexico.

The courthouse was on Grayson Street, next to the mayor's office, almost two blocks from the jail. It had been built in the early days and now becoming too small for the town's growing population. Its use hadn't grown in proportion but the number of onlookers gathering for each session of Judge Kellum's calendar had. It was entertainment for many, a way to get out and visit with others, much like Church. But the courthouse saw many who had never seen the inside of the town's place of worship.

Marshal Smith knew the order in which the judge had planned to call the cases. He'd decided to take Lemual White and Harold Quinn there first and shackle them to the large oak defendant's table. Once there, Ernie stood guard and kept them quiet while the Marshal and Deputy Wilcox brought in the eight men and sat them on a bench three rows back, on the left. The thought that Cahoon and his men might try to free them from the courtroom, had entered the marshal's mind. Not something a sane man would do but no one put Larry Cahoon in that category. So far, no legal council had stepped forward, or contacted any of them.

The courtroom filled quickly. Everyone in town turned out for this session, leaving little room for those who had reason for being present. The first three rows on each side were roped off. Once the onlookers began occupying those seats, Marshal Smith cleared them out and closed the front doors, announcing to all others that the court was full. The prosecutor's table, on the right, was occupied by Ron Jarrod, who would soon be joined by Marshal Smith. On the front row, behind the prosecutor, were Bobby Grayson, Mayor EJ Sterns, JT Belcher and Mrs. Emma Willis. It was getting close to 9:00 am and Prosecutor Jarrod was feeling rather confident, with the lack of council at the table to his left.

Moments before the judge was expected to enter from the rear door, the front doors burst open, with the heavy sound of boots, as seven men made their way into the courtroom. In the lead was Attorney Teddy Black, dressed in a finely brushed black suit and wide flat brimmed hat, banded with silver and Bisbee turquoise. Behind him was Larry Cahoon, dressed in his finest attire. He was cold sober and appeared as healthy as the day before he was shot. Behind them followed five cowboys in trail cloths and spurs. Teddy made his way to the defendant's table and introduced himself to Lemual and Harold, before taking a seat, as Mr. Cahoon sat behind them. The cowboys all took a seat behind Cahoon on the second row, in front of their eight friends.

Rod Jarrod was a bit shaken and Marshal Smith was more than surprised. Just by the looks of Teddy Black, a man Ron Jarrod had never met, he knew this wasn't going to be so easy after all. Mayor Sterns had become rather confident in himself over the past few days. But the sight of a cocky Larry Cahoon and this unknown lawyer, was giving him a very uneasy feeling in the pit of his stomach.

When Judge Kellum entered the room, he too was surprised by the number of men, who now sat with the defendants. Thus far, he hadn't seen, nor heard of any defense for the two men. Now they were surrounded by supporters. When he saw Teddy Black, he knew how serious Larry Cahoon had been. Teddy had the best reputation in Santa Fe and was the most expensive. When he got a case, he didn't let it go. Judge Kellum knew Teddy and had been in a courtroom with him on many occasions.

When the Judge walked in, the bailiff stepped forward.

"All rise! The Honorable Judge Franklin Kellum is now presiding." He announced, then stepped back.

"Be seated," said Judge Kellum, as he too took his seat behind the large bench. He looked around for a moment before speaking. He looked at who was present and where they sat, specifically Teddy Black and Larry Cahoon. The presence of those five dusty cowboys behind them, told the wise judge exactly where Teddy Black was taking this hearing. He knew Rod Jarrod didn't stand a chance.

"Good morning," the judge said, as he consulted his Waltham pocket watch for the time. "Teddy, I didn't expect to see you here, how are you?" The judge looked to Teddy Black and smiled.

"Morning Judge," Teddy began, "I'm fine, thank you. You never know where I might turn up."

"That's obviously true." The judge replied, as he shook his head. He knew this wasn't going to go well for the town, or Marshal Smith.

"Mr. Jarrod, are you prepared to begin this hearing?"

"Yes, Your Honor. The prosecution is prepared.

"Mr. Black, are you ready to proceed?"

"Yes, Your Honor." Teddy replied, as he rose to his feet with a smirk.

"Very well, Mr. Jarrod, would you read the charges."

"Yes, Your Honor."

In the District Court of the Third Judicial District
of the Territory of New Mexico and in the town of
Maple Ridge
The
Territory of New Mexico

Vs.

Lemual James White
Harold Ellison Quinn

Wereas the above are herewith accused and hereby indicted by the town of Maple Ridge within the county of Colfax and the territory of New Mexico by oath and this indictment of the crime of murder committed as follows:

That said accused, Lemual James White and Harold Ellison Quinn in or around the town of Maple Ridge on or about the 16th day of June 1879 A.D., did with force of arms and malice aforethought, did intentionally and upon the body of Benjamin Lewis Willis, a human being, discharge with intent to do bodily harm two leaden bullets fired upon said Benjamin Lewis Willis, a human being, with felonious intent, did willfully and with malice aforethought discharge said leaden bullets charged with gunpowder upon the body of said Benjamin Lewis Willis, a human being, giving him then and there a mortal wound of which said Benjamin Lewis Willis, a human being, did instantly die.

Said accused did kill and murder contrary to the statutes and laws of the Territory of New Mexico and the town of Maple Ridge in such a case made and provided against the peace and dignity of the Territory of New Mexico.

"How do you plead?" The judge asked, as he looked toward Teddy Black. Teddy slowly rose to his feet, after making notes during the reading of the indictment, having never seen the actual document. He stood for a moment, as though he was pondering, then with a clear and prominent voice responded;

"Not Guilty, Your Honor."

"Very well." The judge replied.

"Mr. Jarrod, please state your case."

"Your Honor, on the 16th day of June 1879, Mr. Ben Willis was known by his wife to have followed several stray beef cattle, which had wondered onto the Cahoon Ranch. He went there with the intent of retrieving his sovereign property. They were his, Your Honor and he had every right to retrieve such. Sometime later, Mrs. Willis was horrified to see her husband's horse walk up to the house, with Ben Willis' lifeless body tied across the saddle. Mrs. Willis immediately brought her husband to Doctor Henry Rowe, where he was pronounced dead, having been struck by two .45 caliber bullets.

It was later that evening when Harold Quinn and Lemual White confessed to the murder in Jack's Saloon, on Jacob Street. There, they warned the proprietor, that he too, would get 'some of what they'd given Ben Willis if he didn't back off.' Attempts to arrest these men, heretofore, have been futile, with a proper indictment only now being secured and executed. Thank you, Your Honor." Rod Jarrod was nervous in his delivery of the facts but felt he had done so properly. He was now anxious for Teddy Blacks argument and how he would proceed.

"Mr. Black." The judge looked to Teddy for his defense. He knew it as well as if he'd already finished but he didn't think Mr. Jarrod's forethought was quite as perceptive.

"Your Honor," Teddy began. He stepped out, in front of the defense table and slowly walked to the center, between the two sides. "First and foremost, please allow me to express my heartfelt condolences to Mrs. Willis for her loss. From Mr. Cahoon and myself, we wish only the best for you and hope that time will play a healing role in your heart and that you find happiness and goodness in life."

"As for this indictment...It seems to be the fulfillment of a desire on the part of the marshal and others, to get even with someone, especially if that someone could be an employee of the Cahoon Ranch. To make it even more appealing to them, they saw the opportunity to indict two employees of Mr. Cahoon's organization. The unfortunate fact is that they didn't take the time to check on the whereabouts of these two men, at the time in which this tragedy occurred. Your Honor, we understand the exuberance on the part of many to solve this terrible crime but there is no merit to this indictment and no reason to hold these men.

First, I can prove that they were twenty miles from the scene that day, riding with these gentlemen, as they moved a herd of cattle to the north range. Secondly, your indictment states that Mr. Willis was shot twice. Are there any witnesses to this act? Are you prepared to offer any credible evidence as to who actually shot Mr. Willis? Did each man shoot once, or did one man fire both shots? Was the second man, if he wasn't the shooter, complicit, or did he try to talk his friend out of the act? Who is the guilty party here, Your Honor?

And lastly, the confessions, which you feel so strongly about, were the words of two drunken cowboys in a saloon. They were obviously attempting to intimidate a group of men, equally as drunk with no regard for the truth. We would never accept such comments as credible if they were made in this courtroom. I contend they are even less credible, when blurted in the midst of drunken men in a saloon.

Your Honor, I ask that we dispense with this fantasy and dismiss these charges, so we may all go home. That is, unless the prosecution has something else to offer? Thank you, Your Honor." Teddy spoke calmly and never broke a sweat or looked at his notes.

Judge Kellum paused for a moment, hoping it would give Prosecutor Jarrod, time to gather his thoughts. But it seemed he had nothing else to offer.

"Mr. Jarrod?" The judge asked.

"Your Honor, that's all we have but we know those two killed Ben Willis." Ron Jarrod stood speechless from that point, searching for the words and knew he shouldn't even have said what he did.

Judge Kellum had given Jarrod every opportunity but now determined it was time to make a ruling. He paused, with an obvious look of disappointment on his face. He then turned to the defendants with a voice of authority and made his opinion very clear.

"It is, my not so humble opinion, that you both are guilty of a grave offense against Ben Willis and against the dignity of the laws of the Territory of Mew Mexico. If I had my way, I'd take you both out back and hang you myself. But as sure as I am, it is fortunate for you, that the laws of a civil society do not work through such a practice. You may have slipped the noose and you may walk free of this court but justice, I assure you shall prevail and you shall not walk so freely from the court of the Almighty. You men, I am sorry to say, are free to go. Next case." Judge Kellum hammered his gavel on the bench, trying not to show his disappointment in the prosecutor.

The courtroom was quiet and even Cahoon's men sat without comment. Deputy Wilcox unshackled Lemual White and Harold Quinn, as Ernie looked on. He had no comment and really had no opinion. This wasn't his fight; it had happened long before he came to Maple Ridge. For the accused, it had been a close call with the rope and they were just glad to be getting out of there. For the eight who remained, they were on their own. Cahoon knew that even Teddy Black would have no defense to get them off. Cahoon didn't bother to ask. He knew Teddy wouldn't tarnish his reputation with the obvious mess they were in, so he left well enough alone and threw Marshal Smith a bone.

In an effort to time his next statement for its greatest effect, Rod Jarrod waited until the defendants were unshackled and beginning to make their way out of the courtroom, before he rose to his feet.

"Your Honor," the prosecutor began in a loud voice, "please instruct the marshal to return Lemual White to this court and place him on the third row with his friends." Holding up the indictment for the nine men, who'd made trouble in Grayson's Mercantile, he continued. "His name is among those indicted in the matter regarding those rowdies seated here. Without regard to the previous matter, he must be remanded to custody and join his cohorts to answer for their actions of last Wednesday." Ron had regained his standing with Judge Kellum. He grinned in appreciation for his quick thinking and grit in standing before Cahoon and Teddy Black in such a forceful manner. Everyone stopped, as Lem looked toward Larry Cahoon for help but none was offered. He simply shrugged his shoulders and walked away, as Marshal Smith took Lem by the arm and escorted him back to his seat.

The judge was amazed to see Larry Cahoon and his men exit the courtroom, leaving the others behind. Now Lemual White, who had just been well served by a high-priced lawyer, would be forced to return and fend for himself. The judge concluded this was their punishment for botching Cahoon's plan and not delivering on his demands. He would see to it that he fulfilled Cahoon's wish, this one time.

Court adjourned just before lunch, with Judge Kellum having done his part in following the law. His first ruling had been a blow to Marshal Smith and Mayor Sterns but at least nine of Cahoon's men were now heading to Cimarron, for a thirty day stretch in larger quarters. The marshal didn't get a murder trial but locking up these rowdies was the first real legal victory they'd had over Cahoon. That would have to do for now.

As Marshal Smith exited the courtroom, he saw Cahoon and Teddy Black sitting in a large black four-seater carriage, with Harold Quinn sitting in back. He was obviously waiting for the marshal to walk out, before they rode away. With only a look and a grin, Cahoon snapped the reins and slowly made his way up Grayson Street and out of town. The marshal gave the whole matter a second thought and realized it hadn't really been a victory for Cahoon.

The evidence was admittedly weak, leaving the judge no choice. But this time, it had cost him the price of an expensive lawyer. He didn't try to intimidate the mayor, or strong arm the town. This one was lost according to the law. Then he thought, since the shooting, there had been only one instance, where men from Cahoon's ranch, had tried to intimidate the good people of Maple Ridge. Now, all nine of them were in jail. Although Harold Quinn was riding away, Marshal Smith began to think that maybe this was a small victory after all.

-

Marshal Johnson made his way to the Abilene train station, as Mr. Murphy headed for the telegraph office. The railroad had its own Western Electric telegraph system. It shared the main lines but communicated only with the station masters along each route. This made communication faster and more confidential, since messages were relayed only between their own operators. When he arrived, there was no train in the station, with none due until the next morning. This afforded the marshal the full attention of station master, Gene Skinner, without the ears of busy bodies hanging around.

"Afternoon Gene," the marshal began. "I need to know the whereabouts of a train that's in route to Abilene. How close can you get me to where that train is now?" He asked.

"I don't know, that's a bit unusual. What train are you talking about?"

"You had a train leave Maple Ridge, New Mexico this morning, headed this way. I need to know where it is and its next stop."

"Well, give me a minute and I'll see if I can figure it out." Gene replied.

He turned to his schedule and checked the morning departures, looking down the list to New Mexico. He then took a pencil and paper and worked out the distance and scheduled speed of the train, to pinpoint its current location.

"Okay, that would be the 417. Her next stop will be Cheyenne Wells in Colorado, in about three hours. It's the last stop before she hits the Kansas line." Gene replied.

"Does that train stop in Wichita before coming here?" Marshal Johnson asked, with his fingers crossed. If she didn't, then the whole thing would be a waste.

"Yep, eight o'clock in the morning, she'll be here at 1:00 pm."

"Good. Can you get a message to the station in Cheyenne Wells and have them contact three men who are aboard that train, when she arrives?"

"I guess I can. What's this about, Marshal?" He asked.

"Not much I can say about that now. I just need to get these men off the train in Wichita." Marshal Johnson proceeded to give Gene the instructions for what he needed from him.

"First, contact Cheyenne Wells and have the conductor look for Dick Bryant, Toby Harris and Bobby Jenkins. Tell them the message is from me and have them leave the train in Wichita. Have Cheyenne Wells wire back, so I know the conductor has the instructions. Second, send a wire to Wichita, telling them the men will be arriving. Have Wichita wire back when they arrive, so I may then send instructions directly to the men. Got that?" The marshal smiled, as Gene was writing as fast as he could.

"Got it Marshal, I'll be in touch with you as soon as I get a reply."

As soon as the marshal left, Gene began sending the wires, just as he'd instructed. He stayed close and made sure he had a reply from each, before he left for the day. Marshal Johnson was to meet him at the station at 7:30 am, to follow up with Wichita and to be there when the men arrived. He wasn't privileged to the purpose but Gene knew this was important to the marshal and he was determined to do his part.

Marshal Smith's day had gone badly enough but he had managed to salvage some optimism from the outcome. Now, Mr. William Murphy's telegram had taken that away. He was reluctant to tell Ernie, until he had more information. He wired back, asking Mr. Murphy of his condition and how he might help. He knew it would be morning before he heard back and quietly kept it to himself.

When the judge closed the courthouse doors, Ernie tried to return the deputy's badge but the marshal convinced him to keep it for the balance of the day. He felt the longer he could keep it on Ernie's chest, the more used to it he might become. With this news, Marshal Smith was guessing that Ernie just might decide to hold on to it.

Marshal Smith had never seen Cahoon go to such lengths to get even with anyone and he knew the town would be challenged again soon. What's it going to take to convince this man it's over, he thought. He would have to tell Ernie in the morning, once he received a reply. But he needed the facts and decided to wire Marshal Johnson in Abilene. If he was after these men, he wanted to help from his end. Marshal Smith knew they would be Cahoon's men but whom? All of the usual men, who did his dirty work, were either dead, or in jail. He must have recruited some men for this but he had no way of knowing who. He suspected they were the men from Cimarron but he had no way of being sure. Henry Sutton soon came to mind. He had to get in touch with this young man, to find out what was going on out there.

Bobby Grayson was the only one who knew his favor and he couldn't wait for Henry to come back to town. Cahoon may not even send him the next time. He had to get Bobby to the ranch to contact Henry but he'd have to tell him about the trouble in Abilene. Bobby was more than reluctant at first but he realized the urgency. The only way to pull this off was by taking a couple of items from the store and delivering them to the ranch. He'd tell Henry that he'd forgotten to put them with his order. He knew he'd be giving them away but it would be worth the cost of a couple of routine supplies. He specifically remembered two pounds of nails and a box of therapeutic paper being on the list. They didn't cost him much and were items they could easily have left behind. Just after 3:00 pm, Bobby Grayson saddled up and rode out of town.

CHAPTER 11

With William Murphy's money stuffed deep in his coat pocket, Tom Bainbridge lead his men south on the trail to Wichita. They'd run the horses hard for the first couple of miles but had to back them down soon, if they expected to reach Newton with steady mounts. Clayton Emerson was the most experienced in pushing horses' long distance. He'd driven cattle, from Missouri to Mew Mexico and knew how to get the most out of horse flesh, without driving them in a lather.

They'd stopped a couple of times and looked back for a distant posse but never saw one. They expected to see trail dust rise on the horizon behind them but thus far all had been quiet. Wichita was still seventy miles to the south and the sun was beginning to hang low in the western sky. The remaining distance would require them to ride throughout most of the night, if they expected to board the train there at 10:00 the next morning. With no one on their trail, they eased up on the horses, giving both horse and rider the luxury of relaxing for a spell. They expected to reach Newton sometime around mid-night. There, they could pull the saddles and rest the horses a while. Once fed and watered, they would get a much-needed break, giving them a better chance of reaching Wichita on time. For themselves, they needed a good meal and a little time without a saddle as well.

From Newton they would make the thirty-mile jaunt to Wichita and leave the horses on a side street, or alley. They hoped to have time for breakfast. After which, they would walk to the train station, one at a time, to buy a ticket to Cimarron. Each man would travel alone for a while, at least until they were out of Kansas. If the marshal had used the wire to head them off on the trail south, he'd have a hard time, if they were separated. So far, they were unimpeded and riding straight for their destination.

Gene Skinner had a reply from Cheyenne Wells, confirming his wire, with the assurance that they would locate the men. Now they would have to find them and relay the information for the plan in Wichita to fall in place. Wichita had replied as well, asking what it was about. Gene's return wire told them it was the marshal's business and even he didn't know. Marshal Johnson arrived the next morning, after sending a message to Marshal Smith from the town's telegraph office. In his wire, he told the marshal what he knew of the robbery and his plan to head them off. At the train station, he and Gene waited for the arrival of the train in Wichita and a message from Dick Bryant or Toby Harris.

For Marshal Smith, it was still a game of wait and see. There was nothing he could do from Maple Ridge and nothing to tell Ernie Evans just yet. Bobby Grayson had made his run to the Cahoon Ranch the afternoon before. Henry was out by the stable when he rode up. He bypassed the house and tied up at the barn, where a number of ranch hands were finishing up for the day. As he asked for Henry, he saw him walking up and reached in his saddlebag for the merchandise he'd brought along.

"Henry," he shouted, as he saw him walking in his direction.

"I apologize but I forgot to put these in your wagon."

"I didn't know I'd forgotten anything." He replied.

"You didn't, I forgot to put them with your stuff." Bobby stepped up close to Henry and looked around to make sure he wasn't overheard then whispered; "You didn't forget anything; I just needed an excuse to come out here. I need you to come to town as soon as you can. Marshal Smith would like to talk to you. We need your help and you need to keep it very quiet. Will you do that for me?" Bobby asked.

Henry was confused. He'd agreed to keep an eye on the ranch, now he wondered what else they had in mind. He stood there for a minute, not knowing what to do.

"Henry, this is very important and we need you. I'll tell you what it's about when you get there, okay?" Bobby could tell he was reluctant but he was relieved when Henry finally nodded and said, "Okay." With that, Bobby apologized for the mistake once again, for everyone to hear, then mounted up and rode out of there.

He couldn't have been happier, when he crossed the tracks and rode into town. It never occurred to him, that only a couple of weeks earlier, he wouldn't have thought of doing something that risky. Marshal Smith had watched the men of Maple Ridge take control of their town and hoped it would last. Their display of courage, just a few days ago, had reinforced that hope. With Bobby's willingness to ride into Cahoon's stronghold, he now had a sense of assurance that they would stand, when it mattered most.

Although he didn't know it, Ernie Evans had been their inspiration. He hadn't planned it and he honestly didn't understand it. A man stands for who he is and doesn't back down. It's not a matter of cost it's a matter of conviction. He'd never considered the cost, when compared to doing what's right. Standing for what you know to be right, puts a stop to things you know to be wrong. How do you put a price on that? Sounded like an excuse for cowards in Ernie's mind. He'd shown them everything they weren't. It seems he'd made the complacent townsmen see themselves for what they were and it was a picture most of them didn't like.

\-

As the eight o'clock train pulled into Wichita from the east, Cahoon's men were within sight of the town from the north and riding in a slow lope. The sun rising over their left shoulders was a relief. They'd stayed on the south trail, with Clayton in the lead and trusted his instincts. He knew where they were, generally but the night had been dark, with heavy cloud cover, offering no help from the moon. They had pushed the horses as hard as necessary to reach their destination and saw no need to drive them any harder. Now seeing the roof tops and outline of the town, they knew where they were and knew they would soon be out of the saddle.

Just after they pulled out of Cheyenne Wells, Dick Bryant watched the conductor, as he opened the door and walked into the train car. It was a normal sight but when he called his name, Dick sat up like a bullet and shouted; "Over here! How did you know my name?" He asked.

"We got a wire from the marshal in Abilene, wants you to contact him as soon as we pull into Wichita."

"What the hell for?" Dick asked.

"I don't know, they just told me to find you and your friends. I take it you men are the other two I was to find?" He asked.

"Yeah, that's us," Bobby Jenkins replied.

Something had to be seriously wrong. Neither of them had ever been tracked down on a train before. With no additional information, they could only imagine that things in Maple Ridge had gone bad. They suspected that William Murphy was behind this, with plans to turn them around and head back.

After leaving the train in Wichita, the ex-lawmen were approached by the station master. They'd noticed the man in a derby and spectacles looking their way. He'd already picked them out on the platform. As he approached, he became more confident these were the men he was waiting for.

"Which one of you is Dick Bryant?" He asked.

"Over here. What's this all about?"

"I don't know. Marshal Johnson, in Abilene wants you to wire him right away."

"That's the damn-dist thing I've ever heard of." Dick said, as he removed his hat and walked toward the station master.

"Yeah, me too." The station master replied. I ain't never done this before."

As soon as the telegraph operator saw them walk in, he began tapping out a message to the Abilene station. Marshal Johnson jumped when he heard the machine's magnetic coil begin to vibrate. He'd almost dozed off but the tapping of the telegraph key got his attention. With the assurance that he had three law men in Wichita, Marshal Johnson sent back a message that left them all in disbelief. He explained, in as few words as possible; Cahoon sent men to Abilene who robbed Mr. Murphy; stole four horses; made their way south to Wichita with twelve hundred dollars; no doubt heading back to Maple Ridge on 10:00 train; Four men; find them and bring them here. That's all there was.

They all knew Marshal Johnson and there was no doubt he was very serious. He couldn't give them much more. No description or names. It was up to them to watch the ticket office and platform, for anyone who stuck out. The ticket agent was the key. Tickets to Maple Ridge, or Cimarron were what they were looking for. Dick Bryant was betting on Cimarron. He didn't see how they would get off the train in Maple Ridge and not draw attention, especially if any of Cahoon's men were waiting for them. They all agreed.

Each man walked out of the station and spread out to within a block of the platform, then began to do what they did as lawmen. They slowly looked around the street, focusing on the people and their movements. The way folks walk, where they are looking and the pace of their stride, can tell a man a lot, if he's watching. But it would be difficult, not knowing the town. They couldn't pick out strangers, or undesirables. Bobby Jenkins spotted a deputy and quickly told him who they were and what they were looking for. Being too obvious was a concern. If the men saw them looking about, they would become suspicious and duck out of sight. It was a game of looking without looking and canvassing the town, while strolling along.

It was just after 9:00 am when Toby Harris found the horses, tied to a hitch behind the blacksmith's shop, with no one around. They had crossed the Arkansas River an hour earlier and left the horses tied in an out of the way place, as planned. The horses were wet and dirty, it was obvious they'd been rode hard. To avoid being noticed, the men had split up in pairs and walked over to Fowler Street, one block away. Toby asked the man at the anvil, if he'd seen anyone near the horses. He said he'd seen four men tie up and then walk away but that was it. Nothing to go on but Toby was quite certain these were the stolen horses. The riders were nowhere to be found. They'd held to the plan and were currently at the Café, two blocks down and out of sight of the men looking for them.

Toby met up with Dick a few minutes later and told him about the horses. Dick figured it was a waste of time to look for men he didn't know and decided they should stay around the train station and let them come to him. Bobby Jenkins and the deputy caught up with them shortly thereafter and agreed that would be their best bet.

Tom Bainbridge and his men left the Café around 9:20 and slowly made their way to the station. Tom was smart and considered the marshal in Abilene may have wired ahead, knowing this would be their best place to board a train. He'd intended from the start for them to split up and buy their tickets separately. But he had a plan of his own. The twelve hundred dollars in his pocket would never see New Mexico, if he had his way. He'd have the others head for Cimarron, his plan was to leave the train in Cheyenne Wells. They could ride together for a while then he would become bored and decide to check out the next car. When the train pulled into Cheyenne Wells, he'd be gone and they would be none the wiser.

Dick Bryant and his men stood back from the platform but within sight of the ticket agent, to avoid suspicion. When Clayton Emerson stepped up to buy a ticket, the agent looked toward Toby Harris and nodded. They knew the others would be close behind. Toby kept an eye on Clayton, as he boarded the train car from the front. He then walked to the rear and stood near the steps, expecting his friends would soon follow. Moments later, Tom Bainbridge walked up and bought a ticket for Cheyenne Wells, drawing no suspicion from the ticket agent. He slowly boarded the train without being noticed. Minutes later Cahoon's men, Jim Holden and Seth Leonard, walked up, one at a time and bought their tickets for Cimarron. Each time, the ticket agent nodded, alerting the men of their destination.

"That's three." Dick said. "But where's the other one?"

Dick and Bobby held their place, with the deputy close by. Toby stood at the rear of the car, having seen three of these men board the train. They waited until it appeared everyone had boarded and the train began to build a head of steam.

"Where's the other one?" Dick asked.

"I don't know, maybe he slipped by the ticket agent, or we missed his motions."

"No, he either missed him, or he saw us and skinned out." Dick said.

The train would be pulling out in minutes and they had to do something soon or lose their chance. Dick and Bobby made their way to the front of the train car, as Toby opened the back door. Seth Leonard was sitting by the window. He saw the men approach in a fast pace, as they walked through the steam, now rolling across the platform. He immediately turned to see that the man, who had been standing by the rear steps, was gone. He got a bad feeling and quickly bailed out of an open window on the opposite side and walked to the rear of the train. Clayton Emerson tried to follow but was caught by the back of his coat, as Toby reached over the seat and pulled him back in.

"Leaving so soon?" Toby asked. Clayton stood without comment. Dick and Bobby came in the front of the car, as Clayton just stared back. Toby in turn, bolted out the back door and down the steps, on the outside of the train, to follow the one who'd gotten away but he was gone. He hadn't seen anything but his backsides anyway but he knew he was wearing a brown coat. There were a lot of men in town with brown coats and this one had ample time to slip away. Toby knew he was wasting his time.

Dick quickly looked around and spotted the gray coat of one of the men identified by the ticket agent and approached Jim Holden.

"Where's your ticket?" Dick asked.

"It's in my pocket, where it's going to stay." Jim replied.

Dick pulled his sidearm and aimed it at Jim's face. "Now, show me your ticket, I know who you are." Dick was bluffing, just a bit but he knew he was one of the men. Jim showed his ticket and started ranting, as he noticed the man behind Dick Bryant was wearing a deputy's badge.

"This is an outrage! I live in Cimarron and I'm heading home. Deputy, I want to press charges against this man!" He wasn't about to give up so easily.

"What's your name?" The deputy asked.

"My name is James Shelby. I've been in Kansas City, for the past few days. Now I'm heading home. I want him arrested!" Jim shouted.

"What were you doing in Kansas City?" Dick asked.

"That ain't none of your damn business." Jim replied.

"Mr. Bryant, do you know this man?" The deputy asked.

"No but you know as well as I do, that he's one of them." Dick replied.

"No, I don't know that and unless you've got more than a ticket to rely on, I can't let you hold him.

Dick was seething. He knew he'd just been had but they'd caught one and that was a start. Clayton Emerson had tried to escape, something an honest man doesn't do. He hadn't argued his innocence, so the deputy let them have him. But there were still three others, somewhere. Having arrested only one of the men, Dick and Bobby escorted Clayton off the train. The deputy took it upon himself to check the rest of the passengers for tickets to Cimarron, just in case. There were only two others, a man and his wife. He looked again at Jim and still thought he didn't have enough to hold him. When the deputy reached Tom Bainbridge, he proudly produced his ticket to Cheyenne Wells. Jim Holden saw his exchange with the deputy, from several rows back and was more than curious. How did he do that? He wondered.

Seth Leonard had stayed around the back of the train and took up in the last car, when Toby turned back. When he saw the men leave, with only Clayton Emerson, he laughed. He didn't like him anyway. As the train began to roll, Seth just sat tight in the caboose for a while then eventually made his way back to Jim Holden and Tom Bainbridge.

-

Marshal Smith received a wire from Abilene earlier in the day and now knew more about the robbery. They had arrested one man, with at least two others headed for Cimarron. He didn't know who but he did know enough now to bring Ernie in on the events of the past two days. Ernie had been helping Ralph Thomas, with some horses for most of the day. He was usually easy to find somewhere around town. If not, he suspected that he and Abigail would be at the Cattleman's Diner pretty soon. He knew he could find him there. Ernie and Abigail had been together a lot over the past few days and he was growing even more attached to the town. He was now a duly sworn deputy marshal of Maple Ridge and a part of that oath was to be available to the marshal anytime he needed assistance. Marshal Smith had no intention of overly exercising that right. But he now has some strings attached to his new friend and planned to use that authority wisely.

He'd suspected for a while, that Ernie had a desire to stay in town but for some reason, didn't want to make the decision entirely on his own. He knew the conditions of his oath and the marshal expected Ernie would lean on his commitment to the town, to justify his eventual decision to stay. A deputy's pay would never be enough to satisfy Ernie Evans. He lived better than such meager wages would afford and he could never support Abigail to his liking under such conditions. But maybe it would be enough of a start. At least, Marshal Smith hoped it would.

It was late afternoon when Henry Sutton walked into Grayson's Mercantile. He was nervous but knew it must be something important for Bobby to ride out to the Cahoon Ranch just to see him. He wasn't sure what was going on, between his boss and the town. He knew about the shooting and wasn't told much more. He had only been there a short while but the tension around the ranch has increased considerable in that time.

The men didn't say much and stuck close to their work. But he'd noticed times when Raymond and then Lemual, would gather a few men for a talk and soon after, there would be some kind of trouble in town.

Henry was a bit surprised by Bobby's request. He didn't know how he could help, although he wanted to. Marshal Smith was careful as he spoke, he didn't want to take a chance of scaring him away. He followed Bobby's lead, asking Henry about the things he saw at the ranch and how Cahoon was acting. He also wanted to know about the Misses. She hadn't been around and he wondered if she was actually under duress and forbidden to leave the ranch. Henry answered slowly and basically repeated the story he'd already told Bobby. Marshal Smith was taking it slow. He needed to win Henry's trust and that would require patience, while giving Henry a reason to step up.

He was relieved to see Ernie walk through the door. On his way to the mercantile, Marshal Smith had spotted Michael King, hanging around his usual corner by the Café. He asked him to keep an eye open for Ernie if he happened by and have him come to the mercantile as soon as he could. Luckily, he did but Ernie was adamant that he only had a few minutes. When he arrived, the marshal turned to him and introduced Henry. He wanted to include him and Bobby in what he had to say.

"Ernie, I have some news and it's not as bad as it may sound but we have a problem coming our way."

"There's a big surprise. What is it this time?" Ernie asked.

"Cahoon sent some men to Abilene to rob Mr. Murphy."

"What? Is he alright?" Ernie asked. "How did you find this out?" He was becoming both angry and unnerved.

"Give me a minute. Mr. Murphy is fine. They cold-cocked him with the butt of a pistol and knocked him out for a spell but he's okay. I got a wire from Marshal Johnson in Abilene. He said four men from Cahoon's Ranch came up there and robbed him of twelve hundred dollars."

"One thousand, plus two hundred for their trouble, that's my fault. Son-of-a-Bitch!" Ernie said as he took a seat. "What now?" he asked.

"They left Wichita this morning, heading for Cimarron. Way I see it they will bring the money back to Cahoon. Someone will likely need to pick them up at the Cimarron train station tomorrow afternoon. I'm going to wire Marshal Lambert and fill him in. I thought we would ride up there and break up the party."

For the marshal, the threat of another fight was taking shape and he was sure this one would end it.

-

The "Lawmen from Abilene" had very little to work with in Wichita and little time to make it happen. They had cobbled together a plan from nothing and were probably lucky to catch one of Mr. Murphy's robbers and retrieve the stolen horses. On the next train north, they put the horses in a boxcar and shackled Clayton to a post, for their ninety-mile ride. They figured that once Murphy identified the man, they would pressure him to give up the others. It wasn't as quick and clean as they'd hoped but they had the bait and he'd bring in the fish.

Marshal Johnson wasn't dissatisfied at all when they arrived. The owners of each horse were at the platform, when they left the boxcar and walked down the plank. The marshal felt a sense of accomplishment in retrieving the horses, unharmed with all their gear. He had confidence in his plan, in general. The use of the telegraph wire to run them down, had worked perfectly. He was sure the capture of one man, would lead them to the rest.

Clayton Emerson wasn't as worried as they thought he'd be. He hadn't argued much at the train station; which Dick Bryant took as an admission of guilt. Clayton knew what they didn't know. He'd basically used himself as a decoy, to draw them off the others. William Murphy had never seen Clayton and couldn't identify him as one of the robbers. It came as a shock, when Mr. Murphy stood, shaking his head, when facing Clayton Emerson through the bars of the Abilene jail. Three men had entered the KCBA office, while Clayton had remained outside, to round up the horses, to make their getaway possible. Disappointed as he was, Mr. Murphy had to admit that he'd never seen him before. He was not one of the men.

"So, are you satisfied now?" Clayton asked.

"No but there's nothing much we can do about it." Marshal Johnson replied.

"Now I have a worthless ticket home. Which one of you is going to get me a train ticket and a hotel room?" Clayton asked.

"None of us, you're lucky to be getting out of here. The best I can tell you is to go down to the train station and work it out." Marshal Johnson replied.

The black smoke rolled from the west bound locomotive as she built up a full head of steam, putting Wichita to their backs. Seth Leonard sat comfortably in the caboose, until the town was out of sight and the train was at full speed. A few miles out, he began to move forward, car by car, until he was back where he started. He slid in next to Jim Holden and began to laugh with a sense of victory, at having narrowly escaped the law.

"Damn, I thought you had skinned out of there." Jim replied.

"I started to but I ducked in behind the caboose, where that lawman couldn't see me. How the hell did they get on to us anyway?" He asked.

"Damned if I know. That marshal or deputy in Abilene must have wired ahead on us." Jim replied.

"Seth, I got a bad feeling about Tom," Jim began, as he motioned to their riding cohort, sitting three rows up. "You took out of here and they started giving me a hard time, for my ticket to Cimarron. I learned a few things in Yuma prison. They had to know that's where we were going. The deputy asked Tom for his ticket and he ain't say a word when he showed it. The way I figure it, he ain't got a ticket for Cimarron. That bastard plans to ditch us and get off early. He's holding the money and got a ticket to somewhere else." Jim concluded.

"I ain't never trusted him anyways," Seth replied. "What do you want to do?"

"I'm going to make him show us his ticket and I ain't letting him out of my sight. That's why Mr. Cahoon sent us along anyway." Jim replied.

Seth and Jim eased up behind Tom Bainbridge and quietly sat in the two open seats behind him. Jim pulled his sidearm and laid it on Tom's shoulder, where he could feel it and see the barrel from the corner of his eye.

"Show me your ticket, Tom." He said quietly.

Tom turned, surprised that they would question him. "What the hell is wrong with you? I ain't showing you my ticket." Tom replied.

"Yeah, you are. And I want Mr. Cahoon's money, that's why he sent us. He knew you would steal it. Now turn it over." Jim replied. Tom just sat there for a moment, thinking of what to do. He knew he'd been caught and figured Cahoon would come after him in Cimarron, since he went after this fellow all the way in Abilene.

"Give it to me now and I won't say nothing." Jim offered.

"Hell, I can't blame you for trying."

Tom turned in his seat to see both Jim and Seth displaying their iron and decided it was time to give it up. Without a contest, he reached in his coat pocket and produced the money. Jim reached in and stuffed it in his pocket, without an incident.

"Hell, I can't blame you. That's a lot of money and I might have tried it myself, if he'd sent me alone." Jim was trying to ease the situation and was being honest. He probably would have done the same, if he could have gotten away with it. Tom just laughed and figured it wasn't worth shooting each other on the train. At least he'd tried.

-

Cahoon saw the outcome of the hearing, much differently than Marshal Smith. For him, it had been the victory he'd needed for a while, to get things back on his side. The constant pain was gone and the bottle was now something he could live without. He'd tried to make amends with Mrs. Cahoon. Outwardly she went along, giving the impression that all was forgiven but it had gone too far. She had seen things in him that she had never expected. She'd learned things that reached into her deepest fears.

She had always seen him as a hard businessman, strong and unwavering. It was a part of her attraction to him. His strength had been endearing to her and made her feel safe. But she was finding that his ways weren't confined to business, as she had thought. He had threatened and intimidated townsfolk, who she knew and respected. Now she had come to realize that he was inherently ruthless and her sense of security was no more.

She too, had now been threatened. It was the first time in their many years of marriage that he had forbidden her to leave their home. Her beautiful abode had now become a prison. She was glad he was sober but her heart was no longer his. Her thought of visiting the bank was still something she saw as a way to protect herself. She knew Mr. Kinsey would be sympathetic and help her find some avenue of independence. She didn't know how but she had to try. But for now, she had to go along. If Cahoon continued to focus on the ranch, he would lose interest in her whereabouts and soon she'd find a way to slip into town.

Marshal Smith had a simple task for Henry; watch the ranch and report anything unusual. He didn't want him involved in anything covert, just to be aware of what he heard and what he saw. There wasn't much else he could do without getting into trouble, or at least raising suspicion. Henry felt a bit empowered by the marshal's request and the confidence they seemed to have in him. Maybe he could become a lawman, he thought but Henry was young. The chance that he could blow his cover was still of concern to Marshal Smith. The request from the marshal had been simple but Henry knew he was a part of something important. He was only to inform the marshal of unusual events, or if men he didn't know showed up at the ranch. Bobby Grayson also wanted him to keep a close eye for anything unusual concerning Mrs. Cahoon. He was to do nothing on his own, just to report back to them. It was a game of wait and see but the marshal was concerned he might become overly anxious.

Ernie and Marshal Smith knew the men who robbed Mr. Murphy would show up at the Cahoon Ranch. Without the help of the "Lawmen from Abilene", they would be shorthanded on men who had experience with a gun. It was time for Marshal Smith to learn if his faith in the townsmen was justified. He knew Bobby Grayson had the grit. Add in JT Belcher and Ralph Thomas and he had a sound posse. Several of the men who had ridden with them that morning were willing to join in. Their town was now in their hands, not Cahoon's and they planned for it to stay that way.

The utter waste of living in his self-absorbed world had cost Cahoon, more than he realized. Weeks ago, he could have settled an honest debt and averted the unrecoverable losses he'd suffered since. Ernie Evans would have been on the next train east and no one in Maple Ridge would have seen him again. But Cahoon's arrogance, pride and greed had kept Ernie in town. His presence alone had been the inspiration the townsmen needed. When he was shot, they thought he'd surely die. If he had, Cahoon would have regained his self-ordained power over the town, upon his recovery and all would have remained the same. But Ernie not only survived, he prevailed.

He didn't realize it at the time but the day Ernie Evans stepped off that train his life began to change forever. He'd finally been introduced to his heart, through the prodding and patience of Abigail Bainbridge. The trauma of being shot, was the jolt the rest of his being had needed, to come alive. This was new and confusing to a man who'd lived by the dictates of a gun. His decisions were based on the speed of his opponent's hand. Whatever the question, the gun was the answer and he was always the victor. He wasn't comfortable with matters of the heart. Emotions could not be seen, which made them very difficult to challenge. He was beginning to believe they could be more powerful than any weapon.

He'd tried to run, something he'd never done. He would never admit it but his heart pulled him back. Abigail... She was the catalyst of his transition but the familiar feel of a .45cal. in his right hand, was still his security. The gun was battling the heart and Abigail could feel the conflict. The success of the gun is judged by speed and accuracy but success of the heart is judged through patience and humility. It was a paradox which Abigail had come to understand and was willing to confront. She had vowed to heal the heart of the child, so the man could be freed from his past.

He was a man who everyone knew to be dangerous. The life he lived had been devoid of emotion, which left him with a cold view of his surroundings. He was no different than every other gun hand who trailed alone. As a young man, he'd build walls to keep people like Abigail out. Now she was challenging those walls and they were beginning to crumble. But his abilities and confidence with a gun, would not be affected by the tugs at his heart. He knew the gun would keep him alive, where the heart could get him killed. Now, he had to be sure the two would never cross trails.

Ernie had to make a decision and it had to be soon. It would be Abigail or the KCBA, it couldn't be both, she deserved better. But what about him, what would he do if he stayed? He was good with horses and had offered a helping hand to Ralph Thomas and others on several occasions, since his recovery. He could find work and he still had the badge. He'd never considered marshaling. But he had better credentials than most lawmen and he had a reputation. That alone was the backbone of the most effective among them.

Abigail had come to know him better than he knew himself. She had no prejudice and looked to the future, where he had been unwilling to release the past. He was uncomfortable at first and she suspected that was only when she was around. She represented his future, a place of uncertainty, while he was yet unwilling to stray too far from the past and his own security. She'd noticed the change on the night of their first dinner, at the Byron Dining Room. He'd opened up and told her things that she knew were from his heart. She saw that in his eyes. She witnessed his inner struggle each day but she was becoming increasingly confident that his heart would prevail.

CHAPTER 12

Cahoon's men arrived in Cimarron on the afternoon train. Tom Bainbridge and Jim Holden had gotten along without incident and played cards with two other passengers for most of the trip home. Seth Leonard had stayed to himself for most of their journey and chose to sleep instead. He held a different attitude toward Tom, than did Jim Holden. He didn't trust him and knew he would be a problem for them, if Cahoon kept him around.

Two of Cahoon's ranch hands were waiting with the four-seater carriage, when they arrived. Two horses were also along, saddled and tied to the back of the carriage, which was a welcomed sight for Jim Holden and Seth Leonard. Four men had been expected to step down from the platform but three, along with Mr. Cahoon's money would be enough to satisfy the boss. They'd discussed their pay on the train and made a few presumptions, regarding a bonus Cahoon had offered up if they returned with the extra two hundred dollars.

They had no idea where Clayton had ended up. His first stop after Wichita was obviously back to Abilene. Whether they'd held him, or cut him loose, was still a mystery. Jim came up with the idea of talking Cahoon into split his offer three ways, instead of four. They didn't know if he'd go along with it but they would give it a try. No one knew when, or if, Clayton would return. Clayton Emerson had been rather busy back in Abilene and hadn't given them a lot of thought.

Marshal Johnson was furious. He knew Clayton was one of the robbers but without Mr. Murphy's help, he couldn't hold him. He'd turned Clayton loose, to fend for himself in spite of his protest and demands for a ticket back to Cimarron. Marshal Johnson didn't care if he had to walk back, this drifter wouldn't get the price of a train ticket out of him. He'd restrained himself quite well thus far but at Clayton's mention of a hotel room, the marshal collared him. He offered up a jail cell, for the night with no guarantee of a check out time. Clayton took that as a resounding No and left empty handed. He needed to get back and made himself busy trying to rustle up a ticket home and finding a place to bunk for the night. But, he would be on the morning train and back in Cimarron soon enough.

Henry was watching from the doorway of the stable when the men rode in and reined up in front of the house. He knew two of the men were ranch hands. He'd seen them many times but the third was a stranger. He had time to think of how he should handle himself and wisely chose to stay calm and complete his work, without paying too much attention. Henry just watched, like Bobby Grayson and the marshal told him. He kept an eye out for how long they stayed and if Cahoon might come out with them. If he did, Henry hoped he might hear some of what they were saying. Unfortunately, Cahoon wasn't around when the men exited the house. There was a horse in the barn, which had been there for a few days. Henry had seen the animal and thought he was one of their stock. When the stranger came out and saddled the Mahogany Bay, he knew it must be his.

Activity around the ranch was picking up, with Cahoon becoming more involved in the past few days. Most of the foreman's duties were now left up to Harold Quinn. He'd handle that job, until Lem returned from jail, up in Cimarron. They were short-handed, which meant everyone was working more. This would mean more pay, for the next four weeks, until the other nine men were released from jail. It also meant that Henry would have less free time. He didn't mind it much; he enjoyed the work and it kept him busy. He hadn't hung around with the others much, since he arrived. He was younger than most of the men. The attention he'd received so far was usually from one or two of them poking fun at him for something. It didn't bother him and he laughed it off with the others. Henry just didn't seem to fit in their clicks, so far.

Shortly after sunset, Henry heard a couple of the guys talking about going into town. That ritual had curtailed sharply since the confrontation on the trail. Although tensions had eased up significantly, since nine of Cahoon's men were jailed. Those who had little, or no, profile in town, now frequented the saloons a little more and spending money again. Henry asked the guys if he could ride along and have a beer with them. He was sure he would spark someone's attention if he saddled up and rode out alone. They joked at him a bit about ordering milk instead but they were fine with him riding along. He planned to hang around with them for a while and then hopefully catch Bobby at the mercantile before he left for the day.

When the men arrived in town, the saloons were just beginning to get busy. Henry and the two ranch hands found a table at Jack's place and ordered a beer. One of the men picked up a deck of cards and began shuffling, as he looked around for one more cowboy, willing to join in. Henry saw a card game in the making and bowed out. He said they should look for two instead, giving the excuse that he hadn't brought enough money to play. He probably had but he didn't plan to sit there that long. Besides, a card game would keep them busy and distract them from his whereabouts.

They sat for a bit, nursing their beers, when two takers came to the table, ready to strike up a game. Henry gladly gave up his chair and stood next to the table, watching for a spell while he finished his beer. Soon after, he set the empty mug on the table, then slowly turned and started to wander about. He watched the men, to see if they were paying any attention to him, which they weren't, then slipped out the door.

Bobby was sweeping up when Henry walked in. He was excited to have some useful information to offer and felt a sense of accomplishment that he could be helpful. He'd hoped the marshal would be around and looked forward to making him proud. Bobby was startled when he walked in, anticipating what Henry may have to say.

"Henry, how are you?" Bobby asked.

"I'm doing good." Henry replied, with an air of excitement. "I did like you told me. I kept an eye on things and saw something this afternoon I though you ought to know."

"What did you see?" Bobby asked, as he leaned the broom against the counter, to give Henry his full attention.

"This afternoon, I saw three men ride in and go straight to the house. Two of them were men who work at the ranch but they've been gone for several days. Then there was another man I ain't never seen before. They came in with two ranch hands who left in Mr. Cahoon's carriage early this morning. When they left, they had two saddled horses tied to the back. Two men, Seth Leonard and Jim Holden were riding the horses when they came back this afternoon. The other man was riding in the carriage. When they came out of the house, the other man, the one I don't know, saddled up a horse that's been in barn for near a week and rode off. He ain't said nothing and looked like he was in a hurry to get out of there. Last I seen him, he was riding off to the north." Henry was careful to tell Bobby everything he saw and smiled with pride when he was done.

"How long did they stay in the house?" Bobby asked.

"About half an hour, I reckon. The three came out alone, Jim and Seth went to the bunkhouse and the other man went to the barn to get his horse, like I told 'ya." Henry answered.

"I need to find the marshal. How much time you got?" Bobby asked.

"Not much. I rode in with a couple of guys, so I wouldn't draw any attention. We went to the saloon to have a beer, then I slipped out to come here. I can't stay long, or they'll get to wondering where I went." He replied.

Bobby was impressed. Young Henry was obviously smarter than he'd thought and he began to believe this just might work after all.

"That's smart, Henry, I'm proud of you."

Henry just smiled, that was all he wanted to hear.

"You go ahead and join your friends. You're right, they might start looking for you. I'll get the marshal and tell him what you said. You did good, Henry. You keep your eyes open and make sure you come in for supplies next time. I'll have something special for you." Bobby replied.

Henry was proud, though he was disappointed that he couldn't tell the marshal himself. This was the first time in his young life that he'd felt important to anyone. Bobby shook his hand, with a smile, which Henry gladly returned. As he turned to leave, Bobby said; "Here, grab yourself a couple stick of hard candy from the jar." Henry grinned, as he grabbed a few and began sucking on a peppermint stick, as he walked out the door. When he re-joined the men back at the saloon, still enjoying the candy stick, one of the men asked; "Where you been?"

"I went to get some candy." Henry replied, holding the evidence in his hand, for all to see. They were none the wiser.

Bobby locked the door and walked down Grayson Street toward the marshal's office. Marshal Smith had just left an exasperating meeting with the town council and he was in no mood for more bad news. Bobby told him about his talk with Henry, repeating it just as the information had been provided to him. The marshal was both surprised and relieved at Henry's success, the timing couldn't be better. At least he now had the names of two of Mr. Murphy's robbers. But the third was still a mystery. Riding north, he was likely heading to Cimarron, probably one of the cut-throats who lived at the edge of town. He must have come to the ranch to get paid or bring Cahoon the money. The fourth man was still unknown.

He and Ernie had decided against meeting the train when it arrived in Cimarron. They didn't yet know who they were looking for and thought it best to let it play out and take a chance on Henry. It turned out to be their best choice. Now they had names and the marshal was confident that Mr. Murphy's money had found its way to Cahoon's pocket. Cahoon must be feeling pretty good about now, Marshal Smith thought. His men had beaten the murder charge and his vendetta against the KCBA, was obviously settled to his satisfaction. There was no doubt his next stop would be Maple Ridge. He wasn't yet sure of how it would happen. Cahoon had tried to strong arm the town with a stampede of men, which had earned them a stretch in the Cimarron jail. He could use force again, or he might go back to the old tactic of sending two men at a time to cause a ruckus, when things don't go their way. Regardless of Cahoon's plan, the marshal was sure that none of his old schemes would work this time. Unfortunately, the by-product of whatever he did would be bloodshed.

Larry Cahoon laughed, as he counted his money and placed it in the wall safe. It had come full circle. His money was now back, in the exact location it had occupied, prior to him being 'robbed'. He had been successful, in his mind and beaten them all. From the courthouse in Maple Ridge, to the KCBA office in Abilene, he'd exacted revenge on those who had violated the sanctity of his domain. He had the need to celebrate and called for Mrs. Cahoon to join him in the parlor. When she arrived, he was bursting with joy, all smiles with a festive aura.

"Come Darling," he said, as he raised a glass. "Let us don our finest and make way to the Byron Dining Room, for a succulent cut of beef and a bottle of their finest. Not to worry, my dear. I'll not use the bottle to remedy a pain, which no longer exists." He continued to reassure her and was still making amends but did not believe that she had fully accepted his apologies. She would, she must, he thought.

She smiled, that was the only thing she could do. Denying him would send him in a rage and abetting his current exuberance would only fuel his undeserved ego. In reality, she had no choice. With a smile and without comment, Mrs. Cahoon made her way upstairs to prepare for an evening on the town. All the while, she was concerned about their reception, by those he'd obviously abused. She'd come to understand the misgivings of the folks there and had questioned how she might be received as well.

He was now, through all of their difficulty, back in control. When they arrive in town, everyone will show their respect and he will be first in line. He'd won, don't you see? It was settled. He was the victor and all others would concede and respect his rightful place. Mrs. Cahoon was fearful. It wasn't possible for the reality of the evening to play to the picture in his mind.

Cahoon had a young cow hand to hitch up the carriage and drive them into town. The fall air was a welcome compliment to the ride and helped Rachel Cahoon relax a bit. She didn't know how he would react, to whatever reception they received in town. But she wisely decided that she would stand back and let him respond in whatever manner he chose. She had an innate feeling, that they wouldn't see the endearing townsfolk, he somehow was expecting. Her expectation was to be shunned at best, or openly mocked, in the worst of scenarios. Either way, he was on his own. She saw this as her first opportunity to remove herself from him, even if by some small measure. She almost hoped he would cause a scene or get himself arrested. That would surely give her the contrast between them that she now wanted everyone to see.

The young man stopped the carriage in front of the Byron Hotel and quickly jumped down to help Mrs. Cahoon, as she stepped out. Mr. Cahoon walked to her side and extended his arm, which she graciously accepted upon her first step onto the boardwalk. The sounds from inside the building gave the hint of a busy and cheerful atmosphere, one that most diners would be eager to join. The mood did not change, when they entered. Some took notice of them but others went about their business, without a thought. These were nice people and it was a nice town. It wouldn't be in their nature to be openly disrespectful, or to demonstrate bad decorum amongst others.

As they walked to their table, Mrs. Cahoon was relieved that no one had crossed him thus far. As she dwelled on that thought, they both overheard a man at the bar quietly say to another;

"He's got a lot of nerve coming here." It wasn't meant for their ears, nor intended to instigate a confrontation, simply a private statement, from one man to another. It was, unfortunately, overheard by its subject and he didn't take it too kindly.

Cahoon stopped, his smile vanished and his eyes went cold.

"What did you say?" He looked to the man and waited intently for a reply. The man sat for a moment, a bit embarrassed that he'd overheard the comment but didn't run from his statement. "I'm sorry you heard that, Mister, my apologies." The man replied and then turned back toward his friend.

"You're sorry you said it, or just sorry I heard it?" Cahoon asked. The man had become annoyed, as he looked back toward Cahoon, in a less apologetic manner and replied; "I said I was sorry, now let it alone." He was louder this time and the look in his eyes challenged Cahoon to push it further, if he had the balls. He turned and looked toward his wife. She was now standing about ten feet from the bar, having decided to walk away. It was a slight dose of reality, for a man whose impression of himself, was far different from those around him. He no longer had a hold on Maple Ridge, she knew that now. But it wasn't clear if he'd learned anything from that short exchange.

Dinner was quiet, not the festive celebration he had envisioned. No one spoke as they walked by, with no well-wishers expressing their pleasure in his recovery. Their only interaction had been with their waitress, with the exception of his unintended dealings with the stranger. He managed to hold his composure and played it off as one of those jealous little dirt farmers, who wanted to be like him. Mrs. Cahoon said nothing but gained a small splinter of satisfaction from the man's guts. Admit it or not, he'd just backed down and that encouraged her growing disdain for her husband.

The morning air was brisk, with the feel of autumn, as Ernie walked to Blake's Boarding House to meet Abigail. They'd decided to have breakfast together, before she began her day at Dr. Rowe's. Except for work, they were rarely seen apart. She would routinely visit with her friends and Ernie had become a regular at any one of the poker tables at the Alhambra. But at dinner and any town event, you could expect to see them arm in arm.

Ernie had become comfortable with the way his life had changed. Slowly and without any specific intention, he was developing the routines, which most people unconsciously perform in their daily lives. He didn't miss the days of wandering from town to town, hunting down ranches and intimidating them out of money. He'd come to realize that most of these men were honest. They never knew they'd been paid money they didn't deserve. By the time they came face to face, the money was spent and many had no way of settling up. He felt some regret but still, it was his job.

These days, he was working with horses and though he hadn't planned it, he had all the work he needed. Ranchers, from around the area were finding him to be the best around, at breaking horses and training them for ranch work. There's a big difference in a riding horse and a working horse and Ernie was good at separating the two. He always had somewhere to go and a means of making money. It was honest work and he didn't need to worry about getting shot. It was very different from the past.

Ernie and Abigail strolled to the corner of Third Street, within sight of the Early Bird Café, where Marshal Smith was crossing from the opposite corner. When Ernie called out, the marshal immediately turned and walked his way.

"Man, I'm glad to see you", the marshal began. "Morning Miss Abigail." He turned to her as he spoke and politely tipped his hat.

"Morning Marshal," Abigail replied, with a smile. She could see there was something important on his mind and it was obvious that he needed Ernie, for whatever it was. She had been impressed by his growing status in town. Ernie was becoming someone that everyone knew and respected.

"Ernie, I need to talk to you, sometime this morning, if you don't mind."

"Sure, what's on your mind?" Ernie asked.

"The men who robbed Mr. Murphy, I know who two of them are and they work for Cahoon."

"What are you waiting for? Let's go get 'um." Ernie suggested. The marshal now had his attention and he was ready to ride.

"It's not that easy, besides, I want all four and I don't know who the other two are just yet." Marshal Smith replied.

"How about I come by in an hour or so?" Ernie asked. "We're going up to JT's for breakfast, then walk Abigail to work." Abigail smiled. He sounds like he's lived here forever, she thought.

It was around 9:30 when Ernie got back to the marshal's office. He and Bobby Grayson were discussing Henry's involvement when he arrived. Bobby was intent on giving Ernie the whole story, start to finish. Ernie had good instincts for such things, he'd proved that the second day he was in town. Bobby told him about Henry Sutton and how he had spotted the three men, who arrived at the ranch the day before. The marshal had also heard about Larry Cahoon and his wife being in town the night before, having dinner at the Byron Hotel Dining Room. This was the first time they'd been in town socially, since before the shooting.

"The way I figure it," the marshal began, "Cahoon's men came in on the Cimarron train yesterday and he sent men with his carriage, to pick 'um up. Seth and Jim rode back on their horses and the man we don't know, rode back in the carriage. Then after their meeting, he saddled his horse and rode north, I think back to Cimarron. Now, why would he ride down from Cimarron then ride back? I'm sure it was to see Cahoon and get paid."

"That makes sense but there could be more to it." Ernie added.

"Like what?" Bobby asked.

"Like Cahoon was satisfied with this man's work. Now, he wants to hire him for something else." He replied.

"To do what, you think?"

"You don't think he's done with this town, do 'ya?" Ernie answered.

"Yeah, that's what I was thinking." Marshal Smith chimed in.

"We still got a fight coming. His men are in jail and he ain't waiting 'til they get out. He's going to get even with the town."

Ernie couldn't run from the deputy's badge any longer, or the law he'd taken an oath to uphold. He wasn't sure how Abigail would take to it but he was thinking it was time to put himself to good use. It was time to work for Marshal Smith, full time for a while. Deputy Wilcox would be of little help if trouble came their way, he'd proved that. The town needed an experienced gun hand. As an official lawman, he would have the authority to stop Cahoon's men, watch their movements in town, or arrest them if need be. His jurisdiction would spread out for several miles, approximately half the way to Cimarron. This of course, included Cahoon's entire spread.

Ernie had kept the badge in his vest pocket. He'd tried to return it a couple of times but Marshal Smith refuses to take it. He thought about William Murphy and getting even with his assailants. There was a lot to mull over but he settled on what he considered to be right, for the marshal, the town and for himself. Ernie reached in his pocket and removed the badge. He stared at it for a bit then looked toward the marshal. "I think it's time to put this on," Ernie said, as he held his lapel and pushed the pin through the fabric. He looked off in thought, then adjusted his hat and cocked his head. He looked again in the marshal's direction and said; "Okay, boss…It's time to go to work."

Marshal Smith was relieved. Bobby Grayson just smiled. They needed him, not as a backup willing to help out but as the law. No one in town would be surprised. Fact is many of the townsfolk had put their trust in Ernie being the man to finally bring this to an end. Marshal Smith was well respected and had regained the confidence of the townsfolk. But his age and his graying hair, showed a man whose best days were behind him. The recent fights in town had been intense and Ernie had been the strength behind their success. He represented the future of Maple Ridge. He had cleaned out most of Cahoon's men, without a badge. Imagine what he could do with one.

News travels fast in a small town. By the time Ernie got to the Double Deuce Corral, Ralph had already heard that he was wearing the badge. His plan for the day had included a couple of jobs Ralph needed him to cover. Now it was looking like Ernie would be busy for a while. Mayor Sterns may have been the most relieved to hear the news. His early impression of Ernie, as a self-centered gunman, had long since passed. He had come to appreciate the man under that rough and usually quiet exterior. He'd so vehemently confused Ernie's confidence for arrogance. Ernie had been good for the town and good for their spirits.

Not wanting Abigail to hear it from someone else, Ernie made a quick visit to Dr. Rowe's office. He needed to make sure that she would be comfortable with his new job. She had encouraged him before but with the reality before them, he wanted to be certain. He felt himself becoming attached to Maple Ridge and was growing even more attached to Abigail.

"Does this mean you've finally decided to stay?" She asked.

"I think it does." He replied. With his next statement, she knew he was sincere.

"I need to send for my horse and my stuff," he began. "It's been over a month since I've seen Bruiser, he's probably forgotten about me." Ernie said with a slight laugh. But the notion made him a bit sad, for he thought it may be true.

"Oh, I think he'll remember you right off." Abigail replied, with an air of excitement. "We should send a wire this afternoon," she suggested, "he will be here in a couple of days and you can get acquainted again." Abigail was smiling.

"Yeah, I guess you're right," Ernie replied. "I've left him alone long enough."

Abigail knew the dangers of the job he'd chosen, although it was safer than what he had been doing. Yet she was glad he had accepted the responsibility. She had no doubt he could take care of himself and they both knew the town needed him. He'd come to love Maple Ridge, she knew that better than him. He didn't admit it but she also knew their relationship was a large part of that decision and that warmed her heart.

It was early when Mrs. Cahoon walked out to the stable to check on Lillie, her sorrel mare. The sun had just broken above the mountain tops and the cool air gave promise of fall. It would be the first time she'd seen Lillie in days. She was unwilling to comply with his demands any further and left the house to pay some much-needed attention to her bay and herself. Mr. Cahoon was in the parlor when she walked out, mulling over some financial matters. Such things usually kept him busy for the bulk of the morning. She was disappointed in herself for allowing him to exert such control over her. But given his recent turn to the bottle, she'd been afraid to challenge his unpredictable temper.

Their ride into town had been the first time she'd been allowed out of the house in days and he was obviously trying to regain her favor. She would use his current attempts at humility to regain her sovereignty. Henry was there when she stepped up to the gate and was eager to engage her in conversation. He hadn't seen anything new that could be helpful to Bobby Grayson but he knew he was worried about her wellbeing. He was glad to see that she was well and decided that he shouldn't ask too many questions. He had spoken with her a few times and hoped he could build on that enough for her to come to him, if she needed help.

"Good morning, Mrs. Cahoon. It's good to see you out this morning."

"It's good to be out, Henry. I got tired of staying in that house."

"I noticed, ma'am, that I ain't seen you out lately," he replied.

"I've been tending to your mare. She's a good horse, ma'am."

"Thank you, she is a good horse," she replied. "I want to take her out for a ride, Henry. Would you saddle her for me?"

"Yes ma'am, I'll be glad to." He replied.

Mrs. Cahoon was relieved to be out once again; she wasn't accustomed to being told what to do and she'd had enough.

"Would you like me to ride along, ma'am. I ain't doing nothing right now and I'll be glad to come." Henry offered.

"That's sweet of you, Henry but I'll be fine. I just need to get out for a bit, to do some thinking," she replied.

"Yes ma'am, I understand. Ma'am... maybe I shouldn't say nothing but if you ever need somebody to talk to, I'm always around. I won't say nothing. I mean… maybe I could help." Henry just smiled, not sure if he should have said anything. Mrs. Cahoon was surprised by his unusual offer and wasn't sure what he meant.

"Well, thank you, Henry," she replied, "I'll keep that in mind."

Henry hoped he had planted the thought and decided then that he wouldn't ask again. He needed her to know, there was someone close by who would be on her side, if trouble occurred. He was now friends with the marshal and was proud of his new associations. He had to keep it quiet but Mrs. Cahoon now had a friend close by, he only wished that she knew.

The morning ride was a welcomed break for the Misses. She would have time to think as she rode and needed the freedom to begin resolving the many conflicts, which had burdened her heart. The clear sunny sky was a welcome relief from being confined to the house. The thought of which, still made her angry. Sitting on the hillside, on the north range, she dwelled on the magnificence of the place she'd loved. It had been the fulfillment of her dreams but it seemed to have less meaning for her these days. That made her sad.

Much had changed in such a short time but she was stronger for it. What if he was gone, she thought, I could run this ranch. She recalled what she'd learned while he was in Cimarron and the number of people who were willing to help. She'd learned that she could deal with adversity, both without him and now with him. Her inner strength was greater than she knew. And with that, came a sense of self confidence, which she was beginning to recognize. But he isn't gone, she thought, that was silly but what if I left? She'd thought of it before but had no plan for a future alone. They were just fleeting thoughts, as she rode but the answer had to be there somewhere. She needed to be cautious, it would come to her soon, she was sure of it. For now, she would bide her time and just wait. She kept reminding herself that acting on emotion would only make matters worse. She had to be smart, take her time and use her head. The ride had helped to clear her mind but there was much to consider and she realized the future was still as uncertain as before.

Riding back to the barn, she thought of Henry's unusual offer and wondered what he knew. It was odd and there must be a reason for him to ask. He'd heard something. He must have, why else would he offer to share my problems? He was next to the fence, out a ways from the barn when she rode up. Henry and another ranch hand were replacing broken boards and working their way around to the corral, one board at a time. He saw her as she rode in and made his way to the barn, to help her dismount, then tend to Lillie.

"How was your ride, ma'am?" He asked with a smile.

"It was delightful," she replied.

"That's good to hear, ma'am. I'll curry her and turn her out to the pasture, if you'd like."

"Yes please, thank you, Henry."

Henry had hold of the reins and had turned to remove the saddle, when she decided to speak up.

"Henry, what did you mean when you said, I could talk to you and assured me that you wouldn't say anything? Have you seen, or heard anything unusual, that I should know?" Mrs. Cahoon spoke softly and quietly, not to alarm Henry, or to make him think he'd said something wrong.

"Not really ma'am and I didn't mean to be out of place. It's just that...well; I know that you have been put in a spot lately. I mean, if you thought you was in any trouble, I could maybe help, that's all."

She thought for a moment, unsure of what she should say next. Maybe he could help but it wouldn't be today. But what could he do, he's just a kid? He obviously knew something was wrong and had the courtesy to ask, no one else had. He seemed to be a bright young man and obviously cared. Maybe, she thought and then continued, "Put in a spot, that's an interesting way to put it. Things have been different lately. I'll take care of it. I'm fine Henry but I appreciate your concern. I promise, if I need to talk, I'll come to you. Thank you, Henry." She replied and looked at him with a warm smile.

"Yes ma'am," Henry replied, "I'll tend to Lillie for you." Henry tipped his hat, then turned and walked the bay back into the barn.

Clayton Emerson showed up in Cimarron late the next afternoon. He'd convinced the ticket agent at the train station in Abilene to exchange his unused ticket for a new one home. He hadn't bought Clayton's story of being dragged up there by the law. He almost felt sorry for his inability to come up with anything better. Clayton never could convenience him that he was telling the truth. Still, there were an abundance of empty seats when the train pulled in. Sending Clayton along when she left meant one less drifter in town.

It was two morning later, when he ran into Tom Bainbridge. There was a little diner, near the blacksmith shop, on Kerr Street, where many of them spent time. He knew Tom wouldn't be far away. Tom laughed when he saw Clayton walk into the dark room.

"Clayton, where you been?" He shouted.

"I took an unexpected trip back to Abilene." Clayton replied. He seemed to be smiling but it was difficult to tell in the dark room, as they were still several feet apart.

"How did you get out?"

"That old man ain't never seen me. When he came to the jail, I just grinned at him. I was stealing horses, while ya'll was in his office. They had to let me go, I knew it when we left Wichita." Clayton replied, "Where's my money for this deal, anyway?"

"Cahoon's got it, said he wants me and you to come there, after you made it back to town. He's got another job for us, I told you he would." Tom was glad that Cahoon refused to split Clayton's share with him and the others. He'd be in a fight about now and the other two would never give it a second thought. Tom had asked for Clayton's share of the money when they settled up but Cahoon was too smart for that. He'd suggested instead, that the two men return to the ranch, once Clayton showed back up in Cimarron.

With nothing else to do, they saddled up, after coffee and eggs and blazed a trail south for the Cahoon Ranch. The place was busy in the afternoons, from the corral to the north range. Even with ten men in jail, there were still enough ranch hands to run the lines and tend to the livestock. Busy as he was, the riders didn't escape Henry's eye. He saw them when they broke over the north ridge and watched as they rode in and tied up at the house. It took a moment to recognize Tom Bainbridge but he recognized his horse right off. The other man, he didn't recognize at all.

Something is up now, Henry thought, although he had no idea what. This was the type of thing that Bobby and the marshal had in mind. He would do like before, watch the house and whoever went inside, then keep tabs on how long they stayed and in what order they left. He could have no effect on what happened after that. But if he watched carefully and reported the information just as it occurred, the marshal would have an edge. Maybe that would be enough to make the difference.

As Henry kept watch on the door, there was an intense discussion taking place within the confines of Larry Cahoon's parlor. It was certainly more than either man had expected upon their greeting. It was the mention of the name "Ernie Evans" which sent the conversation into a whirlwind. They had done their job in Abilene and Cahoon was feeling an abundance of self-confidence, now that 'his money' was back in the safe. His plan now, was to engage these men in an arrangement to restore his authority over the town.

These men were good with a gun. Probably better than anyone now remaining within his employ. Cahoon was getting the notion that he may have seen the path for replacing Mac and Raymond after all. A productive starting place in the conversation, he surmised, would be a rundown of who Tom and Clayton could expect as their adversaries in town. When he included the name Ernie Evans, Tom Bainbridge went cold.

"Whoa, stop! What Ernie Evans? Where's he from?" Tom was now focused on nothing other than this man.

"He's a gun hand, come from Abilene. He's the man who was sent here to steal my money. The money you went back to Abilene to get." Cahoon answered.

"He's thirty-one, maybe thirty-two I reckon, near six feet tall, is that the man?" Tom asked, as he stared back with a cold eye, which made even Cahoon back off a bit.

"That's the man," he replied. "I take it you know him." Cahoon grinned. He now saw great value in this man's anger.

"Damn right I know him, known him since we was kids. Son-of-a-Bitch shot me in Liberty Missouri, 'bout ten years back. I'd say it's time to make him pay." Tom Bainbridge was as angry as if it had been yesterday. The pain in his shoulder had been gone for several years now and with it went the memory of that event, until today.

Cahoon had been angered by his wife's earlier imprudence in allowing these same men into their home. Now they sat in his parlor at his invitation. Tom Bainbridge was there for his third time. Mac and Raymond were gone. They had been his front men for many years, enough for him to take their efforts for granted. He'd expected they would be there forever. But forever had now arrived and the two pillars who had marshaled his self-imposed authority, were dead. Lemual White had been a disappointment. He truly thought he could fill Raymond's shoes at least but he'd screwed that up. As for Harold Quinn, Cahoon had no intention of giving this idiot any authority.

Now he sat with two Missouri Bushwhackers, one of which obviously had a personal axe to grind, with one of his main antagonists in town. Cahoon smiled to himself. It doesn't get any better than this, he thought.

"What would you say if I hired you full time…. let's say, as my business manager?" Cahoon said to Tom.

"Business Manager, what the hell is that?" he asked.

"Nothing really, it just means that you work for me. You go where I go and be in the room anytime I'm entertaining guest, or business associates. It also means that you dress more appropriately. You will no longer be a cow-puncher, you will be a businessman." Cahoon laughed. It made him think of Gregory McElliott, he wasn't much different. Folks in town were never privileged to Mac's intellect. He was fast with a gun and never showed fear in any adversity. But he didn't have enough sense to rub two sticks together. Tom Bainbridge was a perfect fit for the job.

Cahoon's unexpected offer hadn't distracted Tom's thoughts from Ernie Evans. He didn't know how the two would work together but if this 'business manager' job would help him get even with Ernie, he was all for it.

"What does this job pay?" Tom asked.

"It pays more than you make now, no matter what it is. You will stay here, in the main house. Your room is the one by the back door, next to the kitchen. And if I find that you've stolen anything from this house, I'll kill you in your sleep. We got a deal?" Cahoon asked.

"Tom thought for a moment, especially about that last line. Then he decided to thank Jim Holden for talking him out of the twelve hundred dollars on the train." Yeah, we got a deal. Hell, I got nothing else to do. I might as well become a business manager." Tom replied.

Clayton sat quietly, just taking it all in. Wherever Tom went, he usually went, so it was all sounding good to him. Once the deal seemed to be made, Cahoon turned to Clayton.

"Mr. Emerson, you have a job here as well. It may not have a title but I need you both. I want you around and staying here, in the bunkhouse. I'll pay you to work the horses and of course the job comes with room and board. The main thing is, you be ready to do what I ask, when I ask. Do you understand?" Cahoon asked.

Clayton thought for a bit. It was better than anything in Cimarron and the bunkhouse had to be better than where he was staying. "Yeah, I'll do it," he began. "As long as Tom and I get to ride lead, in whatever you got cooking, I'm for it."

"You will certainly ride lead, that's what I'm hiring you for. Working the horses, just gives you something to do in the meantime. Besides, I'm shorthanded as it is." Cahoon replied.

As they continued to discuss Cahoon's intentions, Tom asked again about Ernie Evans. Cahoon was intent on keeping this quiet until he was ready. Tom was to keep his hands-off Ernie, until he gave them his permission. He was intent on getting a bead on Ernie Evans and had a plan of his own to hang around the edge of town, to scout him out. The information that he was now a deputy marshal hadn't made its way to the Cahoon Ranch. To Tom Bainbridge, he was a halfhearted bushwhacker, who'd shot him ten years ago. To Cahoon, he was the man who'd caused the town to rise up against him. But to Maple Ridge, Ernie Evans was now the law.

CHAPTER 13

It had been just over an hour since Henry heard the thud of the heavy hand carved door as it closed. As it reopened, the men stepped out, still in conversation, only this time Cahoon following them onto the porch. Henry hadn't lost sight of the house, while he continued to work. He had eased his way a little closer down the fence line, when he saw them emerge. He was still too far away to hear any of the conversation. But their demeanor showed three men who were obviously in agreement over whatever they had been discussing. Henry needed names. That was the one thing he was missing when he last spoke with Bobby Grayson. This time he needed that information. He had to be cautious and couldn't risk being caught. That would surely disappoint the marshal and Henry was determined to fulfill his promise.

They weren't so quick to leave this time. That seemed to be the first thing Henry noticed. He stayed busy, not to appear as though he were watching, as they meandered to the other side of the house. Cahoon pointed to the kitchen door, as the men nodded, then turned and walked toward the barn. Odd, Henry thought. He was still replacing boards along the same fence that he'd been repairing the day before, when the Misses came out.

He saw the men make their way toward the bunkhouse. He then slowly walked back in their direction, heading to the barn to grab a hand full of nails. He really didn't need them, he had a pocket full but it was a good excuse to get closer to the men. They paid no attention as he walked by. There, he overheard Mr. Cahoon direct one of the men to the bunkhouse, as he showed him where he would be staying. Henry continued to walk, never looking in their direction. When he left the barn, they were heading back toward their horses, still in conversation.

These men ain't cow hands, he thought. If they were, Harold would be talking to them and they would never have seen the inside of that house. Harold hires all the men. Mr. Cahoon ain't taking his time hiring ranch hands. He didn't hire me,

he thought. Henry was sure that Cahoon had never even spoken to him. These men were staying this time that was for sure. Cahoon had hired them for something but Henry couldn't be sure for what. With only one of the men directed to the bunkhouse, the other must be staying in the main house. It was obvious they were not there to push cows.

In the early afternoon, Tom and Clayton walked out to the edge of the pasture, on the north side of the main barn. They were away from most of the activity, where they could have a bit of privacy. Henry saw them walk that way and then worked himself around the fence, to their side. He was now away from the road and the front of the barn where others were passing by or running in or out for supplies. Still under the pretense of repairing the fence, Henry drove a few nails and straightened a few boards along the way.

Around the back and within feet of the men, Henry thought it would be a good idea to re-set a post, within ear shot of their conversation. He never looked their way, as he walked into the barn and returned with a spade. The men paid no attention and apparently saw no reason to change their tone. Henry was quiet as he dug around a bit, then on his knees packing loose dirt. There, he listened to every word of their conversation.

"I can't believe that bastard Ernie Evans is in this town. I ain't never forgot what he did to me." Tom said. He had, in fact put it out of his mind some time ago. Now the notion of Ernie being in Maple Ridge, made his old feelings boil back to the top.

"You'd better keep that to yourself for now. Don't get too anxious, Tom. We'll get him soon enough." Clayton replied.

"Yeah, maybe so Clayton but finally getting even with him makes this deal a whole lot sweeter."

"That could be but it makes it harder too. If he sees you in town, he's going to wonder why you're there. Mr. Cahoon ain't going to take so kindly to you showing your hand before we pull this thing off." Clayton warned.

"I reckon you're right but I want Cahoon to know that he's mine. I'm going to kill him, before this thing is over." Tom promised with anger in his voice.

"You can't screw this up. We got a sweet deal going on here. Of course, you get to live in the house, while I'm out here. But I ain't complaining. It's a hell of a lot better than we had." Clayton was laughing as he spoke.

"Yeah but I still ain't figured out what a business manager is. That makes no sense to me." Tom replied.

"Don't worry about it," Clayton began. "It is what it is and we'll go along with whatever this old man says, he's got money."

"Reckon so," Tom replied. "We'd better get back to the house and whatever the hell it is that he wants us to do."

They'd paid no attention to Henry, as they hung over the fence jawing. He stayed put, at the base of the post, packing dirt and appearing to mind his own business. Henry now knew their first names but that wasn't good enough. He figured it would be best to wait until the next day, before he made an attempt to get in touch with the marshal. He knew he had what the marshal was looking for but he had to have their last names. With that, he would surely have done a good job and the marshal would be proud for sure.

This was the first time that Abigail had seen real tranquility in Ernie's face. It was quite a contract from the hard look of a wounded gunman, she saw that morning in August. He'd been at Dr. Rowe's longer than he'd intended. When he stopped by, he'd only planned to tell her of his decision to wear a badge. He didn't realize he would come to such an important awareness while he was there. He'd pinned the deputy marshal's badge to his lapel just an hour ago, something he'd struggled with since the day of the trial. Now he'd taken the final step in deciding to stay in Maple Ridge...He'd promised her. It had always been about her.

He'd been careful not to make such an important decision too quickly and now wondered if he was dragging it on too long. He never doubted that she would be good for him but he was afraid of disappointing her. She deserved better than the likes of a gunman. He'd always resented the inference, though he knew that's what he was. But things were different now. He had found a home, a real home. It hadn't sunk in until that moment but he had made his decision to stay hours ago, maybe days ago. He must have, how else could he have removed the badge from his pocket and pinned it to his vest with any sense of conviction. The commitment was already there, he just didn't know it.

Abigail's insight was a bit scary at times. She seemed to know him better than he knew himself. He liked that. No one had ever cared that much before and he was comfortable with it now, though it hadn't come easily. She understood his struggles, without the need for words. She saw them in his eyes. He hadn't figured out how but she'd found her way into his heart. This had always been a place where no one was allowed. It must have been hers all along, he thought. She'd found the key that he didn't think exited. Oddly enough, it must have been there the whole time.

She was comfortable with him as a lawman. A paradox really, or perhaps the only compromise that truly made sense. She'd hoped to be the one who replaced the gun in his life. But, she had come to accept its presence and knew it was not going away. Now she had encouraged him to take the one job which relied upon it. Only now, it was for good and for the protection of others.

Ernie was relieved that his decision had been made. He was confident it was right. For the first time, it was one he wasn't required to make on his own. They'd made it together, that was different and with her, he knew it was right. On his walk back to the office, he thought about Bruiser. He'd be glad to have him back. There's something about the outside of a horse, that's good for the inside of a man. He'd heard that somewhere and he believed it was true. Ernie smiled and had a spring in his step. He'd meet her later, he thought. She would be there when he sent a wire to Abilene, to send for Bruiser and his other belongings. It would be a ceremony of sorts, something to show her that he was sincere.

It was late afternoon when Cahoon called for Tom, Clayton and Harold Quinn to meet him in the parlor. Mrs. Cahoon had been upstairs for most of the day but heard the voices from downstairs. She worried that he was up to something deceitful. She'd lost all faith in her husband and was determined to know what their meeting was about. Unnoticed, she slowly walked down the stairs, out of sight of the parlor and stood near the foot of the steps. She listened, as he began his story of being the backbone of Maple Ridge and how they had shown him an unacceptable measure of disrespect.

He told of how he'd supported the mayor in his election, with an unrealistic account of the modest level of esteem he'd anticipated in return. To listen, one would think of him as a pillar of the community. Harold knew better, he was a part of it all. Or maybe he'd come to believe Cahoon's distortions and thought of the whole thing as normal. Either way, they were all outlaws in her mind and this time she would stand in his way.

She was frightened by what she heard, both for the town and for herself, if he caught her standing there. It was obvious by their conversation, that he was planning some kind of raid on the town. These men he'd hired, this must the reason they were there. Mayor Sterns was mentioned. She couldn't understand a portion of what he'd said but she caught the part about Cahoon wanting to take care of the mayor himself. One of the other men was fixated on Ernie Evans. She knew he was the man who had killed Mac and Raymond. This man was apparently determined to kill him, which was satisfactory to her husband. Her heart was pounding, as she heard the words coming from the other room. They were planning to kill people, as calmly as if they were buying cattle. She couldn't believe what she was hearing.

The men talked a while longer, before she heard the creaking of the leather chairs, as they began to move about. They must be leaving, she thought but they hadn't said when this would take place. Perhaps tomorrow, maybe a week, or a month, he didn't say, or if he did, she'd missed it. She had to know and she had to warn the marshal. But how, she wondered. Her legs were trembling, as she moved from her vantage point. It seemed to take all the strength she could muster to make her way up the stairs and out of danger.

Rachel Cahoon was terrified. Once back in her bedroom, she could hardly stand on her own. She closed the door, then sat on the bed and began to cry. Suddenly, she stopped herself. "No!" She said aloud, I'm stronger than this, I will not stand by and I will not be afraid. It was a promise she'd made to herself up on the hillside and it would now be put to the test. With all the soul searching on her ride, she'd still found no solutions to her situation. She vowed then to find the answer, or perhaps the answer had just found her.

Henry kept watch on the house and saw the men as they left. He was somewhat curious about Harold being involved, especially with this meeting taking place in the main house. It could have been ranch business. There were two new employees and the ranch foreman, in a meeting with the boss, that wasn't anything unusual. But considering who they were and what he'd overheard, he didn't suspect cattle or horses had been discussed in the past hour or so. One more bit of information, for what it was worth but he still needed their full names.

As Rachel Cahoon put all the pieces together, Henry suddenly came to mind. She wasn't sure what he'd meant. Even with time to think, it still hadn't made much sense. But he must have been telling her something. She'd have to ask him, there was no other way and she needed answers. There was no time to play games or dance around the situation. She had to determine for herself who stood where and wondered if anyone on the ranch was honest. She still had doubts about Henry. If he could help, she wondered how. With only one way to know, she decided that he would be her starting place. She'd find out soon enough if he was being honest, or just blowing smoke.

Mrs. Cahoon regained her composure and acted normal at dinner. He was in a cheerful mood, which she used to engage him in conversation, where they laughed and made small talk. She had avoided suspicion and he was obviously unaware of what she'd heard. She was quite sure but his demeanor at dinner confirmed it. She was relieved and considered her first step to be a success. That had been the easy part, she thought. She could still stop here but if she went to the marshal, there would be no turning back. Confident in her resolve, she was committed. She couldn't allow the mayor to be accosted and others killed and do nothing. Her conscience wouldn't allow it. It would fall on her, if she didn't warn the marshal. In her mind, the outcome would make her an accomplice.

Rachel Cahoon was up with the sun, ready to step out and take matters into her own hands. She was afraid of where this might lead but assured herself that she was strong enough to see this through. There were many uncertainties ahead, not the least of which was getting out of the house, then off the ranch. Her last attempt had resulted in house arrest, imposed by him and only lifted with their dinner at the Byron Hotel. He'd been more agreeable over the past few days and she didn't expect to be faced with the same pushback, as when he was drinking. She would need Henry's help. He was the only person she could turn to. She hoped he meant what he'd said and now was the time to put him to the test. If he would hitch the carriage and drive her into town, she could make this work.

Cahoon was in the kitchen, when she walked though, heading to the back door and holding a red and white pleated dress.

"Good morning, Dear. I'm going to have Henry, the new ranch hand, to hitch the carriage and drive me to the dress shop. Is there anything in town I can get for you?" Mrs. Cahoon smiled, almost holding her breath, as she waited for his reply.

"I don't know of any Henry working for me." He replied, without looking up from the papers, which currently had his attention.

"Come on Larry, you've got to learn your ranch hands better than that. He's the young man who usually works the stable and tends to Lillie." She replied.

"Oh, I know who you mean. Where are you going again?" He asked, as he finally looked up and gave her his full attention.

"To the dress shop, I have two places in this dress, which need to be stitches. It's been needing repair for weeks." She held the dress before her, showing him the unraveling stitches, as she spoke.

"Well, I guess it will be okay, as long as someone goes with you." He replied. "I didn't want you going alone, that last time." He didn't argue, as he had before. Once again, he turned to the papers which had garnered his attention before she walked in. She was surprised at the ease of getting this far but still felt he could change his mind, if she wasn't out of sight soon.

Henry wasn't at the barn when she stepped in, which brought her to near panic. "Henry," she called out but heard no reply. She quickly made her way through the back door, into the east pasture but he was nowhere to be found. If she couldn't find him, her plan for the day would be ruined. He has to be here somewhere, she thought. She turned and walked back through the long barn and out into the road. Looking to her left, she saw him coming down the fence line, walking one of Mr. Cahoon's quarter horses back to the stable. "Thank God." She said aloud. She waited for him to get closer, before she spoke. "Henry," she called out.

"Morning, ma'am." Henry replied, as he turned to lead the horse back to the stable. "How are you this morning?" he asked.

"I'm doing fine, Henry. I need you to hitch up the carriage and drive me to town. Do you have time?" She asked.

"Yes ma'am, of course I have time," he replied.

She felt a sense of relief but hoped her husband wouldn't change his mind. She was still concerned that he might come out and force her back into the house. If he did, her chance would be lost.

They were on the trail and had lost sight of the house, before she breathed a sigh of relief. I'm safe now, she thought. They'd only made small talk thus far, each waiting to initiate a more serious conversation. She was the first to change the subject but still felt she was taking a chance involving Henry in her problems.

"Henry," she began, "I have a big problem and I'm going to take you up on your offer to help. But please, you have to keep this very quiet."

Henry was relieved. He'd hoped she would let him help and suspected that her husband's latest visitors had something to do with her decision.

"Well ma'am, I knew something was wrong but I was careful not to say much. I have friends in town and they are waiting to help." He proudly replied.

"Who's waiting to help? What friends?" She curiously asked.

"The marshal, ma'am and Bobby Grayson, at the mercantile. I wish I could have told you before. They asked me to keep an eye on things at the ranch and to keep it quiet. They know there's something bad going on there." Henry knew it was finally time to tell her. She had to know that he could be trusted. She was both shocked and relieved by his reply, she now felt safe for the first time in weeks.

"You know the marshal? How do you know him, you just came here?" She asked.

"Just my good luck, ma'am. They sort of took to me, I reckon." Henry grinned with pride.

"Ma'am, do you know the last names of the men who were in your house yesterday?" He asked.

"Tom Bainbridge and Clayton Emerson," she replied. "They are here to hurt Mayor Sterns and to kill that man who came to our house, Ernie Evans, they said."

Her heart was racing at the thought of finally seeing this through. With Henry's help, she was sure now that it would work. But with all of her planning, she hadn't given a great deal of consideration as to what she should do next. She had to go back, she knew that but it would take her back into danger. There's no other way, she thought. If she didn't return right away, he'd know what she'd done and he would change his plan. He would surely kill her too. He couldn't know and she had to act normal.

"Where in town do you want to go, ma'am?"

"I need to see the marshal." She replied.

Henry reined up and stopped the carriage by the road, under a tall cottonwood tree. Once they were still, he laid the reins in his lap and looked toward her. "You can't do that, Mrs. Cahoon. I mean, what if somebody sees you? Those guys at the ranch, they all have friends in town. You'll be in big trouble, if one of them sees you anywhere near the marshal. You'd better let me do it, while you go somewhere else."

Henry was smart and his plan gave her the ability to retain some degree composure, once back at the ranch. He would talk to the marshal, while she was at the dress shop. That way, she wouldn't know what was said, or how the marshal would deal with his threat. She could fulfill the promise she'd made to herself and still not be involved. It would work, she though and she could still go home, without fear of suspicion.

"You're right, that makes perfect sense." She replied, with an air of confidence in her voice. "Take me to the dress shop on Jacob Street, I'll show you where. You leave the carriage tied there for everyone to see. Then find the marshal and tell him what I heard. Henry, you've saved my life, this is the only way I could go back, without acting suspicious." Mrs. Cahoon was chattering away. It was quite apparent, even to young Henry, that her burden had been lifted. Now, she could see the full weight of her plan go into motion.

"When you leave the marshal's office, come back to the dress shop and I'll take you to the Cattleman's Diner for lunch. You can order anything you like." She smiled with gratitude, thankful to have this young man on her side.

When they arrived in town, Henry tied up in front of the dress shop as planned then casually made his way to Grayson Street. He didn't go to the mercantile, this time. Choosing the marshal's office instead, he walked past Bobby's door and made his way down the street. When he entered the office, Marshal Smith and Ernie Evans were discussing the robbery and still not sure of how they could legally arrest the men. Kansas was a state, where New Mexico was a territory. It was hard to hold a man for crimes outside the territory.

When Marshal Smith saw Henry, he came to his feet. Ernie hoped he might have more information concerning the men who'd robbed William Murphy and shared the marshal's urgency.

"Henry, come in." The marshal said, as he extended his hand.

"Ernie, do you remember Henry? He's the young fellow whose been keeping an eye on the Cahoon Ranch."

"Morning," Ernie replied, as he slowly tipped his hat, with a nod.

"Marshal, we got trouble coming. There are two men at the ranch named Tom Bainbridge and Clayton Emerson. Mr. Cahoon has hired..." Ernie stopped him there. "Wait a minute, did you say Tom Bainbridge?"

"Yes sir," Henry replied.

"Shit...I've known him since we were kids. He was a bushwhacker during the war. Last time I saw him was ten years ago, when I shot him."

"You shot him?" The marshal asked.

"Yeah, he drew down on me and I shot him in front of his wife and daughter. I always hated that." Ernie replied.

"Well they're here and they have a plan to hurt Mayor Sterns and that Bainbridge remembers you, Mr. Evans. He aims to kill you." Henry had done the job they'd asked of him much better than expected but he didn't feel so full of pride this time. This was serious business and he was truly afraid that someone would get killed.

"Any idea of when, Henry?" The marshal asked.

"No sir and that's the other thing. I brought Mrs. Cahoon with me. She's over at the dress shop now, she's the one who heard them talking. I've been getting close with her for the past few days. I told her that she could talk to me, if something was wrong. I ain't said much else, I wasn't sure if I should 'a said that. This morning she came to me, said she wanted to come talk to you. I told her that was a bad idea and took her to the dress shop. I ain't wanted nobody to see her here and told her I would come instead."

"Damn, Henry that was smart." The marshal replied.

"That was smart." Ernie added. "So, she's at the dress shop now?"

"Yes sir, I ain't wanted her here." Henry answered.

Ernie and the Marshal stared at one another in thought for a moment. "We knew it was coming." Marshal Smith said quietly.

"Henry, I'm curious. So, Mrs. Cahoon overheard them talking then came to you? There's something missing here." Marshal Smith still hadn't grasped the entire chain of events.

"She's turned on him, Marshal. He messed up bad when he locked her in the house and that was the last of it, for her. She's out to get him, now that she knows what's going on. That lady's scared but she's tough and I think she's the best friend you've got right now." Henry replied.

"I'd say you are at the top of that list, son."The marshal replied with a grin. Marshal Smith shook his head in amazement at Henry's ability and grounded thinking.

What the marshal didn't ask, was how he'd managed to develop this much insight, at such a young age. Henry had kept it quiet and didn't intend to tell even the marshal, unless he asked. He was the son of an Arizona lawman, who'd taught him a number of valuable lessons, as a child. Henry had watched his father and had come to understand things that most only learn later in life.

He had seen the turmoil at the ranch and knew of the shoot out on the trail. He also knew by the movement of strangers, that trouble was coming. Henry had taken a number of risky walks at night, siding up close to the windows, near the parlor and kitchen. He'd heard her distress and he'd heard Cahoon's boisterous threats toward his wife, as she became a prisoner in her own home. It was a coincident that he'd chosen the Cahoon Ranch to ask for work. He'd left Arizona simply to be on his own, with his father's best wishes and his momma's tears. He would return but Henry wanted to become a man on his own. He'd come to the ranch for that purpose. But it wasn't a coincident that he showed up at Bobby Grayson's when he did.

He'd wanted to help, since he discovered the unusual nature, of his new boss. Figuring out how was the problem. Then he came into town with one of the ranch hands and saw how they treated the town's merchants. When he got the chance to go for supplies, he made sure that Bobby Grayson would be impressed by his manner. He would show Bobby that he was different than the others. He was concerned at first and not sure of how involved he should become. Henry wanted to do what was right and help the town. He was trying to gain favor from the marshal and was truly proud of himself, when he'd successfully delivered information to Bobby. But foremost, he knew it would make his father proud.

Henry had been at the marshal's office for about twenty minutes, when Marshal Smith decided it was time for him to go. It wasn't wise for him to be seen at the office, for the same reasons he'd kept Mrs. Cahoon away. He needed to get back to her, where they hoped he would be seen. Their next stop, after the dress shop, would be the Cattleman's Diner, where they hoped for reports of their presence to make their way back to the ranch.

When Henry left, a curious thought struck Ernie, about Tom Bainbridge and Abigail. He mulled it over for a bit and then dismissed it but it kept gnawing at him. It can't be, he thought. She's about the right age but how could it be? He put it out of his mind for the moment, as Marshal Smith spoke up.

He began to recount what Mrs. Cahoon had overheard and her willingness to come forward. He reminded Ernie of his encounter with her at the ranch, when they went to arrest Harold Quinn. And then how he and Bobby Grayson had come to include Henry in the whole thing.

"How are we going to play this thing?" The marshal asked.

"Well, we have more information than they ever thought we would. So, their surprise is out the window. What we don't know is when. Henry's got to get that somehow. Until then, we need to get the men together and keep them alert, with their weapons close by." Ernie replied.

"Yeah and I'm going to keep the mayor out of this, for a while. He's skittish enough as it is. If he thinks they're after him, he won't leave the house." The marshal added.

"We've got to know what they are up to out there and how many men he plans to bring in. We need to disrupt them somehow but I'm not sure how, just yet." Ernie replied.

"That Bainbridge is coming to town, Ernie. He's got to. He doesn't know this place and he has to get a feel for where things are. I mean, he ain't going to waltz in here one morning and start shooting up the place, not knowing what he's looking for." The marshal added.

"Yeah, that's true and I'm the only one who knows what he looks like, him and Clayton. I'm betting they'll come here together, hit a saloon or two and try to stay low. He'll be looking for me but he won't make a move, 'til Cahoon tells him to. If he did, he'd blow the whole thing, that wouldn't be like him." Ernie was rubbing his forehead and thinking it through, as he spoke.

"Looks like you've got that part figured out." The marshal replied.

"Yeah but that's the easy part." Ernie answered.

Once they'd had time to consider the possibilities, Ernie walked over to Fredrick Street. Ralph Thomas needed to be in on what they knew. He thought of Abigail along his way and once again couldn't seem to put it aside. He had asked her where she was from, just after they met but she wouldn't say. He thought it to be odd at the time but concluded that he wasn't the only one who'd rather leave the past where it lay. Now it was starting to concern him, when earlier it was just a curiosity.He'd never considered checking up on her and still didn't see his concern as anything dishonest. He had to know and Ralph Thomas knew everybody.

When he walked up, Ralph was busy repairing a loose stable gate and paid no attention to the man behind him.

"Good thing I ain't an outlaw, I'd a got you for sure." Ernie said with a laugh.

"Ain't no outlaw mean enough to come up on me." Ralph replied, with a wide grin and his usual chuckle. "What you doing over here?"

"Come to talk to you about a couple of things."

"Alright," Ralph replied, as he knocked the dust off his vest and turned toward the small pasture, behind the corral.

"What's on your mind?" He asked, as he placed his right boot on the bottom board of the fence. Ernie tipped his hat back and began with the most pressing matter.

"We got a fight coming, Ralph. Cahoon has hired two old bushwhackers from Missouri to lead the charge against the town, I'm afraid."

"Bushwhackers, huh, how you know?" He asked.

"Marshal Smith knows a young man, from the Cahoon Ranch, who saw them there and he just stopped by. I know these men and they are killers."

"Damn, that is bad. What else do you know? Like, when and how many men? We 'gotta be ready." Ralph added.

"I know and that's the part we ain't sure of just yet. We're hoping to get more on that, real soon."

"Who's tipping off the marshal?"

"He's a young man, who works at the ranch. You don't know him and we need to keep his presence real quiet." Ernie knew Ralph could be trusted.

"Well, we'd better line up JT and Bobby, then get the ranchers ready to hit this head on, like we did before." Ralph suggested.

"We can't do this one like before. They're going to have to come to us, this time." Ernie said.

"Fight this one in town?"

"I'm afraid so." Ernie replied.

The men talked awhile longer about Cahoon and his men. Ralph made suggestions from his civil war days and Ernie took them to heart. Ralph was getting up in years but he was still a fighter. Odd, he thought, these men used to be on the same side. Before he turned to leave, Ernie said to Ralph. "There's one more thing I need to ask you." He was still struggling with the idea of meddling but thought for a moment and asked anyway.

"Ralph, how long has Abigail lived here?"

"Oh, about a year, there abouts. Why?" He asked.

"Do you know where she came from?"

"Missouri or Kansas, I think. Come here to work for Doc Rowe after her momma died."

"You're not sure which?" Ernie asked.

"I don't remember. Why are you asking me?" Ralph asked.

"Oh, just wondering, Ralph. A man needs to know these things."

"Why don't you ask her?" Ralph inquired.

"Cause I'm asking you." Ernie tried to play it off as a joke but his smile was less than convincing to Ralph.

CHAPTER 14

The ride back to the ranch was a relief for Rachel Cahoon. She'd done exactly what she told him she would do, before leaving the ranch. But she'd also accomplished exactly what she had promised herself. Her mind was clear and she wasn't nearly as afraid as before. She could now look him in the eye, without the burden, or perhaps the remorse, of meeting with the marshal. She had betrayed him, which could not be denied. But Henry had done it for her and she had no knowledge of what had been said. For her, it didn't exist and neither her eyes nor her smile, would reveal any different. Henry had saved her from that and now he would be her currier and she trusted his ability to carry that duty with honor.

It was fortunate for her, that Henry had intervened. For shortly after they left, Cahoon sent a rider to keep an eye on her whereabouts, while in town. Lucky for them, he hadn't come along while they were stopped on the road but did manage to hit town in time to watch her enter the dress shop. He also saw Henry as he made his way down the street but there had been no talk of following him. He'd taken a slow walk to the marshal's office, without being noticed by anyone who would care, while Mr. Cahoon's rider kept a close eye on his target.

Upon his return to Jacob Street, Henry untied the carriage, in clear view of Cahoon's spy. It had all gone to plan. But neither Henry, nor Mrs. Cahoon, knew their change in strategy would so thoroughly dupe her husband. It had perhaps saved her life. Not knowing of the man's presence, they kept any suspicion further at bay by making their way to the Cattleman's Diner as planned. She hadn't made one step in town, that would have alarmed Cahoon, had he witnessed it all himself.

Cahoon hadn't given a thought to his wife going to the law. He would've never imagined such a thing. But after he'd made the blunder of locking her in the house, he was concerned that she would pay a visit to the bank, while in town. The report back from his ranch hand was a relief to Cahoon. She'd done exactly what she said and that would calm any suspicion he may have harbored.

Henry returned with a burden, which he hadn't anticipated. She was now his responsibility, no matter how he looked at it. He'd given her the help she'd needed to expose the motives of her husband. Now she was intent on getting a date for his raid on the town. It would fall to him to protect her, if she went too far. Henry too, would be more vigilant. He needed to know which of the ranch hands were siding up with the two men. He needed a head count. The number of men involved in conversations with Bainbridge and Emerson, would give him a good read on their strength and their strategy. Marshal Smith would need to know the number of men he could expect to see riding in, if he saw them at all.

The mood at the ranch had become more relaxed and upbeat, over the past few days. The men seemed to reflect the attitude which Cahoon had displayed of late. As a result, they'd become comfortable and more content in their work. They were also more talkative and less anxious about those around them and what they said. Henry knew Cahoon would cut a few of these guys out to use as gunmen, for his attack on Maple Ridge. Most of these guys weren't too bright and he knew somebody would slip up and say something. The strategy still bothered him; he hadn't yet figured out what Cahoon would do.

If he was planning to pull more than ten men from the ranch, Henry figured they would ride straight up Grayson Street, in full view of everyone. That could get bloody for a lot of innocent folks. If he only chose a few, Henry saw that as what his father called, a targeted attack. The smaller group would stay out of sight and surprise the mayor, Ernie Evans and likely Marshal Smith. With what he'd learned about Cahoon's last attempt, he suspected he'd stay low this time and try something different. This made a surprise attack more likely but unfortunately, that could be even more deadly.

Henry hadn't learned all this on his own. He remembered his father telling him about the struggles they had up in Prescott, when he was a kid. One story he recalled sounded a great deal like this. It had all played out in his mind, as his father told him each detail of the events, as they began to unfold. Henry could see it in his mind's eye, as clearly as though he were there. This was giving him such an impression of the similarities to that story and helped him understand. But still, he was missing the important stuff… How many and when.

It was evening, when Bainbridge and Harold Quinn came back to the corral. There were three cow hands with them, who'd been on the north end for most of the day. It was obvious that Bainbridge had ridden out to meet up with these men. He'd gone as far as the north side of the ridge, at least. It was a sure sign that he didn't want to be overheard and to keep all this brand of conversation off the ranch. When they dismounted, the five men walked to the edge of the fence line, away from the barn where they were joined by two others. He knew the likes of both men and hadn't trusted them from his first day on the job. Henry saw them gather but was not in a place to walk up anywhere near their position.

Now there were seven and that told Henry a lot, even without the ability to hear their words. The men weren't laughing, this was a serious conversation and the mood was quite morose. He stood back, careful not to be noticed. His concern now was the possibility of others joining in. Henry knew the names of four of the men and now focused on the other three, enough to remember their favor.

It was morning when he saw the seven men ride off together. They rode to the west, away from the ranch and away from town. Henry suspected they'd only confirmed their number the night before and were now riding off to set in on a plan. If this was the total number of men for their raid, he knew what they would do. It was time to get in touch with the marshal. This had to be how they would play it but he didn't yet know when. That was for Mrs. Cahoon and he hadn't seen her since they returned from town, the previous day.

Ernie sat on the wooden bench next to the Early Bird Café and scratched his head. He had enough on his mind with, Cahoon's never ending vendetta against Maple Ridge. Now, he was just hit with the possibility of Abigail actually being Tom Bainbridge's daughter. He hadn't decided how to bring it up but he had to get this off his mind, regardless of the answer. He'd come to the conclusion, that it didn't matter one way or the other, he just needed to know.

It was still hard to believe, that she could be that little girl, from so long ago. He'd thought of her and her mother many times, wondering how they'd dealt with that day. She couldn't have been more than ten, or maybe eleven at the time. That would make Abigail about the right age. She would certainly have changed dramatically since then. It would be nearly impossible for him to remember her favor. Besides, he only saw her that one time and he had a lot on his mind, at that moment.

Then his thoughts made a startling turn. Is it possible that she could have recognized him and kept it to herself? He wouldn't have changed that much and you would expect that she'd remember the man who shot her father. Now I'm really getting crazy, he thought. If she'd known who I was, she'd never given me the time of day...Oh my God. If it is her, what's she going to do when she finds out it was me? The possibility of losing her was making him sick. This can't wait, it's too important; I have to do this now, he said to himself.

Ernie didn't waste a minute. Cahoon completely left his mind, as he headed to Dr. Rowe's office. His thoughts ran the gamut, on the four-block walk, first over to Jacob Street, then to the end where the office was located. He wasn't sure what the next few minutes might bring but it had the potential of changing his life, again. Abigail was sitting with an elderly man, when he walked in. He wasn't sure what was wrong with the old timer but it didn't appear to be very serious. She saw him enter the hallway and smiled. He smiled as well, then turned to the parlor and motioned for her to follow him. This was unusual for him. Even through the smile, she could see there was something urgent in his visit. Not willing to make Ernie wait, she dismissed herself and followed him into the room, where she stood next to him, by the chair.

"What's wrong?" She asked. "You never come here this time of day."

"Sit down," Ernie began, "I've got to talk to you about something."

Abigail's heart began to race and she suddenly felt cold. He's leaving, she thought. This was too good to be true.

With a trembling voice and almost in tears, she reluctantly asked; "What is it?"

"There's something I have to ask you and I need you to be completely honest with me... Do you know a man named Tom Bainbridge?" Ernie asked the question slowly and inquisitively, not accusatory.

Abigail was startled. This was not what she was expecting. Already in an anxious state, her emotions didn't change and her mind was now reaching for something to say. She sat for a moment, with her hand cupped over her mouth, just looking Ernie in the eye. He could see that she was shaken. Slowly, she removed her hand and straightened her posture, then slowly replied; "He's my father."

Ernie watched, as her expression changed, from one of near panic, to someone who seemed to be asking for help.

"Do you know who I am?" He asked slowly.

Again, she sat quietly for a moment, obviously studying his reaction, before she spoke.

"Yes," she began. "I've known it was you, from the first day." She began to cry. "I wanted to tell you, God, I wanted to tell you but I was afraid you would leave."

He sat for a minute, watching the fear in her eyes and trying to understand her logic. None of it was sinking in, it just made no sense. "Why would you think that I would leave? To me, it's just the opposite. Why would you have given me the time of day? I shot your father, in front of you and your mother. But still, you want to be with me? I don't understand." He was both confused and relieved.

"That day, when they brought you in, we all thought you were going to die. I mean, you were in a bad place. I knew who you were, right after Dr. Rowe cleaned the dirt and blood off you. Marshal Smith was there, standing over you like a father and I saw the look on his face. I knew you had been hurt, trying to help our town. Then when you came around and looked at me the way you did, I got to thinking, this is not a bad man. I'd always thought you were and I kept telling myself to stay away, when you were flirting and asking me to dinner and such." By now her heart had settled down and explaining it to Ernie, took a mighty weight off her shoulders. She even began to laugh a bit, as she recalled those first few days.

"I hadn't thought back to that day in a long while, until I saw you. I haven't seen my father in almost ten…wait a minute. How did you find out?" She had become so enthralled in the moment and finally telling him, that she hadn't thought of how he could have known. Ernie paused a bit. He wasn't sure how she would respond to his answer.

"How did you find out?" She asked again.

"He's here, Abigail, working for Cahoon, at the ranch. We're sure he's been hired to lead a raid on the town." Ernie carefully replied.

"Oh my God," she replied, with her hand, now back over her mouth.

"I know this is a lot at once but I have one more question. Well, I have more than one but for now, I have to know. It's very possible that the events of that day could happen again. You know me and you know where I stand but what if it happens again, where would you stand?" Ernie asked.

"I will stand with you, of course… I love you. He stopped being my father the day he left." She quickly replied.

Ernie was somewhat relieved but there was much more they needed to discuss. He had to be sure and wanted a better explanation of why she'd kept it to herself. This thing was coming quick. And for now, they both needed to know where they stood with each other and how she might react to Ernie facing down her father once again.

Abigail took a deep breath, relieved that she could finally tell him what she'd held back all this time. She told him how her father had left them, shortly after his recovery and that she and her mother never heard from him again. She admitted that she had blamed him but realized the truth after they met. It was a relief for Ernie. Although, he was a little put out, that she would keep it from him and chose to bare that burden alone. He knew from her reaction that she didn't realize her father was in New Mexico. And in turn, was sure that Tom had no idea of her whereabouts as well.

Abigail had always wondered why. She'd asked her mother but she had been reluctant to tell her much about her father. Now, after all these years, she could finally ask the one man who knew. Ernie told her that he and her father were friends, when they were young. He too was somewhat vague but explained enough to satisfy her curiosity. He concluded that only Tom knew why he'd gotten so angry and attempted to draw down on him, that day in Missouri.

She was still troubled, as they walked to the door. Ernie assured her that they were okay and he would be back later to get her, as always. Not one to show emotion, he held her tightly and with a soft kiss on her forehead, he whispered; "I love you" then smiled. She felt the weight of the world leave her body, as her remaining tears, were now those of joy. This was the first time he'd actually said it.

Abigail was relieved that he finally knew but never expected it would be him who cleared it up. She had thought of her father many times, especially after her mother died. But she never knew if he was still alive, or if he'd been killed somewhere along the way. She'd never considered that he could be as close as Cimarron. How long has he been there? She wondered. And what's he been doing? Abigail was curious but it didn't seem to come with any sense of affection.

Ernie, on the other hand, was still very concerned. She would soon be facing a very different reality and he wasn't sure how she would deal with the result. He didn't doubt her sincerity but wondered how she would react, if she saw her father, after all these years. He also considered the distinct possibility of facing him down once again. He hoped she wouldn't be around if it came to that but he couldn't let his feelings for Abigail detract from what he had to do.

If Tom Bainbridge led Cahoon's men in an attack on the town, he wouldn't hesitate in taking him down. He would deal with Abigail's emotions, after the fact. Any attempt to avoid that now would cloud his judgment and he had to be focused and determined in his duty. This would be the last stand, of Cahoon and his men, he'd see to that.

He didn't know how Cahoon would stage his raid but to Ernie it didn't matter. He was no stranger to surprises, that's how these things come. No one tells you their plans, it falls on you to figure it out and not get killed in the process. This was nothing new, Ernie had been here before. It made him think of a job he did for Mr. Murphy a year or so back, where he'd been faced with the unexpected.

It was his second train ride, this time heading east, back to Missouri and Benton County. It was a shorter ride than New Mexico but he still became restless, cooped up in a train car. The train left Abilene that morning, bound for Jackson Missouri, then changed tracks to Lafayette and the south spur to Benton. Again, it was easier than riding a horse for the five-hundred-mile journey and the time he saved, made the train a smarter choice.

Keeping with his normal pattern, Ernie first found a livery stable and rented a feisty little bay, about five years old and sixteen hands. The owner said she was the fastest horse he had but most folks were a little shy of her. That suited Ernie just fine. He could handle her and a fast horse, was what he needed. From there, he paid his usual quick visit to the town marshal, to set the stage for his visit to the Finney Ranch.

Anderson Finney, had sold a herd through the KCBA, a few weeks back. He apparently left with sixteen hundred dollars of Murphy's money, that he wasn't owed. When the herd was inventoried, they found fifty-two head, with a different brand. The owner of that brand had reported his herd short, by approximately that number. A subsequent check throughout the stockyard found them in Finney's stock. No one could figure how he'd done it, or if he even knew, with all the commotion of the thousands of cattle, milling in the area.

Nevertheless, they were there, with the rightful owner, now reclaiming his property. At the very least, Finney would have known if his herd tallied out, with fifty-two more cows than he drove in. He didn't say a word. There was no doubt, that he would have made a fuss, if his herd had turned up light, by that number. Stolen or not, he had to know. As was his responsibility, Ernie headed out to make things right.

He arrived at the ranch around 10:00, on that warm Thursday morning in May. It wasn't a large spread but it was well laid out. A large pasture of sweet grass was to the east, spotted with cattle grazing in the distance. To the north, as he looked between two barns, Ernie could see a windmill, spinning in the light breeze, surrounded by a number of cattle milling around the trough.

There was no one about, when he reined up in front of the house. It seemed mighty strange, for a working ranch to be so quiet, this time of day. Ernie dismounted and called out. "Hello! Is anyone around!" but he heard no reply. He pulled his Winchester from the scabbard and slowly walked toward the barns. There was still no sign of life. The only sound he heard at the time was a squeaking barn door. It would open a few inches in the breeze, then close with a light thud. He continued to look for any sign of activity but to no avail.

He could understand if the rancher and his wife were gone for the day. But for there to be no hint, of even one ranch hand, made him think there may have been foul play. He turned and walked in the direction of the house. Slowly, he scoped out every angle around the barns, the sides of the house and even the outhouse, which was set back a ways between the two. Still, the only sounds he heard were the distant squeaking of the barn door and the rocks crunching under his boots.

As he approached the far side of the house, he began to hear voices. Slowly he walked to the sound, where he saw one man behind the house, about to saddle up. The man holding the reins appeared to be a ranch hand, from the dirty chaps and spurs. He was obviously startled by Ernie's sudden appearance. As he walked in closer, it became obvious the man didn't belong there. He made several additional steps, with the intention of calling to him, once he came a bit closer, then suddenly wished he'd done so sooner. At the back corner of the house, Ernie heard three clicks, of a cocking revolver, just as he saw the pistol being pressed into the side of his face.

"You're in the wrong place, Mister." The man said.

Ernie stopped and raised his hands, as he released the hold he had on the Winchester.

"Careful with that thing," Ernie began, "I ain't here to hurt nobody."

"You're right you ain't. Now unbuckle that gun belt and just let it fall." The man said.

Ernie still hadn't seen his face but his voice sounded as young, as the cow hand standing just a few feet away. Slowly, he lowered his left hand and released the buckle on his cartridge belt, dropping it in the dirt.

"Satisfied? Can I turn around now?" Ernie asked.

"Slow, Mister. What do you want here?"

"I came to see Mr. Finney but I ain't expected to get myself shot over it." Ernie replied.

The man had now backed off a step, with his Colt aimed at Ernie's face. The two men stood for a moment, each studying the other. This young man was no match for Ernie Evans. He should have backed off an additional step, out of arms reach. Suddenly, Ernie made a side step, away from the Colt and reached for the man's right wrist. Twisting his arm behind the man's back, Ernie was now behind him and relieved him of his sidearm. The man at the horse quickly drew his pistol and franticly fired at Ernie, driving his round deep into his partner's gut. Ernie instantly returned fire, hitting the man center mass, sending him back several feet. He was dead when he hit the ground.

Ernie dropped the man, who he now held around the neck and quickly made his way to the shooter. His body was now on the ground, with both eyes open and no sign of life. Ernie picked up the pistol and walked back to his gun belt and Winchester. First putting his cartridge belt back in place, he then slid the extra revolver in his waistband. He thought for a moment, then walked back to the front door of the house and knocked as he called out but again heard no reply. From there, he walked to the back of the house, where the door was ajar. Ernie quickly drew his sidearm and walked in, this time keeping his presence quiet.

He entered through a small pantry, which lead to the kitchen, where he heard the sounds of a woman's cry, through the doorway. With his sidearm in position, he made his way through the door. Slowly, he walked down a short hallway, leading to the parlor, where he saw what he'd hoped to avoid. Mrs. Finney was tied and placed against the wall. Mr. Finney wasn't as fortunate. He was also tied but lying on the floor and bleeding badly. He'd been shot in the left side. The gunshot itself wasn't life threatening but the amount of blood he was losing could have been. If Ernie hadn't come by when he did, Mr. Finney would very likely have bled to death, there on the floor in front of his wife.

Ernie quickly tended to the rancher and packed the open wound with a white lace doily, which he'd spotted on a table under the lamp. He untied Mrs. Finney and the rancher and tried to calm her enough, to get some kind of story. Finally, she re-gained her wits and told him they'd been robbed by two men they'd hired a week earlier. She'd also heard gun shots at the barn, before they entered the house.Mr. Finney was now speaking and seemed to come out of the shock enough to sit up on his own, though he was in pain.

"They came in the front door and told me to give them everything I had in the safe. I wasn't going to argue with them, my gun was in the other room. I figured they'd leave with what they had but the bastards shot me anyway." Finney was breathing heavily as he spoke but had the presence of mind to ask Ernie about the shots out back.

"They ain't going nowhere." Ernie replied, to calm the man.

"Go check the barn, Mister, we heard shots out there. I was going to get my gun when the first one came through the door and got between me and it. Please, go see what's out there." Finney asked.

Ernie left Mrs. Finney, to tend to her husband. He quickly walked out back to retrieve his Winchester then made his way to the barn. Entering the open door, which he'd heard squeaking earlier, Ernie saw the bodies of three men, lying in the straw. All with their guns still holstered. They'd obviously been surprised by men they knew and gunned down before either of them could clear leather. He looked around to see if there were others but they seemed to be all there were. He left them where they lay, for the marshal to see then walked to the other barn, where he found nothing suspicious.

He hated this. He'd come here to collect money and then walked into this mess. Now he had to tell those folks, their ranch hands were dead.

When he walked in, Mr. Finney was sitting in a chair with a glass of water, as Mrs. Finney stood by his side.

"Mr. Finney… Ma'am," Ernie began as he removed his hat, "I hate to tell you but your three ranch hands are dead."

Mrs. Finney began to cry, as Mr. Finney hung his head.

"One of those boys is our son." He said in a trembling voice.

Ernie felt such sadness for these folks. He was glad he'd arrived when he did but wished he could have shown up earlier. Maybe I could have saved those young men, he thought. It wasn't what he'd expected when he left Abilene. His job was rife with uncertainty but this was a first. Too often, in this job he'd end up taking a man life, this time he had saved a man's life.

They sat quietly for a moment, as the reality of their loss began to take hold. Ernie stood silently in respect and not knowing what would be proper to say. Mr. Finney eventually looked up and said; "They stole all our money too."

"They may have tried, Mr. Finney but those horses and saddlebags are still out back, with whatever they put in them." Ernie replied.

Without hesitation, Ernie left the room and made his way out to the horses. In the saddlebags, he found a number of items they'd attempted to steal. Among them, was a small canvas bag, holding a stack of money, tied in twine. He thought of the money he'd come to collect and now realized the rancher had enough here to settle up. But he wasn't sure he had the heart to push him over it. When he walked back in, with the saddlebags and their contents, the Finney's were grateful. Mr. Finney looked to Ernie, as the man who'd exacted justice, though it couldn't save his son. It was only then, that he gave Ernie a long gaze and realized he was a stranger.

"Mister, I don't reckon I know you. How is it you came along when you did?" He asked.

"No sir, you don't know me. My name is Ernie Evans. I came from Abilene, to talk to you about that herd you drove in a month or so back. But I think we ought to do that another time." Ernie replied.

"What about the herd?" Finney asked.

"It seems you were paid on a lot more cows than you drove in, Mr. Finney. But we can talk about it later." Ernie suggested.

"No, I think it's best if we talk about it now." Finney replied.

"Well, if you insist, sir. They found fifty head, there about, in your herd that weren't yours, after you'd been paid for them. I have the papers. They were from another rancher's stock, who'd reported them missing, right after you left. They have a lot of questions, as to how they got there but I think the whole thing will go away, after you settle up. But that ain't got to be today." Ernie concluded.

"How much did it come to?" Finney asked.

"The difference comes to, sixteen hundred dollars, you owe back to the buyer." Ernie answered.

"I figured," Mr. Finney began, "I ain't stole them cows. But when they ended up with mine, I ain't said nothing either. I knew it wasn't right but we needed the money. I considered it a loan, at least 'til I was told I had to give it back." He confessed. "I never thought the man who'd come for it, would save my life." He concluded, as he hung his head. He was ashamed but the thought of his boy hadn't left his mind.

"Never mind that right now," Ernie replied. "I'm going into town to fetch the doc and the marshal, before this gets to bleeding again. He's going to have to get that bullet out of there. Now you folks sit tight, 'til I get back. We'll talk about that other thing later."

"Hand me that saddlebag." Mr. Finney asked. Ernie slowly passed him the buckskin leather bag then backed away as Mrs. Finney stepped in to help him, with whatever he was doing. He scrounged around in the bag for a moment, until he came out with the white canvas bag, holding the money. He looked to Ernie and extended his hand, "Here, there should be twenty-eight hundred dollars in here, you take it. It's all yours." He said.

"I can't do that, Mr. Finney."

"You must, I owe you that and much more. I have to get this off my conscience and you are the only man who can help me do that." Finney remarked.

Ernie was quite surprised but he could see the rancher was attempting to clear his soul, should things turn worse before he returned with the doctor. To oblige his confession, Ernie took the money, with the intention of returning the difference.

When he returned with the doc and the marshal, Mrs. Finney had moved her husband to a small downstairs bedroom in back of the house. Although he could walk, she wouldn't take a chance on moving him to their room upstairs, for fear of reopening the wound. The doctor tended to Mr. Finney, as Ernie and the marshal walked out to the barn with the gruesome task of recovering the bodies.

Ernie hitched a wagon and backed it to the barn door. The marshal was careful that the Finney's wouldn't see their son, as they placed him in back. Once finished, they covered the bodies and made their way to the back of the house, where the bad guys lay. The marshal studied the scene for a bit and where the bodies had fallen and then turned to Ernie.

"You did this alone?" He asked.

"Yes sir." Ernie replied.

"You must be pretty fast." He replied.

"No, just lucky I guess."

The marshal looked at Ernie for a moment, with an inquisitive grin, then replied; "I'd say luck had nothing to do with it." Ernie offered no words, just pushed his hat back a bit, with a smile.

They completed the unwanted task of loading the remaining bodies into the wagon, as Ernie checked their pockets, looking for a name, or some sort of identification. He found none, which didn't worry the marshal. He'd ask Mr. Finney, in the slim chance that they'd given him their right names. Then for whatever else he could offer. He'd put out a wire for anything else he could find.

Ernie didn't stay long after that. He spent a few minutes with the Finney's and talked him into taking back the balance of the money. Mrs. Finney tried to talk him into staying for a while, which he declined. He felt that he'd done something good, where his purpose in being there, could have turned out very different. It was one of the rare times, in Ernie's life, when his heart had any influence over his actions.

-

Now, once again, he sat facing the unexpected. But Ernie knew this situation was coming to him with more than a wounded rancher and two young men, who barely knew one end of a gun, from the other. He'd known his adversaries since they were kids and he knew their ways. He knew their strengths and weaknesses and he knew he was faster than both of them. He also knew they were sneaky, with no sense for a straight up fight.

He'd never had a beef with Clayton but Tom Bainbridge was out to settle a score and that made it personal. He'll be rattled from the start, Ernie thought. Anger foils a cool hand and curses a man's draw. That was for sure. This could give him the edge but they would need to be face to face, for that to play out. Ernie knew if Tom still harbored revenge, he was dead already. For its hatred that kills a man, not the bullet.

CHAPTER 15

The mid October mornings were much cooler than Ernie's first days in Maple Ridge, back in August. He was also finding the air to be brisker than Kansas, this time of year, which he attributed to the altitude. But he surely didn't miss the constant winds blowing across the Kansas prairie. He wondered how Bruiser would adjust to the change, once he arrived. Hopefully, he would be on the train, scheduled to pull in around 2:30 the next day. It had taken Ernie a while to adjust to the thin air, of the mile-high altitude and it would be no different for Bruiser. He'd become easily winded at first but his lungs would soon adjust, to the lower presence of oxygen. With each breath, they would soon learn to retain what they required and normal activities would no longer wear him down. Ernie had certainly adapted; he knew Bruiser would as well.

Marshal Smith and Deputy Wilcox spent most of the morning rounding up the ranchers and store owners, who'd ridden with the posse back in August. They were asking the men to meet up at the marshal's office at 6:30 that evening. Back in August, their strategy meeting had been held at 9:00 pm. Most of the ranchers and farmers couldn't afford to give up daylight, making an earlier meeting too costly. Now with the shorter days, a gathering at an earlier hour was more suitable for all. The marshal needed to fill them in on what was happening. He hoped to encourage them once again, to stay close to town. These men had proved their ability and the marshal was now calling on their gun, for a second time.

The townsfolk had become less afraid of Cahoon over the past two months. His men hadn't come around as much. With nine of his harder surrogates in jail, folks were beginning to relax a bit. They were now asking for cash for their orders, from the mercantile, to the cafés. This new rule had been initiated by Bobby Grayson, then one by one, each merchant in town followed suit. They were tired of losing money over Cahoon's demands. Other folks could have used those supplies and paid for them. Their determination was proof that the townsfolk were ready to stand on their own. Their orders became smaller but they paid. It was apparent that Cahoon was sending the 'big-rig' to Cimarron, for the larger needs of the ranch. But remarkably enough, business owners in town discovered they could live without it.

The marshal had seen a surprising change in the attitudes of the store owners and townsfolk in general. He'd always said it began with Ernie's arrival in town, or perhaps more accurately, it began with Gregory McElliott's departure. Ernie had shown that Cahoon's men could be beaten, though he'd gotten himself shot for it. Over that same period, the folks had realized they could live without his commerce. There was little reason to bow to his demands any longer.

The marshal, once again, needed the help of folks like Bobby Grayson, JT Belcher and Ralph Thomas. He was turning to a select few and wanted to keep the majority of the town out of the fray. Most weren't qualified and he didn't like the idea of everyone in town getting involved in some free for all. Good people can get trigger happy in the moment and it becomes hard to hold those involved accountable. You can't prosecute a mob.

Vigilance was Marshal Smith's priority and he had a plan. There were now eight ranchers, three merchants and three lawmen watching every move. Fourteen men covering the town was something the marshal had never seen. He hoped to hear from Henry soon, to get a bead on what he was seeing at the ranch. But for now, the town was covered. Others, like Mr. Dawson at the Dry Goods Store, were keeping a constant eye on the town. The marshal needed their help but had asked for him and Shorty Williams to stay out of the fight. Shorty was pushing to get in the thick of things. He had a lot of payback to rein down on these people. They owed him big time. He'd put up with their abuse and disrespect all his life and the thought of drawing down on one of those bastards, would make it all square. The marshal had managed to talk him out of it for now but he wasn't sure how long that would hold.

He'd provided very little information to Mayor Sterns. He'd told him of the looming threat and included him in his plan to protect the town. But thus far, he'd said nothing about what he knew of Cahoon's intentions. He had become much more assertive of late but if Mayor EJ Sterns knew he was a target of anyone, much less Cahoon, he'd be out of sight for days. Marshal Smith couldn't let that happen. His routine had to be as normal as any other day. Townsfolk, as well as the mayor, had to stay with their routines and carry on without interruption. Ernie had an eye on the mayor, as did JT Belcher. JT's café was the closest to the mayor's office. He could see everything moving in that direction, from the north anyway. Michael King was occupying his usual boardwalk benches and had instruction to watch for "anything Cahoon" that might come into town from the south.

Ernie expected Bainbridge would ride in at any time, he had to. It was a strange place and he had to learn the layout. If not, he couldn't maneuver through the town. There would be no place to hide, no short cuts, no quick corners, nothing. No, he'd be here soon enough, he really had no choice. This at least, would play to Ernie's favor. He hadn't seen Tom in ten years and a quick glance might miss him in the midst of Cahoon's other men. Regardless of the others, Tom Bainbridge would be the shooter and Ernie had to be quick enough to pick him out of the herd. A good look at an older Bainbridge was important and Ernie was hoping to gain an edge.

Again, Abigail came to mind. She had to stay out of this, for her own good. For now, he'd convinced her to stay close to the Doc and Jacob Street during the day. Ernie was still concerned about her reaction, if she saw him. In her mind, he didn't exist. Ernie knew she believed it but he was certain that would come crashing down, if she came face to face with her father. He's blood and that's a very powerful force.

He picked her up each afternoon, which had become their daily ritual. They would walk to supper, at the dining establishment of her choice, usually on Grayson Street, with her favorite being the Cattlemen's Diner. It seemed that one held some special memories for Miss Abigail. Ernie stayed close; he was certain the next few days could change their lives forever.

Henry was pulling straw into one of the stables when Mrs. Cahoon walked into the barn. He saw her slowly looking around but hadn't yet called out. He stepped out, where she could see him and had the presence of thought to take her lead and not to speak. When she saw him, she placed her index finger vertically across her lips and slowly shook her head, side to side. Henry didn't make a sound, only walked up closer to her.

"Keep your voice low, Henry. I'm sure they have been watching me and he's been reluctant to let me out of his sight." She said in a low, shaky voice.

"Are you okay?" Henry asked.

"I'm okay, he hasn't been drinking or anything, it's just that he won't let me out of his sight. I told him I wanted to come out to see Lillie. I'm surprised he didn't come with me." She replied.

"Have you overheard anything, that maybe he thinks, you shouldn't have? I mean, that you are aware of?" Henry asked.

"Yeah, he and Tom were talking last night but I couldn't make out most of it. I acted like I wasn't listening but I distinctly heard Wednesday for something. That's when he looked at me funny and he ain't been out of my sight since. I guess he let me come out here so they could talk more, without the chance of being overheard. If I stay too long, I'll bet he comes after me." She concluded.

"Don't look now but here he comes." Henry warned.

"I can't let him see me, talking to you." She said in a frantic voice.

"Sure, you can." Henry replied, as he stepped over to Lillie's stall and brought her out with a rope halter and lead line. He leaned down and picked up her right rear hoof and began explaining the wear on her shoe, just as Larry Cahoon walked in the door. She tried to appear startled, as he walked up.

"Oh… Hi Dear. Henry thinks Lillie should be shod soon; he was showing me the wear." She said.

"Good morning, Mr. Cahoon. How are you, sir?" Henry said with a smile.

"You're Henry, aren't you?" He asked.

"Yes sir. I don't think you and I have ever actually met."

"So, you think Lillie needs to be shod?" Cahoon asked.

"Yes sir. I was showing Mrs. Cahoon and asking her permission."

"That's good thinking, Henry. Why don't you take her over to the other barn and have Buck make a set to fit her? "Cahoon suggested.

"Yes sir, right away." Henry replied, as he began to lead the bay out of the stable and toward the north barn. As he walked away, he heard Cahoon say; "Come darling, join me for coffee on the porch." Henry didn't look back but heard her reply;

"That would be delightful."

Henry was convinced that Cahoon would ride in with seven men. Once again, he would make a stand against the town. Now it was looking like Wednesday could be it. That was two days away but yet unconfirmed. He hadn't seen Tom Bainbridge or Clayton Emerson since the day before. That's when they came in after a long ride to the west, with what appeared to be the strength of his posse. He'd only seen a couple of those men since, which made him wonder where the others had gone.

He would stay around the ranch for the day, especially now that shoeing Lillie had become his most important task. He was also watching the house rather closely, with the possibility of Cahoon becoming a little paranoid, over his wife's intuitiveness. He'd make it to town sometime after sunset, he thought. This should give the marshal ample time to have his men in town and in place, before Cahoon showed his hand. Until then, he'd keep an eye open, for whatever might turn up.

The balance of the day was quiet. The only thing of interest was the return of Tom Bainbridge and Clayton Emerson, along with three other men. They'd come riding in from the north, just before sunset. That didn't really mean much. They could easily have been in Maple Ridge, getting a good look around. The north road out of town had a trail to the west. It ran about a mile out and then tied back to another trail, which ran from the ranch to the Cimarron road.

They would very likely have taken that route to avoid anyone of consequence, who they might pass on the shorter trail. He watched for a while from the stable as they reined up in front of the big barn. They talked there a bit longer, before pulling their saddles and gear and then walked the horses inside. He didn't see them again for a while. Henry figured they were tending to the horses and still talking about wherever they'd been. When they came out, the three men walked to the bunkhouse, while Bainbridge and Emerson went to the house, no doubt to confer with Cahoon over their plans.

The men gathered at the barn at the end of the day, stowing their gear and ready to chow down. Henry asked if anyone wanted to ride into town for a beer but there were no takers at the moment. He knew they were tired and more interested in grub at the time. As he suspected, they had little interest in his offer. He saddled up, drawing no attention from the other men and rode off alone in the direction of Maple Ridge. He rode in on Jacob Street, to avoid whoever might be milling around Grayson. He tied his horse on Third, next to the Early Bird Café. Henry walked to the corner of Grayson and looked around for a bit. He didn't recognize anyone on the street but chose to be cautious. Finally adjusting his hat low over his forehead, he sauntered across the street to the marshal's office.

When Henry walked in, Marshal Smith, Ernie Evans and Bobby Grayson were there talking over coffee. The percolator was brewing over the roaring fire, in the potbelly stove. Henry quickly poured a cup to warm himself from the cold ride.

"Evening Henry, cold out there, ain't it?" The marshal asked.

"Evening Marshal, gentleman, yeah it is cold. I ain't used to it yet." He said.

"Well, you'll have plenty of time between now and spring to get your bones adjusted." Marshal Smith said, with a laugh.

"So, what's happening out there, Henry?" Ernie asked. The laughter seemed to come and go, rather quickly.

"I think it's going to be Wednesday," Henry began, as he took his first sip. "Mrs. Cahoon heard them talking last night. She heard them say something about Wednesday. That's only two days away. I think it's going to be seven of them, plus Cahoon, eight total. I saw five other men with Bainbridge and Emerson over the last couple of days. Five of them rode out this morning and didn't come back 'til near dark. Bainbridge, Emerson, Jim Holden, Seth Leonard and one other, that I didn't know. The other two rode off with the guys working the west pasture this morning and came back with them. You ain't seen any strangers around town today, have you?" Henry asked.

Ernie thought for a moment, before he replied; "No, I ain't seen 'um. If they've been here, they were quiet about it."

"Are you sure its seven, Henry?" The marshal asked.

"Yes sir, I've seen them together, talking a couple of times. They all rode off to the north yesterday. I figured they needed to talk, where nobody could hear 'um. I ain't seen nobody else around them but they been sticking real close." Henry answered.

"That's a small number, for a daylight raid." The marshal replied.

"It ain't going to be no raid." Ernie replied. "They are going to use an old guerilla tactic. They are going hit their targets independent of each other and try to cause chaos. Of course, that only works when it's a surprise, that's what they're depending on." Ernie said.

"Yeah, that's what I figured, that's why I kept a close eye on their numbers." Henry replied.

"Henry, you've been more help than you know." The marshal replied. He was amazed at this young man's ability and began to think he'd been a gift from God.

"What else have you seen, Henry. Is Mrs. Cahoon okay?" Bobby asked.

"That's about it, sir. Mrs. Cahoon is fine. She's a tough lady, Mr. Grayson."

"Henry, call me Bobby. You're earned the respect to call me by my first name." Bobby replied.

"Yeah, that goes for me as well," Ernie added.

For Marshal Smith, his position deserved the respect of his title and didn't offer the same gesture.

"I guess a time would be a little much to ask for, Henry?" Ernie asked, in a halfhearted manner.

"I don't know what time," Henry began, "you can bet it will be early but after everyone is in town, where a stranger can find them." He concluded.

"I think you're right, young man," the marshal replied. "I'd say you've given us exactly what we need. I'm really proud of you, Henry."

"Thank you, Marshal. I just want to see you get these guys. That's all the thanks I need."

Tuesday was a busy day in Maple Ridge. Marshal Smith sent Wilcox to each of the ranchers who'd agreed to help out, asking them to come to town as soon as possible. Ernie had gathered Bobby Grayson, Ralph Thomas and JT Belcher for a meeting. He needed to be sure everyone was together on this thing. He had to tell Abigail. He hadn't said anything the night before. There seemed to be no purpose in it and she would only worry. But as it drew closer, he needed her to know. He also needed to convince her to stay at Doc Rowe's on Wednesday and not venture over to Grayson, for any reason.

Ernie wondered if they'd been in town on Monday. He'd tried to keep a close eye on everything that moved but Bainbridge could have slipped around without being seen. He'd learned that tactic as a bushwhacker and Ernie knew he was good at it.If he had, he would have gotten a good look at the town, enough to know his way around, if he wanted to hide. He may have gotten a good look at an older Ernie as well. That was something he wanted to avoid. He had hoped to spot him first, now it looked like Tom Bainbridge could have gained that edge.

Fact is, they had been in town that day. Both men wore their hats low, over their face, with their coat collars turned up. It was a cold day and they didn't stand out in the least. Many folks in town had done the same on Monday. They would have blended in without notice. They'd stayed off Grayson Street, where Ernie had spent most of his day. The men walked to the quieter streets, Jacob and Fredrick and then cut through the side streets, to get a good look at Grayson. Tom had looked for Ernie. He saw a couple of men with a similar favor but was never sure if one of them might have been him.

They stayed for about three hours. They never stood in one spot too long and walking the length of the streets and the side streets, without drawing anyone's attention. Both men got a good layout of the town, which they didn't see as any different than most. Lots of cover and a number of places to slip out if it got hot. They were comfortable with what they saw and had the confidence to go back and pull this off, not expecting they would lose even one man.

They were depending on the element of surprise. The surprise they hadn't figured on was Henry. He'd figured them out in plain sight, with their best effort to keep it all quiet. His movements in and out of town had drawn no one's attention. He'd even come in with others, who had no idea of what he was doing. There was nothing suspicious about Henry. He was a young ranch hand, who took care of the horses and put up with the older guys ribbing on him for fun, from time to time. No one could have appeared to be more innocent.

CHAPTER 16

Wednesday morning was cold and gray with a chilling wind that whistled through the streets and around every corner. Folks seemed to be taking their time stirring about, waiting for the sun to warm things a bit. But the heavy clouds were hindering any rise in temperature that may have offered. The streets were eerie quiet, almost abandoned. When Ernie turned from Second Street, onto Grayson, it seemed ghostly but it was early yet. He anticipated the patrons of this normally peaceful street would soon witness a chain of events they weren't expecting, when they arrived.

It would be an anxious morning, for the men who knew what was coming. Marshal Smith hadn't made a big to-do and kept his expectations for the day amongst the select few. It was imperative to keep the town's goings-on, moving on as usual. Abigail was nervous and afraid for Ernie and the other men who risked their lives to protect the town. Still, she held out that her father was gone from her life. She'd reassured Ernie that she was there for him, no matter the outcome. He knew she was sincere but felt a sense of concern for her unavoidable stir of emotions after the fact. He made her promise to stay inside Doc Rowe's house, until he came for her. Grayson Street was no place for her today and he didn't need that distraction, while his focus needed to be sharp.

Marshal Smith made his presence known on Grayson Street, at 7:30. A few folks were stirring about but the street was still rather quite for a Wednesday morning. The Early Bird Café had been open for an hour, with a number of patrons there adjusting to the cold and trying to get motivated. In the quiet, he could hear the distant clanging of an anvil at the blacksmith shop on Fredrick Street. They too, had been busy for a while but had no idea of what might be heading their way. He didn't anticipate the coming fight to spill over to that side and expected it would likely be concentrated on Grayson.

Marshal Smith's first concern was for Mayor Sterns. Ralph Thomas would provide him cover and the marshal wanted him inside and out of sight as quickly as possible. He'd walked down Grayson from Third Street, where he saw Ernie standing a block away. They noticed one another and nodded, just as Ralph walked up, having come from the corral, on Fredrick Street. Others were now beginning to stir, as a few store owners were opening their doors. That included Bobby Grayson, who was placing merchandise on the boardwalk just outside the doors and under the windows. With the exception of Bobby, none of those who'd arrived, thus far, had any knowledge of what was coming. For Marshal Smith, it had to be that way.

There was still no certainty that Cahoon's plan would come to fruition today. But vigilance was the only safe measure in being prepared. Henry hadn't seen anything that stood out on Tuesday. He'd come in late in the evening, to check in with the marshal but had nothing new that would be helpful. He'd seen the same seven men together, once that day. It seemed to be a rather short exchange of words, with the five ranch hands then going about their duties for the balance of the day. It may have served to reiterate their number of men but they'd settled on that the day before and made their plans accordingly.

Henry's plan for Wednesday morning was to stay close to the stable, where he could watch the house. His horse would be saddled early, keeping him in the stable and out of sight. He'd be ready to mount up, should he see Cahoon and his men ride out together. He would take the shorter route to town, through the pinion pines, then over the hill and come out on the back side of Jacob Street. If he was successful, he'd beat them by as much as twenty minutes. Marshal Smith was hoping Henry could give them an early warning but he wasn't relying on the edge that would provide. He had to be ready to move with the information they had.

Each of the ranchers showed up as expected. The first arrived just after 8:00 am, with all of them in town by 8:30. They tied up at Ralph's as planned and left their horses in the back corral. Once they'd made their way to Grayson Street, Marshal Smith called them all together. With one last check on ammo and final instructions, every man was ready. They were confident that time was on their side. Cahoon would need the town to be in full bloom, when he rode in. Whether that would be in plain sight, or by some surprise attack, was yet to be seen. But either way, he would wait until the town was open for business, to make his move.

Ernie walked Abigail to Dr. Rowe's early. It had become their ritual but he especially didn't want her walking alone today. He gave her some basic information about his plans for the day. And again, instructed her to stay in the house until he returned. He offered the same request to Dr. Rowe and asked him to be ready should one of the townsfolk come for his services.

Mayor Sterns rounded the corner of Fourth Street at 8:45 heading to his office with plans for a busy day. He was startled as he approached the building. Ralph, Ernie and Marshal Smith were waiting next to his door when he arrived and followed him into the office. The mayor was concerned when he was asked to take a seat. The marshal had intentionally kept him out of it and he didn't know what was coming. Marshal Smith was becoming accustomed to his new level of authority in town. His work or arrest activity hadn't been mentioned by EJ for more than two months now and at this moment, he was feeling a sense of authority over the mayor.

"What's going on here?" The mayor asked, as he took a seat in his black leather chair.

"Look, Mayor. Here's the deal. We're quite sure that Cahoon and his men are planning to hit town today." The marshal reported.

"How could you know that?" The mayor asked, as he now leaned forward, somewhat surprised.

"I have a man who works at the ranch giving me information." The marshal proudly replied.

"How did you pull that off?"

"By doing my job." The marshal replied, as small swipe at the mayor. The mayor paused a bit. He got the jab but chose not to reply.

"We don't want you to be alarmed but I think he's coming after you, as well as a few others, including Ernie and me." The marshal replied.

The mayor didn't seem shaken. It amused the marshal, when compared to his reaction only a few weeks earlier.

"Ralph is going to stay here and tuck away in back, to keep an eye on things. JT is at the Café, watching from that angle."

"Do you think I should go home?" The mayor asked.

"No, we want to catch these guys. If you're not here they'll turn back."

"I see." The mayor began, "So I'm like bait on a hook, here."

"Yeah, something like that." The marshal replied.

He sat for a moment in thought, then rose to his feet and walked to the sideboard, next to the wall near his desk. He opened the top drawer and revealed a nickel plated .41cal. Colt Thunderer. He laid it on his desk, next to the ink well then retook his seat without words.

"Where'd you get that?" The marshal asked in amazement.

"I've had it since the day I took this job." He replied.

"Why didn't I know about that?" The marshal asked.

"Cause it ain't none of your business." The mayor replied, returning the marshal's earlier jab.

"Well, you got me there." The marshal said, with a smile.

He was surprised by the mayor's calm demeanor. He too, had come a long way in the past two months. It made the marshal think he should have let him in on the plans sooner.

Ralph stayed behind with the mayor, as he stoked the fire. Ernie and Marshal Smith left, to shore up the rest of their plan. There would be men tucked around each corner, in the back of the Mercantile and near Dawson's Dry Goods. Each man waiting, much like the day Cahoon's men tried to take on the "Lawmen from Abilene". Ernie instructed Wilcox to watch the edge of town, up past the tracks. There, he would wait for men tying horses on the outskirts of town. Most of the ranchers were on that end of town. They had a good view of the tracks and platform and ready for a final stand with Cahoon. Most thought the incident in August would have been enough but he kept coming back. Since then, his aura had died and he no longer projected any dominance over the town. He'd become a nuisance really but his self-importance hadn't waivered.

Henry was at the stable early on Wednesday, with his horse saddled and ready to ride. He saw a number of men gather around the big barn about 7:00 am, which wasn't unusual. But they weren't dressed to ride the range. It was cold and the men who were riding the lines this time of year, would bundle up tight before they mounted up. He hadn't yet seen Cahoon and it wouldn't be until he showed up, that Henry could be sure.

He stayed close and walked Lillie out into the pasture toward the barn. Henry stopped occasionally and lifting a hoof to check the new shoes. He never looked their way but hoped he might get within ear shot of their conversation. The gusts of wind were quite strong at times, enough that Henry's hat was holding on by its chin strap. Any opportunity of hearing something of importance was futile. His only chance of confirming their intent was by their movements. He walked away to avoid suspicion, then turned and lead Lillie back to the stable.

Mr. Cahoon hadn't said much at breakfast and seemed rather preoccupied. Mrs. Cahoon expected as much and began to watch him very closely. She continued to make the usual small talk but knew he wasn't listening. It's today, she thought, it must be. She considered going out to the barn to find Henry but quickly dismissed that as too dangerous. Henry kept an eye on the house, expecting Cahoon would join his men. But it was still early, just past 7:30.It would be a while yet before they would show their hand. Henry didn't expect they would saddle up before 9:00. He had to be patient and Mrs. Cahoon had to act normal. If either of them jumped too quickly, the whole thing could be blown.

Cahoon left the kitchen without words then walked upstairs. Mrs. Cahoon walked to the door and pulled back the curtain, hoping to see Henry but he wasn't in sight. She stayed back, not wanting to be around her husband just now and began to feel a growing sense of anger. She began to think of what might be coming and without guilt, hoped he would be the first to go down. The next hour passed slowly but eventually, Cahoon emerged, dressed in his finest.

"I'm going out for a wee bit." He said to Mrs. Cahoon, with a smile.

"Where are you going?" She asked, hoping the nervousness in her stomach wasn't apparent in her voice.

"Oh, just to town for a bit. I'll be back by lunch." He answered. She rather hoped not but smiled and simply replied;

"Okay."

When Cahoon walked toward the barn, in his black suit, white shirt and red tie, Henry knew this was it. His heart raced a bit in anticipation but he held his cool and went about his business. Cahoon walked to the stable and called out; "Henry!"

Henry's heart stopped, as he looked up to see him at the door. He took a deep breath and slowly walked in Cahoon's direction.

"Good morning, Mr. Cahoon. How are you today, sir?" Henry asked.

"I'm fine, Henry. Saddle my horse. I will be riding out for a wee bit." He requested.

"Yes sir, right away," Henry replied. His heart slowed a bit, he hadn't initially known what to expect. He saddled Cahoon's black stallion and led him to the front and out the door, where Cahoon was waiting.

"Here you are, sir." Henry began, "going for a ride on this cold morning?"

"Yep, I'm going for a ride." He replied, then looked to Henry, with a sarcastic grin.

Henry watched, as Cahoon walked the horse out to the big barn, where the others were standing inside the doorway, out of the cold. He walked inside, with the seven others following him and closing the door behind them. Henry stood inside the stable but still within view of the barn and the three saddled horses tied in front. He looked around, to see who else might be about, then looked toward the house. As his eyes scanned the front, he looked to an upstairs window, where Mrs. Cahoon was standing. Once he'd turned, full face in her direction, she looked to him and nodded several times, then walked away. He was certain before but now there was no doubt. This was it.

Marshal Smith had Grayson Street covered, from the train station, to the corner of Fifth Street. The Calvin Hotel stood on that corner and marked the end of the business district. He had one rancher on each corner. Ralph Thomas was watching the mayor, with JT Belcher at the Café, watching the mayor's office from the north. From where he stood, JT also had a clear view of the street, up to Second from the south. The marshal had given Mr. Dawson and Shorty a run down on what he expected. He didn't think the Dry Goods Store would be a target this time. As a precaution, two men stayed close and covered their back. That would be of no benefit to Cahoon this time but he couldn't leave them unprotected.

His instincts were warning him that Shorty could be somewhat unpredictable and cautioned Mr. Dawson to keep an eye on him. Shorty had talked about getting even with Cahoon's men, since the townsfolk began to stand up to them. He'd been pushed around and made fun of for longer than he could remember and he was sick of it. Marshal Smith felt somewhat responsible. He hadn't been allowed to do his job and Shorty had been an easy target, with no one ever held accountable. He only hoped Shorty's good nature would prevail over the anger he must have felt toward them.

As the morning progressed, the sun began to break through the clouds, offering some relief from the gloom. The increase in temperature was a while longer in coming. But once the winds died down, the sun eventually made its mark. It was now 9:30 with the town bustling as normal. It was just what Cahoon would need to feed his ego and make his stand. Marshal Smith walked up on Ernie, as he stood near Second Street. From there he had a good view of Grayson, from the train platform, to the mayor's office.

He was chewing a straw, which seemed to be assisting his concentration, as his eyes scanned the street, with his hat pulled down low. Marshal Smith stood by for a few moments, just watching, without words. He was always amazed by Ernie Evans. His eyes were completely focused and his deportment was dead calm. He was a man devoid of emotion, without the knowledge of fear. He was prepared for the worst and Marshal Smith pitied any man in the sight of his Colt. He was glad Ernie was on their side, if not, they would be doomed.

Henry was waiting when the barn doors opened and the men emerged. Four men walked their horses out of the barn and saddled up, while the three untied their horses from the hitch rail and joined them. He looked to their saddles and confirmed a scabbard with a Winchester tied to each. As best he could tell, they all had sidearms, as did Cahoon, when he came to collect his horse. His stallion was tied to the first rail. Once the other men were in the saddle, he unhitched his mount and saddled up behind them, ready to ride.

They rode off to the north, as Henry would have guessed. If they had a plan for surprising the town, that would be their best move. They would ride up to the short trail, then over to the stage road and leave the horses, just to the north of town. Nothing else made sense, if they intended to stay out of sight. He waited until they were near the ridge then went to the stable, for his horse. When he came out, Mrs. Cahoon was standing at the barn door. She'd watched from the window, as the men mounted up and headed north.

"This is it, Henry," she said.

"Yes ma'am, it looks that way and I ain't got time to talk. If you'll excuse me, ma'am, I gotta go." By now, Henry was in the saddle and ready to rake fur, as he bid Mrs. Cahoon a polite good-bye.

Henry was certain the men were over the ridge and probably close to the short trail, by the time he saddled up. He spurred his horse and headed south, past the road and toward the stand of pinion pines. Cutting through the pines and over the ridge, he ran the distance of the arroyo, to the back side of town. Once there, he came out through the trees to the west of Jacob Street. The brush was thicker than he'd expected, which gave him and the horse a good work out. He caught a small limb in the face, about half way in. It burned like hell but he thought little of it after the next turn. When he reached town, he realized there was a streak of dried blood, which had run down his cheek but had no time to wipe it away.

He tied the horse on Jacob and walked up Second Street to Grayson, where he saw Ernie Evans standing, just a few feet down the boardwalk. Marshal Smith wasn't far away but closer to the mercantile, near a barrel of nails. He saw Henry, as he stepped up to Ernie and made a quick move in their direction. He knew why he was there and his presence alone was all that was necessary.

"What the hell happened to you?" Ernie asked.

Henry reached to his face, then pulled back his hand to see if there was any fresh blood. "I ran into a tree limb." Henry replied.

"Dumbass," Ernie replied with a grin, as they both laughed, easing the tension for a moment.

Marshal Smith soon stepped up and asked the obvious; "I guess this means they're coming," said the marshal.

"Yes sir, from the north. I think it will be another fifteen minutes or so." Henry replied.

"What the hell happened to your face?" The marshal inquired.

"Don't ask." Henry replied, as he looked to Ernie and grinned. Marshal Smith shook his head and walked away. He headed in the direction of three ranchers, he'd positioned on the Fredrick side of Grayson Street. He walked with them to the north side of the tracks, just past the station and in sight of the road leading into town. It was a good spot to see who was coming and going. And this morning, could give them a real edge, if Cahoon's crew was out in the open.

Ernie and the marshal needed to know where they were and how many but planned to give them time to show their hand. Marshal Smith couldn't arrest a man, simply for walking into town, even if he knew he had bad deeds in mind. They needed enough rope to make a move toward the mayor, or Grayson's Mercantile. They were obviously planning to stay out of sight. Marshal Smith and Ernie had to stay back and give them some room. They would need the time to show their intentions and who they were planning to target. Hopefully, it could give the marshal time to box them in, before they knew they were being watched.

Henry had ridden in without a sidearm and that was good news to Ernie. He didn't want Henry in the fray. He was young and this could get him killed, quicker than he could react. Ernie asked him to find a spot in the mercantile and just stay out of sight, until this thing is over. Henry hadn't come prepared to fight but didn't think much of hiding behind a barrel somewhere, until the smoke cleared. Bobby kept him close to the back of the store but gave him a firearm just in case. Henry was smart, he'd proved that. Bobby trusted his ability, if trouble came there way and would rather have him with a gun, than without one.

The dust soon began to rise from the road a ways out and then quickly blow to the west, without leaving a trace. There were a number of riders, no doubt. Who and how many, were questions still in need of a few moments, to find an answer. The marshal watched, as the riders came into full view. This confirmed Henry's information to be right on target. He thought of what could have been taking place this morning, had they not been the heirs of Henry's vigilance. He and Ernie would face them down, with the help of the ranchers who'd volunteered but Henry was the one who would be responsible for saving lives.

Cahoon and his men rode in, just to the north of the train station. The men dismounted and tied the horses to the rails of an abandoned corral, some two hundred yards away. Each man looked around and retrieved his Winchester, then huddled one last time before making their move. They could see folks moving about the platform. This wasn't out of the ordinary but their identities would have caused great concern, if they'd known. As they approached, Marshal Smith and the others moved away. They walked south and took to the allies and behind the buildings to allow Cahoon and his men room to fall in place.

Ernie quickly walked down the boardwalk and alerted Bobby Grayson, then made his way to the corner of Third Street. He stood out of sight, next to the barber shop. JT Belcher was only a few feet away peering out the front window of the Café. Cahoon's men slowly walked past the ticket office, staying to their left, making their way to Fredrick Street and initially off of Grayson. The street was busy, with the normal activity, one would expect, from any Wednesday morning.

The people who filled the street paid no attention, as the men walked by. They had no idea of what was about to occur. Marshal Smith had no way of warning them, without instigating gun fire in the street. He expected a few would take notice of Cahoon quite soon and begin to wonder why he was there. It had to be that way, the marshal thought. He had to give Cahoon enough rope to hang himself. Any move by the law, that came too soon, would let the whole bunch off the hook with no legal recourse to hold them.

Marshal Delbert Smith had no intention of holding Cahoon for anything. In his mind, he'd made the decision to put a stop to him, once and for all. He'd shot him once, that only made him worse and this time, he may not be so lucky. He walked through the narrow alley, back to Grayson Street and caught Ernie's eye. He then pointed toward Fredrick Street, giving Ernie their position. Ernie looked to his right, where JT was standing inside the Café, still watching from the window. He motioned to him and pointed in the direction of the mayor's office.

JT understood and made his way out the back, then quickly to the back door of the mayor's building. It was time to warn him and Ralph that Cahoon was on his way. The mayor's secretary had just arrived, when JT walked in. She hadn't had the chance to take a seat, when the mayor came out and told her to go home. She looked at him with amazement and started to speak but he stopped her before she could say a word. "Go home now and don't come back until tomorrow. I'll explain then." That's all he said. She didn't argue and without a word, she picked up her bag and high-tailed it out the door.

Ernie had seen only one man that he thought to be in Cahoon's crew. They were dressed like everyone else on the street, making them hard to spot. He'd kept his focus on the faces of those he thought to resemble Tom Bainbridge but he hadn't shown himself thus far. Bainbridge in return, was anxiously searching for Ernie. His sense of anger had only intensified since his arrival in town. It was apparent that no one on Fredrick, or Grayson had become alarmed, or even raised an eye to these men. So far, it had been a matter of strategy, with each man looking for a place to gain cover, while executing his part of the job.

Abigail had made herself busy all morning and tried to remain calm and optimistic. It was now just after 10:00 am and so far, Dr. Rowe hadn't seen any patients. The office was quiet, which may have been for the best but she wished that someone would stop in to keep her busy. But busy work was all she could find and it looked like that would have to do. Her mind would focus on whatever task she'd chosen only for a moment and then quickly back to Ernie. She couldn't get him off her mind. Suddenly it happened, the sound of gun fire. She heard a single shot, which unmistakably came from Grayson Street. There was silence for just a few seconds, then another shot and again, then a fourth. It went quiet for a few moments, as she began to cry, then more shots rang out. Abigail could only imagine the worst but as she'd promised Ernie, her fears were only for him.

The marshal had faced one of Cahoon's men, who'd shown himself from the ally, next to the land office. He was set on being the man who got the marshal but he was anxious and fired too quickly. The marshal took cover, just before the second shot rang out, then rose and took aim. He fired with a steady hand and took down the first of the desperados. The townsfolk scattered, making their way into stores, or around a corner, if they were close. With the street thinning out, Cahoon's men would be easier to spot and the marshal's concern for bystanders was lessening.

Ernie was watching for Cahoon to make a break for the mayor's office. He knew he wouldn't be alone, which would expose one, or perhaps, two others. There was no need in giving the mayor any further warning. The earlier shots could be heard around town, as they echoed off the buildings. The mayor and JT Belcher had proper notice, to be on guard. Tom Bainbridge was his other focus. He was faster than Bainbridge and Tom knew it. Ernie had proved that and he didn't expect he would stand up to a fair fight. He kept his back near the buildings, to avoid an ambush but Bainbridge could come at him from a blind side, if he dropped his guard in the least.

Ernie saw two men, slowly emerge from Third Street and then take cover. He didn't know the ranchers that well but he'd studied their coats and hats and was confident he could pick them out in a crowd. These were definitely bad guys, Ernie was sure. He scanned the street and the corners, looking for other undesirables. The only other person he saw was the marshal, nearly a block down, on the left. He got the marshal's attention then surprised the two men. Ernie stood in full view, with his Colt drawn and cocked and called out; "Hey, assholes…Over here!" The men were startled but took the bait. They both stepped out and leveled their sidearms. Ernie quickly took aim, taking out the one to the right. Aaron Riley, one of the ranchers was behind the other man in the alley and caught his attention with a whistle: "Over here"! He shouted. The man turned and raised his weapon, as Aaron's Winchester responded, with a

45-70 round ripping through the man's chest. Three down with five to go, Ernie thought.

Mrs. Cahoon was pacing the floors. She'd given little thought to her husband. Her greatest concern was for Henry. Larry would deserve whatever befell him, she thought. She'd convinced herself that she'd be disappointed, if he returned home. Henry had left the ranch, with his horse in a dead run, planning to take the canyon, then over the hills into town. He was exuberant and wanted to help. She was concerned that he would get mixed up in this mess and get himself into some real trouble. Tired of waiting around, she changed into her riding cloths and had one of the few remaining ranch hands to saddle Lillie. She left in a light gallop, which she rarely attempted and took the trail to Maple Ridge.

She rode into town alone and made her way up Jacob Street a couple of blocks and tied up to a hitch rail, on one of the vacant lots. The street was crowded with folks talking. Some were moving about, trying to get a better look at Grayson through the alleyways, between the buildings. To them, it seemed to be amusing, while the more mature among them realized the severity of the situation. Several inhospitable looks were cast her way but she paid them no mind. Her concern was for Henry and his safety. She was set on finding him. As she walked toward Third Street, another round of gun fire erupted, three shots this time. Even with all she'd heard and seen, nothing had prepared her for the sound of a revolver's report echoing from building to building. This is the sound of a man dying, she thought. God, I hope Henry is safe. The events which were taking shape, only one block away were horrifying but she had to see…she had to.

Aaron Riley stepped though the alley, to Grayson Street, where he saw Ernie standing next to the Barber Shop. He tipped his hat and grinned, as he stood over the body of the man he'd just shot. Ernie responded in kind. He hadn't seen his face but it was Ernie's old friend, Clayton Emerson. With three bodies now on the street, there were still five bad guys wandering around. That is, until they heard three rounds, quickly fired, just a half block up.

One of the ranch hands, who'd been involved in numerous incidents in town, had decided to make a hit on Dawson's Dry Goods on his own. Cahoon had no intention of wasting his resources and ammo on this old man but his hired help could not resist. He walked in and placed his revolver to Mr. Dawson's head, making him plead for his life. The ranch hand's party didn't last long. As quickly, as it was unexpected, he felt a revolver, now on the side of his head with Shorty's unmistakable voice telling him to "drop it." He turned to find him looking up, with both hands on a .44 cal Colt Frontier, cocked and aimed at his face. He laughed at Shorty, as he'd done many times before.

"I ain't dropping my gun, you little polecat." The ranch hand asserted.

"You can drop it, or I'll kill you. I swear I will." Shorty replied.

"You ain't killing nobody. You got a lot of nerve, pointing a gun at me." The man replied, then reaching for Shorty's weapon. As his left hand approached the barrel of Shorty's Colt, he aimed it point blank in his palm and fired. Blood and fragments of flesh spattered on the man's face and cloths. He returned fire without a target, as his lead landing harmlessly in the back wall. He backed away, cursing Shorty and trying to see what he'd done to his hand. As he backed into the doorway, the light from the street cast a brighter image of his injury. Through the shock and anger, he aimed his sidearm toward Shorty but he was too slow. Shorty's close up aim, this time, was squarely on the man's chest. When he fired, the round hit him dead center like a maul, hurling his dead body out the door and onto the boardwalk. Ernie and Aaron looked toward the sound, without breaking into the street and saw the aftermath, as Shorty stood over the man's body.

By now, Cahoon was seriously outnumbered but determined to take out his targets. Cahoon, Tom Bainbridge, Seth Leonard and one of the ranch hands, they called Buck, were still remaining. Ernie had killed Jim Holden, as he showed himself on Grayson. It was Aaron Riley who ended the life of Clayton Emerson. The four pulled back, to a short cut through, at Fourth Street and Fredrick. Their next stand, now that Clayton and Jim were dead, would be the mayor. Cahoon wanted him first. Tom would then surprise Ernie Evans and take him out, once and for all. In his grand stand to regain control of the town, Cahoon had pegged Marshal Smith, as the last to go down.

Grayson Street at Fourth was abandoned. Everyone had cleared out, with no desire to return, until this was over. Cahoon, Seth and Buck crossed there, to the alley behind the building, then up to the mayor's back door. Seth remembered how they'd tried this unsuccessfully before and concluded they'd been too slow. This time they would break in the door, with all three men charging the office and taking the mayor.

JT and Ralph had been watching the front and rear doors, very closely since the men arrived in town. Their vigilance increased with each report of gun fire. The mayor had kept the fire hot and the revolver close by, all morning. He wouldn't wait for someone else to protect him this time. If they came in his door, he vowed to be the first to open fire.

With Cahoon and his men in place, behind the mayor's office, Tom Bainbridge walked through the alley to Third Street. There, he quickly scanned Grayson, looking for Ernie Evans. He hadn't seen him thus far, at least where he'd recognized him. He was itching to make this happen. He would find him, then hold up until he heard the gun fire from the mayor's office and make his move. Ernie was faster and Tom had no intention of giving him any edge. He would stay out of sight and as close to Ernie's back as possible. He wouldn't shoot him from behind but catch him off guard, as soon as he turned.

Abigail was frantic. Dr. Rowe kept her away from the door, as long as he could. She eventually walked out onto the porch, watching as the townsfolk gathered two blocks up. She'd heard every shot and feared with each that it may have been intended for Ernie. Slowly and without alerting the doctor, Abigail walked up the street and joined the others. They all feared for the good men of their town. She saw Rachel Cahoon and thought of how she must be feeling.

Mrs. Cahoon was a good lady, who most folks didn't hold responsible for her husband's ways. Unfortunately, some wouldn't give her the benefit of being of her own mind. Abigail nodded, as they caught one another's eye and recalled how Mrs. Cahoon had always greeted her with a smile. Soon, they were close enough to speak, with Abigail offering the first gesture. "I know how you must feel," she began. "My Ernie is over there too."

"Abigail, I don't care about Larry, he deserves whatever he gets. I'm worried about Henry, my ranch hand. He came in earlier to warn the marshal. That's why I'm here." She replied. Abigail was stunned. It was known, by most, that she wasn't like her husband but this was the first time she'd made such a statement, for all to hear. Abigail just looked to her and smiled.

"We'll get through this together." She replied.

As they stood, consoling one another, there was another round of gun fire, which frightened them once again.

Ralph, JT and Mayor Sterns, heard the rear door, as it nearly came off its hinges. Seth Leonard kicked it so hard, that he had to pull his boot out. Cahoon and Buck rushed past him, with an eye for drawing down on whoever was inside. When he heard the startling noise, Mayor Sterns handed his firearm, ready to burn powder, at the first person to show his face through the back doorway. JT had overturned a table, in the front office, for cover. Ralph had expected them to challenge the front door and quickly repositioned himself, to the other side of the office, ready to return fire.

Buck was the first man to enter, with his gun drawn and trailing for a target. Mayor Sterns was the closest. Without hesitation, he opened fire, hitting the man in the midsection, drilling lead deep inside his gut. He fell back, almost onto Cahoon who returned fire but missed. He turned as Seth entered and aimed his revolver at Ralph. He was only ten feet away and in plain view. Ralph saw the man and immediately dropped to the floor. Shots immediately rang out in the room, adding to the smoke and the ringing in their ears. JT was next to the sideboard and responded to Seth, striking him in the side. Seth stayed on his feet and stumbled outside and down the alley, where he fell against a building in pain. He remained there without moving, as Cahoon bolted past him and away from another failed attempt at the mayor.

Cahoon stopped at the end of the ally, where it came out on Third Street and stood next to Tom Bainbridge. He looked across the street, at the two dead bodies, almost directly across from their position. He looked down the block a ways to another on the boardwalk, then another. Tom had already studied on the bodies and knew the count. He also realized the one nearest the alley was his friend, Clayton Emerson. The two stood for a moment without speaking. They prepared for their last stand, each settling their own individual grudge. They were alone now. With the exception of a bleeding man in the ally, the rest were dead.

Cahoon scanned the street, looking for Marshal Smith, who was too smart to be out in the open. Cahoon had no idea it would be this hard. The marshal was standing on the corner of Second Street, on the Fredrick side, watching for any movement on Grayson. Ernie had taken cover in the doorway of the mercantile, looking in each direction for whoever might show themselves.

The folks on Jacob were aware of the lull in gun fire, each hoping the fight had ended. They weren't aware of the current standoff as some, including Rachel Cahoon, slowly walked to the intersection at Third Street, hoping to get a look at Grayson. She stayed on the far side of Jacob, behind two men and looked down the street. She saw her husband, standing with his gun drawn, then quickly backed away, knowing it wasn't over. She eased back to Abigail and reached for her hand, lending comfort to both women.

"It's not over, I saw Larry standing at the edge of the alleyway." She said. Abigail didn't reply but was surprised by the disappointment in her voice.

Ernie and the marshal knew the count on the street but were yet unaware of the situation in the mayor's office. They'd heard the shots but had no way of determining the result. The ranchers were out of sight, scattered around each corner on Fredrick. The marshal had instructed them to stay off Jacob, to avoid drawing any gun fire in that direction.

This time it was Wilber Scott, who saw Cahoon and Tom Bainbridge on Third, next to the corner but they were out of Ernie's line of sight. Wilber couldn't see Ernie, who was half way up the block but he knew the marshal was on Second Street.

He ran back in that direction and told the marshal of the men's position. Ernie was within sight from there. Gaining his attention, the marshal pointed back to the corner and raised two fingers. Ernie responded with a nod and ambled out the back of the mercantile. Slowly, he walked toward them, as he hugged the buildings. Marshal Smith was reluctant to cross the street and walked back down Fredrick to Third. From there, he had a clear view of both men. He needed to draw them out but was reluctant to fire a shot in that direction. He stood for a moment, wondering what Ernie had up his sleeve. He needed to distract them, he thought, then decided to call out.

"Cahoon, come on out where I can see you."

Ernie heard him call out and knew the men would now be looking toward the marshal. He moved to the other side of the ally, where he could see both men. As Tom turned, he saw his face and recognized him right off. There you are, he thought. I got you now. He picked up a rock and threw it behind the men.Now looking in both directions, they were confused. Neither of them could tell where it came from. They didn't know who was around but they knew they'd been spotted. Unless they made a break for Jacob Street they were surrounded. Ernie decided he'd fire a shot ahead of them to turn them back, if they did break in that direction. Each man stood cold for a bit, considering their next move. Cahoon had a bead on the direction of the marshal, though he couldn't see him. So far, the whereabouts of Ernie Evans was still unknown to the two.

Ernie had to draw them out but it had to be toward Grayson Street. Quietly, he walked back to the mercantile, then out the front door onto the boardwalk. From there he called out; "Hey Tom, come on out." Bainbridge was startled and looked to Cahoon, "How the hell did he know I was here?" He asked. Cahoon was equally as confused but had no comment. If he knew that, what else could he know? He wondered. In the rush and confusion, he'd realized the men were better prepared than he would have thought. Now he finally realized they knew he was coming. How the hell did Marshal Smith know that? He was outraged.

Cahoon was rattled but it only served to fuel his anger. Ernie called out once again to taunt Tom a bit, in hopes of drawing him out. In the quiet, his voice echoed through the buildings to Jacob, where Abigail heard it and knew it was him. Thank God, he's okay, she thought and then realized that her father was only a few feet away. It was an eerie feeling, knowing he was there after all these years. Then her thoughts turned back to Ernie. That was where her love rested and she wished only for his safety. She never doubted her feelings, although Ernie had some reservation. But now she knew and even in the midst of this unease moment, it gave her a warm feeling.

Cahoon now understood why there were men in the mayor's office and how they were beaten back so easily. His anger was raging and Marshal Delbert Smith was all his could think of at the moment. An angry man is devoid of judgment and Larry Cahoon was a prime example. With a mind for killing, he stepped out first, calling for the marshal to do the same. Tom was bewildered by his move and saw nothing good coming from such a brazen act. He stayed back, waiting as Cahoon stepped farther in the open and called again; "Delbert! Come on out let's settle this once and for all." Marshal Smith was amazed, that he would make such a move and watched as he stepped out in clear view. In the past, he'd never faced anyone more aggressive than Mayor Sterns and now Cahoon was calling him out. He was obviously desperate and angry.

The marshal walked to the edge of the street, now in the open where he could see both Cahoon and Bainbridge. Marshal Smith kept his cool and looked to Ernie who was slowly moving in their direction. He too was now in the open but drawn and cocked, ready for whatever the two men might do.

Cahoon holstered his sidearm but Marshal Smith wasn't that stupid.

"Come on Delbert, put your gun back in leather and let get this done." Cahoon said.

"No, I don't think so Larry, now drop your gun, you're going to jail." The marshal replied.

"So now you call me Larry. Where's your respect, I'm Mr. Cahoon to you."

"Not any more. Now drop it on the ground, or this could turn out real bad."

Cahoon thought for a second, as the marshal refused to holster his sidearm. "Okay, there's no point in killing each other." Cahoon slowly drew his Schofield Model Three and cocked it on the way out. Marshal Smith didn't trust his words and held tight to his weapon, ready to fire. Cahoon quickly leveled the revolver and dropped the hammer, Marshal Smith instantly returned fire. Both men went down, with a cloud of smoke swirling around them. Cahoon didn't move but Marshal Smith quickly rolled to his side and aimed his cocked revolver back toward the man.

Tom Bainbridge was even more confused. He was now the last man, with nowhere to go.

"Hey Ernie, you won't be as lucky as you were that last time." He now stood in full view, less than thirty feet away.

"Howdy Tom, glad you could make it." Ernie replied.

"Yeah, I'll bet you are." Tom replied.

In all of Ernie's past, he had only one thing in mind when standing before a man with a gun…Kill him. This time, he actually hoped he could talk him out of it but Tom never gave him the chance. Ernie expected they would dance a bit, each trying to get the other off his edge. But in his anger and frustration, Tom went for his sidearm without another word. Ernie's instincts were sharp, as he cleared leather and fired a split second before Tom. His aim was deadly and his hand was steady. Tom's shot wasn't as well placed. His round grazed Ernie's left arm leaving a gash and two large holes in his coat. In the moment, Ernie hadn't even felt it. Tom staggered a bit and tried to raise his weapon but his arm was too weak. In moments, he was face down, in the dirt, with blood pooling around his dead body.

Ernie walked toward Marshal Smith, who was now on his feet but moving slowly. He was relieved. When he went down, Ernie thought he was dead for sure. The ranchers and the townsmen quickly gathered. JT, Ralph and the mayor had been on the next block, hoping to help but there was no way for them to break cover without becoming a target as well. Each man stood tall, as they looked over the bodies of the men who had wreaked havoc on their town. It was now theirs and no one would ever take it away.

CHAPTER 17

Jacob Street had become crowded with onlookers and those who'd fled Grayson Street, to escape the danger. As the sounds of gun fire finally quieted, the echoes of voices gave notice that the fight had ended. Many stayed back but Abigail and Rachel Cahoon ran to Grayson, to search for Ernie and Henry. They each found what they'd expected and perhaps hoped for. It was tragic how a husband had lost his wife's love and lay dead in the street, without benefit of her grief. And a daughter, seeing the father she'd lost ten years ago, now dead without her tears. Abigail had prayed for Ernie's safety but she was so afraid. With a feeling of such relief, she ran to Ernie and jumped in his arms, now with tears of joy. After a few moments, she returned to her feet and began wiping the dust from Ernie's coat when she noticed the blood on his left sleeve.

"You're hurt!" She shouted.

"What?" Ernie asked, as he looked to his arm. "Ah, that's nothing. Damn, he ruined my coat." He replied.

"Forget the coat. I have to get you to Doc Rowe's."

"Well, let's get the marshal there first, I'll come along with him." Ernie just smiled.

Marshal Smith was on his feet and walking about. He considered himself to be very lucky. He was hit in the side with the bullet lodged in the fleshy part of his rather stout midsection. His coat and vest had slowed the bullet's velocity a bit and prevented a second rather large hole, should it have gone through. He and Ernie waited there for a spell, to make sure everyone was still alive. As Mayor Sterns, JT and Ralph walked over they each breathed a sigh of relief. They'd heard the shots from the mayor's office but until now, didn't know the outcome. Mayor Sterns stood tall as Ralph praised his quick action, in taking down one of the intruders. He'd never killed a man but given the situation, he felt no remorse. Mayor Sterns would now be counted among the brave men who'd saved the town.

Marshal Smith and Ernie walked to Doc Rowe's, in the midst of a grateful crowd of townsfolk, who followed along the entire way. Doc Rowe met them at the door and immediately turned his attention to the marshal. He removed the bullet and tended to his side. Abigail removed Ernie's coat and shirt, then cleaned and bandaged his arm. She was relieved but knew the outcome could have been very different. She began to giggle, then looked to Ernie and said; "We've got to stop meeting like this, cowboy." Ernie laughed.

"Yes ma'am," He replied. "But you're going to have to keep me out of trouble."

"I've been trying but it doesn't seem to get us anywhere."

Ernie paused, thinking of his next words. They would likely be the most important he'd ever speak and he wanted it to be right.

"Well, if you're going to be a lawman's wife, you'll need to try a little harder." She stopped and looked him in the eyes, as hers once again welled up, with tears streaming down her face.

"Are you asking me to marry you?" She asked.

"If you'll have me." He replied, as he wiped her face.

She paused for a moment, never breaking their stare. "Well," she began, "If I have to keep patching you up, I guess I'll just have to keep you. Yes, I'll marry you." She replied. She held him so tightly, that Ernie thought she would break his neck. But now, he too, knew what it was like to completely give his heart to someone else.

The next few days in Maple Ridge were very different. Wednesday afternoon had been a challenge, getting the bodies off the street, with the blood limed and cleaned up. Later in the afternoon, someone found the body of the dead ranch hand in the alley, behind the mayor's office. He'd bled out where he stopped and where Cahoon ran past him. He'd left him there to die. Henry spent most of the afternoon with Mrs. Cahoon, walking her to the bank and helping her to get his final affairs in order. The undertaker had never been so busy. Considering whom they were, he didn't mind and hired the wood shop to help him build all the coffins.

Rachel Cahoon felt completely at peace. She'd watched her husband spiral out of control. He'd killed himself with a heart full of anger and greed. He was the only one to blame and she was relieved that he hadn't taken the life of anyone else that day. Mr. Kinsey couldn't have been more helpful. He was a single man, who'd had an eye for this lady for years. But she was a married woman and he was a man of honor. He'd been her banker and now, he hoped to be more. She was now having similar thoughts. He was a kind man of means and she would explore the idea.

Abigail talked Ernie into going with her to see her father. It was her choice and he couldn't refuse. On the slab at the mortuary his face looked the same, though it was cold and hollow. She had to see him just to get it off her mind and put it to rest. She decided to send him back to Missouri, to her grandparents' place. Ernie sent a wire to her uncle; they would bury him there. She'd been right all along, Ernie conceded. She seemed to have no emotional attachment to him, except for doing the right thing by sending him back to the family. He was a secret she'd kept since they met and it had caused her pain. Abigail now realized she could have told Ernie and he would have understood. This would be a lesson, in being open, with someone you love. One they would use for the rest of their lives.

Shorty never felt bad about killing that cowboy. He'd come there to do harm and Shorty knew that was the day to make things right. No one ever teased him again. He could never be sure if it was the respect he earned by protecting Mr. Dawson, or the fact that all the men who'd mistreated him were either dead, or banished from the town. Either way, James "Shorty" Williams was a new man. Folks in town called him Jim after that, it seemed that 'Shorty' no longer fit.

Rachel Cahoon fired Harold Quinn, the moment she and Henry returned to the ranch and dared him to ever come back. The men who served their thirty days in the Cimarron jail, all returned without a job. Most drifted to Arizona, while others went back to Cimarron to find work but none stayed in Maple Ridge. Mr. Kinsey kept account for all the ranch's finances and guarded Rachel's interest above all others. He returned fourteen hundred dollars to Ernie Evans, to wire back to William Murphy in Abilene. The twelve hundred dollars, they'd stolen from him, plus two hundred dollars for his trouble. It all evened out.

Maple Ridge gained quite a reputation after the shootout. Newspaper men from around the country flocked in to get a story, about this little town that wouldn't give up. Each interview inevitably included Ernie Evans and how the townsfolk had gained their strength from him. Ernie disappointed the newspaper men. They followed him in every direction but he wasn't talking. "I did what was right." That's all he would say. They knew the truth and wrote about him anyway, telling their stories, as told by the people of the town.

Maple Ridge became known as the safest town in New Mexico. Marshal Smith's side soon healed but he'd had enough of being a lawman. He'd thought about it for a while and finally made up his mind on the day of Ernie and Abigail's wedding. The church at the end of Jacob Street was full that day. It seemed to be as much of a celebration for the town, as for the bride and groom. It marked a new start for them as well.

Marshal Delbert Smith realized that Ernie had saved him, before he saved their town. He'd been beaten down and hamstrung for so long, that even he didn't realize how bad it had become. But with Ernie's help, he'd regained his self-respect and that was more important than what anyone else had to think. He should be the marshal, Delbert Smith thought, as he watched them that day. He's young and full of fire and I'm too damn old for this stuff. Yep, he's the new marshal, I'll see to it. He didn't say anything to Ernie right away. He knew when to tell him and he couldn't say no.

Both Ernie and Abigail had finally dealt with their haunting pasts. For different reason but with the same agony, the events of their lives had left a heavy burden. Together, they had let them go. But out of it all, Ernie was sure that Abigail had saved his life. They had both avoided Missouri for years and pushed it away. They decided to start their lives together, by confronting the last hurdle, they both had to face. They were going home.

Ernie was sure the train ride would be much different, with Abigail along. He didn't mind this one at all. He was sure he wouldn't be counting telegraph poles, this time. With a nice ride east, they would spend a few days in Missouri. They actually looked forward to seeing old friends and familiar places. Then with a pleasant ride home, they'd put the past behind them. Now was the time to start building memories.

It was three days after the wedding, when they left. And with much fanfare, many of their friends turned out to bid them a fond farewell. Marshal Smith and Deputy Wilcox were there. They stood on the platform next to Dr. Rowe and Rachel Cahoon, along with Mr. Kinsey, who said Rachel wouldn't miss it. Bobby Grayson, Henry, Ralph and JT were all there.

Their bags had been loaded and the engineer had stoked the boiler, as steam began rolling onto the platform. Just as they were ready to board, Marshal Smith reached to his lapel and removed his badge. He looked at it for a moment and smiled. As he looked up, he turned to the folks who'd gathered and said;

"My friends… say hello to your new marshal."

Ernie and Abigail watched, as he reached for Ernie's coat, with the badge now in his right hand. Ernie tried to back away a bit but the marshal was successful in pinning the badge in its rightful place.

"Now, it's yours, my boy. You deserve it." The marshal said.

"Wait a minute," Ernie replied, as he was completely confused.

"No, we can't wait a minute. You have a train to catch and a town to protect when you get back."

"But Marshal." Ernie tried to speak but the now retired Marshal Delbert Smith, cut him off and replied: "Don't call me marshal, you're the marshal. Now get on that train." Delbert said with a smile. Abigail and Rachel hugged and said good-bye, as they laughed at Ernie's inability to speak. They boarded the train, just as she began to roll, with Ernie still confused and Abigail once again, full of pride, as she smiled and waved good-bye.

Delbert Smith turned to join the others, as they all watched the smoke billow and the train build up steam as its mighty wheels began to turn.

"There goes your new marshal, folks. But don't worry, he will be back."

They continued to smile and wave good-bye, as Delbert Smith breathed a sigh of relief and the train rolled out of sight.

EPILOGUE

It seems a lifetime ago, since I stepped foot off that train. To think, I'd planned to stay one day, then carry my sorry ass back to Abilene, with money from one more rancher. Now look at me, marshal of Maple Ridge, New Mexico. I'd never seen New Mexico, until that day. Now I'm sitting here with my beautiful wife, watching as that red headed boy plays in the yard. I remember the first time Abigail pointed to this little piece of heaven. She told me about the house she wanted to build here. Oh, she had it figured out, down to the rocking chairs, on the porch and a white picket fence.

Well, she got almost everything she wanted. We built the house, all from her ideas, just as she described, fence and all. But I had to overrule the rocking chairs, they would never do. I built a fine wooden swing instead. It now hangs from the porch, facing east, where we can see the sun rise between the mountains. Those chairs would have kept us too far apart. In this swing, I can put my arm around her and hold her close to me. I swear I'll never let her go.

Maple Ridge is growing fast and Grayson Street has been extended by three additional blocks. We even have an ice cream parlor. Boy, little Ernie and Abigail love that place. Okay, I'll admit it, so do I. We stroll down there, in the evenings sometimes. That boy can eat some ice cream.

Henry is turning out to be a good lawman. He's getting good with a gun but I keep warning him, not to get too close. Take it from one who knows.

Rachel Cahoon and Mr. Robert Kinsey married in the spring. The ranch is thriving once again, under the new name 'The RK Ranch'. She and Abigail have become close and spend time together.

I've seen and heard things, that most folks would never believe. As a child, I saw the ravages of the Civil War and the fear in my mamma's eyes, when they told her my daddy was dead. I've seen the look in a man's face, as he lay dying in the street, from a bullet that I'd just sent tearing through his body. And I heard the first cry of my newborn son and saw the love in his mamma's eyes, as she held him to her breast. I felt tears of joy stream down my trail worn face, as she looked at me, bursting with pride. Then I felt the tears of sorrow, when my mamma died. Abigail showed me that I have a heart. It was silent and without feeling but somehow, she brought it to life. Nothing but a good women's love could have done such a thing.

God has smiled on me. I still don't know why; I sure didn't deserve it.
I reckon he did it for her. Abigail always deserved better than the likes of
me. But over time, He has helped me find my way and that's always made
her happy. I still wear a gun but it's no longer my source of comfort. I
remember the days when I'd reach for that grip every few seconds, just to
be sure it was there and in place. But no longer, now a days it is a source
of protection and a part of a marshal's job, no longer the source of my
strength.

Life is unpredictable. It seems that I found myself in a strange place
and wondered how I got here. Then the harder I tried to pull away, the
more attached I became. That's how it started and now I wouldn't think of
leaving. This is my home, Abigail and little Ernie are what I live for and I
have finally become the man I always wanted to be.

THANK YOU FOR READING!

If you enjoyed this book, we would appreciate your customer review on your book seller's website or on Goodreads.

Also, we would like for you to know that you can find more great books like this one from Cold West at www.ColdWest.com

COLD WEST PUBLSHING
An Imprint of Creative Texts Publishers, LLC